The History of Living Forever

The History of
Living Forever

~

JAKE WOLFF

Farrar, Straus and Giroux
New York

Farrar, Straus and Giroux
175 Varick Street, New York 10014

Library of Congress Cataloging-in-Publication Data
Names: Wolff, Jake, 1983– author.
Title: The history of living forever / Jake Wolff.
Description: First edition. | New York : Farrar, Straus and Giroux, 2019.
Identifiers: LCCN 2018045287 | ISBN 9780374170660 (hardcover)
Classification: LCC PS3623.O5585 H57 2019 | DDC 813/.6—dc23
LC record available at https://lccn.loc.gov/2018045287

Designed by Jonathan D. Lippincott

Our books may be purchased in bulk for promotional, educational, or business
use. Please contact your local bookseller or the Macmillan Corporate and
Premium Sales Department at 1-800-221-7945, extension 5442, or by e-mail
at MacmillanSpecialMarkets@macmillan.com.

www.fsgbooks.com
www.twitter.com/fsgbooks • www.facebook.com/fsgbooks

1 3 5 7 9 10 8 6 4 2

For Lesley

One has to pay dearly for immortality; one has to die several times while one is still alive. —Friedrich Nietzsche

It is impossible for a thinking being to imagine his own nonexistence; in this way, every man carries the proof of immortality inside himself. —Johann Wolfgang von Goethe

Question: If you could live forever, would you and why?
Answer: I would not live forever, because we should not live forever, because if we were supposed to live forever, then we would live forever, but we cannot live forever, which is why I would not live forever. —Miss Alabama, 1994

Contents

Author's Note

In the late 1970s, the first edition of a *Woman's Day* cookbook shipped with an error: its recipe for custard instructed readers to place a sealed can of condensed milk into a Crock-Pot for four hours. Chemists, anarchists, and experienced chefs will immediately see the problem—long before those four hours elapse, the can will explode, raining Crock-Pot shrapnel throughout the home kitchen.

The novel you are about to read is not a cookbook but a work of fiction. Still, you will find within its pages a number of recipes, all of which seem to promise great benefits to your health and well-being. To repeat: *this is a work of fiction.* Every recipe in this book, if ingested, will kill you. Every single one.

In this case, that old cliché proves useful: DO NOT TRY THIS AT HOME. And even when it comes to *actual* cookbooks, maybe wait for the second edition.

Yours in longevity,
Jake Wolff

Notable Moments in Self-Experimentation

1727 Isaac Newton drinks mercury (the taste: "strong, sourish, ungrateful") while searching for the philosopher's stone. *Dies of mercury poisoning.*

1801 Johann Ritter, the first to identify ultraviolet radiation, tests the effect of electricity on every part of his body, including the eyes and genitals. *Dies young, his body ravaged.*

1885 Daniel Alcides Carrión, a medical student, injects himself with the pus of verruga peruana to investigate the cause of the illness. *Dies of the disease.*

1924 Dr. Alexander Bogdanov undergoes nearly a dozen blood transfusions over several years, claiming to have cured his baldness and reduced the physical symptoms of aging. *Dies of malaria contracted via transfusion.*

1929 Dr. Werner Forssmann performs cardiac catheterization— the first in humans—on himself. *Wins Nobel Prize.*

1936 Proctologist Edwin Katskee takes cocaine and attempts to record his clinical reaction. *Dies of overdose.*

1984 Dr. Barry Marshall drinks a broth containing the bacterium *Helicobacter pylori* to prove its role in gastritis. *Wins Nobel Prize.*

2011 Ralph Steinman uses dendritic cells, which he discovered decades prior, to develop experimental treatments for his own pancreatic cancer. *Dies of cancer, wins Nobel Prize.*

The History of
Living Forever

Prologue

At 4:00 a.m. on the first day of my senior year, my chemistry teacher overdosed in the parking lot behind United Methodist. He was known by his students as Mr. Tampari, but that summer, to me, he had become something different: Sammy, my first love.

He died in early September—Rosh Hashanah, the head of the year. A month before that, my father collapsed in the produce section at Shop 'n Save after his liver shut off and turned copper-hard like an old penny. He pitched face forward into the avocado display, his skin a similar shade of sullen green. Avocados everywhere. You could judge their ripeness by the sound they made as they struck the checkerboard floor. My dad survived the fall, but he was unlikely, the doctors told us, to survive the winter.

The day before Sammy's death, I asked him how I had earned such rotten luck. I'd lost my mother to a house fire when I was ten years old, so if my dad died, I'd truly be an orphan. Sammy and I were scientists, and he offered me a cold kind of comfort— the statistics. Every two minutes someone dies of liver failure. Every three days someone dies in a fire caused by a cigarette. More people die by overdose, every year, than were killed in the Vietnam War. You look at those numbers and you think, how is *anyone* alive?

When I turned twenty, twenty-one, twenty-two, I imagined myself growing into Sammy, the way a child grows into a new pair of shoes. *When I'm his age*, I thought, *I'll know exactly why he did what he did*. But Sammy died at thirty, I've just turned forty, and I have long stopped believing that answers come with age.

Still, I find myself hoping that if I tell his story, and mine, I'll discover something that explains our relationship and the ways it changed us both. When I first slept with Sammy, I believed it was the most reckless thing I'd ever do. I assumed he felt the same. Only later did I realize I was part of a much longer, larger experiment—chemical, alchemical, psychological—that would transform me into someone new. Someone who would investigate Sammy's death despite warnings from the police, who would build a functioning chem lab in a roadside motel, who would administer a home-brewed immortality potion to a dying man strapped to a dentist's chair. All by the end of the year.

But I want to go back to that morning, the first day of my senior year, as I stood love-blind in the shower, dreaming of Sammy. Look at me, back then: lean and mean, happy and guilty. A boy with a secret. I was sixteen and ready for anything.

1

A Contradiction of Sandpipers

My cousin Emmett pounded on the bathroom door. He was two years older than me and knocked like a man, with the side of his fist: thud, thud, thud.

"Conrad!" he yelled. "It's time to go."

I'd come to Littlefield, Maine, at the beginning of middle school, after my mother died and my dad drove his car into a tanning salon. He'd blown a 0.12 and made the local news, and since then I'd lived with my aunt. When I first moved in, I had expected Emmett to resent me for a million reasons—here I was, occupying his house, sapping his parents' attention, barging into his grade despite being two years younger. But right away he'd seen the benefits. He asked me for feedback on his drawings and stories, and I helped him pass his tougher classes, which conveniently were my strongest: chemistry, bio—basically anything in a lab.

As I opened the door, he was already walking away. "Your dad is here," he said. "I'll be in the car."

I tried to hurry, but I also needed to look my best. Sammy and I had somehow gone the whole summer without discussing *this* day—the day we'd return to school, student and teacher, knowing what we'd done. "You're sexy," he once said to me, and it made my heart beat so fast that I had to sit on the edge of his bed while he laid a cold washcloth over my neck. Would he still feel that way when he saw me squeezed into one of those stupid writing desks with my three-subject notebook and my five-color pen? I studied my face in the mirror, disappointed to find only my usual self: handsome enough but goofy looking, like a sidekick. My tawny eyes were too small to be pretty, my Jewish curls always too long or too short. I dyed those curls blond for one week in middle school, and my civics teacher told me I looked like Art Garfunkel. Although I hated to admit it, I saw my father in the mirror, too. When I was little, my mother would say, "You have your dad's nose," and my father would grab his face, panicked. "Give it back!" he'd cry.

I found my dad in the kitchen working on a bowl of Froot Loops. He'd shaved his beard and looked so much like my grandfather he might as well as have been wearing a Halloween mask. His skin hung loose on his face.

"Why are you here?" I asked, searching the cabinets for a granola bar.

He didn't look up. "They do let us out, occasionally."

After his fall, he'd booked into a twelve-week alcohol rehab facility near Forest Lake. He needed to finish the program before he could make it onto the transplant list, but the doctors didn't believe he'd live that long. Even after the car crash, my father maintained that he did not, in fact, have a drinking problem. I wondered without asking whether he'd used my first day of school as an excuse to escape for the morning.

The cereal had stained his milk a radioactive shade of green. "I don't know how you eat that stuff," I said.

He stirred the milk. "You should see the color of my pee."

"Pass." I headed for the door.

He reached for my arm, and I saw the gauntness of his waxen limbs. He'd lost at least forty pounds from his heaviest, at least ten since his fall. He drowned in his denim shirt like a child playing dress-up. His wrists, delicate like bird bones, were visible past the fabric of his sleeves, and I could see his veins, blue and bloated, beneath the vitreous skin of his hands.

"I thought you'd have visited by now," he said.

I'd spent the summer with Sammy working on my science-fair project—an experiment on memory-impaired rats—or curled up in his bed, testing actions and reactions of a different sort. But even when I wasn't with Sammy, I was too busy thinking about him to do much else. Sometimes, as a dare to myself, I'd pretend that I would be the first to lose interest. *Sorry, Sammy, but I can't be tied down.* Sure, I loved him, but the summer was over. I was a senior, two years ahead of schedule, and soon I'd be applying to college. At this rate, by the time the year ended I'd be forty, with a job and a dog and a fixed-interest mortgage. By the time the year ended, Sammy would be too young for *me.* He'd be a good story, nothing more. "You won't believe what I did when I was sixteen," I'd tell my dog.

My father was watching me through jaundiced eyes.

"I've been busy with friends," I said. "One of us still has them."

He laughed, holding up his hands to signal surrender. "Hey, it's no skin off my back if you turn out mean."

Standing this close to his face, I could smell the dimethyl sulfide in his breath mixing badly with the modified starch of his breakfast. This was portal hypertension—the pressure building in his veins, the stink of his diseased body. The same thiols in a skunk's spray were gathering in my dad's lungs, bubbling to the surface like swamp gas. There's a name for this odor—this sulfurous, rotten-egg smell. They call it the breath of the dead.

I left without saying goodbye and ran out the door to find Emmett waiting in his beat-up station wagon. He'd spent the previous afternoon polishing the hatchback as if it were some vintage muscle car, and the tan paint glistened under the sun like wet skin. He revved the engine, and the feeble sound was still loud enough to chase the sandpipers out of the bird feeder.

My mother once told me that a flock of sandpipers is known as a contradiction. A contradiction of sandpipers. She had always been a bird person. She worked part-time at a youth reform camp in far-northern Maine, just outside our hometown of Winterville, leading hiking and bird-watching tours for the crazy, messed-up boys who dealt drugs or did drugs or called in bomb threats to their schools. When I was little, I hated thinking of her being around those kids. Another youth camp was along the bus route to my elementary school, this one to help little gay boys turn straight. Confronted by the sight of it every morning and every afternoon, I hardened myself against the possibility of change in people. It was self-preservation—I knew I was just like them. If I couldn't change, how would my mother's troubled boys? They were dangerous, plain and simple, and trying to help them would only cause her pain.

At school, Emmett disappeared to find his theater club friends, but I went straight to Mr. Foster's homeroom, as though going there early would make time move faster. I wanted desperately to see Sammy, but I would have to wait until I could steal a few minutes before first-period English. I told myself to be patient, but our secret was a firework inside me, already lit.

I squirmed in my seat within seconds of sitting down. When I first moved to Littlefield, we only went to homeroom to get our report cards, but after the Virginia Tech massacre we spent half an hour there each morning. We'd sit in a circle and talk about the Issue of the Day. Usually it was something benign—the dangers of sex, the dangers of soda—but we knew the deal: our teachers were keeping tabs, monitoring our mental health for signs of violence. We conspired against this system like criminals trying to pass a polygraph. Relax, we'd tell each other. Say a little, but not a lot. It's normal to be sad; it's abnormal to be very sad. Feel, but do not feel strongly. This was the language of a sound mind: the elimination of adverbs.

The small details of that room have stayed with me: an enormous snake plant in the northwest corner, just under the window and the light of the sun; on the ceiling, a brown water stain in the shape of Australia. Littlefield was bursting with money from summer tourism, but all of the rich families sent their children to private school and then made it a kind of hobby to vote down the public school budget. As a result, LHS looked from the outside like an abandoned warehouse. My biology textbook that year was twice my age and had its own water stain bleeding through the inside cover. Someone had circled it with a Sharpie and provided a label: MR. HASKELL'S SEMEN.

Mr. Foster sat behind his desk, tapping his armrest with the eraser end of a no. 2 pencil. He was one of those thick, ruddy time-warp teachers. You could put him in any classroom in the twentieth century and he'd fit in fine: thin hair, the perfectly round belly of the perpetually seated. A fifty-pound mustache.

RJ slid into the desk next to mine. He was my closest friend—my only friend if you disqualified Emmett for being family. Like all of my classmates, RJ was older than me, and you could see this difference in the way he carried himself. He was not classically good-looking, but I always liked looking at him: his face had a strong, narrow shape and an evenness of expression that I found reassuring. He was difficult to surprise.

RJ's family had moved to Littlefield from France—he was the only black kid in our school. Sophomore year, he was joined briefly by an Ethiopian boy who could swear in eight languages. I heard the boy's father was some sort of prince, or war criminal, or spy. Whatever he was, he moved his son to private school before the end of the first semester. RJ's family had money, too. His dad worked in pharmaceuticals for a company that manufactured the stupidest drugs: one that made your eyelashes thicker, one that made your knees smoother and sometimes, as a side effect, triggered spontaneous orgasms. But I remember RJ's father arguing with his mother, a retired catalog model, about the value of a public school education.

"You spend your whole life in public," his dad said. "Better to start early. Private school is for assholes."

RJ's mom shook a carton of orange juice. "Have you seen their textbooks?"

We'd met in eighth grade after being paired together in Home Economics. We baked brownies and wrote a children's book together for our final project. It was a little domestic partnership, and I was so, so in love with him. But RJ thought about nothing but girls.

"Who's hotter," he once asked, "Bryce or Amanda?"

I shrugged, my brow furrowed. "It's too hard to say."

He nodded gravely. I'd spoken a deep truth.

For the first year of our friendship he was clueless about my sexuality. He forced me to join the baseball team, taught me to spit the juice of my shredded bubble gum in a long, masculine stream. At the end of freshman year, we were hooked on *The Rocky Horror Picture Show*. One night when we came to the scene where Frank-N-Furter fucks Brad on a canopied bed, RJ nudged me and pointed at the screen. "That's you, right?"

I froze. I had an erection, and it made lying seem impossible. "That's not me. That's Tim Curry."

RJ snorted. "No crap it is. I mean, you'd do it with a guy."

"I'm not doing it with anyone. Ever." I stared straight ahead.

"I don't care," RJ said. "My sister said you were gay and that I should talk to you about it because gay people need lots of support."

RJ's older sister, Stephanie, was a pretty, bug-eyed girl with a rare form of muscular dystrophy known as Emery-Dreifuss. I went through a period of hating her for telling him, but it was a good lesson on life in the closet. I could play baseball, I could talk about breasts and the things I'd do to them, but no matter what, I was always one weirdly intuitive sister away from being outed. It's hard to explain the importance of this. We treat lies differently, the more delicate they are.

The bell rang. In came the final wave of chatter and seat-picking, the great spectacle of teenagers in heat. Emmett pushed through the doorway and frowned when he saw RJ and me slouched near the front of the room. He liked the back, where he could read Tolkien and draw without anyone noticing.

"Senior year!" he said, flashing his fakest smile. Behind him, Mr. Foster was writing something about grief counseling on the blackboard.

"Have you seen the freshmen?" asked RJ. "They don't look right. I really think there's something wrong with them."

Emmett turned his head toward the hallway and did a thousand-yard stare. God, was he handsome, and it had happened so fast. The usual story: braces came off, acne cleared up, face filled in. Voilà, duckling becomes swan. But I loved watching the girls try to cope with this change in him. Here was a nerd of the highest order—the kind of boy who kept his charcoal pencils in a sheath on his belt, like Elven daggers—yet they wanted him so badly I'd once seen a group of them puzzling over *Lord of the Rings*, glancing furtively from the book to Emmett, as though one might explain the other.

Mr. Foster pressed too hard on the chalkboard, and the squeak sent a shudder through the room. "Now that I have your attention," he said, "why don't we get started."

I pictured Sammy corralling his own students, reading the roster in the drowsy, defeated voice he used whenever he felt put-upon. He'd be leaning against the chalkboard, inviting thick white smudges onto the back of his black shirt. My mind drifted to the summer, and everything we'd done.

I could get in so much trouble for this.

I won't tell anyone, ever.

Mr. Foster scratched his gossamer hair and took a deep breath. "Welcome back," he said.

I left the porch light off so no one would see you.

It's okay. I was quiet.

A girl raised her hand.

"A question already?" said Mr. Foster.

The girl lowered her hand. "Nope."

Laughter.

Mr. Foster began his announcements, but all I could think of was Sammy's head next to mine on the pillow. Lying there, after the first time it happened. Stunned, happy. Afraid to look at him.

"Are you okay?" he'd asked. "What are you thinking?"

"I'm embarrassed to say."

"We're both embarrassed," he said. "It never stops being embarrassing."

"Okay. A line from *The English Patient*. Katharine says, 'I want you to ravish me.'"

Sammy's face darkened. He stood and began dressing. "Oh, God," he said, struggling to put his arm through an inside-out sleeve. "Don't use that word. Don't say *ravish*."

"Why?" I gathered the sheets around me, the way women do in movies when they're naked and their feelings are hurt.

He stopped cold with only one leg committed to his ash-gray corduroys. He fixed me with a stare. "*Ravish* means 'rape.'"

"No, it doesn't," I said, but I was already working my way toward it. *Ravish*. To fill with joy or happiness. To seize or carry by force . . .

He was growing manic. "*Ravish*, from French and from Latin. *Ravish, ravir, rapere, rape*. Oh, Jesus."

"It's not like that in the book. It's romantic."

"The context is different!" He threw his hands up. "They have the desert, East German spies, et cetera. Hitler. Anything goes."

I'd never felt so confused—how could a person's feelings change so quickly? "I don't think you've read it."

He sighed. "Well, that's true. I haven't." He lifted his blue eyes to me. I could see him put the full force of his kindness into them. "Come here."

Mr. Foster was still talking: "You've seen that I've put some information on the board about grief counseling. I want you to write all of this down because I have some hard news to share." He waited while we dug through our bags for notebooks and whispered to each other about borrowing pencils or pens. Homeroom did not usually require note taking. When we were ready, Mr. Foster took a deep breath. "I'm sad to tell you that Mr. Tampari has passed away."

I blinked. What a strange thing for him to say when I'd been thinking about Sammy that very moment. I'd seen him just the previous night, when I'd gone to his house with one of our lab rats that had fallen sick. If the rat had passed away, I would believe it. But Sammy? No chance. Mr. Foster was confused.

"What happened?" I heard someone ask.

Mr. Foster joined the circle. "I don't know the details."

The girl straight across from me started to cry. Melissa, who used to be fat. Melissa, who rollerbladed herself into shape, grew breasts, got a boyfriend. I'd see her skating around town, her blond hair bunched under a pink helmet, throwing heel toes and flat spins for the delight of passing cars. A Franciscan monastery was across from the fire station, a place with paved, wide-open spaces perfect for skating; sometimes I'd see her shoot out of there, laughing, with a line of angry monks jogging behind her.

"Anyone who needs to be excused from class today will be allowed to go to the student lobby," Mr. Foster was saying, "where our guidance counselors are available to you."

"Holy shit," RJ said under his breath. No one knew the extent of my relationship with Sammy, but it was no secret to RJ that Mr. Tampari was my favorite teacher.

"I didn't know him well," said Mr. Foster, "but Mr. Tampari was a very good teacher, a very bright guy."

I nodded, wondering if anyone else in the world knew Sammy as well as I did. I knew he grew up in New York and that his parents died in a car wreck. I knew he traveled a lot and could speak several languages, and not just French and Latin, but weird ones such as Maya. I knew that when he closed his eyes, it meant he was happy. When he cleared his throat, it meant he was falling asleep.

"Do you know what the ancient Mayans called breath?" Sammy once said. He tapped me on the chest, three times, near the heart. "White wind. And when you die, they say your white wind withered."

RJ signaled to Emmett behind my head. I was aware of a silent conversation between them.

Emmett raised his hand. "Mr. Foster, we're going to the lobby."

Mr. Foster understood that *we* meant the three of us. "Of course, boys. You should."

RJ grabbed me by the elbow and pulled me out of the room. At least, I assume that's what happened. I only remember appearing, as if by magic, in a hallway full of snotty, weeping students, most of whom hardly knew Sammy. Near the staircase, a junior named Beth Dennis had attracted a small crowd. It made sense that she would know something: she was a gossip and her mother was a nurse. Her boyfriend stood awkwardly beside her, chewing on the strings of his hoodie.

"He *overdosed*," Beth was saying, her eyes wet. "He overdosed at *church*."

"Was it on purpose?" someone asked, trying to catch up.

Sammy. Overdose. The words did not make sense together; they were like the north poles of two magnets, pushing apart. Drugs were for unhappy people, for hopeless people, for the deeply depressed. They were not for people who had just spent the summer in bed with me, cuddling and kissing and reading mystery novels out loud. They were not for people who had fallen in love.

Beth's cheeks bloomed red from the attention. "I dunno. But my mom said he took an insane amount of drugs, like, a world-record amount of drugs."

I'd only ever seen Sammy take aspirin, though he would swallow several at once with no water. I'd seen him eat ice cubes in large bites when his head hurt, and I'd seen him press his forehead against the cool aluminum of the refrigerator. Just the day before, I'd seen him alive.

"Bullshit," I said, surprising the crowd and myself. "You're full of shit."

The crowd turned to face me.

Beth did not hesitate. "My mom was *there.*"

I wasn't one to make a scene, and this was the worst time for me to draw attention to myself. But I hated her red cheeks, her crocodile tears. "You sound so stupid right now," I said.

"*You're* stupid!" said her boyfriend, one string of the hoodie still hooked in the corner of his mouth.

A couple of teachers down the hallway heard his raised voice and began a deliberately slow walk toward the crowd, hoping we'd disperse before they arrived.

"Okay," RJ said. "Time to go."

He pulled me away and toward the west exit, which opened onto the soccer field. No teachers would follow us. We were the good kids, and by transitive property, all of our activities were good. I don't think troublemakers ever realize this, how often the good kids break the rules. It's a blindness that surely hurts them later in life.

I first met Sammy at the beginning of my junior year. Freshmen at LHS started school one day early to give them a quieter, less intimidating introduction to the building before the older kids arrived. RJ, Emmett, and I had joined a group of upperclassmen who volunteered to hang out in the hallways and help any lost freshmen find their classes or their lockers. Our jobs left us with little to do during class time except stretch out on the dirty carpet and make fun of each other until the bell rang.

Sammy came upon us lying this way, holding our stomachs with laughter. He pulled a rolling suitcase behind him. We'd never seen a teacher do this. They all seemed so *entrenched*. But Sammy was young and ready to run—the suitcase gave him a fugitive quality.

He stopped in front of us and rubbed his eyes. "Look at you guys, all relaxed." He jerked a thumb to the classrooms behind him. "Do you realize what's going on behind those doors?" He had the biggest watch I'd ever seen. It looked like a tracking device, which only reinforced the notion that he'd recently escaped from somewhere.

We exchanged looks. "Are you a teacher?" asked Emmett.

Sammy leaned against his suitcase and stared down the hall toward the teacher's lounge. "They made promises to get me here that I'm beginning to suspect they can't keep."

RJ sized him up. "I heard the freshmen this year have the lowest standardized-test scores since basically forever."

Sammy tilted his head, considering. "That's not really what I meant, but that's interesting." His hair was blond with a hint of red, like a yellow dahlia. It swept up and away from his forehead. Forget best-looking teacher—this was the best-looking *person* I had ever seen.

"Countries with the highest international test scores often have the lowest economic growth," I said, my need to impress him completely transparent.

"I don't think tests tell you anything," Emmett said. "I think we should have longer school days but no tests."

Who knows where he picked up that idea. We stared at him, unmoved.

"What do you teach?" I asked.

"Chemistry."

My heart leapt.

"Conrad's a science genius," Emmett said. "The last guy quit because Con knew more than him."

"That's not true," I said. I had liked Mr. Sevigne. He had heart problems.

Sammy checked his watch. "All right, showtime. Stay there, okay? Exactly the way you are. It will make me feel better to know someone is having fun." He strode off, his suitcase trailing behind him.

After the final bell rang, I tracked him down in the chem lab. He stood behind the podium frowning at his attendance roster. He spotted me through the window of the door, and I had no choice then but to push my way through it. "I think I miscounted," he said as I approached him. He'd written his name on the chalk-board, along with something about ergoline derivatives. He might have been teaching them about LSD.

He closed the book and frisbeed it to the ground near his suit-case. "I'm teaching something for upperclassmen. Are you in it?"

"Yes," I said. "I mean, not right now. But I've been planning to switch in."

"You're a . . . junior?" he asked, trying to parse my age.

"I skipped two grades." Normally I tried not to broadcast this information—it alienated me from my peers and made teachers suspicious—but I liked telling him.

"Hey, same here. What are the chances?"

This commonality froze me solid with joy.

"Here's to escaping high school as quickly as possible," he said, and mimed clinking a glass with me.

It felt like the end to our conversation, but I didn't want to leave, so I asked about his watch. This worked even better than I could have imagined. His eyes lit up, and he waved me in closer. We huddled over his slender wrist. He spun the watch face and tapped his fingers along the embossed keys. He smelled like the ocean and baby powder—like an adventurer, but one who would need taking care of.

"This is a graph of the barometric pressure since I moved here. I can compare this graph with the data from *anywhere else* I've been with this watch. Here's Puerto Rico." He spun the dial again and pressed more buttons. "Here's San Jose." The watch face glowed and combined two graphs into one. He looked up at me, delighted, and I looked back at him, more in love than anyone else had ever been—ever, forever, and anywhere—even in Puerto Rico, even in San Jose.

RJ, Emmett, and I camped out by the equipment shed at the far loop of the track field. I sat dazed with my back against the grained wood, tearing up clumps of grass with my hands. RJ did it, too. Emmett was cross-legged, squinting under the sun. Behind them, heat waves rose from the tartan rubber of the track. A pole-vaulter had left her equipment to cook in the sun on the inner grass.

Since my outburst in the halls, Emmett had been eyeing me as if I were possessed. My stone-faced silence after our escape only baffled him more. "What's wrong with him?" he asked RJ.

I laid the back of my head against the equipment shed and shut my eyes. My fingers and toes were tingling, and I recognized this sensation as the same one I'd felt, years ago, when my father sat me down and said, "Something happened to Mom." In grief, our adrenal glands flood the body with cortisol. A few years after my mother died, I'd written a research paper on the subject.

"Man," Emmett was saying, undeterred by my silence, "so Mr. Tampari was a drug addict. Do you think he bought meth behind the old Blockbuster?"

"He was *not* a drug addict," I said.

Emmett pointed toward the building, toward Mr. Foster and Beth Dennis. "So he just took a bunch of drugs and killed himself out of the blue? Sure."

"He wasn't!" I was up on my feet. Above me, the sky was a blur of spinning blue. "He wouldn't do that. He wouldn't." What I wanted to say was He *wouldn't leave me*, but I couldn't say this, not without revealing too much. I could only stand there shaking, nauseated, totally lost.

"Okay. Jesus." Emmett watched me with only the barest glimpse of the disgust he would feel if he knew everything. "I'm just saying. He was—"

"Why don't you get Con a drink from the vending machine?" RJ interrupted. I can still hear him saying this—the effortlessness

in his voice. It was the moment I knew I would break my promise to Sammy: *I won't tell anyone, ever.* Twice already I had made
too much of a commotion. I would need to be careful, and I would
need someone looking out for me. This was especially true considering what I had to do next. I felt my secret fluttering against
my throat as if it were a bird I'd swallowed. If Sammy was truly
gone, I would need to set it free. RJ, more than anyone else, I
could trust.

Once Emmett was out of earshot, I sat back down. Before
RJ could speak, I said, "You have to take me to Mr. Tampari's
apartment."

RJ looked behind him, as though I were making that insane
request of someone else. "What are you talking about?"

"I have to get Number Fifty."

"Fifty of what?"

"Number Fifty is a rat. I left him at Mr. Tampari's last night,
and he was supposed to bring him to school. I have to give him
his medicine."

RJ's eyebrows went up. "You were at Mr. Tampari's house
last night?"

The pause that followed felt both endless and much too short.
"We're together . . . like, as a couple." To say this out loud was
not a relief. Sammy had only just died, and I was already betraying
him.

"Whoa," RJ said, but in the same even voice he would use to
say *hi* or *chicken nuggets.* I could see his understanding of me shifting in his eyes.

I looked away. "Are you grossed out?"

"I guess not," he said after a moment, but I could tell his own
feelings were not what interested him. "So if he wasn't a drug
addict, what *do* you think happened to him?"

I shook my head—not just as an answer, but as a rejection of
everything that had happened that morning. RJ's words hung in
the air, baking under the sun like the rubber of the track, and I
blinked at them, watched them harden into permanence. It was
my first time hearing the question that I would ask myself a thousand times, a million times, over and over for the rest of my life.

2

The Widow Self

I should acknowledge, for the record, that Sammy's relationship with me was against the law. Sixteen was the age of consent in Maine, but Sammy was my teacher, which made our relationship a crime. Sexual abuse of a minor. If Sammy had been a woman, or me a girl, he would have faced two to three years in jail with the potential for early release. But according to Chapter 11, Title 17-A, Section 257, Subparagraph B, of the Revised Statutes of the Maine Criminal Code, courts could impose a harsher sentence if the victim of the crime was the same sex as the offender. Had someone found out about us, Sammy would have gone away for a decade.

I'll never see him as a criminal, even if my aunt, my husband, and several very expensive therapists have tried to nudge me in that direction. None of them know the whole truth, the full extent of what I would discover about Sammy and the demons that chased him to Littlefield. I was only one of Sammy's secrets, and because not even my husband would believe me about the rest, I never told anyone. To the people who love me, I was victimized, and my unwillingness to paint my memories of Sammy with the dark shades of victimhood suggests that I am still traumatized and still, every day, suffering at the hands of my teacher. But to recognize the wrongness of a thing is not the same as to *experience* it as wrong. In recalling my affair with Sammy, I can only describe it the way it felt to me: like a romance.

•

I turned sixteen on the first day of June. Dana baked me a well-intentioned, uninspired cake—chocolate on chocolate—on which she'd written "Sixteen!!" in a halting, weirdly baroque script. She was not the kind of woman who baked cakes. For Emmett's sixteenth, she had picked up a Dairy Queen cake and decided not to inform the teenager behind the counter that he had spelled both *Birthday* and *Emmett* incorrectly. She baked for me, and only me, because she knew my mother had always baked. She knew I grew up with the sugary smell of a birthday morning, the sight of my mother whipping batter in a large wooden bowl, her biceps flexing in time with my breath. And, in turn, I knew that Dana's concern for me, the way she treated me, was called *love*, even though it made me feel small and different and as if I would never be loved by anyone the way I was meant to be (like someone who deserved love and didn't simply need it, like a blood transfusion).

For most of my junior year, my affection for Mr. Tampari felt like no big deal. Students develop crushes on their teachers all the time. Mr. Smith-Wyatt, the civics teacher who took his wife's name, had to end class five minutes early to account for the line of girls waiting for him after the bell, their impudent B cups pushing against their tank tops, tempting him to look down, though he never did. But as the school year reached its final weeks, I began to sense a change in Mr. Tampari, and at times—though I couldn't believe it—he seemed to be flirting with me. There was the day Principal Dee interrupted our independent study to say the odors from the Briggs-Rauscher reaction were bothering the other teachers. After she left, I asked him if we should stop.

He gazed into the beaker, where the liquid had turned a dark, almost blackish blue, the color of squid ink. "Oh, don't worry about her," he said. "We good-looking people have to stick together."

That night, I spent twenty minutes in front of the mirror, trying to see the person he did. The next week, he told me to stop calling him Mr. Tampari—"You can call me Sammy, outside of class"—and there was no way to pretend *that* wasn't weird.

.

"This is from me," Dana said, pushing a wrapped box across the table. Her face reminded me of my mother's, but softer, more serene. When she had the house to herself on weekends, she played the violin.

I unwrapped the box and thanked her. She'd given me a pair of high-tech, powder-blue headphones, which became popular after the lead singer of a prominent boy band wore them to his court date. From Emmett, I received a copy of Stephen Jay Gould's *Bully for Brontosaurus*. There was nothing from my dad, though later he did call and leave a short, perfunctory message, his words garbled, as if he were speaking with a mouthful of marbles.

I experienced all of this as if in a dream. My mind was already at the next day, when I had lunch plans with Mr. Tampari—with *Sammy*—at 1:00 p.m. The goal of my independent study, which met once a week for an hour and a half, had been to prepare for a serious run at the science-fair nationals the following year. Instead, we had spent that time playing with the school's surprisingly well-stocked, if outdated, laboratory closet. My favorite was the day we made a lightbulb out of a glass jar (also needed: tungsten wire, tinfoil, and a tank of helium), and when the bell rang, and I began to gather my stuff, Sammy looked up from the fiery glow of the bulb and said, "Oh, it's time to go?"—with a look of such genuine sadness that I felt as light as the helium. The last day of school, confronted by how little we'd actually accomplished, he said not to worry, we could just meet up over the summer. "Like, outside of school?" I asked, and Sammy said, "Yes, *exactly* like outside of school."

We met at a small café on Main Street. I arrived first, Sammy second, and he sat and ordered without looking at the menu. When the food came, he ate quickly, as if he hadn't eaten in days.

"I have a new idea for your science project," he said between bites, his voice just a touch too loud for the space.

It went like this: Sammy had a colleague at the University of

New Hampshire who had just concluded a pilot study on the
effect of electroshock therapy on the memory functions of Wistar
rats. Sammy thought we had an opportunity for a follow-up experiment: we could take a handful of the most damaged rats and
try to restore their impaired memories. He told me about a Bra-
zilian climbing plant that had been shown to stabilize the activity
of neurotransmitters in select animal models. *Paullinia cupana.*

"If you can show improvements in their memory using a water
maze, you can pave the way for future studies of *P. cupana* for
people with all sorts of memory impairments."

I wasn't sure. I wanted to say yes to any request Sammy made
of me, then and forever, but I also wanted to *win*. The National
Science Foundation offered prizes of up to $50,000. Sammy's idea
reminded me too much of my last science-fair project, which had
tested the effects of Asian and South American evergreens on
liver scarring. I'd learned the hard way that phytochemical studies were not the path to victory—plant-based medicine was not
in fashion. There were also the rats. My previous study had used
rat *cells*, but I hadn't been handling live rats, subjecting them to
experiments. The judges wanted to see teenagers saving the environment and helping the disabled, not torturing rodents.

"But that's just it," Sammy said, wiping his mouth with a white
paper napkin. "*You* aren't torturing them. They've already *been*
tortured. You're the one who's going to make them feel better."
He took a large drink of water. "I mean, some of them, anyway. A
couple will need to serve as controls."

His insistence confused and excited me. During the school
year, his primary goal was always, obviously, to kill time. We once
spent a full hour of the independent study taking turns playing
Snake on my calculator. Of course, if I said yes, I'd have a whole
summer of research with him to look forward to. If I said no . . .

"Okay, let's do it."

Sammy signaled for the check, and my heart sank. The whole
lunch had taken less than forty-five minutes.

"Can we get those books you wanted me to read?" I asked.
"Are they at school?"

I knew they were not at school.

Sammy shrugged, *Why not*, and next thing I knew I was at his place—a studio apartment on top of a two-car garage. As he opened the door, he complained about his landlord, a widow who left the house only to hassle him. "It's like *Misery* here. One day I'm going to wake up strapped to the bed." Inside, the shades were drawn, the space lit by a sunlamp on its dimmest setting. I had to inch by his bed to enter the small area of carpet he referred to as his living room, which contained a television and the smallest possible love seat. Sammy was dressed in cotton, coffee-colored slacks and a T-shirt that landed just above his waist. When he bent to clear a seat on the couch, I saw a sliver of skin.

"Here," Sammy said as I sat, handing me a stapled packet of papers. "Some light reading material." It was a copy of the electroshock study that had produced the memory-impaired rats. The first figure showed a sedated Wistar with electrodes stuck to his little skull. While I read, Sammy went to the bathroom but left the door open. I could see him rummaging through his medicine cabinet. "My head is killing me," he called through the doorway. Soon, I would learn he said this every day, as though in a perpetual state of agony. Ironically, the only days he didn't say it would be the truly bad days, when he went to a dark place that was alien and unknowable, like deep space or deep ocean. On those days, he was so joyless it reminded me of the morning in Winterville I saw a baby goldfinch dying in a soft pocket of snow and, standing above it, its golden-brown mother pecking herself in grief, refusing to migrate.

Although he had promised me science books, I couldn't see a single textbook in his apartment, only paperbacks with embossed lettering on the covers—mysteries, mostly, and legal thrillers.

"Something to drink?" he asked when he returned from the bathroom. "Water? Cognac? Kidding."

"No, thank you," I said, missing his joke. So I added, too late, "That's funny."

Sammy raised an eyebrow. "You're kind of weird about laughing out loud, aren't you?"

"What do you mean?"

"Like, you don't really like to do it."

I considered this. I was still at an age when people can tell you things about yourself that (1) you didn't know and (2) are actually true. This stops happening, forever and with no exceptions, at twenty-five.

"So," I said. "Those books?"

"Right. Please follow me to my office."

This was another joke, because his office was exactly one step to his left and only a writing desk. He began moving papers from one side of the desk to the other. I recognized tests and answer keys from his classes, long lists of boiling points and multiple-choice questions about the periodic table. Above his desk, I saw a postcard with a photograph of a harpy eagle in flight, its white, owl-like head squawking in profile.

"'The Cooperative Republic of Guyana,'" I read out loud.

Sammy looked up from his desk to say, "Oh, that's nothing," and I will remember the way he said it (too quickly, defensively) until the day I die.

"Aha." Sammy lifted two textbooks with broken spines: *The Laboratory Rat, Second Edition*, and Walter Cannon's *The Way of an Investigator*. "Don't be frustrated if you can't understand all of this. I'll help you."

I had never read a book and failed to understand it, not once in my life, but I didn't tell him this. When it came to Sammy, I liked the idea of being helped.

He began to hand these books to me, but then he pulled them back against his chest. "Have you ever heard of Ignaz Semmelweis?"

I had. Dr. Semmelweis was a key figure in the history of germ theory. In the midnineteenth century, he argued that hospitals could reduce infant mortality simply by requiring doctors to wash their hands.

"Correct," Sammy said, his eyes sparking with the delight of my knowing this. "But no one believed him. They said he was insane. He died in a mental asylum, raving about childbed fevers."

"That's really sad."

Sammy held the books out to me again. "Sad, yes, but is it too high a price? To be *right*, even if it means dying alone, or being called crazy? Would that be worth it to you?"

I tucked the heavy hardbacks beneath my arm. "I don't know

if it would be worth it. But if I knew something was true and could save lives, I would fight for it."

Sammy nodded and closed his eyes, as though this answer was a great relief to him. But then he said, "Well, I should probably take you home."

I couldn't tell if there was a question mark at the end of that sentence, but I could only head for the door, where my shoes were waiting on his tweed entry mat. On the way, I brushed the edge of his bed with my fingertips and imagined the two of us under the covers. I *could* imagine it, at least partially; I was not entirely green. At a weeklong science fair the previous summer, I'd administered two hand jobs and received one—an inequity I'd dwelled on for months. But the way I felt around Sammy was so much more.

"Con?" Sammy said, when I reached the door. "I think you forgot something." When he saw me searching my hands, he asked, "What's missing?"

I turned, and he was holding the electroshock study out to me with a faux-disapproving stare. I'd left it on the couch, as though just holding it had affected my memory.

"Sorry." I retraced my steps around the bed. I took the article and slid it between the pages of one of the textbooks.

And then the strangest thing happened: We just stood there, the two of us. Doing nothing.

If a timer had been running, it may have reported only three seconds passing, maybe five, but it felt like much longer—as if standing so close, allowing that closeness to be the only thing happening, was a decision we'd made together.

It was Sammy who broke eye contact. "You know," he said, "Hugo Grotius wrote that the care of the human mind is the most notable branch of medicine."

"Hm," I said, unsure why he was pitching me on the memory study when I'd already agreed to do it. I looked up at him, and the loneliness I saw in his face was like an undertow, pulling me to sea. It's hard to explain how I found the courage to do what came next, except to say that it *wasn't* courage, or cowardice, or anything to do with strength. It just felt necessary, like breathing.

"So," I said, and closed the inches between us to kiss him.

How did I experience this kiss? Was it dry and nervous, our lips meeting together like a pair of paper plates? Was it moist, passionate, his soft lips inviting my own, drawing me into him, enveloping me? Was it actually how I had dreamed, or was it so much better that only then could I recognize my complete failure of imagination, my inability to conceive of what it means to love someone, and to be loved by them, and to get exactly what you want, when you want it? Was it long or short? Was it right or wrong? Was it him, or me, who made that little noise halfway through, that little moan, like an animal who had fallen asleep in the sun? Was it the end of the world, or the beginning?

Then the kiss was over. Worse, *I* ended it. I lowered my head, felt his lips separate with a sting from mine. Neither of us spoke. I knew that by pulling away, I put the onus on myself to decide what happened next. I could tell him to take me home, and he would. That was option one. Option two was more complicated. If an older woman and a teenaged boy were caught in bed together, people would say, "That's wrong . . . but way to go, kid!" If an older man and a teenaged girl were caught in bed together, people would say, "That's wrong . . . but have you seen those Facebook pics of the girl in her bikini?" For the two of us, Sammy and Conrad, it would only be wrong, and if someone found out, both of our lives would be ruined.

So I said to myself, *In three seconds, I will put my hand on his hand. In three seconds, I will take his hand, and he will know what this means. In three seconds.* I closed my eyes and took the deepest, longest breath of my life. *One, two, three.*

It took some convincing, but eventually RJ agreed to drive me to Sammy's apartment. "If we see any cops there," he said, "I'm not even slowing down." But as we parked on the street, the view from the car showed a surprisingly peaceful tableau. The widow's house sat undisturbed on its manicured lawn. The wide driveway was empty of cars, save for her wood-paneled Oldsmobile. A forest of birch trees encircled the house, their leaves so full and green I could barely see the whites of their trunks.

RJ cut the engine. "Seems pretty quiet," he conceded.

Despite my reassurances, I, too, had been picturing the widow's house surrounded by cops, maybe a fire engine, a SWAT van, a chopper overhead. Littlefield was a small town, and it reacted to drama with breathless excitement. An errant Fourth of July sparkler once set off a small brushfire behind the Dairy Queen, and every volunteer firefighter in a twenty-mile radius descended on the scene, their walkie-talkies hissing and interfering with one another. The DQ ran out of Dilly Bars.

RJ stepped out of the car and eased the door shut, but I stayed in the passenger seat, watching him—this all seemed to be happening very fast.

"Come on," he said. "If we're going to go, let's go."

So we followed the tree line around the far side of the garage. We kept low, RJ in front, me trying to mimic his lithe, graceful movements. I peered at the widow's house, which was the color of pavement and extensively, ominously windowed. I strained my eyes, watching those windows for signs of movement. Sammy's landlord was a bored, fussy woman—the kind I could imagine peering suspiciously out into the yard from behind her curtains, regularly and for no good reason.

At the back of the garage, a flight of stairs ran up to Sammy's apartment. In unison, we stopped at the bottom step. There it was, crisscrossed over his door: police tape. I let out a gasp, RJ at my side, watching me with a frightening intensity. I'd climbed these steps so many times, my fingertips numb with anticipation. I used to pause at the door and listen to the sounds of Sammy inside: the tap, tap, tap of papers being evened and cleaned off the coffee table; the whoosh of a comforter spread over a mattress; the clink of dishes being cleared from the sink. This was the most beautiful music—the sound of Sammy preparing to greet me.

We ascended the stairs together. As we neared the top step, I imagined the police bursting through the other side of the door, dragging me down the stairs, and hauling me to jail. An officer in white latex gloves grabs me by the collar and forces my mouth open: "We're taking a buccal swab. Your DNA's all over that place."

RJ peeled one end of the police tape off the door. I removed the key from my pocket, but as I approached the door, I saw I wouldn't need it—the lock was busted. RJ and I stared at it as if it were a rattlesnake. Silently, and with only the pressure of a single finger, I nudged the door open. Through the narrow slit, I could see the corner of Sammy's red-oak mission bed, where once, when we were supposed to be working, we'd sat side by side and taken turns reading to each other from a murder mystery about a cheese shop: *The Long Quiche Goodbye*.

We stayed at the entry for several long seconds. When still we heard nothing, I opened the door wide, and RJ and I looked at each other. Sammy's apartment had been destroyed.

To the side of the bed, the couch cushions were ripped from the sofa and sat flattened on the floor like deflated balloons, the stuffing torn out and piled in a separate corner. From the doorway, I could see a fist-size hole gaping above the sink, a faint cord of wiring visible in the darkness. Closer to me, Sammy's recliner lay tipped on its side, the guts exposed, the built-in footrest pruned from the chair. Everywhere, *everywhere*, I saw papers and books and folders, spread around the room as if they'd been dropped loose-leaf from an airplane. RJ took three tentative steps into the apartment. Seeing the fear in his face made me dizzy.

"Did Mr. Tampari do this?" he whispered back at me.

"No way," I said, but the truth was that I'd seen him, only a month ago, put his fist through a wall.

"The police?" RJ offered.

I could imagine this: the police finding his body and then rushing to his house for information, breaking the lock to gain entry. But why wouldn't they ask the widow to let them in? And what were they looking for? I entertained a brief, insane thought: that Sammy had *another* sixteen-year-old lover, and he'd come here, just like me, to search through the remnants of Sammy's life.

I watched RJ wade into the wreckage, wincing as he trampled my memories. "You would . . . stay here?" he asked. He was showing his typical restraint, asking me questions about my relationship with Sammy in small, digestible doses.

"Sometimes," I answered.

I'd been standing in the doorway, but I forced myself into the room, stepping over the coatrack and the little white computer desk Sammy used as a dining room table. The last time I'd seen Number 50, he'd been in his cage on the love seat, but Sammy could have moved him—perhaps to the bathroom, where it would be easier to refill his water and where the smell of his feces could be ventilated by the fan. On my way there, I stepped over Sammy's long, colorful tennis racket and two cartons of tennis balls. On the floor on the other side of the bed, I saw two silk ties, sandy gray like cherrystone clams, and a pair of black dress socks turned inside out. Next to those, one ballpoint pen, cap missing, and a pile of ancient books: *Knight's American Mechanical Dictionary* (1874); *Aging as a Disease*, by Dr. Leopold Turck (1869); *The Proceedings of the New York Society of Numismatics: 1887–1889* (1891).

Seduced by their unfamiliarity, I knelt to examine these books, ran my fingers over their deckle edges. Sammy's apartment was truly, impossibly small, and over my many hours there, I'd helped myself to every inch of it. How had I never seen these before? I flipped through the first of them. In the margins of the dictionary, Sammy had diagrammed an early medical experiment in which the investigator swallowed sponges attached to threads and then pulled them back up through his throat. I was drawn to the soft pencil marks of Sammy's sketch, the way he'd shaded the little sponge. I could feel him in the room.

RJ snapped his fingers and motioned for me to keep looking. I set the books aside and redirected my attention to the bathroom. Blocking the door, a box of Sammy's papers had been overturned and searched through so quickly that many of the pages were torn. Sammy often left his quizzes and tests out in the open, and I always delighted in seeing the poor grades of my classmates. But these, like the old books, were papers I'd never seen before, filled with charts and diagrams and spreadsheets of indecipherable data. And there were *thousands* of these pages, piled so deeply in places that I could bury my arm up to the elbow. As I cleared a path to the door, I realized RJ was standing over my shoulder.

"Wow," he said quietly, diplomatically. "What is all this stuff?"

I knew what RJ was thinking because I couldn't deny my own

thoughts: everything here—the papers, the destruction—made
Sammy seem crazy.

I had cleared just enough space to squeeze through the bathroom door. Inside, I flipped the light switch, and as my eyes adjusted to the ultrabrightness of the neon overhead, I saw the sunny
orange of Sammy's shower curtain, the taupe laminate of the tub,
and the open medicine cabinet, which had been ransacked, with
several over-the-counter-pill bottles left open in the sink. I swept
aside the shower curtain, and there, lying awkwardly on its side,
was the cage of Number 50. His bed was there, and his water
bottle, and his gray pellets of food. But the door to the cage was
open. He was gone.

I was only beginning to register my heartbreak when RJ poked
his head into the doorway.

"Quiet," he whispered.

Below us, from the garage, I heard a woman mutter to herself,
followed by a kind of crackling. A mechanical noise. It sounded
like a fax machine or a dial-up modem—the ancient equipment
a very old woman might store in her garage and sometimes use
to connect with the world. Sammy and I heard her downstairs,
occasionally. Back then it seemed funny, and we would hold our
fingers to our lips as we listened to her shoo squirrels out of the
garage with a broom.

It wasn't funny anymore. RJ and I exchanged glances: There
was still time to run. We could head back to school and no one
would know we'd been gone. We had not yet committed any
serious crimes in front of a senior citizen. We were still the good
kids.

"What now?" he asked softly, gesturing with his hand to the
empty cage, and it was clear what he meant by this: *Let's leave.*

"Number Fifty could still be here," I whispered. I imagined
Number 50 hiding, hungry, as lost as I was. "I have to look."

If I expected resistance from RJ, I shouldn't have—he was
ready, always, to help me. As quietly as we could, we continued
our search, this time with our focus directed to the floor. RJ crept
to Sammy's bookshelves and rifled through the books and papers
that lay in tatters and loose piles on the carpet. I checked the lower

cupboards of the kitchen, hoping Number 50 had sought out their quiet, sheltered darkness.

RJ pulled a comforter off the floor, revealing Sammy's writing desk, its little legs broken. He motioned for me to help him lift it, but I tripped on the way, the teeth of the coatrack biting at a hole in my jeans. I took several out-of-control steps and fell in a heap of limbs, my knees and elbows hitting hard against the furniture. We held our breath, waiting to hear movement from below.

"*Shh* and get up," whispered RJ.

I lifted myself off the floor. The desk had been paid a particularly violent brand of attention. Notebooks in shreds. Desk calendar ripped to bits. A pen had exploded, and the blue ink gathered like an oil spill in a divot of the hardwood. Sammy's papers had been turned to confetti, a collage of words and color, of nonsense and abstract meaning. His papers arranged themselves in random layers to create new, cryptic sentences like refrigerator poetry: *around town Around below. I am. The floor, but—A+.* The postcard from the Cooperative Republic of Guyana lay among the wreckage, its corners bent. I flipped the card over. It read, *Dear Sam: Saw one of these eat a baby kinkajou. It sucks here. Miss you, Sadiq.*

I held the card neatly and evenly between my fingers, in two hands. I used to read it when Sammy was in the bathroom. I'd obsessed over Sadiq, wondering whether he was an old flame, whether he was a better kisser than me, better in bed. Whether Sammy would lose all interest in me once Sadiq returned—at last!—from the Cooperative Republic of Guyana. Everything was different now. *Lucky Sadiq,* I thought, *who doesn't know Sammy is dead, who hikes and sightsees and dreams of their joyous reunion. Who fantasizes about Sammy from a canvas tent in the rain forest. Dumb, clueless Sadiq.*

RJ put a hand on my shoulder. "Are you okay?" he asked.

"I'm fine," I said. Since I'd told him about me and Sammy, RJ had been looking at me this way—as though I might, at any moment, hurl myself into an open grave. He was waiting for the tears to come, for the gnashing of the teeth. I wasn't going to do that.

I've always found that grief hits hardest in the light: when you can see clearly what you've lost, and why, and you can list all the ways you'll never be whole again. If Sammy had killed himself, if he had *chosen* to leave me, that would be one kind of pain. If something violent had happened to him—the way something violent had happened to his apartment—then that would be another. An overdose? I didn't believe it. Where was Number 50, and what the hell had happened here? My grief was a nighttime animal. I could hear it and smell it and see its yellow eyes, but it wasn't yet upon me.

This was something I learned when my mother died: There's no rush. She'll be dead your whole life.

"Keep looking," I said.

RJ nodded and lifted the desk, grunting, so that I could check beneath it for Number 50. There was no sign of him, but I did find something else: *The Long Quiche Goodbye*. I was picking it up when the door behind us swung open. I hoped it was only the wind, but I knew from the way RJ dropped the desk, no longer trying to be quiet, that we weren't alone.

I spun around to face the widow. She stood in the open doorway, her flannel nightgown rippling in the breeze. She was much taller than I expected—I'd only seen her from a distance—but lean, so lean, with a mountain of gray hair piled loosely on her head. An emergency-response pendant hung from her neck, and she held a baseball bat in one hand, her grip choked up high. She'd wrapped duct tape around the meat of the barrel, as though she'd already cracked it once over some poor teenager's skull.

"We didn't do this," RJ said, gesturing toward the destruction.

She squinted at me. "I know you. You come around."

Rather than seeing this as a possible way out, I took it as an accusation. "Nuh-uh," I said stupidly.

She held up the pendant. "I'll call the police."

It was the first time I'd seen one of those devices used for the purpose of intimidation.

"We'll leave," I said.

The widow shook her head, though I couldn't tell if it was in direct response to my promise. "I've got enough problems without teenagers breaking in."

I didn't know what to say to this. I stared at the floor, where her shadow cast its asymmetrical shape over the wreckage of Sammy's life. Had he ever seen in her what I saw in that moment—a dark future, my *own* dark future? At sixteen, I was already burning through loved ones. In another sixteen I could be just like her, alone and uptight, grabbing my Louisville Slugger to check on strange noises in the attic.

Some of the rubble shifted behind me, and the sound of it helped the widow remember herself. She moved out of the doorway. "Just get out," she said.

As we tried to leave, my foot caught again on the coatrack, and I stumbled. *The Long Quiche Goodbye* slid from my waistband and landed with a thud on the carpet.

The widow's eyes went wide, and she steeled herself back in front of the doorway. I'll never forget the look she gave me: such betrayal! She pressed her emergency pendant.

"Connecting . . . hold for operator," said the device.

RJ put his hand on my back and pushed me toward the door. I stepped over the book and advanced on the widow, palms out, the way I would approach a feral dog. She remained steadfast in front of me, the bat resting on her shoulder as if she were posing for a baseball card. As I drew near, she reached out for me, grabbed at my sleeves with a wrinkled hand. I waved my arms, trying to shake her off. The widow bounced off me and went hard to the ground.

"Uff," she said.

"Hold for operator," said the device.

As we left the apartment, the widow didn't get up.

"Thieves," she said simply, damningly, as RJ turned to slam the door shut.

When I was four, maybe five years old, my parents took me to Santa Clara for a wedding. It was my first time out of New England. On the way back to the hotel, we drove our rented sedan through the Santa Cruz Mountains. I remember the headlights catching in the fog, the way the road bent, like a river, like a jet stream— like something with a current. There's no way my father could see, but he kept his speed up, refused defeat.

"Ned Aybinder," said my mother. "Use your brakes."

"Nasya Aybinder," he said. He craned his neck to look back at me. "Conrad Aybinder."

I adopted his tone. "Dad Aybinder. Mom Aybinder."

"Ned!" my mom screamed. An animal appeared in the road. This, we would argue about later. My parents said it was a deer— "that poor, *tsetummelt* deer"—but I maintain to this day it was a mountain lion. I saw its eyes in the lights.

The car spun out and hurtled toward the guardrail. None of this really matters—we almost went over the edge of the mountain, and a truck almost hit us, and my mom said *"Fuck!"* so loud that she didn't swear again for six months. But we lived, and my dad steered us back onto the road and drove the rest of the way to the hotel with his hazards on. What felt important to me, even then, was how wrong this felt—this cold carrying on.

"We should go to the hospital," I said from the backseat.

My mother turned to make sure she hadn't missed a head wound. Seeing me safe, she asked, "Why?"

"Because we almost *died*," I said.

My parents laughed, but I still wanted to know why life was proceeding as though nothing had happened. We'd teetered on the edge of a mountain. A truck almost hit us. We should need weeks of therapy. We should leave the country, take a long vacation from school and work. We should buy all new clothes. What did it say about life if we could come so close to disaster and my parents would act as if it were nothing?

RJ dropped me off at my aunt's house, the air in his car thick with the heat of a cloudless sun. Since I'd left that morning, the place had shrunk in size. If this was grief warping my view of the world, it was only the beginning of my reenvisioning of Littlefield, of my life there, without Sammy. The house was still white with gray shutters, the cream-colored curtains still fluttered in the open window of my bedroom, but nothing was the same.

Dana was sitting in the kitchen, home for lunch. The room smelled of yogurt, granola, and more faintly of her lavender perfume. She was small and tan, with pointy, birdlike elbows, so she always seemed more perched than seated—as though she'd only landed for a minute. But after my visit to Sammy's apartment, I found myself labeling her with a word I'd never applied to her before, even though, literally speaking, it had been true: *widow*.

My uncle Jeff had died less than a year after I arrived, following a short, ugly battle with breast cancer. (Every seventy-four seconds, someone dies of breast cancer.) To me, his death was such a natural extension of my arrival that I lived for months in a state of constant over-apology, begging forgiveness for even the smallest transgressions, before I realized that neither Dana nor Emmett seemed to blame me. Still, despite their kindness, I couldn't help but feel like a visitor, as if I were living the wrong life. Sometimes when she would hear me refer to "my aunt's house," Dana would say to me, "Can't you please call it *your* house?" And I would say it for her sake, the words feeling clumsy in my mouth.

She was licking her spoon clean and working halfheartedly on a crossword, the pen held limply between the fingers of her free hand. "Home for lunch?" she asked, only vaguely concerned, and I searched her face for whatever it was I'd seen in the widow. It was the beginning of a habit I would carry throughout my life, to wonder about people's second selves, their widow selves—*How would you look, how would you be different*, I'll wonder about the gum-snapping girl in the checkout line, about my postman, who wears women's glasses, *if everyone you loved went away, and you were alone? What kind of ugliness would reveal itself?*

"Free period," I lied, hugging her with one arm.

"Your dad just called." She looked cautiously at the phone on the counter, as though she was afraid that mentioning my father would cause him to call again. "He was rambling about tombstones. I think he was trying to upset me."

"I'm sorry," I said, and that was true.

"I found a package for you on the back porch. I put it on your bed."

I shuffled, exhausted, to my room. The box was there, filled with the supplies I'd ordered for my rat study, which I certainly wouldn't finish now. I slumped on the floor and pulled my laptop from under the bed. The e-mail icon on the computer screen jumped in its tray—Dad had written. He was still going on about his tombstone:

How's this for an epitaph: "I spent a lot of money on booze, birds, and fast cars. The rest I just squandered." Look that up. The guy who said it was a REAL alcoholic. They've got plenty of those here. Make one joke about drinking and they all just frown at you. This might be hard for you to understand, but it's very unusual for adults to openly frown at each other. —Dad

I deleted the e-mail without responding. The science fair project I'd completed before I met Sammy had been my final, sad attempt to impress my dad, to win him back in my life as someone who loved me and who could show me love. I even thought I could save him, maybe—that I could discover a way to help him reverse the damage he'd done to himself. The centerpiece of my study was the soursop—the fat, spiny fruit of the *Annona muricata*. The con men of alternative medicine had been advertising soursop as a treatment for cancer, and I felt that medical research, in its efforts to debunk these fraudulent claims, had overlooked the real potential benefits for patients with cirrhosis. My results showed the promising but slow-acting effects of soursop on TGF-β1, and I made the national finals in Washington, D.C. When I returned from the trip, my dad never even asked if I'd won a prize—I hadn't—and today, he was closer to death than he'd ever been.

Exhausted, I curled up on the floor, still in my school clothes. *Mr. Tampari died. He died of an overdose.* I shut my eyes and repeated those sentences in my mind until I knew, when the time came, I could say them out loud to Dana. As I fell asleep, I remembered that question I'd heard whispered by a student in the crowd: "Was it on purpose?" And I heard Beth's casual, torturous reply: "I dunno."

By the time I woke, it was nearly four in the afternoon. I heard, as my eyes adjusted to the light, a faint groan of pain rise from my throat. It seemed to outpace even my conscious memory of the day. *Sammy.*

I grabbed the bed frame and hauled myself up to the mattress. I hefted the box Dana had left for me and flipped it right-side up. There was no return address, no postage—it had been delivered by hand. These were not lab supplies. It was addressed to me, and I recognized the handwriting.

I ran to the door and checked and double-checked that I'd locked it. I ripped through the tape on the package with my hands, my stomach churning. I lifted the flaps. Inside were a key chain with a single key, a brief, handwritten note, and an enormous stack of notebooks.

The note had been scribbled hastily in dull pencil:

con,
use key at southern maine self-storage, unit 335
if trouble, call +1-202-555-0106
$10 \times ((0.957 \times \ln(4)) + (0.378 \times \ln(24.5)) + 1.2 \times \ln(5))) + 6.43 = \underline{50}$
—s

I squinted at the note, deciphering its faint letters and numbers. By the time he'd reached the end of the equation, the lead of his pencil was a thick, flat smudge. For most people, that equation might as well have been a foreign language, but to me it was recognizable—and also baffling. The formula wasn't about Sammy, and it wasn't about me. It was about my father.

The day Sammy died, I'd shown him the results of my dad's latest round of blood work—results my father had texted to me, as he always did, with some sarcastic, cynical message. Sammy had somehow remembered these numbers, and he'd used them to calculate what's called a MELD score: Model for End-Stage

Liver Disease. MELD scores are used to prioritize patients in need of liver transplants based on their three-month risk of death. I ran my finger along the formula, checking Sammy's work. MELD scores are typically capped at 40: a 71 percent chance of death within the next three months. There's no clinical need to calculate a higher score; all patients at 40 are already extremely unlikely to survive their stay on the transplant list. But Sammy had uncapped the formula, revealing my father's true score and emphasizing just how certain he was to die before he even left rehab: 90 percent, at least. I understood the math, but not the motive. Why had he written out this formula? What good did it do?

The phone number was just as much of a mystery, and while I was aware of the storage facility—it was only fifteen minutes away—Sammy had never mentioned it. That simple phrase *if trouble* sat in my stomach like spoiled milk. Yes, there was trouble—Sammy was *dead*.

With trembling hands, I removed the notebooks one by one, spread them out on the floor like tarot cards. I counted them as I went: twenty-two in total, each a few hundred pages long. I opened one at random, and it said, "The Journal of Samuel Tampari, 2002–2003." Every notebook I opened said the same, for another year. The earliest was dated 1988, when Sammy was eight years old. His entire life story, and he'd left it to me.

At the bottom of the box, I found another book—a cheaper thing, spiral-bound. My late grandma Ela had one just like it and passed it down to my mother, and now it was lost, probably, since her death. It was a recipe book, the kind with separate, delineated spaces for lists of ingredients and instructions. The front cover showed a black-ink drawing of a mixing bowl and wooden spoon, the art folksy, the image fading from time. There were no words on the cover, but inside, on the first blank page, Sammy had provided a title: "The Elixir of Life."

3

Model Boy

Sammy Tampari lies on his stomach on the floor of the living room, pretending to read. He is eight years old, and it is Saturday, early afternoon. He turns the pages of the book, licking his fingers, keeping a steady rhythm (*too* steady, if anyone paid attention), but what he's really doing is observing his father, a man he calls Don. Don is *actually* reading. He's a psychiatrist. When he comes home from work, he talks about his patients into a tape recorder, and then a transcription service turns these recordings into huge towers of paper, which Don can read silently, for hours, with no breaks to pee. Sammy likes to watch him, to study his face as he reads, but Don has said, repeatedly, "Stop spying on me, Samuel." This is one of his father's Traps, which is the best word Sammy has for it. Because Sammy *wasn't* spying, not at first; he was just watching, right out in the open, not knowing it was wrong. But now that his father has told him to stop spying, Sammy has no choice but *to* spy, to watch his father secretly, to feel the shame of this disobedience.

Once, in reference to an important painting—six flowers surrounding a tomato—his father said, "Don't even *think* about touching this," and then it was all Sammy could think about, for that day and the next.

Sammy turns another page, sighing as he does it, and this makes Don look up from his papers. "Are you bored?" he asks.

"No, sir," Sammy says.

Don grunts and returns to reading. He is a small man but handsome, even *very* handsome, with thick honey-blond hair and a broad dimpled chin that seems to lead Don from place to place, that seems to have—if this is possible for a chin—an awareness of its effect on people. On weekdays Don wears black suits, gray suits, or black-and-gray suits, but on Saturday, he dresses in a sweater and slacks. Sammy only sees his father in a T-shirt at bedtime, and it is hard to see him this way, like a turtle without its shell.

Directly behind Don's office sits a smaller room, cavelike and cold, where Don stores his coin collection. For Sammy, this collection is twice over a source of consternation. First of all, the coins are used, again and again, as example par excellence of a *hobby*, which Sammy's parents feel he most urgently lacks. It's true: Sammy does not have hobbies. He takes no pleasure in them. Second, despite its use as a rhetorical device, Sammy isn't even permitted inside the collection room. He has been allowed, only once, to see the collection from the doorway. When he did, he was surprised to find the room filled not only with coins but also a very many books, which he presumed (incorrectly, it would turn out) to be *about* coins. Indeed (his father had used that word), it was the books, and their preservation, that rendered the room off-limits. Coins, his father explained, were very hard to destroy, even by children, and this was part of their appeal. With surprisingly little effort, Don said, you could find a coin that would be the oldest thing in your house, oldest by several hundred years. But *books*. Oh, no. Children, especially boys, must not be allowed to handle old books.

As for the coins themselves, they came in sizes large and small, bronze, silver, and gold, mostly circular, some more square. Sammy would admit that the sheer number of them was impressive— two whole walls full, plus several smaller displays—and he would admit that there was a certain magnetism to seeing, this close together, so many objects alike in size and shape and yet, in a profound way, completely foreign to one another. And it's true, this nearness without exactness produced an interesting visual effect, so that when he tilted his head, a kind of shimmer passed over the coins, like the sun traveling quickly over a river, like a wink, a raise of the eyebrows, the promise of a secret.

Don grunts again, this time to himself, and Sammy thinks, *What's wrong with me?*

From across the house, the long, empty hallways report the sound of the front door opening. His mother is home. The Tamparis live in a Manhattan brownstone, a building so old that Sammy can't re-create it with LEGOs; he's found the right colors, even a plastic door with a fake stained-glass window, but the shiny plastic simply can't reproduce the history of the place. He hears his mother drop keys into her purse and kick off her shoes in the landing. He hears the sound of her bare feet in the hallway. The entryway is rich with windows, and the house is bright, but as you proceed, the rooms darken, so that coming home is, for Sammy, like falling asleep.

His mother, Leena, sweeps into the room, patting his head, inspecting the wall hangings—she's an art appraiser—as though she hasn't been home in years. Leena is plainer in the face than her husband but much taller and thinner; from behind, Sammy can see the beginning of her spine form below her neck and disappear into the low back of a cotton dress. Sammy knows he has inherited the best of them both, at least physically; he will be tall, thin, and pretty, and everywhere he goes, people will look at him. They already do.

"SonAndHusband," Leena says, acknowledging them. She bends almost in half at the waist to kiss Don's head, and when he looks up at her, there is warmth between them. Sammy can recognize these feelings in others, which he thinks must be good, must be a sign that he is not totally, irreversibly broken.

Leena adjusts the slider for the ceiling lights, which are recessed like the eyes of a doll, and the room brightens. Her hair is curly and red—last week it was brown—and she grabs a strand of it now, examines its color in this new light.

When she's done, she catches Sammy's eye. "Your friends are outside. The sun is there, too. Go play and be free."

Sammy closes his book. This is his mother's version of a Trap, except it's not a Trap really, just a Sadness: she tells Sammy to do the things that *she'd* like to be doing, but never does. His mother dreams of playing basketball for the New York Knicks. He knows this because when she naps on the couch, she updates the score in her sleep and sometimes, like a peaceful sigh, says, "Swoosh."

He has accepted that his parents don't love him.

Those boys outside, whichever boys she's seen, are not his friends. They're just neighborhood boys. To Leena, all young people know and admire one another. Sammy wonders if this assumption comes from some great happiness in her own childhood or whether, instead, it has formed in response to some *un*happiness, some old wound. Sammy does not have any friends. At school, he is so much smarter than his classmates that he feels the weight of their stupidity on his chest—even after the bell rings, like waking up from a nightmare to find yourself suffocating, still, under the heart-crushing burden of your fear.

Nonetheless, he stands and stretches. With Leena home, Don will read in the bedroom, away from the noise of the television (which Leena is turning on now, checking the *TV Guide* for schedules) and away from spying eyes. Sammy might as well go outside if it will make Leena happy.

"Hey," Leena says to him. "How many three-pointers did Trent Tucker make in 1986?"

"Sixty-eight."

She laughs with delight. This is the one thing he knows can make his mother happy: his memory. Words, faces, field goal percentages, he can just . . . remember things.

"How about you teach him something *useful*," Don says.

Sammy trudges down the hall, Leena calling to him to take his skateboard, so he does, though he's never actually used it. On good days, he would confess that it does bring him pleasure to carry the board around, to be seen with it. He thinks it suggests to strangers some hidden swiftness, which he has chosen not to show them.

Outside, the sun is high and hot, the sky a distant river blue. There are boys, yes, four of them, playing four square in the street. This is a relief to Sammy: they will have no use for a fifth. He tucks his skateboard under his arm and sits on the shaded bricks of the stoop. His mother likes to say Manhattan is changing— she likes to say it even though it pains her—but to Sammy, everything looks the same as it always has, except maybe for the coffee trees planted along the sidewalk, which for some reason, this summer, have not grown leaves and now sit naked under the sun like skeletons. The cars in front of his house are parked very close together, their bumpers nearly kissing, and it gives Sammy a sick, shuddering feeling, as he imagines the drivers trying to extract these cars from their spaces.

Three stupid pigeons—one white, almost dovelike, the others as dirty and gray as the street—land near the neighborhood boys, who are hurling a spongy red ball across the chalk lines of the playing field. The pigeons line up in single file, as though they are waiting to play, and this distracts the tallest, oldest boy—who is not wearing a shirt, who has a thin line of hair emerging from his nylon shorts and rising to his belly button, it's really something— and so he loses the point and throws the red ball at the pigeons, who scatter. Sammy looks away from the boy's hair and follows the white pigeon as it flaps—in the inelegant way of pigeons— toward his house. He worries it might fly directly into his bedroom window, but at the last moment it thrusts upward, into the camouflage of some fast-moving clouds.

How high above the street is my bedroom? Sammy wonders, and the urgency of this question frightens him. He's always being struck by thoughts like this, that arrive seemingly out of nowhere but *desperately*, with an insistence that reminds him of his father's chin. He stacks imaginary versions of himself on top of each other until his hypothetical head has reached the window. His bedroom, he decides, is four and a half Sammies off the ground.

When he returns his attention to the street, there is a man standing in front of him, blocking his view of the boys. The man is wearing dark jeans and a green collared shirt. Wiry tufts of chest hair sprout from the neckline of this shirt, and it is not like the hair of the neighborhood boy—Sammy does not want to look at this.

"Hey, kid," the guy says. "Got a minute?"

Here is why Sammy spies on his father.

Every Wednesday Don receives the package from the transcription service—delivered in person, it *must* be signed for, "And not by a kid, please," said the delivery boy, once, when Sammy opened the door—with a box full of patient files. Every Thursday evening Don meets with the New York Society of Numismatics, i.e., coin collectors, and of course Sammy is not invited, while Leena goes to something she calls Fun Club. This Sammy *has* seen, and it's just women smoking cigarettes. The babysitter hired to watch Sammy—a college girl with polychromatic eyes—doesn't care what he does so long as he doesn't go "out of sight," the mere thought of which makes the girl breathe so frantically that Sammy can map the shape of her breasts.

This means that every Thursday evening, for four hours, Sammy can read his father's files. The coin cave Don locks, but the files, miraculously, he leaves unprotected, perhaps assuming they're too dry, or too complex, to attract Sammy's interest. The first time, he read them out of boredom. Sammy really doesn't have anything, not one thing, he particularly likes to do. He plays with LEGOs when ordered, but they make his mind anxious and his fingers feel raw. Reading books is okay, but only when they're about science, and even then he could take them or leave them. In bed each night, he cries from 10:00 to 10:15 (he sets the timer on his bedside clock). It's almost a relief, this crying, though he can't explain from *what*. To use a phrase of his mother's, "It's just one of those things." Why did the pigeons land near those boys, and not some other place? Why did they arrange themselves in a line?

These things could not be explained: the behavior of pigeons, the crying, his lack of pleasure in activities that drive other boys into frenzies of excitement (video games, cap guns), that his parents loved each other (proving they were capable of love) but not him, that if he listened carefully, in a quiet place, he could hear something rattling in the space between his shoulder and neck, as if a part of him had broken off. He did want to touch the babysitter's breasts, and he did want to do . . . *something* with that neighborhood boy, but even these things he wanted vaguely, indifferently—he wouldn't give up anything to have them. Or was it that he *had* nothing to give up? That there was nothing in life he valued?

All of these, he had thought, were questions without answers. But then he read his father's files, and he found stacks upon stacks of pages of his father *trying* to answer them . . . for other people. He read about someone named Edna, who cried so much in public she lost her job, which made her cry even more, so then she lost her kids. He read about William, *who felt unloved by his parents* (this was Don writing this!), and for whom Don had prescribed medication. Sammy read about Christina, who told Sammy's father—and these were her actual words, though Sammy could barely believe it—that she had always felt *broken*. To solve these people's problems, Don had to take a *cross-sectional view*, plus a *longitudinal view*, to create a *working hypothesis*.

Sammy, too, would do this. He would read the files. He would watch Don read the files. He would figure out, once and for all, what was wrong with him.

"Seriously," the guy with the chest hair is saying, "you're a real beautiful kid."

Sammy clutches his skateboard. He wonders how tall the man is, how many of him it would take to reach Sammy's bedroom from the street.

"This is your house?" the guy says, responding to Sammy's glance back at the window. The man has bad teeth, but his clothes look expensive, or at least they seem to have been chosen carefully. "Are your parents home?"

Like all children, Sammy has been instructed not to talk to strangers. But one of his thoughts comes to him, and he can't help himself. "Are you a patient of Don's?" he asks.

The man's eyebrows narrow. "A patient I am not," he says, very seriously, but then he smiles his crooked smile. "In fact, I've been told I'm rather *impatient*." This makes him laugh. Behind him, the red ball escapes the playing field and goes bump-bump-bump down the street.

Sammy has lost his curiosity and stands to go inside. He tries to turn his back to the man, but the man has his arm.

"Wait," the guy says. "Do you want to make a lot of money?"

Sammy considers this. It's not a question he's ever been asked before. "I think I already have a lot of money."

The guy casts his eyes over Sammy's house. "That's probably true," he admits. "But there's more to it than money."

"No, thank you," Sammy says. "Goodbye."

"So polite!" The guy still has Sammy's arm. "Let me give you something." The man fishes in his pocket with his other arm and produces a small business card, the kind Don keeps in his wallet. "I photograph kids. Beautiful kids."

Sammy's right arm is holding the skateboard, so the man has no choice but to release Sammy's left and press the card into his hand. Sammy grips it tight, bending the paper, and the man grimaces. "Just show it to your folks."

Sammy climbs the steps to his door. It has not occurred to him before now to meet one of his father's patients, but now he wants to, badly. He imagines meeting all of them in a warm, public place—there are coins, and there is four square, and there is the smoking of cigarettes. It would be their own Fun Club.

"Hey, model boy!" the man yells from the street as Sammy opens the door. "Tell your folks to call that number. The world needs beauty."

Sammy says nothing and enters the bright foyer of his house. The sound of televised basketball wafts like a smell from the living room, and Leena has often dragged him to live games, so he really can smell it: the popcorn, the beer, the sweat from the players, which runs and runs down their muscled arms until the ball is slick with it and they start missing shots. Sammy wonders if athletes would ever need a psychiatrist or if their minds are too simple. He has heard his mother call Patrick Ewing a "head case."

He goes upstairs to his bedroom, which is across the hall from his parents' bedroom. Don is in there with the door closed, not to be disturbed. Sammy's own room stays clean because of the housekeeper who comes once a week, but it is also cramped with his bed and bookshelf and homework desk and neon-colored beanbags, the fabric of which develops a weird film in summer. The walls are white, with a hint of yellow, and he's covered them in glossy posters of the Ferrari Testarossa, a fast and flat car. This is one of those things he can't explain. He has no interest in driving this car—no interest in driving, period—but something about its pancake geometry, its simplicity of form, excites him.

He goes to the window, opens it, and looks out at the neighborhood boys, still playing. The strange man is gone. The air smells of gasoline and heat. All of the cars parked in front of his house, he notices from above, are the same shade of blue. One of the boys makes a violent motion with the ball, and the tallest boy says, "Hey, no spikesies!," and an argument ensues. The bleached limbs of the coffee trees cast fingered shadows over all of this, and it is pretty—actually, *so* pretty—and just one more reason for Sammy to go on living, to take pleasure from this good city, this good house, his good parents. What was it the man said?

The world needs beauty.

Sammy jumps out of the window.

Several weeks later, on a Thursday evening, Don takes Sammy to his first meeting of the New York Society of Numismatics. Sammy's arm is still in a cast, his left arm—broken right where that strange man, the photographer, had grabbed him. It wasn't the man who broke it—that was the fall, four and a half Sammies to the sidewalk. When he landed, the world went white with pain. Sometimes he thinks he never left that world, the pain world, as though his jumping flipped some switch on the universe. But still, the two events—the man grabbing him, the jump—have become linked in Sammy's mind.

And not just his. Don and Leena have tried to convince him that he didn't *jump*, exactly—the man scared him, and he ran, and he fell out of the window. An accident. Sammy is not convinced by this, nor is the psychiatrist he now visits once a week: Dr. Gillian Huang, an interesting woman—interesting because she seems to watch people, including his parents, with an intensity he recognizes as his own. She has black hair with heavy, side-parted bangs and thick-rimmed glasses that she adjusts constantly, forward and back. She does not buy the panic theory, but she did agree (reluctantly?) to consider his fall an act of "self-harm," rather than a "suicide attempt," considering his young age and the short distance from the window to the street. (It would take a drop of seven or eight Sammies, he's since calculated, to ensure a fatal outcome.)

Dr. Huang did echo his parents on one central issue: hobbies. "You need some," she said to him, and in their first group meeting, Dr. Huang suggested that each of them—Sammy, herself, and his parents—propose one such hobby. He would be allowed to veto one of these proposals; the others, he would have to try.

Sammy suggested reading. He was already doing it anyway.

Dr. Huang suggested journaling. Every day he would need to write about his life: what he did, how he was feeling. This didn't sound so bad to Sammy, relative to his mother's suggestion.

Leena said he should join a basketball team. VETOED.

When the needle landed on Don, he shifted uncomfortably in his chair, bereft of ideas in a way that seemed embarrassing— what kind of psychiatrist was he?

"How about this," Dr. Huang said patiently. "Why don't you tell Sam some of the hobbies *you* enjoy."

"He collects coins!" Leena said, relieved to break the tension. She was sitting between Don and Sammy on the small couch that faced Dr. Huang's chair. The office was carpeted, clean, and slightly too warm. A well-manicured-but-dehydrated ficus tree sat potted in the corner, the tips of its leaves pointing to the ground.

"Good." Dr. Huang's voice had a liquid quality that contrasted with the dry air and produced, in Sammy, a pleasurable hum. "Does his coin collection interest you, Sam?"

"He doesn't let me near it." It made Sammy feel good to say this to her, in front of them.

Don lifted his chin, defensive, but Leena interjected before he had the chance to explain himself. "Maybe you could take him to one of your coin meetings?"

"The New York Society of Numismatics," Don clarified, in response to a single raised eyebrow from Dr. Huang. He clenched his teeth. "That's a good idea," he said, chewing the words.

Dr. Huang smiled, indifferent to his obvious displeasure, and focused her eyes on Sammy. "Reading, journals, coins." She ticked them off on her fingers. "Showing up is half the battle."

The coin is gold, or at least the color of gold, and the size of a half-dollar. The side of the coin that Sammy would call heads— though he now knows it's called the obverse—shows a man standing on a pedestal, striking a pose that reminds Sammy of the ballet dancers he can see through the window of the studio near his house, their heads lifted, arms raised, fingers and toes extended. The man has wings like an angel, but he wears a hat that *also* has wings, and so do his boots. This, Don says, is a poetic redundancy. The man is actually a god, Mercury, and below him an inscription reads *Arte de Industria*—"art by industry."

The tails ("The *reverse*," Don corrects) is nothing but text, a full paragraph but circular, coiling around the coin like a sleeping snake. But now the coin collectors have lost interest in walking Sammy through his first close reading of a coin, and they only summarize it for him. "It basically says mankind can make stuff that is just as beautiful as found in nature," says a much-older man, whom Sammy has identified as the leader of this group, even though he was not introduced this way. They are sitting in a circle, maybe twenty of them, but everyone's chair—including Don's—points toward this ancient fellow.

They are in the library of a house on the Upper East Side— whose house, Sammy isn't sure. No one seems to be acting as host, the way his mother does at home, arranging seating, fixing drinks (or telling someone else to do those things). The air is thick with dust and wine (which everyone is drinking) and the smell of old books and old people. Sammy wouldn't call it stuffy, exactly— the room is quite large—but there is a sense of permanence, of objects and people that either don't move at all or move slowly. There are three walls of books, floor to ceiling, and their age gives them a uniformity of color, just as many of the men, even the Asian one, share an ashy, faded complexion. (Don is one of the youngest.) In the middle of the circle is a table, and on it are more books, several bottles of wine, and a sign-in sheet with a pen attached by string to a clipboard.

What there isn't much of, surprisingly, is coins. "There's a bit more to it than that," Don says when Sammy remarks on this, and even the gold coin he now holds between his forefinger and thumb was produced offhandedly and without much interest. "Does anyone have something he can look at?" Don had said, and now Sammy feels the way he does at a restaurant when the waiter hands him a children's menu.

"We approach the subject of coins obliquely," the ancient man explains, and Sammy likes that he uses this word: *obliquely.* It's clear he does not speak often to children. "We approach the subject . . . alchemically."

"Alchemy," Sammy says. "Like chemistry?" At home, he has a chemistry set. It's just a toy—used to make volcanoes or monsters that foam at the mouth—but Sammy has hacked it to test the paint in his house for lead. So far: negative.

Apparently his question was loaded because all of the adults, except Don, begin to laugh.

"There's no difference between alchemy and chemistry," the ancient man says quickly, as though to immediately curb debate.

He's not fast enough. The Asian man clears his throat. "The continued existence of the two words—*alchemy* and *chemistry*—suggests there *is* a difference."

The ancient man throws up his hands, but the subject has broken loose.

"For me," says another man to Sammy, "chemistry is more practical, while alchemy is more *thinky.*"

Don leans forward in his seat, fingers caged, and Sammy wonders if this is how he talks to his patients. Sammy's gut says the answer is no, that the way Don is acting is a performance for Sammy's benefit. But why? "I believe you're referring," Don says in a low voice, "to what Goltz calls the *science* of matter versus the *philosophy* of matter."

"Alchemy is a subset of chemistry," says the only woman in the room, a white-haired wrinkle-face (that's what Leena calls old women) with a faint Long Island accent. "Alchemy is chemistry with a specific purpose."

"What purpose?" Sammy asks, his interest piqued by the dissent.

He is startled when several of the coin collectors answer this question at once, in unplanned unison: "The elixir of life." This word, *elixir*, makes no impression on Sammy, but it clearly means a lot to these people. He picks at his cast.

"This leads us back to our proper subject," continues the old man, trying to end the unwelcome digression. "Last week we examined the manuscript that claims to be the fourth volume of the *Steganographia*, proposing a fuller recipe for the elixir than that described in Trithemius's other work. Do we have thoughts on the veracity of this manuscript?"

"The recipe's use of spikenard root is consistent with Trithemius's research," Don says, glancing sidelong at Sammy in a way that seems—though this can't be true—almost shy. Sammy's thoughts keep being pulled to his cast, which is so itchy he could scream, but something in Don's voice, a smallness, moves Sammy to alertness. In spite of himself, he's drawn to it, the same way a distant plane, a fleck of white against a blue sky, makes him stand on his tiptoes. He wants to see that shyness again.

So he says, "I don't get what this has to do with coins, even *obliquely*."

Don's face goes red—there it is!—but the white-haired wrinkle-face laughs. "There's a centuries-old bond between alchemy and numismatics," she explains.

"Look again at the coin you're holding," says the ancient man, so Sammy does. "'Art by industry.' The coin commemorates the supposed transmutation of mercury into gold."

"It's all fiction, of course," Don says quickly, his face still bright. Seeing this, Sammy feels as if he were lighter than air, as if, if he jumped out of his window now, he would rise.

"So you talk about the history?" Sammy asks.

"Not history in a general sense," says the Asian man. "The history of the elixir."

"It's just for fun," Don says. "A thought experiment."

The ancient man has been writing something on a slip of paper torn from the sign-in sheet. He holds it out to Sammy, who has to stand and cross the circle to take it with his one good arm. "There's your homework. Next time, you can tell us why this is important."

The paper says:

$$HgS + O_2 \rightarrow Hg + SO_2$$

Sammy takes the formula to his chair. Everyone is staring at him, but not seriously—to them, he's just a kid. A baby historian. "What is the elixir of life?" he asks. "Something that makes you immortal?"

"That depends on whom you ask," says the ancient man, "and when they lived. But in most modern cultures, true immortality is not the objective. Do you know the word *panacea*?"

Sammy does know the word. "So if there was something wrong with someone, even if you didn't know what it was, the elixir would make them feel better?"

Don is watching Sammy hard. "It's all just stories. A hobby, remember? Don't get excited."

Sammy nods, but one of his thoughts comes to him, as hot and urgent as fire.

It's a Trap.

4

Assembly

Number 50 was a Wistar rat, and as far as rats go, Wistars are some of the cutest. They're albinos, with soft, white coats. They have pale-pink noses, like the inside of a strawberry. Their ears, which are the same color, tend to be slightly asymmetrical, giving them an eager, attentive appearance. Their eyes are red, but they are too small and offset to seem sinister; the rats look, each day, as if they've just woken up with a cold.

But on Sammy's last day alive, Number 50 really did get sick. I'd gone to the chem lab to gather data for our experiment, but I found Number 50 huddled in the corner of his cage, lethargic, hardly lifting his head as I reached for him. I held him up to the light and inspected him for any obvious wounds. Nothing. He looked at me with his red, tired eyes, and I felt the truth of that look in my chest: Number 50 was dying.

I put him back in his cage and called Sammy once, twice, three times, without answer. I debated what to do. The right thing was to leave him in the lab, where Sammy could examine him in the morning, but I wasn't convinced he would live that long. The other option was to bring him right away to Sammy, who had much more experience with lab rats. I hated the idea of being judged for this, but I hated even more the thought of losing Number 50. I began to prepare his travel cage, and as I did, he started to sneeze—four or five sneezes in succession, so hard his little legs were shaking.

Before I left, I texted my aunt that I was going to RJ's. I didn't always lie to Dana about the time I spent with Sammy, but it was a *lot* of time, and a few weeks prior, when I was headed to see him for the third morning in a row, Dana looked up from her toast and said, "Tell me again what you're working on?"

I carried Number 50 downstairs, strapped his cage to the handlebars of my bike using electrical tape, and then I rode, like Elliott carrying E.T., the mile and a half to Sammy's apartment.

Once I arrived, I knocked for a minute before letting myself in. I kicked off my shoes and set Number 50 on the bed. Fading light through the lean casement windows turned the white walls the color of corn silk. Sammy was standing in the kitchen with his head in the freezer. I wasn't sure if he knew I was there, but then he said, "Sorry, my head is killing me!" without turning around, his voice echoing out of the freezer.

"Did you take some Tylenol?" I stepped around the bed.

"No! I mean, yes! I mean, I took something else!"

"Okay, good." I was right behind him.

He turned, startled. "Sorry for shouting. My head is killing me."

"I heard." I kissed him.

He put his arms around me and held me in this kiss before pulling away. His eyes were big and bright like headlights. I was caught in them like a deer. Before I could look away, he tightened his arms and hoisted me up over his shoulder. "You're so light!" He laughed and carried me around the room.

I grabbed the back of his shirt and held on. "You're in a weird mood." My words came out in a breathy staccato as I bounced against his body.

He set me down and clapped his hands together. "I haven't eaten," he said, as though that explained anything.

"Do you want me to make you something?" I asked, eager for the chance to take care of him.

"I want you to relax, and to always be happy when you're here."

"I am," I promised. "Is something wrong?"

"Not at all. I actually had a really good talk with my parents today."

"What?" Sammy's parents were dead.

"Oh. Not like that. Don't you ever talk to your mom?"

"Sometimes." I would lie in bed at night and tell her what life was like in Littlefield. I would picture our life in Winterville, me in the living room, cooking myself in front of the pellet stove, my mom trudging in from the snow with several big bags of groceries, her body wrapped in soft, puffy layers of winter coats and snow pants. She looked like a purple synthetic snowman, and it always made me smile. Then she would remove those layers and become my mother—my skinny, strong, quick-tempered mother—and tell me to get off my butt and help put away the food. I would say, "Did you get me anything special?" And she would say, "That depends. Is kale special?"

Sammy was watching me, waiting for me to come back to him. "So"—I gestured to Number 50—"I could use your help."

Sammy followed my finger to the cage, and upon seeing Number 50, he had a strange, singultus reaction, like a hiccup. I was certain that he was angry. His eyes were all pupils, the sky on a starless night. Behind me, on the wall, was a framed print of Joseph Wright's *The Alchemist Discovering Phosphorous*, and behind that, hidden like a safe, was the hole Sammy had punched into the wall earlier that summer. He was older and wiser, but of the two of us he was also the more intrinsically delicate; I imagined his heart as a little glass flute and, inside it, a hummingbird.

He knelt in front of the cage and poked one finger through, tousling the spiky hair between the rat's ears.

I sat on the edge of the bed. "I'm sorry if I shouldn't have—"

"I told you not to get attached." To my great relief, Sammy didn't sound angry. "I'll keep an eye on him tonight."

Sammy placed the cage on the love seat and sat next to me on the bed. Our elbows were almost touching. I was going to kiss him again when my phone buzzed with a message, a text from my father, the screenshot with the results from his last round of blood work: bilirubin, creatinine, INR. Appended to the image, my dad had written, *Hasta la vista, baby.*

In response to a questioning look from Sammy, I handed him the phone, and only a slight twitch of his lips betrayed his understanding of my father's bleak future. Part of me wanted Sammy to tell me that everything would be okay; part of me loved that he would never say such a thing when it wasn't true. Still, between my mother, my father, and now Number 50, I was feeling sorry for myself and asked, "What did I do to deserve this?"

Sammy took this question seriously, and rather than saying, "Nothing, you did nothing," he talked to me about the terrible odds of survival. The ash from a troubled teenager's cigarette catches the curtains of a closed window, killing my mother on the second floor, and this happens so often that there are people *keeping track* of it, creating graphs and charts to map its every occurrence: Deaths by Fires Caused by Cigarettes of Underage Smokers. Every second we're speaking, he said, two people die. One Mississippi, two Mississippi, three Mississippi. For a boy of sixteen to lose both his parents was truly, cosmically unstrange.

"The real question is whether you *want* your father to live."

I recoiled as if he'd slapped me. "What?"

"You said yourself he doesn't love you," Sammy answered plainly, not realizing how much it hurt to have these words— which, yes, were my own—reflected back at me.

"That doesn't mean I want him *dead*. He's still my dad." I didn't say that it was partially Sammy himself who made the idea of losing my father so real. Sometimes, in quiet moments, I felt that I could *see* Sammy's loneliness, as if it were some distant island that came into view in calm weather. He had no mother, no father, no siblings, no friends. It meant he was all mine, but it also frightened me.

"Okay. He's your dad."

I said nothing, and there was nothing I could say. Sammy wasn't apologizing. That I still wanted a father was simply information Sammy had processed, which was somehow enough for me—to be learned about by this man.

"Anyway," he said. "I can't believe the summer is over." Real sadness was in his voice, and maybe he was just mourning the end of warm weather, of the vacation from school, but his sadness produced an ache in me, one that dissolved any lingering anger like a solvent. I wanted the summer to last forever.

I said, "I love you."

I had never said this before, and I could see the words pass through Sammy like an electric current. A long second passed, then another. I was humiliated, searching for ways to take back what I'd said, but then Sammy stood up, and it was as though a switch had been flipped. Without a word, he peeled off his shirt and tossed it overhand to the hamper, where it caught the lip and hung off the side, half in and half out. He put his hands on my face and kissed me, hard, as his hand slid below the waist of my jeans.

I knew he was dodging my declaration of love, but I was also sixteen, and I spent every hour with him in constant agitation. The sight of his bare chest and the feel of his hand pushed all thoughts from my head.

I reached for him. But even though he leaned his head back as though seized by pleasure, he was soft and unresponsive. "Sorry," he said after a minute of effort.

"No rush," I said, even though there *was* a rush—I *needed* him.

"It might not be in the cards."

"Just relax."

"Seriously. This isn't helping."

"It will," I said, because it had to.

"Stop!" He pushed me away, standing, pulling up his plaid boxer briefs. "Jesus."

"I'm sorry." Then, foolishly, I said again, "I love you."

He threw a cardigan over his bare shoulders and began to jimmy his tight jeans over his legs. "I'm going outside." His voice was needlessly loud. He was searching his desk in a tizzy, and I knew, from how he lifted papers and pulled drawers, that he was looking for his phone.

"It's in your pocket."

"Oh." He was too upset to say thank you or even to be embarrassed. He stuffed his bare feet into his sneakers and marched to the door, shoes untied, like a child. He opened the door. Over his shoulder, I could see the sun setting into the woods behind the widow's house, the birch trees filtering the light and sending speckled shadows onto the porch.

In the doorway, Sammy paused. "I'm not angry at you," he said angrily, and shut the door.

I stood up and went to the window, watched him descend the stairs and stand in front of the woods with his hands on his hips, as if he were scolding the trees. His spine was straight, his posture infallible—a habit drilled into him from boyhood by his father, who told him the brain sags when the body does. Under the low, pink sun, his blond hair was orange. I couldn't see it, but I knew the face he was making, his eyebrows gathered together, his mouth pinched.

I dragged a chair to the window and sat. Sammy's face glowed in the light of his phone; he stared at the lambent screen and put it to his ear. Whomever he'd called had answered. I couldn't hear the conversation, but Sammy paced along the tree line, gesticulating with his free hand. He was animated but not angry. It was something other than an argument. Sammy spoke with his head down, his chin almost in his chest. He toed the sod with his still-unlaced sneakers. His mannerisms were all apology—someone else was getting the sorry that belonged to me.

Who was that someone? What was Sammy saying to him? I would have given anything in the world to know. They talked for long enough—at least twenty minutes—that Sammy grew tired of pacing and leaned against the railing of the stairs. He surveyed the sky, which was turning cinereal silver, like granite, and seemed to track with his eyes the path the sun had taken into the trees. It reminded him of something—me, perhaps—and he checked his big, expensive watch. He glanced at the window, and I ducked and returned to the bed. As I heard his footsteps thudding toward the door, I rearranged myself on the mattress, pretended to be engaged with my own phone. The doorknob turned, my stomach with it.

He opened the door. "Sweetheart. I'm sorry."

I had steeled myself to stay angry, but his voice was a snakebite. Happiness filled me like venom. "Are you okay?"

In answer, he kissed me. "I'm ready now."

And when I pulled him onto the bed, my legs circling his waist, my heels on his back, he was.

Emmett came home from school around four, but I stayed in my room with Sammy's notebooks until Dana called us to dinner. I ran my fingers over the earliest journals and tried to resist the urge to just dive in, to consume his life uncritically. Before he died, he had left me this gift, and to understand it I would need to approach the journals as he would have—as a scientist first.

On the outside, each journal was identical to the last. The front and back covers were made of fine full-grain leather with an aubergine suede interior. They were secured with a metal clasp and a nude leather tie. Inside, Sammy wrote single-spaced and mostly in print. As a child, his preferred writing instrument was a black pen, but as I thumbed through a journal from his teenage years, I saw more randomness in his choices. One entry from college was written in crayon.

The first journal was in good condition, with only slight creasing of the suede and a few ripped pages demonstrating its age. Had anyone other than Sammy ever seen a word of it, before me? I opened to the first entry:

> My name is Samuel Tampari, and I am eight years old. I will try to write clean, but my arm is broken. Dr. Huang said I should start right away, even though my arm is broken. Don and Leena took me to her because of what happened with my arm, when I jumped out the window. I will tell what happened, and then I will tell more about my life.

I read to the end of this first long passage, as he described his encounter with the creepy photographer and the jump from his bedroom window. The next day, he talked more about his parents: their work, their personalities. He knew he was not like other boys. *I don't think I have met anyone like me. Who is always pretending. But maybe I have and didn't know.*

It was his second week with the journal when he attended the

numismatics meeting with his father. This received a long and de-
scriptive account; his slanted prose showed the excitement I'd
seen in him when we worked together in the lab. *The coin collectors don't talk about coins!* he wrote, using his first exclamation point
in twenty-odd pages. *They talk about the "elixir of life."*

On a legal pad, I jotted down the formula Sammy had received
from the old numismatist during that initial meeting:

$$HgS + O_2 \rightarrow Hg + SO_2$$

I didn't share Sammy's gift for memorization, but I did know
the periodic table the way he, at that age, knew the free-throw per-
centage for every player on the Knicks. I put names to the symbols right away.

$$HgS + O_2 \rightarrow Hg + SO_2$$
cinnabar [heat] mercury

Chemistry 101. Mercury, also known as quicksilver (*quick*,
from the Old English *cwic*: "living, alive"), is the stuff you find in
old thermometers, the stuff—if the thermometer breaks—your
mom tells you not to touch. It comes from a mineral ore known as
cinnabar, which is a red, evil-looking rock found in only a handful
of places. The formula Sammy received from the numismatists—
let's call it the Mercury Formula—described how to extract liquid
mercury, quicksilver, from cinnabar.

Quicksilver was discovered by an ancient Chinese alchemist
known as Ge Hong. When Ge Hong applied heat to the quicksilver, it produced a red powder known as mercuric oxide. This
compound is remarkable because just as heated quicksilver produces mercuric oxide, heated mercuric oxide turns right back into
quicksilver. It's an endless loop of production and reproduction,
of blood-red stone to living silver and back again. No matter how
much Ge Hong burned mercury, he could not destroy it.

For this reason, Ge Hong identified mercury as the key to
immortality. By giving the Mercury Formula to Sammy, the numismatists were inviting him into the earliest traditions of alchemy,
chemistry, and the search for the elixir of life.

·

Eventually I began to hear the sounds of Dana in the kitchen. She was on a health kick, and I could smell the sweet potatoes roasting on the stove, hear the static hiss of millet poured into a cast-iron pot. She was not a confident cook, and she would do this work nervously, always keeping one hand on the large, glossy spread of some vegetarian cookbook, holding the pages flat.

In this way, that evening, we were alike. I had just received a cookbook of my own.

ELIXIR OF LIFE #1
Yield: 100 pills

INGREDIENTS
Quicksilver (8 g)
Licorice root powder (4 g)
Honey (1 g)
Sugar (7 g)
Rose water (2 g)

PREPARATION
Combine honey, sugar, and rose water and stir until smooth. Combine mixture with quicksilver and stir until silvery globules are invisible. Add licorice root powder. Pound until solid, cut into yield.

HOW DID IT TASTE?
almost died.

According to the date in the top right corner, Sammy had written this first recipe when he was only thirteen years old: not an "elixir" at all, but a pill. Along with its lists of ingredients and instructions, the book provided a section for notes after each recipe, titled "How did it taste?" Sammy's use of these spaces left little doubt that he'd been ingesting the concoctions himself: *felt good but briefly*, said one of his notes; *slept all day*, said another. And that alarmingly casual first review: *almost died*.

There were just over a hundred of these recipes, each modi-
fying the last. As I flipped through them, I felt a rising nausea, as
though I had left Earth entirely and found myself subject to unfamiliar gravity. I *was* on a brand-new planet, one on which the
man I loved had been searching for something out of a bad fantasy novel: the great panacea. It had begun as the desperate quest
of a troubled, suicidal boy—that, I could understand—but it had
continued, and continued, until he was gone. I felt as if the box
of journals had been dropped on my head rather than delivered
to my doorstep.

There is no such thing as an elixir of life! I would have shouted if I
weren't so afraid of Dana's hearing me. For people such as Sammy
and me, scientific truth is a heartbeat, a bass line—it is the rhythm
by which we walk and breathe and live. Sammy's death felt like a
betrayal—he'd *left* me—but the recipe book was itself an infidel-
ity. Behind my back, he had abandoned reason. As I turned the
pages, I was surprised to find my hands trembling; even in the
worst of times, I could usually rely on them. It felt like a silly
thought, in light of everything that was happening, but I kept
thinking it: *I don't want my boyfriend to have been crazy.*

Yet something else, too, added to my dizziness: relief. The boy
in the hallway had asked, "Was it on purpose?" I forced myself
to imagine that the answer was yes. I forced myself to picture
Sammy saying goodbye to me our last night together, the last night
of summer. How could he not have been thinking of everything
we'd shared? I had told him I loved him: that was the truth I left
behind when I kissed him good-night and said, "See you tomorrow." If his death held even the slightest bit of intention, it meant
he had looked at everything I offered him and said, *No, I'd rather
die.* It meant I was irrevocably, fatally, not enough. I could only
think these thoughts for so long because I couldn't catch my
breath when I thought them. I had to choose between believing
he'd killed himself and breathing.

The recipe book, as crazy as it was, offered me what I desperately needed: a way of understanding Sammy's death that did not
involve his deliberately discarding the love we shared. My boyfriend wasn't crazy. He was sick, and it seemed he had tried for a

long, long time to find a cure for that sickness. Sammy had "almost died" once pursuing an elixir of life, so it stood to reason that he may have done it again, only this time he'd *really* done it. But he would also have known, from experience, the risk he was taking. Thus the package, hand-delivered to the back porch in the middle of the night. And the note, which I imagined him scribbling hastily in his car, closing his eyes to calculate my father's MELD score.

"Sweetheart," he'd said, when he treated me badly, "I'm sorry."

Yes, Beth Dennis was right: Sammy overdosed. But it wasn't on purpose, not if the recipe book could be trusted. Sammy didn't kill himself. He tried to live forever.

The year before I met him, when I conducted my experiment on liver scarring, my hypothesis had been that treatment using the fruit of the *Ardisia elliptica* would show the greatest beneficial effects. Ultimately, though, the data steered me away from A. *elliptica* and toward the soursop, which consistently proved more effective. I found no reason for soursop to be the better treatment. It just was.

Only science could offer such a thing: unexpectedness without disorder. There were surprises, always, but they *led* you somewhere. A new point of data could emerge in a place you weren't looking, but once it did, it shined a light on the next point, and the one after that, until these points formed a kind of constellation, revealing a picture, a shape, that held meaning. At the time, I would have explained my love for science as the product of aptitude: science was hard, and I was good at it, and those two in combination gave me pleasure. But it was also the feeling of losing control of the truth and then regaining it, over and over, that made me feel more at home in a lab than I did in any house since my mother's death—a *true* act of randomness that took no shape and held no meaning.

So even though the information in the recipe book ran counter to my understanding of Sammy, I remained attuned to the pressure building in my ears, guiding me another way. *The Way of an*

Investigator said that the goal of scientific investigation is to learn whether facts can be established that will be recognized as facts by others. This was a fact, as I saw it: Sammy had been in search of an elixir of life, and in delivering his notebooks to my doorstep, he had passed this search on to me. This was a thrilling revelation— what mattered most to him, his life's work, he'd gifted to me. But my natural skepticism crashed headlong into this knowledge.

I glanced at the note, with my father's MELD score. A MELD score that said, *Your father will be dead before winter.*

"Okay," he had said, the last time I saw him. "He's your dad."

Sammy was telling me to use the recipe book to save my father.

It was a truth both electrifying and nonconductive—like being hit by lightning while in a rubber suit. Sammy wanted to help my father, but Sammy was also *dead*, which meant his final experiment had failed. In that way, I told myself, what he had done was heroic: Sammy experimented on himself before involving me or my father. All I had to do to accept that version of events was rearrange my entire understanding of the world. I had already done exactly that, several times over, since the day I met Sammy. But when I imagined leaving the confines of my bedroom and explaining this to someone, even to RJ, I found no way to do it without sounding insane.

The day Sammy first pitched me the rat study, his voice carried a persistence that seemed to come from some foreign place, from a room in his mind he normally kept locked. I had felt confusion then, but also a bright, hot need to be part of that place, to be invited inside and allowed to stay. I hadn't realized it, but he was showing me the path to be with him. Reading this strange book, I didn't know what to believe. I did know, as I had always known, what I would do: whatever he asked of me.

ELIXIR OF LIFE #101
Yield: 1

INGREDIENTS
THE APPETIZER
1. Dor (1 sp)

THE ENTRÉE
1. Quicksilver (200 ml)
2. Tribal medicine (100 ml)
3. B. *rossica* (3 oz)
4. Rapamycin (15 mg)
5. P. *cupana* (100 mg)

PREPARATION
Inject Appetizer. Combine Entrée and drink.

HOW DID IT TASTE?
still not strong enough. what's missing?

Sammy's final recipe made even less sense to me than the first. In a cheeky nod to the recipe book's true function—a cheekiness that struck me as totally unlike him—Sammy had split the ingredients for his final recipe into two stages: the Appetizer, an injectable, and the Entrée, an ingestible. The Appetizer was a substance Sammy called Dor, but I'd never heard of such a thing, and the recipe book offered no help. I checked the internet, but it, too, revealed nothing useful: *Dor* was the word for a flying insect that buzzes, it was the acronym for the Department of Revenue, it was the Romanian word for "nostalgia" and the Portuguese word for "pain." I could not find a single result that had anything to do with a substance a person could inject into his veins. Even the dosage made no sense: 1 sp. The only unit of measure I could think of with that abbreviation was screen pixels.

The rest of the ingredients made varying amounts of sense. Quicksilver I knew, but I knew it, like most people, as poison. The tribal medicine could have been anything, and how annoying that he'd used such a generic name! B. *rossica*, a Web search revealed, was a rare parasitic plant native to China and Alaska. Rapamycin was an antibiotic discovered, in all places, on Easter Island.

Compared to the previous recipe, Sammy's final elixir contained two changes: a dramatic increase in the amount of quicksilver, and the addition of P. *cupana*—the extract we'd been studying all summer. Apparently, I'd been part of this for longer than I realized, but part of what, exactly? I stared at that final note, with its frustrating, frustrated question: *still not strong enough. what's missing?*

What's missing, I told him, *is* you.

"Conrad!" Dana called, startling me. "Dinner!"

Before she could send Emmett to get me, I slid Sammy's box under the bed, straightened my shirt, and reentered the world of the living.

Dana and Emmett were already seated at the table, taking turns lifting salad out of a large wooden bowl. She passed him the French dressing, its top open, and placed the cap by his plate so he could refasten it when he was finished. In return, he handed her the ketchup for what appeared to be homemade veggie burgers. My uncle had built the table and installed the laminate floors, and they were both cheap, ugly, and perfectly crafted—my uncle, a man with bad taste and steady hands. The whole scene had a workmanlike quality: the work of being a family. I was surprised by the part of me that wanted to enter the room by telling them everything, by revealing every secret. Instead, I entered silently.

"Nice to see you," Emmett said, sarcasm adding a jaggedness to his words. RJ and I had driven to Sammy's apartment without alerting him. "Where did you guys go?"

"Just here," I said softly, in some impossible hope that Dana would not hear this conversation despite being seated at the same table, in a quiet room.

"Well, thanks for the heads-up," Emmett said. "I looked for you."

"What's happening?" Dana asked. "You didn't go back to school?"

Emmett looked at me with annoyance. "She doesn't know?" He waited for me to answer and, when I didn't, put down his fork. "Mr. Tampari died today."

"Your teacher with the rats?" Dana asked. "Oh, Conrad."

To brace myself against the questions and condolences to come, I let my mind drift to Sammy's elixir. *P. cupana* was the one thing that contained even an ounce of familiarity. I'd seen him hold it, test it, administer it to a sick patient. To understand his elixir, I would need to understand the recipe in relation to the life he'd been living. The recipe book was a code, and his journals were the method to break it.

"How sad," Dana was saying. "What a sad thing."

Emmett poured himself more soda. "The whole day was weird. Like a fake day."

My aunt put a comforting hand on my arm, and I managed to smile vaguely in the direction of that hand. Already I felt closer to Sammy, as if I were tugging back on the rope he'd used to descend into whatever depths had claimed him.

It was close to 10:00 p.m. when my aunt went to bed. If I pulled an all-nighter, I'd have eight hours with the journals before my alarm clock rang and I needed to shower for school. Dana had offered me a "mental health day" after Emmett broke the news, but a part of me felt that the safest option was to go about my normal life. Nothing in the recipe book explained the ravaged state of Sammy's apartment—if someone other than Sammy was responsible for the destruction, that person might have been looking for the very materials he'd given me. This sense of danger added voltage to my grief; it was like holding a funeral on an active volcano.

I went to my bookshelf and removed a toxicology textbook I'd received from my father the year I turned twelve. It hadn't been a gift meant kindly. Not long after he surrendered me to my aunt, my father briefly became convinced that the real cause of his decline was not drinking but poisoning, by some unseen enemy. The textbook contained an entire chapter on mercury intoxication.

Quicksilver was the one constant in all of Sammy's elixirs; it appeared, in some quantity, in all 101 recipes. He didn't doubt the toxicity of mercury; his use of the element was based on that toxicity. Scanning the first few journals for mention of the elixir, I found this, written by Sammy when he was only twelve years old:

There is nothing more valuable to the life cycle of a forest than fire—through destruction, it creates the *conditions* for life. Mercury is the same. I don't know what the elixir of life will be, but I do know this: it won't be Superman, hands on his hips as the bullets bounce off his chest. It will be the snake who sheds his skin and slithers on. It will be the lizard who loses his tail and grows another.

Mercury's toxicity comes with a special power: it can bypass the blood-brain barrier. This is *important*. To understand Sammy's elixir of life, you must understand this small but essential part of our biology.

The blood-brain barrier is a membrane that protects the brain and central nervous system from the blood that circulates throughout our bodies. Why would the brain need protection from our own blood? Because lots of bad stuff can get in there—pathogens and toxins that can destroy the delicate and complex systems of the brain. The blood-brain barrier works a bit like a moat and a bit like a greenhouse, maintaining a steady, constant environment to protect the organisms inside.

It also causes problems. Sometimes doctors do need to send medicine to the brain, but the blood-brain barrier is so effective that it makes delivering these drugs difficult. For Sammy, this was a challenge to be solved.

His answer was mercury. As it nears the blood-brain barrier, mercury pretends to be an amino acid and sneaks its way into the central nervous system. Sammy aimed to use mercury as a kind of cargo ship; if he could load it up with a bunch of helpful agents, the mercury could smuggle them into the fluids of the brain.

I set the book down, trying to square my sense of Sammy as a genius with the recklessness of this idea. It was no surprise that his first attempt had nearly killed him, and it was no surprise his final attempt, which used even higher doses of mercury, had finished the job. Using mercury as a transport was like sending food supplies to an impoverished country—but strapping those supplies to a nuclear bomb.

He'd left me in an impossible position: *what's missing?* If Sammy couldn't figure that out—if he'd died trying—how on earth was I supposed to do it?

•

That next morning at school, we had a classwide assembly to honor Sammy. We filtered into the oddly shaped gym—too long and too narrow, like a basketball court stuffed in a hallway. I hadn't slept at all. I was bleary-eyed, sick to my stomach, and seeing Sammy *everywhere*: in doorways, in the bleachers, in the blond hair of a classmate with his back to me. I wasn't in denial—he was dead, and I knew this—but I'd also just spent the night with him, with his words. Our story wasn't over.

Principal Dee stood with the microphone near the three-point line, the student council fanned out behind her. We took our seats in the bleachers. To my left, Emmett hid his phone between his legs and swiped along the screen, playing some game where a muscle-bound avatar killed a demon with a Viking sword. To my right, RJ tried to whisper to me about Sammy, but I shook my head hard and fast. *Not here.* I'd told RJ about the package, briefly, before homeroom, but as much as I wanted to tell him everything, we didn't have long to speak: Number 5, Number 7, Number 37, and Number 42 needed to be fed. Even with Sammy gone, the rats were my responsibility, and they, too, had lost someone. As I refilled their little bowls, I couldn't help but feel they were looking up at me with their tired red eyes and asking, *Where is Number 50? Where is our brother?*

Principal Dee tapped the microphone and congratulated us for how well we'd handled the tragedy yesterday, and during the first day of school no less. "Give *yourselves* a round of applause," she said, which a few students did, sarcastically. Principal Dee talked about how Sammy's death underscored the way shared grief can bring a community together. "It's what Mr. Tampari would want us to learn from his death." The irony of the whole display was that Sammy hated assemblies, hated any gathering of more than fifteen people, including in his own classroom.

"No one will ever," he said to me once, "and I mean *ever*, say anything important to a large group of people." He pointed to me and then pointed to himself. "This is where everything of value happens. Between people who are sitting so close they could kiss."

The principal explained that there would be a slideshow as well as a student speaker. First, though, she handed the microphone to Captain James Carson from the Littlefield Police Department. The newspaper that morning had run a story on Sammy's death, including a statement from the LPD. They were treating the case as a "suspicious death" but "likely suicide" and were waiting on a report from the coroner. The article said nothing about the state of his apartment.

Captain Carson took the microphone and said good morning. For years, he'd been the police representative for school assemblies on drinking and driving, bomb threats, domestic abuse— the usual small-town issues. He was an older guy, midfifties. The rumor at LHS was that he'd been shot in his younger days and spent the rest of his career doing desk duty, trainings, and, well, this kind of stuff.

"I'm here to reassure you that we have no reason to think there's any danger to anyone," he was saying. "That said, if any of you have any information about Mr. Tampari that you think we might want to know, I'm here to listen."

I could feel RJ making a concerted effort not to look at me. I stared forward, eyes on Captain Carson, trying to avoid the mistake bad students always make when they don't want to be called on by the teacher: looking away. I knew I should tell the police, or someone, about my relationship with Sammy, but no way was I going to do that. Not ever. I imagined the breathless articles that would run in the newspaper. How long would it take before the story went viral? Headlines swirled in my head:

Small-Town Teacher Overdoses After Molesting Student

Sex, Drugs, Suicide?
Pervert Chemistry Teacher Kills Himself at Church

Report: Gay Student Fucks Teacher . . . to DEATH!

I imagined my father reading those things. When we lived in Winterville, in the good days, he used to read me the headlines from the local paper, laughing at the trials and tribulations of small-town Maine. Once, a moose interrupted an outdoor hockey game and ate the puck—that was the front page. Another day, a police officer dropped the keys to his cruiser in the snow and, when he couldn't find them, nearly froze to death walking back to the station. My dad would mock these things, and it was mean, but I was *inside* that meanness. It was a joke that included me.

As Captain Carson finished his remarks, Principal Dee signaled to someone, and the slideshow began, projected onto a large screen they typically rolled out for graduation. Music began to play from the speakers: a pop song about saying goodbye. I'd been wondering how they managed to find enough pictures of Sammy, from his one year at the school, to fill a slideshow of any length. The answer was that they hadn't. The first picture was the one Sammy had taken for the yearbook; it was him and the rest of the science department standing shoulder to shoulder in the lab. Sammy was on the far right, wearing a peach-colored button-down.

But after that, whoever put the slideshow together had to get creative. Someone had made a poster with Sammy's name written in calligraphy and surrounded by flowers, and there were *two* photographs of this, with a fade-in, fade-out effect. The next picture was an up-close, low-resolution photo of Sammy's face. His eyes were a blur of pixels. I suspected that this photo had been taken at an assembly like this one, with Sammy in the background, and they'd simply zoomed and cropped the image.

The rest of the brief slideshow continued this way, with a mix of bad images of Sammy and bad images *not* of Sammy. But as the song reached its coda, and the final photo appeared, I felt all of my blood rush to my head. The last picture was of us—Sammy and me. We were in the hallway talking to each other. We were standing close. Sammy was gesturing with his hand, and it appeared, maybe, as if he was touching my arm. I was gazing up at him with a look that seemed, from where I was sitting, to be a completely transparent expression of love. And it wasn't just me: Sammy was *beaming*. It was a picture of two soon-to-be lovers, and I couldn't imagine anyone seeing it any other way.

I cast nervous glances around the gym, expecting everyone to be staring at me. But other than RJ, who was watching me out of the corner of his eye, no one seemed to register the photo at all. Emmett was still swiping at his phone. As the music faded out, I hoped I was in the clear, that the picture was only interesting if you knew what I knew. But then I saw Captain Carson take a step toward the screen, and I thought, *Uh-oh*.

Just like that, the image was gone, the lights were up, and Principal Dee was saying, "I'd like to introduce our student speaker. One of your student council representatives, Natalie Domney, has offered to share her experiences with you today."

This elicited some genuine murmurs of interest. Natalie Domney was famous for trying to slit her wrists on a band saw at the end of her freshman year. Since her return to school, she was always finding some odd way to embarrass herself in class—tripping, farting, calling the teacher "Mom." Everyone had a Natalie Domney story.

Prompted by the principal, she stepped forward, her shaking hands visible even from our spot in the bleachers. She was a plain, round-faced girl, dressed in a knee-length skirt and a thin black shirt that covered her arms to the wrists. She took the microphone from Principal Dee and breathed loudly into it. Any of us could have told the principal that this was a bad idea: you don't shine a spotlight on Natalie Domney.

"She's gonna pee her tights," someone said behind me.

"I hope she shits them," said another. "She ratted me out last year."

"Stop, you guys," said someone kind.

Natalie lifted the microphone back to her lips. "It's very—" she started to say, but then sneezed, with no windup, all over the microphone. The noise reverberated throughout the auditorium like a thunderclap. Natalie stared at the microphone in obvious, abject horror. Later, reports from the first row of the bleachers would clarify what she'd seen: Natalie Domney had just sneezed blood all over the microphone. It was slippery with the stuff, and she lost her grip on it. The microphone dropped from her hands and cracked against the hard court, its plastic casing shattering into pieces. Feedback whistled through the air. Natalie took two steps back, her footing unsure, and collapsed in a heap of limbs under the basket.

Chaos. The teachers screamed at us to remain in our seats, but forget it, we were already up. We stampeded. Some of us went for the doors—school, for those students, was over for the day—and some went for center court, just hoping to stay part of the action. RJ and Emmett wanted to stay and watch, but I was thinking of that photograph, of Captain Carson, and I wanted to get away. I forced them out of the gym and into the parking lot. It was still early morning, and the lemony sun was low and warm.

RJ shook his head. "What's going on in this place?" What he meant was, how could two bad things happen so close together?

I loved RJ, but his life had been easy.

Eventually, we would learn what had happened to Natalie: deep vein thrombosis. A blood clot formed in the anterior tibial vein of her left leg and traveled upward to her heart and lungs. In the 1700s, doctors believed this condition was caused by the accumulation of milk in the legs of lactating women and prescribed frequent breast-feeding as the only method of prevention. If we'd lived in the eighteenth century, Natalie would certainly have died, and her medical chart would have listed the cause of death as *Milk Leg*.

As it was in 2010, Natalie lived, and at my insistence, RJ, Emmett, and I finished out the school day. Looking back, the image that sticks with me most is not Natalie's body or even the photograph of Sammy and me—though I wish I had that picture—but something I saw as we followed the herd out of the gym. Only a few yards from the principal, standing under the 2002 BOYS' LACROSSE STATE CHAMPIONSHIP banner, Tracy Bean-Upshaw lit a cigarette. She was a senior, a tiny thing, with sand-colored hair and a fondness for diet iced tea. She was a straight-A student, captain of the debate club, and despite the opportunities this gave her, I'd never, not once, seen her break a rule. But that day, as thirty or forty people simultaneously called 911, and as Principal Dee sat on her knees in front of Natalie, crying into the crook of her elbow, Tracy lit a cigarette and smoked it for at least as long as it took me to leave the building. For all I know, she had time to finish it before anyone noticed. I don't know why I remember this so clearly; I suppose it struck me as incredibly brave. Maybe it reminded me of something I shouldn't have forgotten, something my father taught me years ago and Sammy was teaching me again: no matter what you may think, you never really know anyone.

That night, after everyone was in bed, I caved. I thought of Captain Carson, of the photograph, of Natalie's bloody sneeze. I abandoned my methodical approach to the journals and skipped to the most recent volume—to the summer Sammy and I spent together.

I didn't pretend this was a proper part of the investigation. I left my legal pad on the desk, shut off my computer, turned off the overhead light. I lay in bed with the journal and a reading light, which shined a wide whitish glow. Rationally, I was prepared that I might not see much of myself in these entries. Even in a private journal kept in a locked drawer, it would be risky for Sammy to commit our affair to print. My own papers and e-mails certainly made no mention of what we'd done. In my heart, he was Sammy, but everywhere else, he was still Mr. Tampari.

I was not prepared for what I *did* find: no mention of me at all. Not one. No reference, even, to an unnamed student, an advisee with special promise. If all you had was Sammy's journals, you wouldn't even know I existed. What was I to make of this? There were thousands of pages of journals, a recipe book, a MELD score, a phone number, a key. I was important enough to receive them but not to trust with them while he lived. I believed he was trying to help me, but damn him: he was doing it in the least helpful way possible. He'd left me, and with what? An "elixir of life" that probably killed him. An apartment torn to shreds. A secret too big to keep, an "I love you" he would never say back.

This was all he wrote the day our affair began:

June 2, 2010
    When I woke up today I was colorblind. My bedspread, which I know to be blue, was the color of pancake batter.

It was probably the pamidronate disodium, which I've been playing with in small doses.

Good night.

All this time, I had wanted to think of myself like Tracy smoking in front of the principal—a good kid breaking the rules. But as the sun came up on another day without Sammy, I allowed myself a harder thought: maybe I'm just the thing you use and cast away, the thing that makes you feel good until it doesn't.

Maybe I wasn't Tracy. Maybe I was the cigarette.

Ge Hong Reflects on
the Discovery of Mercury

Mount Luofu, China, AD *330*

Ge Hong opens his eyes. A swallow has landed on the foot of his bed. It stares at him with its big white irises, its feathery white eyelids. Swallows look surprised by everything they see. The bird hops once, twice, three times, on the floor. Ge Hong watches it dance. Sometimes he finds himself gazing at birds expectantly, as though they might open their colorful beaks and speak to him. But nothing is to be learned from birds except by catching them and taking them apart. He has studied the locomotion of their wings, the way their brittle wing bones fork in the middle like a river around a rock. He has dissected their tiny hearts.

He rolls off his mat and stands slowly, his legs creaking and popping. He is forty-seven years old, a decade older than his father lived to be. He died before Ge Hong turned thirteen.

TEN WAYS THAT GE HONG HAS SEEN A MAN DIE
1. Febrile disease
2. Too old
3. Execution by sword (At first: "There is not much blood?" Then: "Oh.")
4. Arrow (in two cases, arrow fired by Ge Hong)
5. Stabbed in battle (thousands, but never by Ge Hong)
6. Trampled by horse ("Ge Hong, we must go back for him!" "We cannot go back for him.")

 7. Drowned
  a. Accidental ("Help!")
  b. Self-inflicted ("Stay away!")
  c. Inflicted ("No!")
 8. Stillborn (". . .") (no silence like this silence)
 9. Fire (*seen* and *smelled*)
 10. Unexplained ("Father, what is wrong?" "Agh!" "Father, can you breathe?" [no reply] "Sister, fetch Mother!" "Father, sit and take water!" "Father, can you hear me?" "Father, wake up!" [Father does not wake up])

Ge Hong goes to his food room. The dried roots of sweet flag dangle in bunches from the walls. He inhales their aroma, at once sugary and acidic and of the earth. He will mix it with ginseng for his morning drink. This will increase the flow of his liver blood and enhance the potency of his vision. If he had already consumed his morning drink, he would be better able to see the boy who is approaching his home, at a full sprint, from the east.

The boy draws closer. He is making such a racket with his running—his feet hitting hard against the path, his heavy breaths echoing in all directions—that the sun seems to rise faster into the sky, as if to say, *Well, it must be morning.*

Ge Hong curses under his breath. It is Cai Ju, who is only five years old. The villagers always do this. When someone falls ill, they send their dumbest boy in a panic, with no real information. By the time the first boy has turned to make his descent, a second boy will be cresting the final hill, sweaty and panting, with an update.

"Master!" the boy calls. "Master!"

Whoosh. The fire starts for his morning drink.

Ge Hong peers down at the boy. "Yes, Cai Ju. What is it?"

The boy wobbles on his feet. "Mother. My mother. It's my mother."

"Easy."

The boy takes a deep breath. "Mother has the hot sweaties."

"Are you saying her face is hot and wet, like from a fever?"

The boy turns red. "She threw up," he says softly, "onto Father."

Ge Hong pours some morning drink for himself and the boy. Cai Ju's mother has the febrile disease described by Emperor Huang Ti in the *Nei Ching*, which is bad but also lucky—Ge Hong is the only one in the world who has successfully treated it. It is the same disease that killed Bao Gu, wife of Ge Hong.

Cai Ju drinks gratefully. "Father says she is sick from the swamp air."

"That is incorrect."

Cai Ju frowns. "Father said she is sick from breathing swamp air."

"Well, what do I know. I've only written an entire book on the subject."

Ge Hong tells him to return in three hours for medicine. Just as Cai Ju disappears from sight, his older brother crests the hill with an update.

Ge Hong gathers *qinghao* plants at the edge of the forest. He presses their leafy stalks to his face. They smell like mint and pepper and camphor laurel. The sky is cloudless but the color of clouds, so blue it is almost white. It is the season of sulfur, when the changing wind currents carry swamp air up the mountain. The villagers associate this smell with the fever of Cai Ju's mother. Swamp fever. They are half-right: The fever *does* come from swamps, but not from the air. From bugs. For years he has heard that faint mosquito whine, a special hum, that tells him people will die. When the fever strikes a village, it does not strike one person and leave, like lightning. It is a sickness not *of* people but *among* people. A sickness that spreads.

KEY MOMENTS IN GE HONG'S ENCOUNTERS
WITH SWAMP FEVER

1. The year 304, just outside Luoyang: Ge Hong's first encounter with the disease. Twenty infected with swamp fever. Twenty die. A mother tries to follow her daughter's

body into the fire and must be knocked unconscious with a stone.

2. The year 310, Lurong: Ge Hong discovers mercury.
3. The years 314 to 316, Lurong: Almost seventy infected with swamp fever. Fifteen live! Ge Hong rushes home and kisses his beautiful Bao Gu. "Progress!" he tells her. "Husband," she replies, "I love you and your crazy ideas."
4. The year 320, Mount Luofu: Ten infected. Ge Hong discovers that *qinghao* should be steeped in cold water, not warm. Six live.
5. The year 321, Mount Luofu: Bao Gu infected.

Ge Hong discovered cinnabar in the hot springs of Lurong. He heard stories that if you bathed long enough in the springs, you could see small pieces of the world's beating heart float to the surface. It was the usual folktale nonsense spouted by Common People. But he went to the springs and waited until a piece of the crystalline mineral bubbled to the top. Immediately he saw the misguided logic of the folktale: cinnabar looks like a quartz covered in blood. He took it home. He placed the cinnabar over fire and watched, in horror and amazement, as the rock oozed blood, a silver liquid that emerged like tears from its blackened pores. He collected this blood and called it quicksilver.

A metal that runs like water even in the cold; a substance that cannot be destroyed but only *transformed*. He has burned it a hundred times, two hundred, three—it only grows more beautiful. All earthly things carry the *xuan*, the Mystery, the embryo of the Original One. In quicksilver, Ge Hong has found the source of the Mystery, the river that feeds the ocean. He needs only to master it, and Ge Hong will never die.

Except: Bao Gu. How long does he wish to live without her?

His thoughts are interrupted by the return of Cai Ju. Ge Hong gives the medicine to the boy, but the boy is weakened by running and worrying and tears. He will never make it down the mountain. Ge Hong puts on his walking boots and swings the boy up onto his shoulders. They begin their descent.

FIVE SIMILARITIES BETWEEN CAI JU'S
MOTHER AND BAO GU

1. Big, wet eyes—midnight dark like new moons.
2. A way of laughing so that everyone laughs, even Ge
   Hong when he's flattened by writer's block, even Cai
   Ju when he stubs his toe and can't find the words to
   express his disappointment ("Why is life so full of
   small humiliations?").
3. Often saying to her husband, "I know there was something I wanted to tell you" (and then looking away, a
   little sadly; it was probably some minor thing, a chore
   to be done or an observation that will come back to her
   later, but what if it wasn't, and what if now, unspoken,
   it grows fat and tumorous in the silence between them?).
4. Pretty (not true beauty, the kind you want to observe
   from a distance, but true prettiness, the kind you want
   to run straight into, like a field of canola flowers).
5. Killed by swamp fever (despite the best efforts of Ge
   Hong).

WAYS THAT CAI JU, AFTER DEATH OF MOTHER,
RESEMBLES GE HONG, AFTER DEATH OF BAO GU

1. Where the Mystery flows, happiness follows. Where
   the Mystery ebbs, happiness recedes—and the bright-
   est soul turns to dust.

The Cave of Gloom

I woke up the next morning with the recipe book draped across my face. I'd slept for less than an hour. In the kitchen, I found Dana standing tiptoed on a footstool, cleaning out the cupboards. When she heard me come into the room and pull the orange juice out of the fridge, she said, without looking over her shoulder, "How are you feeling?"

I poured the OJ into a tall plastic cup. "Fine."

She turned to toss an ancient, half-used box of spaghetti into the trash bag at her feet. "You've hardly talked about Mr. Tampari. You can talk to me." I'm not sure how many times, in the years since I moved in, Dana had said this: *You can talk to me.*

"I know."

She put her hands on her hips. "Do you? Because you haven't said one word about this man, who died, who you spent all this time with. That's not healthy, Conrad."

"I'm fine." In a strange way, this was actually true. My mother had burned alive. My father abandoned me and drank himself sick. Sammy made love to me and said nothing about whatever dangers were at the door. That's what I couldn't communicate to Dana: I was sad and lost and *fine.* Grief is an emotion, but it is also a skill. I was simply more practiced at it than most.

Dana let out a frustrated sigh and returned to the dusty reaches of the cupboard. "On Monday we're having dinner with your father."

I finished my juice.

"You can't not visit him."

"I know," I said again. As I went to the front door, I passed Emmett, eating breakfast in the living room.

Emmett looked up from the television. He was watching anime. "Don't you need a ride?"

"I'm heading to RJ's. I'll ride with him."

"Sure." He increased the volume on the TV. "Whatever."

Fifteen minutes later, I sat with RJ in his bedroom, catching him up. RJ lived in a big house—his father had to pay a "mansion tax" and complained about it—but RJ's was the only bedroom on the second floor, and this made it feel private. The sun rose slowly into the skylight window. RJ was wearing a plain white T-shirt and a pair of khaki shorts, belted with blue fabric, and he was sitting cross-legged on the bed with his back to the headboard. I sat at the other end with my feet on the floor, watching his closed door with apprehension. He had just finished breakfast, and his whole family was downstairs, his sister watching TV, his parents making a grocery list in the kitchen, the pair of them dressed in matching tracksuits that rendered them more alien to me than the mother's French accent.

Today, we'd be skipping school to visit the storage unit.

"You have the key?" RJ asked.

I showed him. It was a stubby yellow thing—the kind of key that comes with a cheap padlock, not the kind you would use to protect an object of value.

"Elixir of life," RJ said in a voice of wonder. He had the recipe book in his lap. "You think he kept the ingredients there?"

Sammy had given me the recipes, but without the ingredients, what good were they? Still, I was having a hard time saying *elixir of life* out loud. So I said, "I just know he wanted me to go."

RJ swung his legs over the side of the bed and began putting on his shoes. Where once he'd been reluctant to visit Sammy's apartment, this morning he was a bundle of eager, impatient energy.

"Wait," I said. This was the dynamic RJ and I had established over years of friendship: he would need to talk me into it.

But before he could say anything else, his door swung open, revealing his sister, Stephanie, eyeing us from the doorway. "What are you two talking about?" Her eyebrows were pinched, her voice slightly slurred by her condition, which affected the muscles of her neck and jaw. She was still in her pajamas—ankle socks, silk shorts, a white tank top that said, in gold letters, LOVE IS STRONGER THAN HATE.

"Nothing," RJ said, and although he filled this word with annoyance, I knew how much he loved his sister. No matter how often or relentlessly she pestered us, I had never seen him tell her to leave.

"Nothing?" she said, slightly out of breath. "Nothing, really?" She looked at me (the weaker of the two). "You're just in here saying *nothing, nothing, nothing?*"

I reddened under her gaze. Stephanie's muscular dystrophy meant she had to turn her entire body to look at you, and I partially attributed her intuitiveness to this. For her, watching someone, listening, wasn't casual—it took her whole self to do it.

"Why are you breathing so hard?" RJ asked.

Stephanie's eyes went small. "The doctor said my leg muscles."

It was the kind of sentence fragment one hears when dealing with a fatal condition; if spoken in full, every sentence would have the same ending. We all looked at her legs together, which were short and thin, her dark skin shaved smooth. In a moment of my own intuition, I knew she must be thinking about the work of that shaving, and how, in a not distant future, she might not trust herself to do it.

Shaken by these thoughts, Stephanie said, "You dipshits are gonna be late for school," backed one step out of the doorway, and slammed the door shut.

RJ and I stared at each other in the hard silence that followed her departure. "Look," RJ said, "when someone gives you the key to a mysterious door, you open it."

We headed north out of Littlefield, tracing the Little River toward the storage facility. The river was shallow, slate blue, and curved to the southeast before emptying into the bay. Our route took us through Main Street, which was wide and still busy, though emptier now that summer was over. We drove by a lobster restaurant, a beachwear boutique, a chain sandwich shop with a CLOSED sign in the doorway. The sun was overhead, so we could feel it, but we couldn't see it.

The GPS on RJ's phone directed him away from the streets we knew and toward the storage facility, which lay in an industrial part of town we never had reason to visit. RJ guided the car down a one-way side street, his eyes focused on the road. He was not classically handsome in the way of Sammy or Emmett; in fact, I wonder if RJ was, to a neutral observer, a bit homely. His forehead was high, which gave him the appearance of a receding hairline. His lips were slightly too narrow for his wide cheeks. But I certainly didn't feel that way about him, and I admired how he could be completely serious in one moment—as he was then, driving me to this unfamiliar place—or completely silly in the next, as though he had full control of his emotions. His face, handsome or not, registered this confidence. For me, everything always seemed jumbled together: my loves, my fears, my hardest questions about the world.

When we arrived, RJ parked in the lot among a handful of other cars—we would not be alone. I pictured the violent appearance of Sammy's apartment and felt a stab of fear. It was one thing to read Sammy's journals at night in my bedroom. But there in the parking lot, in the sun, I was exposed. I didn't know if we were in danger, and in this not knowing, I felt Sammy's absence most painfully.

The storage facility was broad and several stories tall, covering half an acre of fenced-off pavement. We made our way toward the wide double doors of the entrance. As we went inside, I was aware of footsteps on the sidewalk, getting near. RJ heard them, too, and indicated with his chin for us to walk faster toward the elevator, which sat around the corner and was large—as it would need to be, for people and their furniture.

We hurried into it, and I mashed the button to close the door. I've since read that these buttons rarely do anything—they're installed to provide the illusion of control—but I didn't know that then, and I pressed and pressed, not wanting to share the elevator with whoever was behind us. Only when we could really hear the footsteps did the door begin to close, and by the time it shut, we glimpsed the shadow of a figure making the turn around the corner. As the elevator rose, I imagined again the other-Conrad, Sammy's second lover, tracing my steps. Then I entertained an even worse possibility: that the figure was Captain Carson, spurred by the intimate photograph of Sammy and me, hunting us like a dog.

At the third floor, we began the walk to Sammy's unit, counting the numbers as we went. The walls of the storage facility were bright white, the color of tooth enamel, and the rows of identical units made the place feel endless. We twisted our way through the corridors until we were on the far end of the building. The elevator, having deposited us on the third floor, had been called immediately back down to the first.

I extracted the key from my pocket, but in a moment of horrible déjà vu, I once again didn't need it.

"What in the actual fuck?" RJ said, running ahead of me—only a few yards ahead, but it was enough that I almost cried out to him. Instead I watched, frozen, as he picked up the pieces of the broken padlock and showed them to me. Whoever had beaten us to Sammy's apartment had beaten us here, too, and the path they were forging was not peaceful. My lungs were a tightening knot in my chest. Someone really was out there, *doing this*.

RJ crouched into a squat, inspecting the steel roll-up door of the unit. When I came to stand next to him, he looked up at me. "Let's be fast," he said, leaving no time for me to question the wisdom of staying.

He slid the door up easily, quickly, the metallic sound of it echoing off the walls. As the storage unit received the light of the hallway, I expected to find total destruction. Instead, we found uncertainty.

RJ frowned, his arms still extended over his head. "Is it like his apartment, or is it just *messy*?"

The storage unit was packed with boxes, and while some were overturned, I saw no evidence of the violence enacted on his studio. The space was a mass of equipment, clutter, and cardboard, and only my aptitude for chemistry allowed me to make any sense of the scene. Immediately through the door, several rolls of dialysis and thistle tubing were coiled like garden snakes under a hedge of filter paper. A $3,000 immersion circulator, which must have looked to RJ like a microwave with arms, lay on its side, its wires dangling pathetically over the console. Sampling bags and sponge probes surrounded the pump housing of a fluid aspiration system, its nipplelike tube connectors standing at full attention. Under another empty box, I saw a $500 incubator. Based on a quick mental calculation, Sammy's storage unit contained over $10,000 worth of equipment. Whoever had broken the padlock wasn't motivated by money—having left behind an elevator-ful of expensive laboratory devices.

"What next?" RJ asked.

I didn't like that he was asking—he was the one who was supposed to know. "Should we leave in case they come back?" I asked, gesturing to the broken padlock, and what I meant was *Play your role.*

"Just look for a few minutes." This was what I expected him to say, but his tone surprised me with its uncharacteristic plaintiveness, almost desperation. I didn't recognize it.

I began to search. RJ stayed near the entrance to the unit, picking at some open boxes, keeping his eyes on the hall. He pulled a reaction flask from a plastic crate and held it absentmindedly to his nose. He gagged and dropped it back into the box, his face contorted. I could smell the thiols—the same ones in my dad's fetid breath—from the other side of the locker. Along with the laboratory equipment, the only immediately visible items were easy-to-find materials with no obvious relation to the recipe book: twenty boxes of baby aspirin, a gallon of lye, a box of sparklers. In a pinch, Sammy could have used these materials to build a bomb.

"What's this?" RJ had reached into an open box and removed a small plastic vial. He held it horizontal, and the metallic liquid inside settled into a shallow pool. It was the first ingredient in Sammy's Entrée: quicksilver.

Seeing my face, RJ grew excited. "There's lots more stuff in here."

He was holding the flaps of the box apart and looking up at me expectantly, as though I might be able to tell him, with only a glance, if the box contained the secret to immortality. I crouched down next to him. Along with the mercury, an unlabeled herb was wrapped in computer paper, which looked like the *B. rossica* of Sammy's elixir. We found a pill bottle labeled RAPAMYCIN, though it was nearly empty. At the bottom of the box was a thick vial with only a tablespoon or so of a clear green liquid. The vial was circled in masking tape, and on it, Sammy had written CATHERINE in blue Sharpie.

"Who's Catherine?" RJ asked.

"No idea," I said honestly. I tipped the vial on its side, letting the green sludge slide slowly down the clear walls.

"Do you hear that?"

I listened. The heavy fumes of the storage unit had filtered down the hallway, and they were just then rounding the corner, hitting the nose of the figure whose shadow we'd seen on the first floor. The stranger coughed, barely audible. Before I could stop him, RJ began to creep in the direction of the sound. I followed, trying to wave him back. We approached a bend in the hallway. RJ pressed his spine against the wall and inched forward as if he were navigating the edge of a tall building. At the corner, he took a quick peek, and then he was running, at full speed.

"Hey!" he called, disappearing around the side.

"RJ, wait!" I yelled, giving chase. As I rounded the corner, I saw, at the end of the hall, someone's legs as he sprinted away from us. RJ and I charged forward, but before we reached the second corner, I heard the sound of the elevator. We arrived just in time to see it depart.

"Stairs," RJ said, and he was running again.

We traced the exit signs to the stairwell, which we descended quickly, reaching the bottom just as the slow, heavy door we'd opened at the top thudded closed. I followed RJ breathlessly, terrified—what on earth were we doing?

We ran through the unmanned lobby and into the light of the

sun. To my great relief, the parking lot was empty of people. RJ threw up his hands and leaned against his car, breathing hard.

"Sorry I couldn't catch him," he said between breaths.

"I didn't want you to."

He coughed the air back into his lungs. "You need to call the phone number."

I looked into the sky. A prop plane flew under the clouds, leaving a faint white contrail that faded as soon as it appeared.

"What else are you going to do?" RJ asked. "Let's go back for that box and then we'll call."

I heard it again in his voice, the desperation. I grabbed the sleeve of his shirt, holding him in place. "Why do you care so much?"

RJ looked at me as if I'd asked him for the solution to one plus one. "Don't you want to help your dad and Stephanie? Don't you want them to get better?"

I let go of his sleeve. Of course. Without a miracle, Stephanie would be lucky to see her thirties. I'd been focused on the mystery Sammy had left for me, but to RJ, there was no mystery. If Sammy had given me the chance to save someone's life, even the smallest chance, then that's what we would do.

He was taking small steps toward the building. His face was serious, urgent, almost panicked—and for a moment, behind his confidence and his courage and his endless reserves of optimism, I glimpsed it: his widow self. It was like quicksand, pulling him under, into the world of pain and loss.

"This is all bullshit," I told him, even though I, too, wanted to believe. "You know that, right?"

RJ waved me on. "Mr. Tampari's work must be worth something if someone is trying to steal it."

6

How I Got Here

For my fortieth birthday, my husband threw me a party, just a little thing in our backyard. One of our neighbors had bought me a T-shirt that said IT TOOK ME 40 YEARS TO LOOK THIS GOOD! We all laughed at how bad it was, and my husband pretended to kick him out of the party.

In fact, I first met my husband at a birthday party—a high-end, rooftop affair in New York City, celebrating the birthday of blond-haired, blue-eyed twin sisters who had once been my room-mates. I knew almost no one there, and it certainly wasn't my kind of scene. All of the other guys in attendance wore such tight button-down shirts you could see their nipples, and the women, God help them, could barely stand on their towering heels. Every time they tottered near the edge of the building, I fought the urge to pull them to safety. A three-piece band of impossibly young people were playing noncommittal electronic music on what looked to me like a row of color copiers.

I had found a relatively quiet space for myself on a bench be-tween two tall green succulents when a man I didn't know, and who was, honestly, a little big to share the bench with me, sat down with a thud. He turned to me and smiled, and it was a nice smile—wide, unafraid.

"Do you mind if I just sit here quietly with you?"

Hearing this, and reading his gentle face, I felt something happen in my chest—not an awakening, necessarily, but a kind of move to alertness. My heart *attuned* itself to this man, the way a cat's ears adjust to distant noises—just a little tilt, the rest of the body staying perfectly still. I told him yes, you can sit with me, and I hoped he heard that what I meant was *Yes, please sit with me, I need exactly you.*

We watched the party together. After a moment, I realized he was looking at me.

"Do you like animal fire?" he asked.

That didn't make any sense to me.

"Animal fire," he said louder, as though volume had been the problem. "Do you like animal fire?"

I grimaced. "Is that a drink?" I showed him my glass. "This is just Coke."

He laughed, but it didn't feel mean-spirited. "Animal Fire is the band you've been listening to all night." He gestured with his chin to the waifs behind the copy machines. He shook his head, still laughing. "How on earth did you get here?"

I don't remember how I answered that question—my answer was good enough, whatever it was, to keep him sitting with me all night—but it's one of those questions you can't think too much about, or it gets too big for you. How did I get here? How far back do you want me to go? To earlier that week, to earlier that decade, to the creation of man?

For the sake of this story, let's go back to Ned and Nasya, a couple of overachieving undergraduates who had been groomed their whole lives to find each other: two New England Jews, exact same age, exact same GPA. How I got here starts with them.

Ned Aybinder was an only child, a small and sensitive boy from Milford, Connecticut. He wept at his bar mitzvah not because he was nervous but because he *felt* something. A connection to his faith. A love for his family. I remember two folders he used to keep on our desktop computer: one where he saved articles about anti-Semitism and one where he saved his poetry.

Meanwhile, Nasya Beckmann was a high school tennis star in Newport, Rhode Island. If we can call a five-foot-two-inch Jewish girl a jock, that's what she was. I've seen the pictures from her team portraits. She stands to the far left, her long wooden racket gripped in both hands and her white Teddy Tinling skirt just a tad dirtier than everyone else's. She liked to aim her ground strokes directly at her opponent's body; if she came to the net, you were better off protecting yourself than trying to win the point. She didn't just want to beat you, she wanted to kill your love of the game. She continued to play tennis in college, but her opponents were fiercer and her lack of size caught up to her. Those gentiles from Amherst *averaged* five feet seven inches. They hit serves that seemed to come from the heavens. In a different body, my mother could have become a tennis pro, but in the body of Nasya Beckmann, she became a psychology major with a mean streak.

The two of them met as juniors at Connecticut College and were married soon after graduation in America's oldest synagogue. They tried immediately for a family, but my mother couldn't conceive—polycystic ovary syndrome—and they had to wait for the fertility research to catch up. I was born June 1, 1994, a miracle of modern science, the product of five hundred milligrams of metformin, fifty milligrams of clomiphene, and a decade's worth of patience.

Winterville, Maine, was a quiet town, population two thousand. They say it's the kind of place you can hear the snow falling. I loved our house there—a lean, rustic one-story on three acres of moss and mud. The peaked roof was the color of bruised strawberries. In winter, the ice would catch the roof's reflection and give the snow trapped in tree branches a sanguineous hue. We lived in a big, beating heart, the three of us, protected by the bones of the house and the cold of the air, which kept us inside and everyone else out.

We'd moved there after my father found a job teaching math at the high school. My mother worked a couple of days each week at the reform camp for troubled boys. Winterville and its neighboring towns were full of camps—for healing, for fishing, for sobering up. For learning how to hunt with a bow.

I only lasted a month in kindergarten before I was promoted to first grade. It was news to me that I was smart for my age, but I do remember a unit on the solar system, and how I was the only kid in my class to know that the sun was a star. When I reported this to my mother, she said the children up there didn't get any sun and couldn't be blamed for not knowing much about it. But later that night, I heard her talking to my father behind a closed door, and I knew then that I was different and that this difference was meaningful. Two years later, I skipped third grade.

I existed this way—friendless, too young for my grade—until I was ten years old. That was the year my mother died. A fire caused by a cigarette. She'd spent the night at the youth camp, filling in for someone, and it was her first time doing this—she'd never slept there before. When she woke to the smell of fire, she was disoriented. The fire inspector said she did everything wrong: she went up when you're supposed to go down, she traveled toward the heat and not away from it. The fire spread slowly, and there were plenty of safe exits. No one else died.

I remember standing with my father outside the funeral home after the service, shaking hands with people as they walked to their cars. My mother was in an urn. From the front lawn of the funeral home, I could see, just down the road, the entrance to the conversion camp for homosexual boys. While I waited for my father to take me home, I watched as a green SUV stopped at the gates of the camp. The driver's door swung open, and a man stepped out. He was tall but a little mousy, dressed in a button-down shirt that didn't quite fit. From the front passenger's door, another man emerged and stomped the ground, shook the feeling back into his legs. The first man walked around the car and popped the trunk, pulled some luggage from the back. The other man opened one of the back doors, reached inside the car, and dragged a boy outside by his wrist. The boy wasn't crying, but you could tell he'd *been* crying by the way he watched the ground. He followed the men to the gate, and they waited there for admittance. After a minute or two, a camp counselor appeared and opened all the locks.

The counselor waved hello to the boy, and I could see the men apologize for the boy's shyness. And that was that—custody of the child was exchanged. The kid didn't look back as the men drove away and the counselor guided him inside. He knew full well that neither direction was better than the other. That's the crazy thing about those camps. It's all just *shame*, and trust me, your gay child can get that anywhere. You don't need to pay for a wilderness retreat.

Winter in Winterville. It's as bad as it sounds. Snow piled up to the windows. Snowmobiling and ice fishing and the inevitable, graphic injuries of snowmobilers and ice fishermen. Sometimes there'd be a twofer, such as when Bobby Segal, Jr., drove his snowmobile into the ice-fishing shed of Bobby Segal, Sr. Both lived, neither were ever the same again.

Nor was my father. The first night our house was empty, Ned and I played Jenga until three in the morning and then fell asleep in the living room, me on the couch and him on the floor. We shared, at that point, a wounded camaraderie, and we indulged each other in our grief. We ate ice cream for dinner. We belched and farted and never said excuse me. We watched all the scary movies my mother would have made us turn off.

My father's mysterious transformation began during one of these movie nights. We had microwavable burritos laid out on tray tables in front of the TV and a movie in which Kate Beckinsale, a skinny Brit with vampire-pale skin, played an actual vampire. The camera loved her. She wore a skintight black leather suit that hugged the contours of her body. She opened fire on a group of bearded thugs we would later learn were werewolves. She jumped out of a window, landed on her feet, and bared her fangs at a stranger. She didn't do much for me, though looking back, I wouldn't have kicked some of those werewolves out of bed.

My father turned up the volume by several notches and immediately back down by the exact same amount. He was drinking a glass of wine; me, a tall cup of Vanilla Coke. "I don't think I'd wear black leather if I were a vampire," he said. "I'd just wear regular clothes."

"It's camouflage," I explained. "They only go out at night."

My dad finished his burrito and folded his paper plate in half. All of our real dishes were piled high in the sink. "What? They don't make cotton in black?"

Kate Beckinsale infiltrated a werewolf lair. For a people at war, the werewolves seemed overly preoccupied with chemistry experiments involving their own blood.

"Anyway," my father said, "I'd fuck her for sure."

I was ten years old.

My father punched me on the shoulder, too hard. "I'd even let her keep those teeth in."

I turned my attention to my meal. I drank, before the movie was over, six full cups of Coke—the whole bottle. By the time the night ended, I was so hyped up on sugar that I just lay in bed, covers up to my chin, debating the difference between having sex with someone and fucking them. The best I could do was that you have sex with your wife and fuck a stranger. She didn't even have to be human.

Sometime after midnight, I heard my dad in the kitchen and crept to my door to spy on him. He was standing in front of the sink. He removed a plate from the pile and held it up to the light. It was truly filthy—these dishes had been gathering for weeks. My father held that pose and then smashed the plate on the floor. The pieces scattered across the linoleum and surrounded his bare feet. He picked up a soup bowl and this time with less ceremony whipped that, too, against the floor. I closed the door and returned to my bed, more awake than ever, but I could hear him continue this work for the next half hour.

Here's what that scene suggests: a depressed, widowed father. Later, this depression feeds the alcoholism, and the alcoholism destroys the liver. But there is more to the story, so much more happening in his body than any of us, including his doctors, understood. For now, I'll take a cue from the New York Society of Numismatics and offer, in place of an explanation, a bit of homework, a formula that doubles as a clue:

$$Cu^+ + H_2O_2 \rightarrow Cu^{2+} + \bullet OH + {}^-OH$$

Let's call it the Copper Code. The human body produces data like this all the time—most of us just don't recognize it. We certainly didn't for my father. The chemical balance of the body is always the slightest glitch away from disaster. It's a small thing, but also big. So many of his problems started with that simple string of symbols, and with transport protein ATP7B2.

Hanukkah 2005. The year I turned eleven. My father took me to dinner at the only restaurant within two hundred miles that served latkes. He'd started on antidepressants after he tried and failed to return to work, but I'd still come home from school to find him crying into the couch cushions, his eyes open and blank. It was his first time out of the house in weeks.

The restaurant, coincidentally, was called Little Ned's.

"Big Ned is here," my dad said as we came through the door.

We sat at a booth near the window with a view of the Penobscot River. This was Bangor, Maine, and we'd driven three hours to get there. The teenaged waiter came for our drink orders.

My dad put on his reading glasses. "Everything here is kosher, right?"

The waiter leaned forward. "Like, is everything here good?"

"Coke, please," I said.

My dad ordered a glass of pinot noir.

The waiter fled. I watched my dad fuss with his napkin. I'd had this idea that he was going to drive me all the way out here, get me into the restaurant, and sprint back to the car and abandon me like an unwanted dog.

"We don't even keep kosher," I said.

My dad laughed. "Just trying to provide some *hashgacha*. I'm the closest this place has to a rabbi."

I didn't know what that word meant, but said nothing. Lately he'd been using a lot of words I didn't know.

"Hey," my dad said. "A Frenchman walks into a bar with a

parrot on his shoulder. The bartender says, 'Hey, that's cool. Where'd ya get it?' The parrot says, 'France.'"

"That's funny."

The waiter came back with the drinks, and we ordered our latkes. We were alone in the restaurant, and I remember feeling bad that we had only given the chef one dish to make.

"Do you have any paper?" my dad asked me.

I didn't, but our tablecloth was paper. My dad ripped off the corner and began to draw on it with the red pen he always kept in his breast pocket, even though he hadn't graded a test in months. I looked around to make sure no one had seen him. It was upside down to me, but I could tell that he was making a line graph. The x-axis said *Age*. The y-axis said *Death*.

"Did you know," he said as he drew, "that an anagram for *a decimal point* is *I'm a dot in place?*"

"Yeah."

"Of course you did," he muttered, and this was a new feeling: that my intelligence annoyed him.

He polished off his wine, and the latkes came. We tasted them and looked at each other. These were nothing like what my mom used to make. They were ropy and strange. The applesauce was pure sugar.

My dad flagged down the waiter.

"Don't," I said.

The waiter came. My dad pointed to our food with his middle finger. "These are pretty disturbing."

"Oh, man," said the waiter.

"I was just going to eat them anyway, but my son demanded we speak to the chef."

"I didn't!" I said.

The waiter gathered our plates. "Okay. One sec." He disappeared into the kitchen.

I refused to look at my father.

"Hey. Lighten up." He reached across the table and grabbed my wrist. He spun his line graph around to face me. "Look."

I did. The graph showed the risk of dying according to age.

"When you're first born, your odds of dying are about one in two hundred. At your mother's age they were one in four thousand. At your age, they're one in eight thousand." He traced his finger along the line. "But look. By the time you're a teenager, your chance of dying goes all the way up to one in two thousand. Do you see what I'm saying?"

"Yeah."

"I'm saying lighten up. You'll never be safer than you are for the next two years. Do whatever you want. Drink, smoke, fight. Take up hitchhiking. Be mean to waiters. Send back your shitty latkes."

"Okay. Jeez."

The waiter returned with the chef, an older guy, gray hair, maybe in his sixties. Odds of death: one in a hundred.

"Latkes no good?" he said.

"The Force was not strong in them," my dad answered.

"I'll be honest. I don't really know how to make them. There's an old couple down the street who eats here like three times a week, and they asked us to put them on the menu."

"They're really wealthy," explained the waiter.

My dad scratched his head. "You just described a plutocracy."

"I'll make something new up for you," the chef said. "Drinks on the house while you wait."

So we waited, and my dad drank for free. I forget how many glasses he had. By the time we left, I could see he was unsteady on his feet. By the time we pulled out of the parking lot, I could see he wasn't fit to drive. By the time he careened off the road and into a tanning salon, I could see that my father, as I'd always known him, was gone.

Christmas lights and police lights. Everything lit up in the night. My father was charged with driving under the influence. This would be bad for him later. When your liver fails and you have a DUI on your record, no one is inclined to believe you when you say alcohol isn't to blame. Here's that clue again, the Copper Code:

$$Cu^+ + H_2O_2 \rightarrow Cu^{2+} + \bullet OH + {}^-OH$$

I gave the police my aunt's phone number, and she drove all the way up to spend the night with me in Winterville. The next morning, she told my dad that she was taking me to Littlefield to live with her. I didn't hear the conversation—they went into his bedroom and spoke in hushed voices—but it didn't last long, and my aunt emerged looking no worse for wear. I don't think my dad fought for me, and one thing's for sure: he never asked for me back.

My fortieth birthday party ended at 11:00 p.m.—by my standards, practically an all-nighter. As the last of our guests filtered out, I collapsed onto the sofa and moaned into the cushions. My husband laughed and rubbed my back until I stopped complaining.

"You had fun," he said, not a question. He had told me, early in our courtship, that I was out of touch with my feelings. *Out of touch.* This was a common phrase even when I was a teenager, but now we say it all the time, and more seriously. More literally. It's easier today to live a life without touching—even technology doesn't have to be touched. But my husband meant it in the old-fashioned way, the figurative way. "You're happy to see me," he'd say when he came home from work and I didn't do enough to acknowledge him. When he annoyed me and I retreated into silence, he'd cast a rope and pull me back out: "You're mad. You're mad at me right now." And I'd say, "Yes, of course I'm mad," as if I didn't need him to tell me.

"Come on," he said now. "Let's go to bed."

I followed him upstairs, and we lay down in bed, him on his back and me basically on top of him. He smelled like a birthday party in Maine—beer and smoke and blueberry frosting.

We'd bought this house together. We had been living in New York City, where I'd completed a graduate degree in science writing. I had written an article on Ge Hong for a monthly magazine about life extension. It did well, so I wrote another piece on the history of immortality research, and then another, and then another. I even appeared on TV once, as a talking head for a PBS special on the Fountain of Youth. After a year or two of this, I thought, *You know, I could do this from anywhere.*

I huddled against my husband in bed, pulled the blanket up

over my face. Soon I was asleep. I still dream of Sammy. I'm always the age I was then—sixteen, skinny, love struck. We don't have sex, but the dreams are sexual, with a hot, liquid quality. My therapist says someday I'll be an adult in these dreams, and apparently that will mean something.

In the middle of the night an alarm sounded. I assumed it was my phone, telling me to wake up. But then I sat up in bed and saw my husband staring at the underside of his forearm, just below the elbow. His medical chip had activated.

"Keep sleeping. It's probably just my cholesterol."

I burrowed my face into the side of his leg. "I told you not to eat so much cake."

He took his phone with him into the bathroom. I saw the light go on beneath the door. He would scan the chip and get the report. It would tell him what was wrong and what to do about it. We laughed at the chips when they first came out. Medical chips were for nerds and hypochondriacs, we told ourselves, even though I was both. But ten years later, almost everyone had a chip.

The bathroom door opened, and I waited for the comforting feel of my husband sliding into bed, looping a leg over mine, and breathing warm air onto the back of my neck. But moments passed and I was still in bed alone. I rolled over and opened my eyes. He was standing motionless like a ghost in the light of the doorway.

I held out a hand to him.

He didn't move. He was still staring at his phone. "Cancerous tissue."

His words registered and did not register. I sat up and straightened my T-shirt. I could feel my toes tingling under the covers, waking up too fast as my heart began to beat. "Where?"

He touched the screen. "My brain." He looked up at me, lost. "It says I have brain cancer."

7

Brain Burn

Sammy sat in a circle of numismatists, falling asleep. He liked to do simple math as he drifted off—his version of counting sheep—and as he began to multiply the ages of all members present, he perceived a strange phenomenon. Although society meetings had no assigned seats, his fellow members had arranged themselves perfectly in order of age. As the youngest member, Sammy was sitting next to the second youngest on his right and the oldest on his left. Was this the first time it had happened, or only the first time he'd noticed?

"Samuel, are we boring you?" asked Andres, the chairman of the society.

"Yes, a little." Sammy was thirteen years old.

He'd joined the society after that first trip with his father, when he realized the numismatists had much wider interests than the collection of rare currency. But sometimes the group actually wanted to talk about coins. The following week, Sotheby's was auctioning a pair of silver half-dollars believed to have been placed over Abraham Lincoln's eyes following his assassination. The numismatists were debating the value of these coins. They were of obvious historical significance, but they were also damaged: to keep the coins together, someone had drilled holes into them and connected them via a black silk ribbon.

Sammy wasn't sleeping on purpose. His antidepressants made

him tired, and when there was nothing to occupy his mind, he would rest. In school—where he was a high school upperclass-man, having skipped two grades—this made the long days of class an endurance test. In the feedback for one of his English papers, his teacher wrote, *You're as smart as you are sleepy.*

In the first couple of years after his jump out of the window, Don and Leena pushed hard for him to be medicated. Dr. Huang held them off for as long as she could, arguing that he was too young to abandon nonpharmaceutical approaches. But by the time he was thirteen, he'd been dosed with combinations of imip-ramine, amitriptyline, nortriptyline, and desipramine. When those didn't work: phenelzine, tranylcypromine, isocarboxazid. *What's wrong with me?* His parents' answer was that he was de-pressed. But if the tools used to treat depression had no effect on Sammy, then eventually the word must lose its meaning. This is one of those secrets you learn when happiness eludes you: a lot of the words people use don't mean anything.

"We can't cure mental illness," Dr. Huang had told him. "We're trying to determine the best path to palliative care." This was an example of what she called "brutal honesty," but where, Sammy wondered, was the honesty in the palliative? (*Palliative*, from the Latin *palliare*—"to cloak, to disguise.")

"Well," Andres was saying, "I'm ninety years old, and *I* manage to stay awake."

"That's because you decide what we talk about," Sammy said. "And when you get bored, you change the subject."

The numismatists made eye contact with one another. It had been less than a year since Don stopped attending, and though no one said out loud the reason for this, everyone knew it: Don's interest began to wane *because* of Sammy's interest.

The numismatists continued their discussion of the Lincoln half-dollars, and Sammy tried to keep his eyes open. If he of-fended them too badly, they would avoid the topics that inter-ested him out of spite. Well, the *topic* that interested him. In his bedroom, he'd replaced the car posters and beanbags with book-shelves, and these held many of the books that once belonged to his father, locked up in the coin cave: Leopold Turck's *Aging as a*

Disease; Trithemius's *Immortal Liquor*; *Alkahest, of Philalethes*; Ge Hong's *Traditions of Divine Transcendents*.

He often tried to explain this fascination to himself, to make sense of it. Don said it was natural to be afraid of death, that Sammy took comfort in the idea of an elixir of life the way some children took comfort in night-lights. But Sammy knew that wasn't it. Death, to him, was like an obligation, a dentist appointment— it was a thing you sometimes wanted to put off and sometimes wanted to just get over with. Dr. Huang said the elixir represented hope for Sammy, hope of a cure for the incurable condition of his mind. That was closer, maybe, though *hope* was one of those words that held no smell or flavor—he knew the definition, but he'd been born without the receptors to feel that quickening of the pulse, that rising of the hairs, when someone "gets his hopes up."

This was the secret to his fascination, one he would not admit to anyone but himself: he expected to die pursuing it. Don and Leena and Dr. Huang said he needed a hobby. Well, he'd found one. It was like falling, falling, falling, out of the window—a thing you do until you hit the ground.

"You know," said the chairman, and his condescending tone meant the *you* referred to Sammy, "Lincoln actually has ties to the elixir of life."

"Blue mass," said someone in the circle, and the chairman frowned—he'd wanted to build to the reveal.

"Blue mass?" Sammy repeated.

"Lincoln was a depressive," Andres said. "Henry Clay Whitney wrote of Lincoln's tendency to enter the 'Cave of Gloom.'"

"Blue mass was an antidepressant that derived from experiments in search of an elixir," said another member. "A combination of mercury, licorice root, and . . . other stuff. Does anyone remember?"

"I don't. Arny's *Principles of Pharmacy* has one recipe." The chairman gestured toward the walls of bookshelves behind him. "It's around here somewhere."

"It's there." Sammy pointed to the bottom shelf of the second bookshelf on the left wall. His first year as a member, when

Don would shush him if he spoke, he'd spent each meeting on the floor or atop the stepladder, mentally cataloging every book in the room.

"You can take it home," Andres said dismissively. "It's not rare."

Sammy thanked him and, two hours later, sat in his bedroom with the book. Don and Leena were downstairs, finishing their dinner and watching the Knicks on the thirty-six-inch Zenith Smart Set. When he was six years old, Sammy and his mother were at Madison Square Garden to see a rookie named Patrick Ewing put up thirty-seven points against the Bulls. They had courtside seats for that one, and the TV cameras caught them over and over. Leena had a tape of the game and liked to watch it when there wasn't anything live. The best shot of them came near the end of the first quarter, when Ewing backed down the Bulls' center beneath the rim. Little Sammy was watching them collide with his face upturned, lips pursed. His white-and-orange team sweatshirt was two sizes too big for him. He could have been just Jell-O under there. Next to him, Leena was up on her feet, fist pumping. She was wearing a yellow top and had insane, gravity-defying hair.

Sammy was remembering this—not the game itself, but the moment afterward when Leena dragged him to the TV and showed him the footage, as happy as he'd ever seen her—when one of his thoughts came to him: How much would it cost, *today*, to buy mercury?

Several months later, after a two-day stay, Sammy came home from the hospital. It was November, and the air was dense with cold. From the street, his bedroom window was a pane of ice.

His memories of the overdose were hazy, but Don and Leena had returned from a charity dinner to find him slumped on the floor of his room, tongue out, a long line of drool bisecting his shirt. His skin had turned stygian gray. He did remember waking up in the ambulance with a mouthful of charcoal. His mother rode alongside him, exhausted in formal wear, listing all the things he had left to live for: a college degree, the chance to finally beat his father at chess, a Knicks championship. Sammy smiled weakly at his mother through charcoal-blackened lips. He could still taste the blue mass. He'd swallowed the pills whole, but his tongue registered the flavor, and it was bitter and stannic and sweet, like candied metal.

"I already beat Don at chess," he murmured, but Leena didn't hear him.

Dr. Huang visited him in the hospital, along with the hospital psychologist. Sammy knew there would be consequences— more therapy, more meds. The worst was the judgment handed down by his mother: Sammy was no longer a member of the Numismatics Society. It was an unhealthy influence, Leena said, and Sammy needed to spend time among boys his own age. The irony was that when Sammy jumped out of the window, he was trying to hurt himself, but his parents refused to see it that way. When he took the blue mass, he was trying to *help* himself, but this, they decided, was a suicide attempt. He just wished he could remember how much he'd taken; he would need to be more careful in the future.

When Sammy arrived home, he found a visitor waiting for him in the living room: Andres. The old man was sitting in the corner of the sofa, one arm up on the armrest. The bottom of his thick beard rested against his chest, and he was wearing dark jeans and a sweater the color of tennis balls. Seeing him this way, reclining casually outside the library, was a bit like seeing Don in his undershirt. The chairman rose stiffly as Sammy entered the room, but Andres had no nervous energy around him, none of the unctuousness that clung to so many of the people in the hospital, people unsure how to act around a boy who had *tried to kill himself*.

"I heard you won't be joining us anymore," Andres said as he shook Sammy's hand. "Your father said it would be all right if I came to say goodbye."

Leena was standing in the doorway, and Sammy thought he saw her mouth tighten. The living room was one of the lighter rooms in the house, with cream-colored walls and a ten-bulb crystal chandelier, but compared to the luminescent whiteness of the hospital, it seemed dark.

Sammy was prepared to endure a long, awkward conversation with Andres, but instead the old man gave a brief, satisfied nod and said, "Well, goodbye."

"Oh. Bye," Sammy said.

Andres took the long way around the couch, and Sammy and Leena followed him to the front door, where Sammy recognized the man's heavy coat hanging in the foyer. He put this coat on slowly, grunting, as Leena's impatience filled the room like gas.

"Thanks for stopping by," she said before he had it on fully, then she opened the door and held it for him. If Don were there, he would have said, "Don't let the heat escape," but he was upstairs in his office, bothering neither to entertain their guest nor welcome home his son. So Leena held the door, the cold air hitting them hard, until the chairman was all zipped up.

As he left, he handed Sammy a small, rectangular present, wrapped in gray tissue paper. "A little get-well gift."

"Thanks," Sammy said, and it was the last time he would ever see the man.

Once Andres was gone, Leena charged upstairs to scold Don for letting the old man inside. Adults loved to talk about young people being *influenced* by things: violent movies, violent video games, and, yes, in this case, an elderly group of coin collectors. But Sammy knew he could watch the most gruesome movies, play the bloodiest games, every minute of every day, and he would never be anything other than what he was. How he chose to fill the hours was no more meaningful, really, than when Leena chose the crystal chandelier over the wide Roman bronze.

It was good she was angry: the front door was only just latching shut and she'd already forgotten about the gift. He trailed her upstairs and closed his bedroom door behind him. A small card was attached to the tissue paper with Scotch tape. Sammy lifted the flap. The note, which was unsigned, read, *Speak of things public to the public, but of things lofty and secret only to the loftiest and most private of your friends.* The quote was from Trithemius.

Sammy unwrapped the gift. It was a book, a small book— neither old nor expensive nor rare. The sticker on the back, which the chairman had neglected to remove, said it cost him $18. Sammy opened the front cover and flipped through the pages. He'd seen something like this, he thought, in one of the rarely used drawers in the kitchen.

It was a recipe book.

Sammy rode the subway to the hospital, and it was dark in the train car, or—no, he was wearing sunglasses. He was sixteen years old, and he was wearing sunglasses to hide the color of his eyes. That morning, in the mirror, they were so red from sleeplessness he thought instantly of the day he saw a family of deer dead on the side of a parkway—three of them together, a mother and two fawns, and the eyes of the smallest one had burst.

The previous night, he couldn't sleep because he was hungry. He was hungry because he hadn't eaten. He hadn't eaten because Dr. Huang told him not to. So, too, did the informational pamphlet she gave him.

> Q: What should I do to prepare for my electroconvulsive treatment?
> A: First, do not eat the night before. . . .

Electrotherapy. Shock treatment. In the spirit of Ken Kesey, Sammy had taken to calling it "brain burn"—"a free trip to the moon"—but this upset Dr. Huang. "That's a terrible way to think of it," she said. "No one is going to burn you."

He shifted in his seat. The subway car rattled, the muffled beat of dance music came through the oversize headphones of the boy sitting next to him. The air smelled of exhaust and baked bread. He was dressed in a red hooded sweatshirt and blue jeans one size too big.

> Q: What should I wear?
> A: You will be placed in a hospital gown upon arrival.
>   You will be tired when you wake up from treatment,
>   so we recommend clothes that are easy to get back
>   into, like loose-fitting sweatshirts or jeans.

This was his first brain burn, and he was not scared, exactly, though somewhere within the deep space of his mind was a kind of trembling—a psychic arrhythmia. As a boy, he would wonder, *What's wrong with me?* As a teenager, he pictured that boy and said to him, *Your life is going to be impossible.*

Then he thought of the Mercury Formula that had got him into all this trouble:

$$HgS + O_2 \rightarrow Hg + SO_2.$$

Andres had known, somehow, the very first day they met, that Sammy would respond to an idea presented this way: as a formula, as a puzzle to be solved. After the overdose, he'd used the recipe book as Andres clearly intended, to refine his search for an elixir, to keep track of the recipes as he consumed them. The overdose had been a bad mistake: for a year or two after, he had no independence, little unsupervised time with which to experiment. He was more careful now. At NYU, where he was a freshman chem major, he tested his recipes rigorously and took them only in the smallest doses. He heeded Andres's inscription and spoke of his work to no one. He told Dr. Huang he was finished with the elixir, kept his books and his materials hidden. His actual antidepressants he deposited, one tablet per day, into the toilet.

What he hadn't anticipated was Don cheating on Leena with a Peruvian hypnotherapist he'd met at a conference. Sammy had a small apartment in the East Village, funded by his parents, walking distance from NYU's shared instrumentation facility. When Don confessed the affair to Leena, she'd grabbed the spare key to this apartment, which they kept for emergencies, packed an overnight bag, and let herself in while Sammy was at class. When he came home, he found her in tears, and he still wasn't sure which was the primary cause: Don's cheating, or that she'd found, in Sammy's bathroom, close to a gallon of quicksilver.

Thus: the brain burn. Either he agreed to this or he gave up school, his freedom, everything. Even Dr. Huang seemed hurt by the news. "I really thought we were making progress," she said, "but has it occurred to you that your self-experiments are the reason we haven't made more?" It was the closest he'd ever come to feeling guilty.

Q: How will I feel when I wake up?
A: Hopefully, you'll feel better. . . .

By the time he reached the hospital he was ravenous. Even the nauseating smell of apple juice and pudding, which was so heavy there it stuck to the walls, made his stomach growl. Through his sunglasses, Sammy watched old, sick people push their IVs like a reluctant friend down the hallways. In his room, he put on the papery gown and lay flat on the bed. The nurse zip-tied his clothes into a plastic bag, which she hung by a cord around the bedpost. "Relax," she said, but there it was, so close to his head: the ECT machine. It looked like a microwave or a video game console. But he could see the little pads that would go on his head, the little dials that controlled the strength and duration of the shock. One button said BEGIN, another said STOP, and why was this worse than ON/OFF? He wasn't sure, but it was.

He lay that way for what seemed like a long time until he felt a hand on his shoulder, and it was Dr. Huang, smiling down at him. She had a slightly oval face, a smile that was almost a frown. She squeezed his shoulder and told him she would be there the whole time, would be there when he woke up.

"Will *I* be here?" he asked.

"I promise you will be," she answered.

The nurse hooked up his IV.

"Count backward from ten," said the anesthesiologist.

"Ten . . . ," Sammy said, and he was sleeping.

Dr. Huang connected the oxygen mask and inserted a mouthguard to prevent Sammy from chewing off his tongue. She placed electrodes at each temple. When everyone was ready, Dr. Huang pressed BEGIN, and the electrical stimuli surged through the electrodes. A muscle relaxant administered with the anesthesia prevented Sammy's body from thrashing against the restraints. In the 1940s, some brain burn patients would shake so bad their femurs would snap and their shoulders would pop out of their sockets. But Dr. Huang could see only a flutter in the eyelids, a trembling in the feet. Goose bumps emerged on Sammy's arms and neck.

When he woke up twenty minutes later, he told the nurse, "I have to go to bed."

She adjusted his pillows. "Mission accomplished."

He fell asleep for another minute and woke to see Dr. Huang standing over him. She had a slightly oval face, a smile that was almost a frown. He began to remember where he was and why.

"You had a really good seizure," she said. "Are you going to throw up?"

He blinked at her. "Maybe." But then he yawned and the feeling passed. The darkness lifted. His thoughts ping-ponged between happiness and the remembrance of becoming happy. He'd gone to the hospital. Three flavors of pudding.

Count backward from ten.

Ten. Ten. Ten.

Everything was light and right in the world.

Four years later, Sammy was a graduate student, still at NYU, in organic and inorganic chemistry. He wasn't the standout he used to be. His undergraduate career had been underwhelming, and he'd only been accepted to the graduate school off the wait list. Every year since he was sixteen he'd required "maintenance" brain burns—like rotating the tires of a car—and whenever he was in the middle of a regimen, his memory just wasn't the same.

That day, he was staying late in the lab, which had so much equipment, and so little desk space, that a casual observer might wonder where the work was done. There was the matrix-assisted laser desorption/ionization unit, which looked like an air conditioner, and the elemental analyzer, which looked as if it would talk if you pressed the right buttons, and the infrared spectrometer, which had an arcadelike joystick. There were no windows, and the air smelled of ethanol and coffee. He was proofreading the manuscript of an article on the structures of carboxylic acid reductase, which was part of his adviser's research—nothing that especially interested Sammy, but it paid the tuition, and eventually some offshoot of the project would grow into his own dissertation.

His obsession with the elixir wasn't gone, per se, but the ECT had shocked it into some deeper part of his limbic system, where he only sometimes felt it, like an ancestral pain. On "happy" days—in the immediate aftermath of a brain burn—he would say he'd lost his obsession because the ECT had fixed him. But then it would wear off, and the darkness would come, along with his memories. For most people, memory loss after a brain burn was slight, brief, and occasional. "I won't claim to understand why it's worse for you," Dr. Huang had said. "We'll figure it out." But he knew the answer, even if she didn't: *everything* was worse for him; that was his condition in life. *What's wrong with me?*

Sammy was pondering this question when a young woman entered the laboratory with a Styrofoam cooler and said, "Hey, I could use your help." She was small, maybe five feet three, and her hair was dirty blond and cut short. She was wearing a tank top with the logo of a potato chip company, jet-black jeans, and a worn leather messenger bag, the strap of which cut diagonally across her body and accentuated the shape of her breasts.

He was too startled by her forwardness to say anything but "Okay."

She dropped the cooler on the table and began to remove the electrical tape that held the top shut. Her dissertation, she said as she picked at the tape with her fingernail, involved the traditional medicines of pre-Columbian tribes in Central America, and she said this, Sammy noted, as though she was only reminding him, as though he should already know. She had recently smuggled home a tribal medicine made from *Zamia nesophila*, a beach-loving cycad she'd first seen on the southern coast of Panama. There, she noticed the locals stripping the skinlike bark from the fern's narrow trunk and grinding the leaves into paste. She tracked down a Ngäbe-Buglé healer, who told her that they used the tree to create an elixir of eternal life.

Her use of this phrase excited Sammy, and his excitement was sexual.

She wanted to know exactly what was in it. She pulled the last strip of tape off the Styrofoam, lifted the lid, and removed a ⅛-dram vial, clear glass, filled with a thick green liquid. Sammy studied her as she held the vial up to the artificial light of the laboratory and examined the contents from below. He did not make a habit of comparing women to cars, but she reminded him—the thought was there, he couldn't unthink it—of the Ferrari Testarossa.

His ability to feel this attraction, he knew, was the result of the brain burns. They did help. If nothing else, the ECT eliminated a doubt he'd had in his mind since his jump out of his window—that is, he'd often doubted his father's cold reassurances that his disorder was chemical and not an indictment of his character. The real torture of mental illness is this lingering sensation that normalcy is a thought away, that if only you were strong enough, you could *think* your way out of it. But if that were true, something so visceral as the brain burn wouldn't help at all. A paradox emerged from the convulsions: the ECT left him both happier and weaker. Imagine that. It turned out strength had nothing to do with it.

"I'm not a phytochemist," he told the woman. "I don't think I can do anything."

She snorted. "You know how to use the equipment and you're here on a Friday evening. You obviously have nothing better to do." She handed him the vial.

"Actually, I *am* interested in the elixir of life." It was the first time he'd said this out loud since he was sixteen.

She gave him a funny look. "Right," she said, but something was different. Her confidence had faded. She was the one who'd barged in here and started making demands, and yet somehow, as always, he was the one who said the wrong thing. "Well, anything you can tell me would be helpful."

"Sure."

She lingered near the table. "So . . ." There was a long pause, as though he was supposed to say something. "I'll see you tonight?"

Sammy cocked his head, nose scrunched. "Do I know you?"

The woman licked her lips. "I can't tell if you're being funny or mean."

Her name was Catherine, she was a graduate student in anthropology, and what the fuck? Why was Sam pretending not to remember her? She'd met him a week ago, in this very lab, and he was so different then: brighter, more attentive. When she told him what she was studying, he told her to sit, and she watched him find a stool for himself, and then he sat very close to her. He asked so many questions, about her dissertation, about her time in Panama, that by the time he asked a different kind of question—*Would you maybe want to have dinner with me?*—it seemed like a natural, inevitable extension of that interest. It was not like with the other guys she'd met at NYU, whose compliments were too horny to be sincere.

Long before they'd met, she'd seen him around campus—Christ, had she seen him. Those eyes! Up close, he looked like a feminine Kurt Cobain—like a *gay* Kurt Cobain, to be honest, but she knew gay men, she'd even kissed a few, and none stared at her with such intensity. He wanted her.

Or he *used* to. Now he was staring at her like an entrée he didn't order and was about to send back. He was playing some sort of game, and because the human heart is absolutely useless, this made him all the more alluring. She was aware of the pickup strategy men called negging—"You'd look so much hotter with long hair," she once had two men tell her, in the same night, at the same bar—but this was something different. There was too much confusion in his coldness. He was lost in it, like a little boy.

"I can't tell if you're being funny or mean," she had said, but watching him, she thought it was something else.

He brushed the hair away from his eyes and looked down at the floor, his cheeks red. He was a beautiful blusher, and she actually entertained the quick, breathless fantasy of interrupting the awkwardness of this encounter by tackling him to the cool, chemical-smelling floor and fucking him until he remembered her.

"We had a date tonight," he said slowly, with a hint of a question mark.

"I guess I'm not that memorable."

"Catherine?"

"That's me." She was twenty-three and had never trusted men. Sure, she'd slept with them in a mechanical way—it was something to do on the weekends, she couldn't afford cable—but she'd never come close to a relationship. So what was she to do about this strange, beautiful man? This man she'd been thinking about since she'd met him and who had now forgotten and remembered her in the space of a minute?

"I hope I haven't blown it, but I should tell you something about myself, and you can decide." He pulled a stool out for her, as he did the first time they'd met. His wrists were thin like a woman's. "So, have you ever read *One Flew Over the Cuckoo's Nest?*"

Over the next few months, Sammy saw Catherine almost every day. After their embarrassing meeting in the lab, he'd gone home to check his journal, and sure enough, there it was:

Met an anthropology student studying ancient medicine. Catherine said the Ngäbe-Buglé don't believe that any medicine, even the elixir of life, can actually cure diseases. "They don't believe the elixir itself heals the body," she told me. "They believe it gives the *mind* the strength to heal the body." How great is that?? She said they'd take the elixir not only when they were sick, but also when they became jealous or angry or sad. I asked her to dinner, and she accepted.

Never in his life had he spent so much time out of the house. Catherine held his hand and blew on his neck during brunch at Cafe Mogador. Catherine took him to a nightclub in Alphabet City, where the strobe lights hit her sandy hair and gave him a new kind of brain burn. Catherine leaned against him and laughed as he waved helplessly at passing taxis along Avenue C. Where did this woman come from? That some *other* self, some self he'd forgotten, had initiated their romance cast a semimagical, semi-strange sheen over their time together. It was like being set up on a date by a mutual friend, only the mutual friend is yourself.

The first time he took her back to his apartment, Sammy removed her coat and threw it with his over the arm of the sofa. He gave her the grand tour—the living room, with the leather sectional he'd bought from the previous tenant; the kitchen, which seemed fifteen degrees hotter despite its distance from the radiator; the bedroom, where the bed was. The contrast between Sammy and his apartment baffled her. She wondered to herself where this money came from, how he could afford such a nice place but wear such terrible clothes. He couldn't even offer her wine or a cocktail, only ice water served in a coffee cup. But when you date a man who forgets you a week after asking you out, there's no obvious place to draw a line. She didn't know it then, but she would keep pushing that line back, redrawing it, until her heart was broken.

They met at the foot of the bed. Sammy was a twenty-year-old virgin. He kissed her, openmouthed and awkward. She chewed on his lip, shoved him a little, challenged him to loosen up. He let her push him to the bed and then pulled her down, too, onto the brown-and-kiwi comforter. He gathered the edge of it and yanked it over them both, buried them in blankets. There, the darkness excused his clumsiness. He could paw at her bra like an idiot and it only meant he was blind, not inexperienced. Once their clothes were off and piled high on the carpet, she lay on her side with her spine against his chest and her left leg raised and curled back across his thigh. But the geometry of this was too advanced, too complicated, so he turned her around to face him. It was now or never. He positioned himself on top of her, pressed his face against her clavicle, and hoped for the best.

The next morning, when she woke with her hand pinned under his back, Catherine rose and searched Sam's refrigerator for something to drink. There, alongside an empty bottle of orange juice, a hugely expired carton of milk, and two eggs sitting loose in the butter compartment, was the tribal medicine she'd smuggled from Panama. *Smuggled* was overdramatic; she just liked the way it sounded. In truth she had all the paperwork, but when the customs people asked her if she had anything to declare, it was three in the morning, and she hadn't slept at all on the plane.

She stretched her back and took in the sight of his apartment for the first time in daylight. The floors were dark natural wood, extending from the bedroom to the living room before turning to speckled slate in the kitchen. The counters were marble, white, smooth. She could see straight into the bedroom from where she was standing. Sammy was asleep in there, and he was a quiet sleeper, which surprised her. He seemed too anxious for easy dreams. Last night, she'd texted a girlfriend from the bathroom: *I think he's rich?!* And the girlfriend was, like, *cha-ching!* But Catherine didn't care about that—she was just taken aback. Only in the clearer light of day did it seem less strange. Erratic behavior such as Sam's was, in its own way, a kind of privilege. Not everyone could afford it.

She took the vial from the fridge. Almost all of it was gone.

"Good morning," Sam said from behind her, still in bed, and she turned, still holding the vial. He'd arranged the sheets carefully over his groin, but his torso was exposed, and she wanted him again. He had not been very good, but it took a long time for him to come. He apologized for that, but she wasn't complaining.

"Good morning, darling," she said, making it clear in her voice that *darling* was used ironically. She showed him the vial. "What happened to this?"

"Oh." He gathered the sheets around his chest, which seemed unfair—she'd put her underwear on, but she was topless in the morning sun and the almost-definitely unflattering light of the refrigerator. "I'll have those results for you soon."

"No rush. But what happened? Did you spill it or did you drink it?" This, she thought, was a joke.

Sam didn't laugh. She would learn that though he was capable, sometimes, of laughter, it was rare. He was not even a smiler, though *when* he smiled, it was as if she were a girl again, and her mother—who was kind but strict—was allowing her, once a year, to have ice cream for dinner. It was an important lesson she learned from her mother, who raised her alone: anything withheld is the best thing.

Sammy stared at her, his face slack. "You asked me for a favor," he said sharply. "I had better things to do, but I did it."

"I know. I wasn't . . ." She didn't know how to finish that sentence. She didn't even know what he *thought* she was doing.

He *had* taken some for himself, locked it away in a cooler in the storage unit where he still had (unbeknownst to Leena) the rest of the quicksilver. He wasn't planning to do anything with it, necessarily, it was just . . . a rainy-day fund, a fire extinguisher secured behind glass. *Break in case of emergency.* "I used what I had to use," he lied, "and I only bothered to help because I felt so bad for forgetting you. I still don't remember asking you out, by the way. I'm just taking your word for it that I did. For all I know you've tricked me into this."

Catherine put the vial back into the fridge, closed the door, and moved stiffly into the bedroom, hands over her breasts. At the foot of the bed, she knelt to hunt for her clothes, which was hard to do, kneeling while covering her chest. But she wouldn't cry. Not for this prick.

She found her bra and her tank top and was trying to put them on, still crouched at the foot of the bed, when she felt his hand on her still-bare shoulder.

"I'm sorry."

When she looked up at him, so much sadness was in his face she wanted instantly to rescue him from it. He was lying stomach down, reaching for her, and God, where, all her life, had this lust been hiding? She'd never wanted anyone else the way she wanted him.

"That was awful," she said.

"Yes," he said immediately. "I get like that. Maybe it's good you know."

She made a noise that was kind of like *Hmm*, as if she were deciding whether to get up, dress, and leave, as if she hadn't *already* decided to stay.

"Come to bed," he said, "and I'll tell you how wonderful you are and how I'm falling in love with you."

So rather than leaving, she went to him, felt his long arms encircle her waist. *I'm falling in love with you.* She felt as if she were drowning, only it was good. This was something her mother couldn't teach her: a bit of cruelty makes love taste sweeter, and it's always the not-cruel people who suffer for this, who feel, most acutely, the hypnotic effect of the pendulum as it swings from cruelty to love.

On His Deathbed, Trithemius Dictates the Elixir of Life

Würzburg, Germany, AD *1516*
The abbot says black-tailed night birds are born with their eyes open. "Very unusual for birds," he tells us. "They require hardly any care and leave the nest early." We don't say anything out of respect for the abbot, who is dying, but secretly we're thinking, *Why is he talking about birds?* According to Brother Marcus, the abbot's mind is gone: "The abbot thinks he's ten years old and delivering a report on birds to his schoolteacher." According to Brother Fridl, who heard from Brother Dietmar, the abbot spent the whole night singing an inappropriate song in his sleep. Brother Fridl would only repeat ten words of this song, but we bargained him up to fifteen:

The tits of a cow are like the tits of a woman, ready for the

We first met the abbot when he arrived at St. James's Abbey in the spring of 1506. It was a warm spring, and we'd spent much of the season outdoors, tending to the gardens, chopping wood. We'd gone unsupervised since our last abbot died of ergotism (his skin turned black and fell off his bones). We prayed, but we prayed right there in the fields, on our knees in the freshly tilled soil. The Benedictine Order is no place for softness. Joining the brotherhood is like opening a heavy door—you have to lean your whole body into it, keep pushing and pushing until it gives.

We knew all about the abbot. We knew everything there was

to know. When he was assigned to Würzburg, the other monas-
teries were merciless:

"Oh, Trithemius will be your abbot? Good luck with *that*."

"I heard he reads in the nude!"

We soon discovered the abbot reads fully clothed—but the
books he reads! Tomes on alchemy and medicine and magic crys-
tals. Brother Fridl lifted the cover of one such book and saw a
naked man on the *first page*, with arrows pointing to all his secret
places.

We'd probably be celebrating if it weren't for Brother Georg,
who is heartbroken over the abbot's poor health. Brother Georg
stands in the corner, near the fire, crying into his robes. We love
Brother Georg, who is an orphan of Sponheim. He is sixteen and
easily startled. If you touch him on his shoulder, he jumps right
out of his skin and says in a high-pitched voice, "Praise God!"

We don't hold his affection for the abbot against him. He was
so young when he came to St. James's. He didn't know any better
than to bond with Trithemius, whose avuncular fatness does have
its charms. When Brother Georg calls the abbot "father," it has
a different sound than when we say it. For Brother Georg, it
has two meanings.

The abbot moans and sweats onto his pillow. We stand in the
doorway and study our sunburned feet. Before he lost his mind,
the abbot diagnosed his own disease as a fever of the Sensual
Spirit. There are four spirits, he told us. The Sensual Spirit lives
in the brain. The liver and kidneys house the Natural Spirit. The
groin shelters the Generative Spirit. The Brutal Spirit belongs to
the heart.

Brother Georg nurses a weakness of the Brutal Spirit. He
loves too strongly and without self-preservation. Brother Marcus says Georg never learned to protect his heart. Brother Fridl
says only God's love is safe. Brother Heinrich, who is so old he
sleeps standing up, says, "Look, life is hard. There's no one way
to get through it."

The abbot's last words are a recipe:

One cup quicksilver
One-half nutmeg and mace
Two handfuls aniseed
One gentian root
Copious cream of tartar
Oil of three spikenard plants
Lots of good cinnamon
Slag of iron

Brother Zobeslaus writes down the recipe, and we all know what it is: the elixir of life. The abbot has been working on the elixir since before he came to Würzburg. His second year at St. James's, he consumed a hallucinatory dose of black henbane and nearly killed Brother Heinrich with a chair.

Later, after we've buried the abbot, Brother Zobeslaus holds up the recipe. "So who wants to go first?"

We don't laugh out loud because of the abbot, but it's a pretty good joke.

"Elixir of life from a dying man," says Brother Marcus. "That's rich."

But later, when Brother Marcus gathers the abbot's papers for the archive, he can't find the recipe anywhere.

After the abbot died, we had two days of quiet before Brother Bartilmebis complained of noises from the basement—smoky sounds, he said, like liquids coming to a boil and solids burning to ash. When Brother Marcus caught Brother Georg sneaking from his bedroom in the early hours of blackness, Brother Georg shouted, "Praise God!," and dropped an armful of spikenard plants onto the cold stone of the hallway.

Brother Donat says Georg will kill himself making the elixir, but Brother Fridl, who is Brother Donat's actual brother, says Georg is only mourning and won't do anything foolish. We aren't so sure. We say, "Isn't mourning the kind of thing that *makes* you foolish? Isn't grief, in large quantities, a kind of madness?"

•

The day before the arrival of our new abbot, we find Brother Georg on the roof of the stables. He has a goblet of elixir in his shaking hands. We gather below and stare up into the sun. It is early morning, and there is no wind.

"Easy there," says Brother Oswald, as if he were talking to a horse.

Brother Georg is crying so much it's hard to hear him. "He's *dead!*" he shouts, as though this were new information.

A bit of the elixir sloshes over the side of the cup. We gag when we see it. There is the smell of cinnamon and ash and melted horseshoes. Brother Georg says the abbot was touched by God and makes a long speech about geniuses who went unrecognized in their own time. "It's a test of faith," he says. Snot runs from his nose. He's using a lot of words to make his point, but all any of us can hear is "I'm alone, I'm alone, I'm alone."

So we tell him he is not alone. He has a house full of brothers who love him. We promise to always watch out for him, like a big bunch of dads.

He seems to consider this, but every one of us can see what's happened: His mind is already gone. His brutal heart is elsewhere.

"Don't," we say.

But he does.

We bury Brother Georg next to the abbot. It's against the rules, but who's going to know? Our new abbot was supposed to arrive a week ago, but there is no one, and we are alone. Brother Bartilmebis received a letter from Brother Arnold of St. John's, which said he heard from Brother Goswin of St. Stephen's that our new abbot died of swamp fever on his way to Würzburg. If this is true, they'll send another. If that one dies, they'll send another. We're interchangeable, we brothers. We don't all wear the same clothes because it's fun.

Still, we miss Brother Georg. We try to remember him as he lived, but for now it is impossible to forget how he died. The way he coughed blood through his swollen, ulcerated lips. The way the skin of his hands peeled off his bones like banana rinds. The way he cried for a father who abandoned him. Brother Donat says Brother Fridl has been waking up screaming, his mind filled with nightmares.

"Don't gossip," we tell him. "There's no comfort in that."

8

Problems in Living

In an entry from his first year in college, Sammy discussed his conception of the elixir's purpose:

> This morning, my psych professor started class by announcing that everyone's greatest desire—greater than love, money, power, *anything*—is to be bitten by a vampire. We thought he was joking, but then he wrote "vampire" on the whiteboard, double-underlined, and we stopped laughing. He explained that humans, by nature, are afraid of death, and yet, paradoxically, research has shown that people respond negatively to the idea of living forever. According to a study at Yale, if such an option were available, an overwhelming majority of people said they wouldn't take it. Their reasons were typically moral: to live forever is against the laws of nature or God, to wish for it hubris, to attain it would mean watching those you love grow old and die. (No one ever mentions that you'd find *new* people to love.)
>
> This was the crux of his Vampire Theory, that human beings want to live forever but regard choosing to live forever as a moral or spiritual failing. If those things are true, then the ultimate fantasy is vampiric embrace: to have immortality *forced* upon you, to live forever but be spared the guilt of choosing.

When class ended, I had ten minutes to get to Origins of Literature. We're reading *Gilgamesh*. The professor spent almost all of class focused on a single passage from Tablet IX, in which Gilgamesh begins his search for immortality after the death of a comrade:

Gilgamesh for Enkidu, his friend,
Weeps bitterly and roams over the desert.
"When I die, shall I not be like unto Enkidu?
Sorrow has entered my heart.
I am afraid of death and roam over the desert."

Gilgamesh misses Enkidu, but what pains him most is the realization that he, too, will die. The professor argued that this is the moment—as Gilgamesh learns to fear death—in which he becomes fully human. I sat there in the back of the room, wondering, "What does that make me?"

Next, I had my appointment with Dr. Huang. She asked me today if I really believe in immortality, if I believe true agelessness is an attainable goal. We were in her office, but I'd only just sat down. She was wearing these blue eyeglasses. They must be new, or at least she's never worn them in front of me. She does this on purpose: small surprises, unexpected questions asked at unexpected times. There was no "How are you?" or "How are you feeling?" Just: "I want to ask you about immortality."

Here's what I told her: I don't believe in immortality, of course, and my interest in the elixir of life is purely theoretical.

Here's what I really believe: Everything in our body is connected. We learn this from our earliest encounters with anatomy. I'm thinking of that childhood song: the thighbone connects to the hip bone, the hip bone connects to the . . .

If everything is connected, it follows that there is some way to treat everything at once. I'm talking about what the

Greeks called *panakeia*, the all-healing. My goal is not to live forever but to live *happily*—to figure out what happiness even means. Can it be done? I don't know. At least it keeps me busy. An old colleague of my father used to say that the only true panacea is work.

He wouldn't like me much, that man. He believes mental illnesses are a myth, a metaphor. They are not "real diseases" but simply "problems in living." The words don't interest me. I do know that people who have searched for the elixir of life have often suffered from "real diseases": cancers, malaria, what we now call Alzheimer's—stuff that shows up on an MRI or autopsy. Their search for the elixir is a response to an alarm sounding in their bodies.

But that's the problem. Their dying bodies pollute the data and place too short a timer on the search. No one has ever searched for the elixir in response to a mental illness. *What's wrong with me?* I've never found the word for it, but that same indefinability makes it the ideal condition on which to experiment. What's wrong with me doesn't clear up on its own, as malaria sometimes does; it doesn't kill you, like cancer.

Who knows what's *possible?* Any question about possibility is just a sanity test in disguise. That's what Dr. Huang was really asking this morning: "Are you crazy or are you sane?"

I believe I'm uniquely qualified to search for the elixir of life. Whatever that makes me, that's what I am.

Good night.

It was one in the morning, and I lay stretched out in bed, the tips of my fingers sandpaper dry. On the floor, I had the stuff we'd taken from the storage unit. The box contained at least some of the materials described in Sammy's elixir, and though it was slow going, the journals were helping me make sense of them. I read as much as I could each day, in every spare, private moment. I'd reached his grad school years, and it wasn't until I read his first entries about Catherine, for example, that I understood the CATH-ERINE vial we found in the storage facility to be what Sammy called the "tribal medicine" in his recipe book.

CATHERINE. It was appropriate that I'd first seen her name that way—all caps, thick ink. Her name had reverberated in my mind since reading Sammy's account of their courtship. He'd been with a *woman*. It was ridiculous to be jealous of a dead man's ex, but I couldn't help searching his entries for signs of insincerity, for hints that he was only faking with Catherine. It's not uncommon for closeted gay men to date women, even to marry them—just look at Congress. But nothing in his journals suggested reluctance, displeasure, bared teeth. It didn't read like playacting.

I set the journal aside and moved from the bed to the floor, where I had a half gallon of quicksilver sitting in a carton as if it were leftovers raided from the fridge. I turned the plastic container upside down, watched the quicksilver travel from one side to the other. I was trying to see it as Sammy did—as the centerpiece to an elixir that could save my father. Instead, the more I looked at the stuff, the more my bedroom felt poisonous.

The mercury reminded me of a day in spring, Sammy's second semester at LHS. That was baseball season, the Littlefield Yellow Jackets. My position was right field, where no one ever hit the ball, and if they did, I was too surprised to chase it. Back in the dugout, our coach would pat me on the back as if he were about to console me, but he hated to lose, so in the heat of the game all he could manage was "At least no one's here."

That day, though, I'd invited a special guest: Mr. Tampari.

"Do you have a game this afternoon?" he'd asked me, after the bell rang and I said goodbye to him. We were in his classroom. Our relationship had been, if not always professional, at least strictly platonic, and I allowed my affection for him to grow only because I considered him unattainable.

"Yeah. We're playing Saco. You should come watch us."

Sammy pretended to consider this. "Are you going to hit a touchdown?"

"You know that's not what it's called."

"Are you going to hit the ol' four-bagger?"

"Stop."

"The grand salami?"

"I will if you come."

He closed his grade book. "Are you serious? Because if I sit in the sun with strangers watching sports, and you don't do anything impressive, you will fail this class."

I refused to crack a smile; I was serious about wanting him there. "Okay, I promise."

He sighed in a long, dramatic way. "Fine," he said, stretching the word out. "I'll go."

But these were not promises either of us could keep. As I walked back to the dugout after another strikeout, I searched the stands for any sign of Sammy. Nothing. I found only the bored, stiff smiles of overtired parents, the dirty, sun-kissed faces of little brothers and sisters. By the time I missed another ball in the outfield, I was despondent.

The next morning, I searched for Sammy in the hallway. When I found him, walking in the opposite direction from his classroom, something felt wrong. He was too sweaty for seven in the morning, and his blond hair looked almost leaden in the bad light of the hallway.

"You missed my game."

"Oh." He had no idea what I was talking about.

"I hit the winning home run, and my team carried me off the field on their shoulders."

"Awesome. Really good." Then, when it was clear I wanted more: "Something came up."

"Big plans last night?"

"Sort of." He tried to move past me.

"It's just that you said you'd come."

Sammy fixed me with his cloudy eyes. "I know you think you want to know everything," he said, his voice gravelly and cruel, "but trust me that you don't."

I stared at him, dumbfounded.

"I'm your teacher. Not your cheerleader." He walked away.

I ignored him for the rest of the day. I even skipped our third-period independent study. I spent that hour in the bathroom, imagining him alone in the lab, wondering where I was. What an idiot! I was so in love with him, and whether he liked it or not, I believed that affection made him responsible for me. Someday, I decided, I'd have a young protégé who wanted to fuck me, and I'd be nice to him. I'd show him how barium chloride, sodium silicate, and varying concentrations of carbon dioxide could be used to create microscopic crystal flowers, a whole garden of color, right there on the slide, visible only to us. The flowers would serve as a metaphor for the bond we shared—a special intimacy, but not a boundless one. An intimacy that followed the rules of the experiment, and the first rule of the nanocrystal flowers, I'd tell him, is this: don't touch them, or they'll break.

After school, I went to the lab and watched Sammy through the window of the door. I don't know why I expected otherwise, but he looked the same as that morning. He was hunched over his desk. He had the colored chalk from his blackboard and was pounding it into powder with his fist. It puffed into the air around him. He removed a container from his bag and poured something slow and serous onto the chalk—it was mercury, though I didn't know that then. His desk was covered in a sticky gypsum goo, and he rolled his hands over this mixture as if he were making the dough for bread. He picked up the dough, rainbow colored from his assortment of chalk, and bit off the end of it as if he were biting the head off a snake. He swallowed. I watched him struggle to keep it down, which he barely did, and then I ran away.

I never asked Sammy about that day. It was strange enough that I could pretend I'd misunderstood, and the next day at school he was back to normal. He called on me more than once to answer a question, even when other hands were raised. After class, he asked me to stay behind for a "quick chat" but was interrupted by a boy, whose name I can't remember, who had just failed the midterm exam. He didn't understand why.

"Well, look at your diagram in number four," Sammy said. "What's missing?"

The boy scrunched up his face but couldn't find the answer. To help him, Sammy mimed taking deep breaths.

"Ah, dude," the boy said. "I forgot oxygen. Can I get another try?"

"No can do."

"Dude, please."

Sammy shook his head. "In the words of Eminem, you only get one shot."

"Dude. *Dude.*"

"The sooner you stop begging me for something I can't give you, the sooner you can start studying for the final."

The boy stood quiet, possibly trying to make himself cry. But no tears came, and he zipped up his bag and left.

The moment the door closed, Sammy burst into laughter. "Thanks for staying after, dude." Sammy's eyes were wet from laughing. "I have a question for you."

"Dude, hit me with it."

He blotted his eyes with his sleeve and asked if I had any interest in a field trip the next day during our independent study. He wanted to take a tour of a local company that manufactured, of all things, organic deodorant and toothpaste. Of course I agreed.

"All right, dude," he said. "It's a date." Only after reading his journals did this moment, and the way he smiled, come back to me. It was a wild, reckless smile—a smile that, in hindsight, marked the start of our affair as much as our first time in bed. All of the things that had once been barriers between us burned up in the light of that smile like fog being cleared by the sun. The rules of the experiment had changed. Now, we could touch the flowers.

I'd been keeping these two sides of Sammy separate: my lover, and the eccentric who wrote the recipe book. But as mercury began to seep through my memories of Sammy, I had to face the reality of its influence. We had not grown close, as I'd thought, in the halls of the high school, in the chemical-rich air of the lab, in the cramped confines of his studio apartment. No, we made love in the cave of gloom.

In his journal from the day after my baseball game, he wrote:

Scary couple of days. Yesterday's entry contains several paragraphs of illegible words. I don't remember writing them.

I do remember waking from a nap, in the early afternoon, to the sound of the Widow sending a telefax in the garage. I also remember deciding, awake and angry, to drive to the storage unit. I can only speculate on what happened next. When I finally came to, back in my apartment after a school day that I apparently *did* attend (!), I woke up with a mouthful of blackboard chalk. I waited for a phone call telling me that I'm fired, but none came.

When I first recovered, I found something new on my desk: a postcard from S, from the Cooperative Republic of Guyana (!). He wrote to say Hello, I Miss You. How he even found me here I don't know. But now it all makes sense: I was woken by the Widow, checked the mail, found the postcard, went crazy. Is that an oxymoron, to say going crazy makes sense?

Good night.

PS: Where does the word "dude" come from? The OED attributes it to the late nineteenth century but does not know its origins. The *Boston Journal*, on June 2, 1885, refers to the "intense dudeness of Lord Beaconsfield."

Although the box from the storage unit contained none of this so-called Appetizer, the Dor, it did contain the Entrée: quicksilver, tribal medicine, *B. rossica*, rapamycin, and *P. cupana*. The problem was quantity. I had everything I needed of the quicksilver, but the tribal medicine, the CATHERINE vial, was nearly empty—if it were a jar of peanut butter, I would have thrown it away. The *B. rossica* had been wrapped in computer paper secured with tape, but I didn't even need to unwrap it to know I had much less than the three ounces required in Sammy's recipe. The same was true of the rapamycin; I needed fifteen milligrams and had, based on the dosages listed on the bottle, less than five.

Why had Sammy left me with so little to work with? There were two possibilities, as I saw them:

1. Someone had broken into Sammy's storage unit and stolen the bulk of the ingredients.
2. The same Sammy I saw eating blackboard chalk and punching holes into the wall was responsible for the destruction—was likely mad with mercury poisoning—and I couldn't trust anything he said.

It was early in our summer vacation when he'd attacked the wall, the third week of June. It was the same day our rats arrived: Number 5, Number 7, Number 37, Number 42, and Number 50. Those were the numbers they came with, and Sammy advised me not to name them.

"Don't fall in love," he told me. "There's no place for love in the lab."

That first day, Sammy spent a good eight hours teaching me how to care for them. He showed me how to hold the rats in one hand with their belly up, firmly but gently, and he showed me where the needle would go to inject the *P. cupana*: in those bellies, just below the liver. I was too hesitant at first, too afraid of hurting them, and the rats fought me for it, squeaking and snapping. Eventually, I learned.

I did love them—their tired eyes, their wiggling noses, the way they slept on top of one another and sometimes, most adorably, in their little hammocks. They didn't *look* traumatized. Their coats were white and full, their appetites normal. Even though Sammy preached the value of scientific distance, the rats' arrival had obviously excited him. He showed me how to set up the water maze, humming as he did it. We cleared out the supply closet to make space for the maze, and so we were surrounded by shelves and boxes and file cabinets, all pushed to the far edge of the wall.

I watched Sammy work, and now and then I would have mental flashes of his naked body, just small pieces: a bead of sweat on his lower back, a round belly button, a bare knee. If I pictured his body all at once, I would lose the ability to think. The school was completely empty, but we would never, ever touch each other outside his apartment. That was something we'd agreed upon without needing to say it.

The water maze looked like a kiddie pool but with a hard acrylic shell. It was five feet in diameter and one foot deep. We filled the maze using a rubber hose connected to a tap and stirred tempera paint into the water, watched it darken in a slightly sinister way. A water maze isn't a "maze" the way we usually think of one; there is no way out of it. Instead, it has a hidden platform—obscured by the dark paint—where the rat can stand and rest. Once you place the rat in the water maze, you time how long it takes him to find the hidden platform. If the rat is healthy, he'll get better and better at it over time—he'll remember where it is.

"We used to use milk powder instead of paint," Sammy said. We were crouched in front of the maze, and I could see our reflections slowly disappear as the paint spread. "You haven't smelled anything until you've smelled sour milk mixed with rat shit."

I wrinkled my nose and watched the hidden platform *become* hidden, vanishing under the dark water. "Did you ever do a science fair?"

He shook his head. "Never. Are they actually fun?"

I told him they were. My favorite part was talking to the judges, being judged by them, but not the way my high school classmates and even some of my teachers judged me. These judges were *my* people. A few of them actually wore dark-plastic pocket protectors, the kind you usually only see in "nerd" Halloween costumes. Once, in the middle of my explanation of hepatic stellate cells, one of the judges closed his eyes and said, "Mm, I love learning," as if he were biting into a piece of chocolate cake.

"Huh," Sammy said. "I've never really fit in anywhere."

I looked at him, delighted that he was opening up to me, but also somewhat disbelieving. He was so beautiful. I couldn't imag-

ine him ever feeling alone. Sometimes I did feel bad for the popular girls, the really pretty ones, who seemed to be drowning in
attention. I thought of Jody Girardi, a senior, and how every time
she opened her locker, a thousand eyes fell upon her perfectly
round backside, muscles straining as she went tippy-toes to reach
her history textbook. I had always thought she didn't notice—
she seemed to operate in a cloud of beauty-induced careless-
ness. But one day I was leaning against the wall near her locker
as she searched through her bag for soda money. Behind her,
Shaun Bowa punched his friend on the shoulder, gestured to
Jody's ass, and mimed biting into it like a hamburger. They were
perfectly silent, even in laughter, but I watched as Jody's face
turned red, her eyes shut tight in exhaustion. She knew everything
and always had.

Sammy clapped his hands together. "Let's get our test subjects
and see what's been done to them."

I opened the cage and lifted Number 50 out of his bed.
Number 50 was the smallest rat, but his tail was a full centime-
ter longer than that of the others, and this gave him a toylike
appearance—it was easy to imagine him being dangled in front
of a cat. He was also our primary test subject: Number 50 would
be receiving the highest dose of *P. cupana*.

I scratched his ears through the rubbery fabric of my gloves
and carried him to the water maze. Sammy held the stopwatch,
and when he nodded for me to proceed, I lowered Number 50 into
the water. He began to swim a lap around the perimeter of the
circular pool.

"Why is he hugging the walls like that?" Sammy asked, and
this was not a sincere question—it was a quiz.

"Thigmotaxis," I said, drawing upon a textbook he'd given me
on behavioral neuroscience. "His impulses tell him to remain in
contact with the vertical surface."

Sammy said nothing, which meant I was right. Number 50 was
looking for a way out of the maze, but there was no such exit. He
swam quickly, propelled by doggy paddles around the perimeter.
Eventually, his survival instincts pushed him away from the wall
and toward the center of the pool. In Sammy's hand, the stopwatch

ticked the seconds. We were timing Number 50's *escape latency*; that is, the time it took for him to reach a full stop on the platform.

When a minute had passed, I grabbed him by the tail and pulled him to the platform, held him there, allowed him to see where it was.

"Even if you put him back in the water right now," Sammy said, "he wouldn't be able to find the platform again."

"Okay." I began to lift Number 50 out of the water maze.

Sammy grabbed my wrist. "Wait. Never just take my word for it. You have to see for yourself."

So I lowered Number 50 into the water maze for a second time, and he began to swim. Sammy was right. If Number 50 had been a healthy rat, he would have shown at least some improvement on this second try. But Number 50 wasn't healthy. In the previous study, he was electroshocked so many times—the electrodes placed near his dime-size brain—that his memory functions were shot. He couldn't remember where to find the platform. He simply began his lap anew, hugging the walls. Without my intervention, he would have drowned.

When we were finished, Sammy invited me back to his apartment for dinner. "Have you ever made sushi?" he asked, and I didn't tell him that I'd never *eaten* sushi and had only the barest conception, from cooking shows, of its shape and color.

It was just after five when we arrived, which meant his little apartment had received a full day's worth of summer sun. The air inside was hot and dry, and this bothered Sammy more than it bothered me. I remembered what he'd said—"I've never really fit in anywhere"—and it was true that he never seemed comfortable. He was always too hot or too cold, always adding or removing layers. I watched him walk to the kitchen and fish an ice cube out of the freezer, which he ate in four loud crunches.

Once he cooled down, he started the rice cooker and stretched out on the bed. I stood awkwardly and indecisively in the kitchen. I wanted to have sex as soon as possible, but I liked, too, that he seemed to want me around even when we *weren't* having sex.

Sammy caught my eye and motioned me over. He was holding a thin manila folder, and he placed it next to him on the bed. "Check this out."

I scooted onto the mattress and opened the folder. It contained a couple of images, and I knew I was looking at MRI scans of two brains—human brains, not rat. The brains were white and gray, set against a black background. It was like an inkblot test, and you could see so many things depending on your mood—a smiley face, a family of upside-down bats. Each image had a couple of red arrows pointing to different areas of interest, but no labels indicated what those areas were. Behind me, Sammy was sitting up so that he could see over my shoulder.

"It's actually the same brain," he said, reading my mind. "One is before electroshock therapy, the other is after. Can you tell which is which?" Another quiz.

I considered this. They looked awfully similar. Neither one had any obvious abnormalities, none of the big white spaces that would indicate a tumor or lesion. But the arrows were pointing to mirrored places on either side of the brain, and this was a clue.

I held up one of the scans. "This is after?"

Sammy looked at me the way he sometimes did—with an intensity that was flattering and strange. "Are you guessing or do you know?"

As far as I could tell, the arrows were pointing to the hippocampi—the thin, seahorse-shaped ridges at the floor of the brain. In one image, these ridges seemed slightly larger, and I assumed this to be "after." If electroshock therapy could improve a person's mood—and that was the goal—then it would happen there, and it would maybe be visible.

"Good," Sammy said, when I finished explaining my rationale. "Our P. cupana, if it works, will activate the NMDA receptors in the hippocampus, thus strengthening memory."

I handed the photos back to Sammy, and he looked at them for only a second before placing them in the folder, shutting it, and tossing it to the floor. He'd been impressed by my answer, but he seemed far away.

After a moment, I asked him if he was okay.

"The truth is," he said, ignoring my question, "no one truly understands how ECT works. Is the hippocampus where happiness lives? Where memory lives? If so, how can electroshock improve one but decrease the other, and what does this say about our relationship with time?"

He sometimes spoke like this in the classroom, and just as in those moments, I didn't know if his questions were rhetorical or if I was supposed to answer. I would learn, during my project, that ECT really worked for people. It made them feel better. But Sammy was right: there was so much we didn't know, and every time someone was hooked up to one of those machines, it was a bit like sending a message into the deepest parts of space, not knowing who or what would answer.

"It's just sick," Sammy was saying. "Those rats are lost in their own minds." He was staring at his hands, as though he had conducted the earlier study. Then—this happened fast, in an absolute blur of motion—he turned at the waist and put his fist through the wall.

A hole appeared above his headboard, his arm vanishing into it as if he were being eaten alive. The sound it made—like a basketball being run over by a car—echoed throughout the studio. Sammy retreated to the floor and tucked his fist into his stomach. He sat cross-legged, eyes wide, nursing his swollen knuckles. His stunned expression was that of a man waking up from a seizure.

I hadn't moved from my position on the bed. The hole loomed behind me, dark and out of place. I imagined an MRI of the apartment, the hole a bright white lesion.

When the shock wore off, Sammy went to the bathroom and closed the door. I sat that way for several minutes, waiting for him. Eventually the rice cooker dinged, and the starchy smell of it infused the still-warm air of the apartment. Two little black boxes of seaweed were lined up on the counter, a rice paddle, a chef's knife, a cutting board.

When the bathroom door finally opened, Sammy emerged with a warm, apologetic smile.

"Dude," he said. "*Dude.*"

"Dude," I replied, because I knew this was his way of apologizing.

"Listen, dude. That was, like, totally crazy, dude."

I stifled a smile. "It's fine, dude."

As though this settled the matter, he went to the kitchen and prepared the sushi rice. The smell of vinegar and sugar filled the air. Thirty minutes later, we made sushi—California rolls, with avocado, cucumber, and sticks of fake crab—and when my rolls came out looking like sad, dying mushrooms, we abandoned the endeavor and threw ourselves onto the bed, the rice left hardening in the bowl, the avocado left oxidizing on the counter.

It was hard not to lose faith, remembering Sammy's strangest behaviors. I actually thought about it: closing the recipe book, putting away the journals, going to bed. I was very, very tired. If I gave up now, I would be failing Sammy, but I would also be protecting my memory of him.

I was distracted from these thoughts by an odor emanating from the box of ingredients. The B. rossica was unsealed, contained as it was by a single sheet of paper. This meant the smell of it had entered the room—mild, earthy, but with a hint of sweetness, like dark chocolate. I lifted the groundcone out of the box and removed the paper covering. The herb was long and purple-brown, with rows of flaky knobs and a chunkier, knotted root. It looked like a pinecone's gangly younger brother. Drowsily, almost absentmindedly, I searched the scientific literature for references to the herb and was surprised to find, almost immediately, an article about the herb's effects on aging in the *Journal of Ethnopharmacology*.

ANTI-AGING ACTION OF *BOSCHNIAKIA ROSSICA*
ON WISTAR RATS
by L. Xianming

Abstract: This study aimed to determine the anti-aging properties of the dried herb of *Boschniakia rossica*. The herb's extract was administered to Wistar rats, and its free radical scavenging ability was analyzed using electron spin resonance spectrometry. The results showed that plasma from the test rats demonstrated statistically significantly higher free radical scavenging activity than that of the control population. Clinical observations of the test rats included improved appetite and endurance. Within the limitations of this study, the author suggests that *B. rossica* offers potential anti-aging function(s) via mechanisms of free radical scavenging and the prevention of age-related disorders.

As I came to the end, I nearly glossed over the paper's acknowledgments section, which usually contained thanks to research assistants or department secretaries. L. Xianming's acknowledgment read as follows: *The author thanks Samuel Tampari, New York University, for his ideas and feedback on this study.*

My drowsiness lifted. It was a small thing but also big, to see Sammy's name this way, in a published study. It took everything I was reading and placed it back in the world of the living. I was beginning to search for other references to his name when I noticed something on the floor. The computer paper holding the *B. rossica*, I had thought, was blank—just an ad hoc wrapping Sammy had thrown together. But as it flattened out on the carpet, I saw that it contained images and a bit of handwritten text. I picked up the paper. Two photographs appeared to have been taken with a digital camera and printed out, probably on the old inkjet Sammy kept under his bed and plugged in only when he needed it.

Both of the images were of Number 50.

The first picture showed Number 50 in his cage, and I could recognize Sammy's bathroom in the background—the picture had been taken the night Sammy died. Number 50 was lying sideways on the floor of the cage, but he wasn't sleeping. His eyes were open. I couldn't tell if he was dead or merely in the final stages of death, but either way, it was not a pretty picture. Next to the image, in pencil, Sammy had written, *11:55 p.m.*

But in the next picture, Number 50 was out of his cage and sitting in the palm of Sammy's hand. (You could have shown me pictures of a thousand hands and I would have been able to identify Sammy's—the long fingers, the strong sun line, the little scar below the pinkie where he'd cut himself dissecting a frog.) Number 50 was awake, alert, *alive*, with his nose lifted and his lopsided ears pointed in Sammy's direction. His long tail dangled over the side of Sammy's index finger and disappeared into the border of the image. Sammy's time stamp said, *12:35 a.m.*

All of this would have been more than enough to excite me, but a final note was on the bottom of the page, in the exact same space where, if the paper had been part of the recipe book, you'd find the *How did it taste?*

In all capitals, with the pencil pressed hard to the page, Sammy had written, *DUDE*.

9

Black Sites

The morning after finding the photographs of Number 50's res-urrection, I went to school to give RJ the news: I was ready to call that number.

Once I fed Number 5, Number 7, Number 37, and Number 42, I walked the halls to homeroom. There, I spotted RJ through the window of the door. He was sitting in the back row, unusual for him, and I understood that he was doing this to keep an eye out for me. His leg bounced an uncharacteristically anxious rhythm. He had been waiting for me to decipher more of the recipe book, and it was almost thrilling to be wanted this way, to be needed. I caught his eye, and his face flooded with hope—and with a question: *Are we going to save my sister?*

As I began to turn the doorknob, I felt a hand on my shoul-der. I saw a note of concern in RJ's eyes, and then I was looking up at the familiar, kind, terrifying face of Captain Carson.

"Conrad Aybinder. Can we have a chat?"

I was a senior at LHS, had volunteered on multiple occasions to serve as a tour guide to lost freshmen, and I'd never even *seen* the room in which I found myself sitting face-to-face with Captain Carson. It turned out there was another office *past* the principal's office, deep in the administration annex, and that's where he led me, saying little along the way. The room was small and round and brown—it was like sitting inside a chicken egg. The circular table had chairs for five, but it was only the two of us. Was that even legal? For him to speak with me alone? Our government teacher had told us about secret CIA black sites where suspected terrorists could be held and interrogated, for years at a time, with no paper trail.

Captain Carson sat in the chair across from me, his left leg held splayed and straight away from his body. He looked tall during assemblies, standing next to the principal, but up close he was not that big—an inch or two shorter than I was. Still, he had the thick body of a man, a shiny badge, and the steady eyes of someone who knew what was happening, who hadn't just discovered the existence of this room.

"Sheesh," he said, settling in. "I've never seen a school year start like this one." He had the thick accent of Downeast Maine, which is sort of like a Boston accent, except if you make that mistake, you'll offend both Mainers and Bostoners: *I've nevuh seen a school ye-ah staht like this one.* Few of my classmates spoke this way, but my uncle Jeff always had, so I was used to it.

Captain Carson pretended to examine his fingernails. They were short and clean. "What did you think of Mr. Tampari?"

The photograph in the slideshow. The two of us standing close, smiling, eyes locked. The distance between us collapsing.

"He was nice."

Captain Carson drummed his fingers on the table. "He helped me move this in here. Stronger than he looked."

There was a pause, and it was deliberate: he was seeing how I responded to quiet.

"How well would you say you knew him?"

If only he understood how loaded a question that was. "I don't know. I'm pretty good at chemistry."

"I hear you're pretty good at every subject. I hear if the year ended today, you'd be valedictorian. You ever been to his house?"

The suddenness of the question was designed to catch me off guard. It worked. I hesitated too long to say anything other than "Yeah." Then, after another beat: "A couple of times."

"Oh yeah? How come?"

"We were working on a science project." I began to point in the direction of the chem lab before I realized that I didn't actually know, from the chicken egg, where it was.

"Yuh, okay, but I never went to a teacher's house." He said this as though he were just musing out loud. When I didn't say anything, he smiled. "I'm not givin' you a hard time. There's nothing wrong with going to a teacher's house." He looked me right in the eyes. "Unless that teacher makes you do things you shouldn't be doing."

All of the air went out of the room. I could feel the blood rushing to my head, along with a million questions. How did he know about Sammy and me? How *much* did he know? I saw everything unraveling at once. If word got out, I would have to switch schools—I couldn't walk the halls with everyone knowing. Dana and Emmett would never see me the same way. The search for Sammy's elixir would be over, and so would my father's life, and Stephanie's. In a very real way, *my* life would be over. Captain Carson was watching me, reading my face, and I felt as if I were failing a lie detector test.

Before I could speak, he said, "When was the last time?"

"Last time what?"

"You were at his house."

"A few weeks ago," I lied.

"Okay. That's not what Mrs. Donahue told us."

"Who?"

Here I experienced some luck; my genuine confusion undermined, just a touch, Captain Carson's confidence. Despite how many times I had been to Sammy's apartment, I'd previously known Mrs. Donahue by only one name: the widow.

"She says a couple of boys were in there the day he died. Scroungin' around."

I felt an unexpected surge of confidence. If the widow was his source, he might know less than I feared. I met his eyes. "I was looking for my rat. Our rat. For the science project."

"Oh yeah? Like an actual lab rat?"

"There's more in the chem lab."

"You find it?"

"No. His apartment was all torn up."

"I noticed that."

"Do you know who did it?"

Captain Carson had an incredible ability to keep his expression neutral. His face was blank. "Do *you* know who did it?"

"No."

"You weren't looking for anything else?"

"No." But then I was hit with a pang of guilt and the memory of the widow lying on the floor. "I mean, there was this book, it's about a cheese shop, and Mrs. Donahue saw me—"

"Conrad," interrupted Captain Carson. "Everyone tells me you're a good, honest kid, so I'm just going to come right out and ask you."

I held my breath.

"Did Mr. Tampari ever give you cocaine?"

"What? No!" There was a rush of relief: Is that what he thought Sammy was making me do? Is that all?

"He never gave you drugs, or sold you drugs, or asked you to try drugs?"

"Never."

"You never gave or sold *him* drugs?"

"Is that how he died? Cocaine?" I didn't know how to square this information with the ingredients in the recipe book.

Captain Carson exhaled a long breath. "That's not for your blogs or Facebook. That's a private conversation between you and me."

"You're *sure* it was cocaine?"

Captain Carson gave a short, single chuckle—amused, but only slightly, by my attempts to switch roles with him. "You've been skipping school. If you're grieving, talk to somebody, but you can't just skip."

"Okay."

"And do *not* go back to his apartment. Roger?" Captain Carson began to stand, and I followed his lead.

"Roger," I said, and left.

Homeroom was over by the time I escaped Captain Carson, so my next chance to see RJ was study hall in the computer lab. We sat next to each other in the back, pretending to waste time. In front of us, on rows of flatscreen monitors, our classmates checked that dreaded Facebook or watched short, loud videos of people hurting themselves doing backyard stunts. I had the recipe book and photographs of Number 50 in my backpack and showed them to RJ, filled him in on what I'd learned. If Sammy had really brought Number 50 back to life, he may have thought he had finally done it—that it was time to test the latest recipe on himself. But that didn't explain what I'd just learned from Captain Carson.

"Cocaine isn't even part of the elixir," I complained to RJ, holding the recipe book open for him.

"Hm," RJ said, half-listening. For all his excitement over the prospect of saving Stephanie, he was happy to leave the "science-y stuff," as he called it, to me. So he surprised me by saying, "I mean, you don't really *know* that cocaine isn't part of it."

"What do you mean?"

He pointed to the Appetizer, the Dor. "You said you don't know what this is, but the instructions say you have to inject it. And cocaine . . ."

He was right. While I was silently scolding myself for missing this, RJ was opening the Web browser on the computer. On the search bar, he entered *Dor + cocaine*.

The results came back, most of which were irrelevant: Indiana's Department of Revenue, for instance, had a section on its website about "drugs of abuse." But a few were interesting. The addition of *cocaine* as a search term had revealed a definition for the acronym *DOR* that I had missed: "delta-opioid receptor"—a member of the brain's opioid system heavily involved in its response to cocaine.

"Is this something?" RJ asked.

"Maybe. But if Dor is cocaine, why not just call it that?"

RJ moved the cursor back to the search bar and modified his terms: *Dor + Cocaine + Tampari*. "What the hell, right?" He clicked the mouse.

The results came back: one hit.

"Whoa," I said.

The lone website had a strange address, a long string of seemingly random numbers and letters. That website is long gone, but it looked something like this: www.btlfiud23rbgy83.ro. There was no description or summary of the link, just the address itself. In a separate browser, we searched for *.ro* and discovered it to be the country code domain for Romania. I recalled another of those definitions of *dor*: the Romanian word for "nostalgia."

RJ clicked the link. A website with a black background began to load, slowly, but before we could see any of its contents, a command prompt appeared on the screen: *Enter Password*.

"Awesome," RJ said, but I felt a jolt of frustration. Why did everything have to be so difficult?

RJ scooted over, allowing me to man the keyboard. I stared at the empty box, thinking. Lines from Sammy's journals and recipe book danced through my mind, creating a mental word cloud: *elixir, quicksilver, Catherine, brain burn*. I knew nothing, and I knew too much. After a moment, one careful letter at a time, I typed, *Tampari*.

After a flicker, a message box appeared. The first line of the message was in a foreign language that I assumed to be Romanian. The second line, helpfully, contained the English translation: *Nice try, fuckface!*

Instinctively, I tried to click away from the website, not wanting the study hall monitor to see those words on the screen. But no matter how feverishly I clicked, the browser wouldn't close, and fifteen painful seconds later, the entire monitor went blue. The website had crashed the computer.

When the day was over, RJ and I met in the chem lab. I stood by the window, where the reception was better, and entered the number Sammy had given me into my phone. The Romanian website hadn't just frozen the computer—it had completely fried it, hard drive and all. It was *so* fried, thankfully, that no one knew we'd been the last to log in.

"Put it on speaker," RJ said.

I can see this more clearly than a photograph. RJ was standing near the fume hood, dressed in black slacks, a button-down shirt, and a loosely knotted skinny tie that lay crooked on his flat stomach. He'd had a presentation earlier that day in College Prep History, and his parents made him dress up for it. The lab tables had black tops, but the surfaces near the window had bleached a little in the sun. I watched through the window as my schoolmates maneuvered their parents' oversize cars through the narrow corridor of the exit.

It may seem strange that I would remember it so well, among all the other, more interesting things that had happened. But not long after I dialed that number, I would do a bad thing, and it helps me forgive myself to remember that I was just a kid, a sixteen-year-old boy, who had never so much as placed an international call.

I pressed the green button and waited. I heard the soft static of the call being answered.

"Hello?" said a man.

I deepened my voice. "Hello."

There was a pause. "Who's calling, please?" He sounded like a British diplomat.

"My name is Conrad. I was a friend of Sammy Tampari's."

I could hear his breathing stop. "Has something happened to him?"

I wasn't ready to speak the answer, not over the phone to a stranger. "He gave me your number. Who is this?"

So he told me his name, only now Sadiq's voice had lost its European authority—he spoke with the high-pitched urgency of someone pleading for information. He told me his name, then he said again, "Has something happened to Sam?"

10

Aposematism

The circular room was sort of doughnut-shaped, with the doughnut hole being the central podium where the Belgian stood, lecturing. The conference center was located on the border of Chinatown and Little Italy, and Sammy could smell this confusion wafting through the large overhead vents: spicy cumin lamb, gnocchi alla romana. He took a slow, quiet breath and decided he would find pleasure in these smells, even though it did not work that way. All those years ago, the man had said, "The world needs beauty," and he had meant that the world is not, itself, beautiful.

The Belgian paced the edges of the podium, saying, "All the rats lived. Every. Single. One."

That day on the street, the man had also meant that Sammy was physically beautiful, that his beauty enriched the world around him. Empirically, yes, he was beautiful—his whole life had been evidence of this, including the woman, right then, who kept glancing back at him from the row below, hoping to start a conversation—but no one was better off for it. No one had been enriched.

Just ask Catherine. She was stuck with a sulky grad school dropout who had literally tried to kill her. That *happened*. Yes, he was beautiful. But so were the poison dart frog and blue-ringed octopus, and their beauty was a message: don't touch me, or you'll die. Aposematism. Warning coloration. In the animal kingdom, predators heeded this warning. So why did Catherine come back to him, time and again, no matter how much he stung her?

The Belgian—that's what he called himself—said, "Medical ethics don't apply to the *self*. The Hippocratic oath doesn't apply to the *self*."

Sammy was thinking about the smell of food because of the test he used to run—an experiment to gauge his happiness. A tea shop was across from his apartment ("*Our* apartment," Catherine often reminded him), just a little place, locally owned, with a deep green awning and a tall, wide window that allowed you to watch from the street as the little Lebanese woman who owned the shop brewed loose-leaf teas in big bullet-shaped vats. If Sammy lingered outside the door, the smell of those teas would hit him like a gust of wind: mint truffle, blueberry merlot, lemon vervain. On his dark days, the feel of this was like smelling a stack of printer paper. But on certain days, the smell of those teas made him feel like Dumbo with the feather—smiling, stupid, about to take flight. Then he would know the brain burn had worked.

The day it happened, sure enough, he had grinned at the woman through the window and floated up to his apartment. The elevator opened with a ding, and he held his key out in front of him as if it were leading him to the lock. He swung the door open, humming to himself, dropping his bag. He was so thirsty he drank out of the faucet with cupped hands, watching the cold water gather in the grooves of his fingers, feeling the wetness on the ends of his nerves. He splashed his face and used his T-shirt to dry his forehead. When he opened his eyes, a woman was standing in front of him, someone he'd never seen before.

"Hey," she said.

What happened next Sammy could not remember—he had it told to him, first by the police, then by the woman.

"Are you okay?" the woman said, seeing the confusion in his face.

Sammy stepped away from the faucet and stared at her with his back to the refrigerator. "Who are you? What are you doing here?"

"What?"

Sammy ran to the living room and began to rummage through his couch. He was looking for his cell phone, though the woman didn't know this, or why he wanted it.

"Sam?"

His breath caught. Something in having a stranger know your name, in having a stranger *say* your name, with such confidence, in your own home, is uniquely terrifying.

His voice rising, Sammy said again, "Who are you?"

Catherine realized that Sam wasn't playing, wasn't doing a bit. It was just like the day in the lab, only back then he'd only met her once. Only known her for a week. Now they'd been a couple for a year. They lived together, said "I love you" before bed, fucked in the morning, ordered stationery with both their names—and he'd forgotten her. Again.

Sammy found his phone—it wasn't in the couch cushions, but in his pocket—and dialed 911. Catherine would later blame herself (it amazed him, her endless reserves of self-recrimination) and say that she should have let him call—that's what he *should* do if he finds himself disoriented and scared. But she also said that when someone is calling the police on you, and you haven't done anything wrong, your instinct is to intervene. She ran to Sammy and tried to take the phone from his hand, to explain: Sam, it's *me*.

Even if her name would have meant anything to him then, he was too panicked to understand it. He wrestled with her over the phone. He pushed her against the wall, and because the human brain shows no mercy, this he *does* remember: the sound of her head hitting the wall, the look on her face—pain, horror, and, worst of all, love—and the way doing more violence to her seemed so real a possibility, so easy a one, like turning up the burner on a stove. With one hand holding her to the wall, he raised his other hand, and they would argue about this later: she would say his hand was open; he would say his fist was closed. Catherine wrenched herself from his grasp. In the struggle, she lost her footing and fell to the floor, hard, the coffee table leaving a long, dark bruise on the underside of her arm. Imagine what could have happened if instead of her arm it had been her head, her neck, her delicate face. He *did* imagine this. He imagined it and imagined it and imagined it, sharpening the idea until it was a fiery-hot poker in his mind.

It didn't take long, once the police arrived, to sort things out. Sammy's memories began to return, and Catherine explained everything. He knew it right then and there, before he even fully remembered his life with Catherine: he would never, under any circumstances, subject himself to another brain burn.

There was no telling why the ECT affected his memory so badly. Sometimes he wondered if his earlier experiments with the elixir, when he was just a boy, had damaged his brain in some permanent way, made him more vulnerable to the negative consequences of electricity. He preferred that explanation to the one that felt, in his heart, more true: that he was simply broken, as he'd always believed, and nothing that worked for others would ever work for him. He was incompatible with the world.

That very night—while Catherine stayed at a friend's house—he tore up his bedroom until he found his long disused recipe book. He took a trip to the storage unit where he kept his mercury and that old sample of Catherine's tribal medicine. The search for the elixir of life was back on.

The Belgian said, "So if the rats could survive it, I decided to see if I could, too."

Something stirred in Sammy: the warm feeling of not being alone. The Belgian—a medical doctor and molecular biologist—had recently admitted to injecting himself with a bacterium being studied at his home university. They'd discovered the bacterium in the permafrost of Siberia, and in preliminary trials, it had shown rejuvenating effects on sick and aging rats. The Belgian's willingness to experiment on himself had made him a cult figure, and he was the keynote speaker at this, the Symposium for Outsider Science.

After the incident with Catherine, Sammy dropped more than the brain burn: he was no longer a Ph.D. student at NYU. His doctoral studies were too much of a distraction. To Catherine, he told a half-truth: he wanted to write a book—one for regular people, not for the stuffy academics in the lab—on the past, present, and future of immortality research.

"But can't you stay in school and do that?" she'd asked. "Wouldn't staying in school *help* you do that?"

"It's not that kind of book. No one in the program would take me seriously." That was true.

Catherine scrunched her nose. "So it's a general-audience kind of thing?"

"Sure."

"What's it called?"

Sammy considered this question for the first time. "*The History of Living Forever.*"

The audience began to applaud, alerting Sammy to the end of the Belgian's lecture. Sammy stood with the crowd, arching his tired back until it cracked. He expected the Belgian to be mobbed with admirers, but a free lunch was in the cafeteria. Sammy had to stand in a line only three people deep before he found himself face-to-face with the man, who was pale and thin but also square at the shoulders, unusually so, which gave him a grounded, perpendicular appearance. Sammy shook the Belgian's hand and introduced himself.

A flash of recognition passed across the Belgian's face. "You're the potion guy," he said in perfect English. "The alchemist."

"You read my letter."

Sammy had written to the Belgian soon after the news broke about his bacterial injection. In truth, Sammy didn't see much potential in the bacterium. It hadn't killed the Belgian, but it hadn't helped him, either. The rats, yes—the old rats started fucking one another as if they were five months old. But foreign bacteria can stimulate host responses that seem temporarily beneficial, and the rats didn't live any longer than they would have otherwise. They fucked and died.

No, Sammy's interest in the Belgian was more psychological than biological. If Sammy confessed his self-experiments to Catherine, she would leave him, and if he confessed to his parents, they would have him committed. But the Belgian had done it! And he still had his job and his wife. Here was someone who could understand. Sammy had written to him with a simple question: Should I tell the truth?

Sammy took the subway to his secret apartment. It was actually his *parents'* apartment—his mother sometimes used it as a gallery space—but no one knew he was using it. The sixteen Wistar rats he kept there were a secret, too, in the sense that they were stolen. He'd lifted them from NYU's biology department the day he dropped out.

Sammy threw the key on the empty kitchen counter and heard the rats stir. They knew this sound meant food. He checked on them every day, and he hadn't been entirely successful in hiding this activity from Catherine. She'd asked him the other day if he was cheating on her, and he said no. But how true was this? Recently he'd made his own contact in Panama, and he'd been importing small quantities of the tribal medicine for his own use. Was this worse or better than sleeping with someone else?

Catherine knew he was finished with the brain burns, but not that he'd returned to flushing his antidepressants down the toilet of their small, windowless bathroom. As in his teenage years, he was supported only by his elixir. Most people would laugh, but for Sammy, this was his way of taking responsibility, of taking ownership of his own mind. So far, the elixir was just barely enough. His moods were unstable, and importing the ingredients was difficult and costly. He was like a man trapped in a cave, quenching his thirst on a drop of water that falls once every hour.

The Belgian had said, "I don't think a potion alone will do it." (Sammy hated that the man kept calling it a potion!) The Belgian had said, "I think you'll need an injectable to go along with your ingestible. An appetizer to your entrée."

Thinking of the recipe book, Sammy had almost laughed out loud at the Belgian's choice of words. He had no idea how appropriate that was. And how *right*. An appetizer, an entrée. Of course.

"Good afternoon, Number Eighty," Sammy said, crouched down in front of the first cage. Prior to their relocation, the rats had been used in a study of H. *pylori*, a bacterium causing gastritis and ulcers. These were rats with upset stomachs, and Sammy had been treating them with his elixir. Number 80 had received the heaviest dose, and he was looking good, with a bright white coat, alert eyes, and clear, pink ears. Sammy was monitoring the rats' digestive health based on their fecal output, but he would eventually have to kill them and study their stomachs up close.

He scooped Number 80 out of the cage and checked his skin, his feet, his tail. He'd been treated with the elixir over two weeks prior, and he still seemed cured of the H. pylori infection. The effects of the elixir on Sammy's mood never lasted for more than a week, which meant the elixir was acting more powerfully—as the Belgian suspected—on the stomach than on the brain. Only a fraction of the elixir was getting past the blood-brain barrier, but when Sammy had tried adding more quicksilver, his rat subjects had died from mercury poisoning.

This made him remember the Mayans and their phrase for death: *white wind withered.* The Mayans made no distinction between the atmosphere and themselves—the same forces that rustled the leaves of the *uva de playa* also animated the human form. When the rain stopped, your crops died. When the wind stopped, your body died. Sammy wished we could return to this way of thinking, this connectedness. But when he'd told Don about it, his father only waved his hand in dismissal: "Yeah, yeah. All foreign cultures will seem more beautiful than your own. Don't be covetous."

Sammy returned the rat to his cage. The role of H. pylori in gastritis had been discovered by an Australian physician who drank a sample of the bacteria to test its effect on his own body. For this, they gave him the Nobel Prize. So what was the difference between him and Sammy and the Belgian? Was it that Sammy and the Belgian were trying to make themselves stronger, while the Australian was deliberately causing himself pain? What did it say about the world that one was valued over the other?

That evening, Catherine came home with a bag of groceries tucked in one arm and a wide, flat package in the other—Sam's master's degree, which he'd earned before dropping out of the doctoral program. NYU had sent it when he ignored his department's e-mails to pick it up. The package said DO NOT BEND, but their mail-man had bent it, twice over, before shoving it into their tiny mailbox.

Sam was sunken into the couch, so low she didn't see him when she came into the apartment. He was lying on his back, and he tilted his head up to look at her, so that his face was upside down.

She tossed the package onto his stomach. "Your diploma."

She'd recently turned twenty-four, Sam was twenty-one, and that made it easier, this current phase. She hadn't realized he was so young when they first met, that he'd once been a sixteen-year-old college student. If she examined it from that perspective, he was currently the age most people are when just finishing their bachelor's. He had time.

He examined the creases in the box, but he didn't open it. "How was class?" She'd been TA-ing an introductory course on endangered languages.

She shrugged. "A student asked if he could write his paper on pig latin. How was the symposium?"

"A lot of weirdos."

"Can you help with the groceries?" She didn't need help, just wanted him to get up. She could handle the mood swings, but she didn't like this version of Sam: the sunken couch guy. Anger, sadness, cruelty—okay. Just get off the couch.

He did, yawning and stretching. It was late evening, but the bright city lights lit up the living room and gave him an electric glow. There he was, her Sam. She kissed him as he padded barefoot into the kitchen, and he put his arm around her waist, and, yes, there he was. Everything was fine. He'd dropped out of school, and he wasn't telling her something, but everything was fine.

Sammy began to stack the cans of garbanzo beans in the bottom cabinet, one on top of another. Catherine grabbed two of her gigantic anthropology textbooks from the bedroom and took out the diploma, laying it on the kitchen island and stacking the textbooks on top.

"Did you meet the Belgian?" She was torn on that guy. What he had done with the bacterium was irresponsible, but he hadn't given up his job to do it. She hoped Sam could see that this so-called outsider science didn't actually require being *outside*. For sure, write a book about immortality. But first, get tenure.

"I did."

The period at the end of that sentence felt, to Catherine, like a heavy one. He was dressed in a sweater she'd never seen—an uncharacteristically bright color, with orange stripes. She felt that he was slipping away from her, so she reached out for the sleeve of that sweater and pulled him close. He smelled of curry and the fabric cleaner she used on the sofa.

"Hey. You wouldn't do what the Belgian did, would you? You wouldn't do anything stupid?"

"Of course not," he said, heeding the Belgian's advice. *A true obsession is always a secret, always withheld, no matter how much we try to explain it.* He couldn't bring himself to drive Catherine away. But he'd also dressed that day in orange and black, warning colors, the banded pattern of the coral snake, and he hoped, as Catherine regarded him with fear and love, that she would see how dangerous he could be—and run.

Leopold Turck Describes
His Antiaging Machine

Paris, France, AD 1850

It is snowing in Paris. Dr. Leopold Turck watches through the window as the snowfall dusts the street. He has not left the window since he woke, but he decides he'd better check the little mailbox again, just to be certain he did not miss a letter. He opens the front door, still in his bare feet. The ironwork box is empty. He closes the door, shivering, and this is how sane men know they are sane: they cannot endure the cold. Leopold has seen lunatics run naked through a Norwegian blizzard and then, when offered a warm blanket upon their return to the asylum, say, "What for?"

He returns to the window. He lives alone with his dying father on a street that has no name but *does* receive mail, he has confirmed this. He mailed himself a letter, and it arrived six days later, which is an extraordinary wait but hardly any time at all compared to the six long months he has waited for a response from the *London Journal of Medicine*. It was summer, and the sky was blue and round like the egg of a starling, when Leopold submitted to the journal his most recent article, "Immortality and the Electricity Machine."

The journal's response to his article will determine whether his father lives or dies.

Leopold discovered the cure to death during his studies in Strasbourg. When he returned home—beckoned by his father's declining health—he proposed the treatment to his father, who received the proposal with the same disdain he typically reserves for Gypsies.

"I do not understand this rubbish you are speaking," his father had said, when Leopold explained the procedure. "What is this rubbish?"

"Papa"—Leopold always calls his father Papa, even though Leopold is no longer a boy but a man of middle age—"what evidence do you need beyond the word of your son, who is a doctor of medicine?"

"But how can this be? That you are the only doctor in Paris, in the world, who knows the cure for all disease, and only you possess this knowledge, and no one else? Where are the accolades that would accompany such a discovery? Where is the medical textbook that says, 'Throw away all previous editions! Dr. Leopold Turck has conquered death!'"

Eventually, they reached an agreement. If Leopold could publish his theories in a reputable scientific publication, his father would consent to the treatment. Otherwise, and on this outcome they found no disagreement, he would die.

Leopold watches a horse clop past his window. Zoology has much to teach us about the life span of the mammal. The African elephant can live for a hundred years, and the females remain fertile for the entirety of their lives. Hippopotami, it is believed, can live 150 years and are immune to all diseases found in nature. A large breed of arctic whale has a life span of over two centuries. What do these beasts share, beyond their long lives? Not climate, not diet, neither temperament nor size. No, they share only an epidermis of unusual thickness—the skin!

"Imagine a house," he told his father. The exterior of the house has crumbled, and the inside has fallen to ruins: the floors are swollen from rain; the unchecked sun has bleached the furniture; all manner of critters have staked claims. There would be no use in solving these interior problems if you didn't also rebuild the walls.

When Leopold returned from his medical studies, he was startled most by the change in his father's appearance. Gone was the strapping, olive-skinned man of Leopold's youth, replaced by

a pale, wrinkled figure. As the skin ages it becomes dry and un-
elastic, and this allows the veins to expand. When the external
pressure on the blood reduces, the blood moves more slowly and
leaves the organs dehydrated. In turn, the skin loses its power to
control the secretion and retention of the electricity needed to
power the bodily functions.

Electricity! If the ancients had known the wonders of Electricity, they would have built temples to Him—they would have
worshipped Him as the most powerful of the gods. There is only
one way to restore the proper electrical balance of the body, and
this is what he proposed to his father. This is Leopold's life's work.

The immortality machine:

His father would be submerged to the neck in water in a
bathtub. Leopold would run positive electrical currents through
the base of the tub. The tepid water would soften the epidermis, allowing the excess negative electricity to escape, while simultaneously restoring the positive electricity required for healthy
organs. Leopold did not mince words: his father would need to
enter this bath for days, weeks, possibly months, at a time. Leopold could not promise that much of the remainder of his father's
life would not be spent in water.

Leopold finds himself so lost in thought that he nearly misses
the arrival of the postman, who slides an envelope into the mailbox. Through some odd impulse of bashfulness, Leopold waits
until the man is out of sight, then hurries to extract the letter from
the box. It is from the *London Journal of Medicine*.

Leopold takes the letter to the kitchen, where he sits at the
table with his back to the stairs. He breaks the seal of the envelope and removes the single sheet of paper. The letter begins, *Dear
Dr. Leopold Turck*, and he skims the rest, picking up words and
phrases that piece together, in mosaic, the overall tenor of their
response:

 . . . shocked by the barbarism of your approach . . .
 . . . these treatments, as you call them, are tortures, and wretched . . .
 . . . quarrelling with your "evidence" is like boxing with a shadow . . .

When he is finished, Leopold folds the letter neatly and places
it back inside the envelope. He sits for some time—long enough

for his father to descend the stairs and snatch the letter before Leopold thinks to destroy it. He watches his father read: *We reject your article, and we reject all premises upon which you have based your conclusions.*

Leopold's father takes a seat across from his son and says, with infuriating tenderness, "Leopold, I was half your age when my father died. I promise you, life goes on."

Leopold stares at his hands. "Papa," he says, his voice soft. "Enough. Enough now."

But there will never be enough, not of time. It is enough to make a man laugh. The skin is the body's largest organ, its most visible, and for that reason its most overlooked.

How very hard it can be!—to see what is right in front of you.

11

Family Night

The Monday after I called Sadiq, Dana drove me an hour north to Cumberland. It was Family Night at the St. Matthias Rehab Alternative.

Dana and I left Littlefield shortly after four. The day was warm, but with wind, and it carried the salty smell of the ocean into the cul-de-sac. We'd been warned about the mosquitoes where my dad was staying, so we were dressed in jeans and long-sleeved shirts—mine a dark shade of blue, hers a lighter one. We followed the same route, at first, that RJ and I had taken to the storage unit.

While Dana drove, my thoughts turned to Sammy and his relationship with his father. "We're both orphans," he told me once as we lay in bed, and I loved that we shared so much and hated that he would talk about my father as if he were already dead. I'd reached the year 2001 in Sammy's journals—the year he dropped out of NYU to pursue the elixir full-time. On his twenty-first birthday, he wrote:

The first present I remember receiving from Don was a chessboard, for my sixth birthday. I'd seen him play with his friends, but I didn't even know how the pieces moved. He showed me in his usual way: quickly, with the assumption that I would either catch up or fall behind.

My mother came into the room and shook her head.

"I don't know why you're playing board games when you could be outside, practicing your jump shot in the *actual sun*."

"The boy doesn't want to play basketball," Don said. "No, Samuel, don't treat your queen like she's fine china. She's a killer, see?"

I did see. But I was more drawn to the little horse, which moved in a strange, herky-jerky pattern, not like a horse at all. I moved it up and over, as my dad had shown me.

"Okay," he said, disapproving. "I can see how much you favor the knight, and that gives me an advantage."

"Oh, Don." Leena watched with her brow furrowed as he swept my horse off the table with his pawn. "Let him keep it."

"Why?" He seemed genuinely curious.

"It's an interesting lesson that liking something is a weakness because your father will take it from you."

Once she was gone, my father earned checkmate and showed me again how to reset the board. We played another game, and this time he beat me so quickly that most of my pieces were right where they'd started.

As we neared Cumberland, the air lost its brine and grew drier, pine-scented. We turned onto one of those little Maine roads that's two-way only in name: when you meet another car, it's a game of chicken, and someone has to pull over. We passed a sign that said HIDDEN DRIVE, and there it was, the long dirt driveway that led to St. Matthias. I listened to the crunch of rocks under the tires as Dana steered the car at five miles per hour to the wide, unpaved lot. She parked between two pickups, one of them painted a bright shade of army camouflage. My dad had described the place as some sort of prison camp, but all I saw as we stepped out of the car was an adorable stucco Cotswold cottage flanked by a few rectangular bungalows. I could smell food cooking on the grill, but I couldn't see it, only the smoke rising in a narrow column into the trees.

We followed a walkway lined with wood chips to the back-yard, where we found my dad waiting for us near an empty firepit. He waved us over. In the dying light of the evening, his skin was gray and green. He gestured to our new surroundings, his hand gripped around a can of sugarless soda. "What do you think?"

"Nice," said Dana.

"It's literally the opposite of how you described it," I said.

My dad held up his free hand. "We have the whole night to bicker. Let's pace ourselves."

The smoke from the grill rode a fresh current directly into our eyes. St. Matthias owned a good four acres of shoreline along Forest Lake and loved nothing more than to barbecue. Down by the water, a fleet of kayaks lay belly up on the dock. I heard splashing behind a fence of trees, the sound of grown men play-ing, of water sports. *Therapeutic* water sports—everything for that purpose. Therapeutic kayaks. Therapeutic hot dogs. A raft was tethered fifty yards or so into the lake.

To my right, a man emerged from a thicket of trees with a stack of wet towels draped over his shoulder. The weight of them turned him lopsided, forced a hitch into his gait. I recognized him from the website as the director of the program. He wore several layers of flannel, and they gave him, like the pickup truck, a kind of camouflage. He was hard to follow with your eyes.

"I hope you're hungry," the director said to me. "We make enough food for everyone's family, even those who aren't quite ready to come." Something about this made him laugh. "We make an optimistic amount of food." He adjusted the towels to his other shoulder and limped away from us. Before he went, he gave my father a fast thumbs-up.

"That means I did well on the piss test," my father explained. "It's a pass/fail situation."

I watched as the director entered the main house. It was about the size of my childhood home. The last time Dana, my father, and I had been in Winterville together was the day Dana came to get me.

My father began the grand tour. He pointed to one of the bungalows. "That's where I sleep, but I e-mail you from the main house." He led us around the firepit. "Over here is my second-favorite log."

"Great," I said. "I like it."

"I'd show you my first favorite, but it's very hard to get to."

"Another time," I said.

He continued on. His sneakers crunched against the pine needles. "I refuse to swim here because I can tell the lake has leeches. Do you remember when we were camping and your mother found that leech in her armpit?"

I did remember.

My dad shrugged. "I also forgot to bring a bathing suit. But the dock is a good place to contemplate my poor life choices."

"Ned," Dana said, and she sounded so much like my mother that my dad and I both stopped short, abandoned the game we were playing, and stared at her like lost children.

Chastised, my father grew quiet. We followed the carpet of wood chips around the perimeter of the retreat. As we walked, I could hear the sounds of other people's sicknesses echoing across the camp. Wet, troubled coughs reported from inside the bunga-lows; labored breathing mingled with the sound of the lake water hitting the shore. Cigarette butts lay squashed like bugs along the path—one addiction exchanged for another. Dana lagged behind, slowed by allergies, by the molds of the balsam fir: aspergillus, penicillium, Cladosporium, Alternaria. They call it Christmas tree syndrome. In the woods of southern Maine, it's year-round.

We circled back to the grill. I walked alongside my father, count-ing both my steps and the seconds, eager to get back to my re-search. Sadiq had not said much on the phone—"We should speak in person," he told me—and before I even knew what was happening, we were discussing his trip to Littlefield.

The ground was littered with pinecones, and their chocolaty scales reminded me of the *B. rossica*. I'd found, in Sammy's journals, the entry that explained his appearance in the acknowledgments section of that article. Soon after he dropped out of NYU, Sammy had traveled to China, to the villages surrounding Longkou, along the Laizhou Bay, to investigate stories of the elixir of life spread among the descendants of the alchemist Ge Hong. Sammy had arranged in advance to meet with a student from the Life Sciences Department at Shandong University, Lee Xianming, to act as Sammy's guide and translator. I found Lee Xianming online and wrote to him about Sammy, asking if he could tell me what they talked about. To my surprise and disappointment, he responded immediately but ignored my requests for insight: *I took Mr. Tampari to Bianqiao* was all he wrote. *I am very saddened to learn of his passing.*

He attached a picture. In it, Sammy stood in front of a battleship-gray tricar factory, bundled in a black-and-blue winter coat that gave him a clumsy, top-heavy appearance. He wasn't smiling. Next to him, Lee stood with his hands in his pockets, and he was laughing—a big, open laugh. The picture was taken at a distance, from across a narrow road that runs through the center of the photograph. The round edges of a frozen lake extended beyond the factory.

Lee drove Sammy to a small house at the base of Mount Feng. There, Lee introduced him to an older woman who claimed to have been saved from stomach cancer, as a child, by an elixir of life prepared by a traveling healer. She dictated the recipe to Lee: quicksilver, morning dew collected near the lakeshore, and an herb the healer gathered from the mountainside. She gave them some of this dried herb, which still grew along Mount Feng. Sammy didn't recognize it and neither did Lee.

They returned to the laboratory. Together, they injected the herb's ethanol extract into lab rats and examined the results in the department's ESR spectrometer. Almost immediately, the herb made the rats act younger, healthier, more vibrant.

The key to this improvement was the herb's scavenging of a type of atom called a free radical. In simple terms, free radicals are bullies. They're missing an electron, so they go around stealing electrons from other cells. This interrupts the function of those cells and, worse, converts them into free radicals themselves (as I said: bullies). Sammy believed that the accumulation of free radicals in the body was synonymous with a common phrase: *growing old*. This is known as the Free Radical Theory of Aging. Sammy and Lee discovered that *B. rossica* hunts these free radicals and eliminates them before they can do further damage.

A year later, Lee published the results of their study. He couldn't give Sammy full credit for his contributions—Sammy wasn't authorized for scientific research in China—so the brief note in the acknowledgments was all he could offer.

"Con?" my dad said. "Pay attention. Everything I'm telling you is going to be on the quiz."

We returned to the main group. People were gathering around the picnic tables, claiming seats, pouring soda into tiny paper cups. The director had taken control of the grill; he worked the spatula as if he were in a race with someone.

"The more you flip the burgers, the better they taste," he was telling another counselor. "That's just science."

My dad pulled up on the periphery of all this commotion. I recognized his hesitation. He didn't have any friends, and he was scared to go to the cafeteria.

"Well," he said. "That's the end of the tour. Not sure what else to say."

Dana brushed the pine needles out from beneath my collar. "You could start by asking Conrad about *his* life."

My dad checked his watch. "Sorry about that, kiddo. I've been distracted by my imminent death." He led us to one of the picnic tables and sat on the outer edge of the bench, forcing me to act as a buffer between him and the other adults. I didn't see too many kids there, just a lot of tired grown-ups. A thirtysomething couple was holding hands near my dad's second-favorite log. The woman laid her head on the man's shoulder. Tattoos of much-sexier women snaked up his arm and disappeared into the sleeves of his shirt. His girlfriend traced these with her finger. They were the kind of people who had been through a lot of shit together and were trying, every day, to make that into a strength rather than a weakness.

My dad poured me some soda and pulled a bowl of potato chips over to our side of the table. "Dana told me about your science teacher. You didn't even get a day off?"

I stiffened. "It's fine."

Dana rubbed between my shoulder blades. "This is where you tell Conrad he can call you whenever he needs to talk."

"Sure, what the hell," my dad said. "Day or night, any hour. It doesn't have to be an emergency."

I tried to remember what I'd read on the website. "I don't think that's true."

My dad considered this. "Maybe not, but I'm pretty sure it is." He closed his eyes, thinking. "I know I've heard the phone ringing when I'm trying to sleep."

"We'll ask them," Dana said. "It's not something we have to wonder about."

The director banged the side of the grill with a metal spoon. "Food's ready! If you haven't started eating, you're doing it wrong."

We lined up in silence and carried our plates back to the table. Aunt Dana used the hot dog toppings to make a salad for herself and pushed it around the plate until it looked half-eaten. My father ate nothing and refused to try. He said it would come right back up, and at a place such as this, one act of vomiting can lead to another, like dominoes falling.

After a minute of silence, my dad said, "I bet you're glad you came."

"Great food," I said. "Worth the drive."

He laughed and turned to Dana. "I don't know why you make us do this. Skyping with him is awkward enough."

She made a small, exasperated noise. "I don't make you do anything. I thought you might want to see your son, who loves you."

"You know what I'm saying," he said to me. He thought I was an ally in this line of attack. "I don't mind seeing you. But you're better off in Littlefield, even if Dana is still doing the depressed-widow thing."

Dana's breath caught in her throat. I could see a shudder run through her. She wasn't an angry person, and when my father made her into one, her body tried to reject it. "Don't take this out on us," she said. "Everything that's happening is your fault. It's a result of *your* behavior."

My father looked away from the table. "I do not have a drinking problem," he said. Everyone heard him. "Once, when I was drunk, I *caused* a problem. That is not the same thing."

Silence fell over the dinner. No one moved.

"Ned," said the director from behind the grill, "how does it help you to say that? How does that bring you closer to your family?"

My father started to argue, but the director stared him down. The director had the spatula in one hand and tongs in the other. He was wearing an apron that said I DO ALL MY OWN STUNTS.

Everyone was looking at us. Dana smiled at them. "We're sorry. Please don't stop eating." She was crying.

The director waved her off. "The first month is tough. Really tough. It gets better. And then worse. And then better. And then worse . . ." He moved the spatula back and forth as if he were flipping imaginary burgers. A few people laughed at this.

My father stood up, his knees knocking against the table and disrupting people's food.

"Ned," the director said, "do you want to go talk somewhere?"

My dad snorted. "No, thank you, I'm fine. I mean, I feel like puking all the time and I'll probably die here surrounded by these fucking drunks."

I waited for someone to be insulted. Nothing. Everyone there had heard much worse about themselves. My father stormed down the path and disappeared into his bungalow. Dana and I sat there like idiots, humiliated, until she gathered herself, took my arm, and pulled me from the table. We walked down to the shore and stood side by side on the dock. In the middle of the lake, two old men were baitfishing from a canoe. Their yellow slip bobbers danced in the ripples of the water.

"I know I've said this before," Dana said, "but I'm sorry about your father. I'm probably not always easy to be around, but I'll never act toward you like he's acting."

"I know."

She shook her head. "We should say goodbye."

So we walked back up and headed for his room. Along the way, I received a handshake from the director and several consoling glances from the other campers. This was not a group of people you wanted to pity you, but I tried to be polite, to smile through their expressions of solidarity.

Eventually we made it to my father's door, and he opened it immediately. He'd been standing right there waiting for us. "Next time we'll eat out."

Dana balled her fists as if she were going to sock him. I would have paid to see it. "If you want him to visit again," she said, "you'll have to do better than that."

My dad began to respond but lost the strength for it. Even the jaundice seemed to drain from his face. He moaned and pressed his forehead against the doorframe. His feet stomped the floor. I could see him trying and failing to relax his breathing, to take control of the pain. His hands reached out, grasping at air.

All I wanted to do was abandon him the way he'd abandoned me, to leave him here, hurting. Maybe, if walking away meant returning to the summer, to Sammy's open arms, I would have done it. But the summer was over. Sammy was gone. And here was my dad, still alive, still reaching for me. In spite of myself, I took my father's hand.

He gripped hard. "Ouch." His voice was barely audible.

"Ned?" Dana said. "Do you need me to get someone?"

"Just give me a second."

So we waited together. I imagined what was next for him, how much worse it might get. His skin was yellow, but without a new liver it would soon turn blue and then purple. The darkness would start at his fingertips and spread inward, like a lake freezing in winter, until it reached his neck, his face, his lips. His spleen would triple in size—a man's fist transformed into an agave heart. His stomach would swell like a pregnant woman's. More migraines, more nausea, more nosebleeds. Engorged veins would crisscross his distended belly like the root system of a diseased tree. If I didn't save him, he would die.

But that day, my father recovered from the attack and wiped

the cold sweat from his face with his sleeve. Dana told him to lie down and disappeared into the bathroom to pour him a glass of water. He reclined on the bed with his eyes closed, and Dana took off his shoes, folded the blanket over his legs. He didn't thank her, that asshole, but the whole time, he also didn't let go of my hand.

12

Autopsy

Sammy and Catherine arrived in Belize City in the spring of 2002. Ostensibly, they were there for a chapter in Sammy's book on supercentenarians—people who live past the age of 110. He'd arranged to witness the autopsy of Anna Flowers Magaña, a native Belizean who had, before her death, claimed to be 123 years old.

A driver was waiting for them outside the airport. He was big, bordering on fat, and maybe of Indian descent, maybe Middle Eastern. He took Catherine's bags and handed her a Tupperware container filled with oatmeal cookies. "Thank you for arranging all of this," the driver said to Sammy. His accent was British, his voice slightly too high for his size. He looked like a bass but sounded more like a tenor. He wore khaki pants with sandals, a cotton button-down with several buttons open. His eyelashes were very long.

"Thanks for the cookies," Sammy said.

In the car, Sammy and Catherine sat close together in the backseat. They drove west out of the city toward the Cayo District, but the driver didn't know where he was going. At Princess Margaret Drive, he rode the roundabout three full times before picking a turn at random.

"Sorry," the driver said. "I'm a postdoctoral fellow."

"You drive like it," Catherine said.

"You work with Dr. Radkin?" Sammy asked.

"Yes. I don't even own a car."

Sammy had paid for Joseph Radkin to conduct the autopsy. As the leading expert in the field of gerontology, Radkin had made a lot of money promoting himself as the man most likely to defeat aging. He traveled the world conducting autopsies of supercentenarians with his research group, the Association for Gerontology Exploration.

The driver pulled onto Central American Boulevard and straight into a police checkpoint. They waited in a row of cars. The driver watched Sammy and Catherine in the rearview. "Do either of you have a watch?"

Catherine held up her wrist. "Are we about to bribe someone? Because I would be okay with that."

The driver laughed. "I just want you to time something."

They pulled up to the gate. A policeman in sunglasses approached the car, hand on hip.

"Either he'll wave us through immediately," the driver said, "or he'll stare at us in silence for exactly thirty seconds and *then* wave us through. Time it. You'll see."

Sammy and Catherine exchanged a look. In his journal, Sammy would complain that Radkin had sent a moron to pick them up. The policeman walked to the driver's side window. He waved them on immediately.

"Damn. You would have been impressed if he'd waited the thirty seconds, yeah?"

"We can circle around and do it again," Catherine offered.

"I'm sorry," Sammy said. "Who are you, again?"

The driver turned half in his seat to smile at Sammy. "Sadiq."

Sammy, Catherine, and Sadiq arrived after sundown at their resort hotel—an upscale lodge along Privassion Creek. Radkin would only fund these trips himself if the deceased's date of birth could be supported with valid documentation, but Anna Flowers Magaña didn't have anything like that. So Sammy lured Radkin to Belize with a free rain-forest vacation. The resort was situated in a pocket of the Maya Mountains, at the edge of a forest preserve. Palm trees and kraabu shrubs lined the gravel driveway. A row of thatched-roof cottages horseshoed the infinity pool. Catherine and Sammy would be staying in the Honeymoon Cabana.

Sadiq led them to the main lodge. There, in the dining room, Radkin was holding court for a wide circle of resort staff. It was Sammy's first sight of him in person. He was short and thin, dressed in khaki shorts and a powder-blue polo shirt. He wore one pair of glasses on his nose, another perched on his head, and yet a third hooked in the pocket of his button-down. His graying beard couldn't quite hide the craters of severe childhood acne, and his mouth seemed always to be moving, regardless of whether he was speaking.

"I want you to imagine," he was telling his audience, "that your body is a book. And here is the first line of your book, listen close: 'Year after year and night on night I keep / On the Atreidæ's roof, like house-dog true, / My weary watch and scan the host of heaven— / Bright powers that shine along the sky.'" Radkin surveyed his audience and switched out one pair of glasses for another. "I trust that someone recognizes this passage?"

No one spoke.

"Correct. Your body's book was written by Aeschylus. But we know what happens to a book over time. First you spill some coffee on the pages, and the stain blots out one of the words. Instead of 'on the Atreidæ's roof' we now have only 'on the roof.' No biggie, okay? That word is hard to say and no one's going to miss it.

"Years pass. Now the ink begins to fade, hastened perhaps by the acids in that coffee accident you've long forgotten. Now we lose 'like house-dog true.' It's unreadable. And we're a little sad at this point because that's a lovely phrase, a lovely analogy for a man who feels affection but lacks true *freedom* of affection. *C'est la vie.* The sentence still makes sense.

"We're getting older now. 'Weary watch' fades to 'watch,' and those 'bright powers' lose their brightness. You're ninety years old—a good long life—and all that's left, basically, of that long, poetic sentence, is 'I am on the roof.' And you're just waiting for any of those last five words to disappear and for the sentence to lose its meaning. That's my nice way of saying time's up, curtains, you're dead.

"And here's the amazing thing. Whenever that last word does fade away—let's say you're in the hospital and you spill some Jell-O on it—the doctors will say *that's* how you died. Cause of death: spilled his Jell-O. But we know better. We know that the final spill was just the last in a long series of spills that started with that hot cup of coffee.

"My friends and I, my friends who are doctors, call this *informational entropy*. That's just a fancy way of saying that aging is a loss of information. Right now you lovely young people are like a very complicated, very beautiful sentence—a sentence written by Aeschylus, by Melville, by Walter Abish. As you get to be my age, that sentence becomes simpler and simpler—if you want the truth, we're talking not about sentences but intricate physiologic processes—until one small accident, an accident you would hardly notice as a twenty-year-old, up and kills you as a ninety-year-old. What we're trying to do, myself and the AGE, is figure out how to restore those words as you lose them, how to retrace those missing words with new, fresh ink."

Radkin's assistants initiated a polite round of applause. The resort staff eyed the doors. They had horses to feed and cabanas to restock with champagne. Lizards the color of pool water climbed the walls and puffed their necks at one another. Sadiq led Sammy and Catherine through the tables and caught Radkin's attention with a raised hand. Radkin grabbed a glass of wine from his table and moved to meet them halfway. As he neared, Sammy could see that he was wearing, below his shorts, a set of midnight-blue shin pads.

Radkin clasped Sammy's hand and said, "I hope you have strong stomachs. Tomorrow is going to be gross."

Sadiq opened the hatch of the cooler and pulled out the corpse of Anna Flowers Magaña. He wheeled the body bag to the autopsy table, where Sammy, Catherine, and Radkin were waiting in scrubs and protective masks. The city morgue had just been renovated, and it sparkled in stainless steel like a new American kitchen. The renovations came after a lawsuit in which a woman claimed her husband's body had been stored in the same unit as another corpse, their unripe faces pressed together in a sallow kiss.

Sammy scribbled notes on a legal pad as Sadiq unzipped the body bag. Catherine watched through her fingers. Anna's face appeared first, her eyes and mouth closed beneath a curly bob of chalk-white hair. Her thin lips, unsupported by teeth, had collapsed inward and left her cheeks hollow. Photographs of Anna as a young woman showed a dark-haired, fair-skinned Belizean, the daughter of a white mother and a father who, before his retirement, had been the only trained fireman on Caye Caulker.

Sadiq pulled the zipper down to her toes, exposing her body. Her arms were hairless and thin; they finished at the shoulder in a knotted mass of bone. Her breasts lay small and flat across her chest. Her hands had been taken by arthritis. The pinkies bent inward toward the thumbs, pulling all of the other fingers down with them. To ease the pain of this, for the past three decades Anna had kept her hands balled in a fist.

Radkin turned on a digital voice recorder and announced the start of the autopsy. As he did, Sadiq slid his arms under the body, with one arm at the buttocks and the other at the base of the neck. He grunted, lifted with his knees, and dumped the body with a thud onto the autopsy table.

"Oh," Catherine said from behind her hands.

Sadiq placed a rubber block under Anna's back, arching her spine and revealing the outlines of her ribs against the skin. She reminded Sammy of the sacrificial sculptures he'd seen in the ruins outside Mexico City, those little Chacmools with their bellies offered to the gods. Sadiq removed a large scalpel from the instrument tray and, with no hesitation, plunged it into Anna's left shoulder. He leveraged his weight onto the handle and guided the blade down under the curve of the breasts. The sound of the incision was like scissors passing through wet paper. Blood emerged at the wound and cascaded down the rib cage into the spigot of the autopsy table. Sadiq terminated the incision at the xiphoid process and moved around the table to draw an identical line from the other shoulder.

When the two cuts had joined below the sternum, Sadiq brought the blade straight down toward the belly button. Here the sound gained, somehow, additional moisture—this was a dish sponge squeezed again and again over an empty sink. Anna's stomach wept blood. Sadiq carried the scalpel all the way to the pubic bone.

Radkin had acquired a smaller blade. He pressed his thumb into the wound at the sternum and began to peel the skin up toward Anna's face, slicing at the muscles and connective tissue.

"Fuck me," Sammy whispered.

"Worst vacation ever," said Catherine.

Radkin continued this way until the chest flap had been pulled entirely over Anna's head, hiding her face and exposing the bones of her rib cage. She looked like someone who had swallowed a live hand grenade. Sammy came in close to observe the strap muscles of the neck. They reminded him of the cordage on a sailboat—sinewy and strong, tangled and overlapping in an intricate bouquet that only made sense to an expert.

To crack the ribs, Radkin used what looked to Sammy like common pruning shears—the kind his mother used to trim her azalea bushes. Sadiq followed behind with the scalpel. They attacked the rib cage and then lifted it off the body, lickety-split, as if they were removing the case from a desktop computer. Anna's heart and lungs came into view.

The human heart, Don once told Sammy, is like the Grand Canyon. You've heard a lot about it, you've seen a million pictures, but when you're finally there in person, you still forget to blink. This was Sammy's first. He circled the body. A healthy heart looks like a bloody biceps, all flexed muscle and coiled energy. You'd want it by your side in a bar fight. But this was the heart of the world's oldest woman. The intricacy was there, but none of the power. Anna's heart resembled leftover turkey.

Radkin and Sadiq removed the organs en masse and dissected

them at the foot of the autopsy table. Sadiq opened the intestines
and emptied their contents into the sink. It was as though he had
tipped a Porta Potti upside down. The smell of shit and bile gey-
sered out of the drain. Radkin and Sadiq continued, undisturbed,
to butcher the organs. They took tissue samples for microscopic
evaluation.

Later, they'd get the results: diverticulitis in the colon, fibro-
sis and atrophy of the pancreas, acute congestion of the liver. In
the lungs, bilateral bronchopneumonia with pleural adhesions.
Pyelonephritis of the kidneys and a trabeculated bladder. None
of this was surprising. Her body showed the expected, desiccated
wear of a long life. She was born in the nineteenth century. She
had seen her parents die, her brothers die, and four of her five
children. She had seen her first husband ripped in half, literally,
by the hurricane of 1908. She did not age gracefully, and she did
not see her longevity as a gift. She asked her daughter, months
before she died, if she had been forgotten by God.

After they'd finished with the torso, Radkin and Sadiq came
for Anna's brain. Sadiq sliced from ear to ear and then scalped
her. The skull came into view. Radkin applied the electric saw.
As Sadiq returned to the sink, he slipped and dropped his scalpel. It clattered to the floor near Radkin's feet. Instinctively,
Sammy knelt to retrieve it, and so did Sadiq. They looked at each
other. Sadiq's eyes were small but expressive. He smiled beneath
his mask. Sammy started to feel something, and then, from above
them, Radkin turned off the saw and separated the top half of
the skull from the bottom. There was a loud sucking sound, and
Sadiq and Sammy stood together to watch Radkin place the brain
in a jar.

That night, Sammy and Catherine caravanned with Radkin's crew
to a party at Altun Ha, a set of Mayan ruins located an hour north
of Belize City. The governor-general (a significant financial
backer of the AGE) had arranged for the group to have private
access to the site after hours. Radkin invited colleagues from all
over the region to attend, including some from as far as El Salva-

dor. There were a lot of scientists, a lot of alcohol, and a little bit of food.

Sammy and Catherine stretched out on the grass drinking beer in front of Structure B-4, the Temple of Masonry Altars. Catherine draped her legs over Sammy's lap. She was twenty-five years old and had the tan, angular face of the perpetually outdoors. She kept her dirty-blond hair cut short so that it would stay out of her face in the jungle. To some she might have seemed like a tomboy, but for an anthropologist she was positively elegant.

Sammy felt something slither across his ankle. He shot up and made a noise. The sound of his scream attracted Radkin, Sadiq, and another man—a biochemist from Mexico City with a massive LED flashlight. The man shined the torch at Sammy's feet.

"Are you bit?" Sadiq asked.

"No. But I wish you hadn't said that as though it's a real possibility."

"Come join us by the fire," said Radkin. "We're talking about existence."

So the five of them walked together to tomb F8/1, where someone had built a makeshift firepit that was very much against the rules. There, twenty or so scientists were laughing and arguing with one another over the future of gerontology.

Radkin opened a fresh beer and saluted those gathered: "To the singularity."

They drank. The biochemist put the flashlight under his chin as if he were about to tell a ghost story. "Once upon a time," he said in a dark voice, "there was a soluble protein that became . . . insoluble."

Laughter. Radkin, sitting across the fire from Sammy and Catherine, said, "My friend isn't too impressed by my research."

The biochemist waved him off. "It's fine enough in the short term."

"And in the long term?" someone said.

"Alien overlords," said another.

The biochemist chuckled. "Radkin's work will help those of

us currently living to live a little longer. No doubt about that. But the future of longevity isn't in medicine, or pharmaceuticals, or even biotechnology."

"Nanotechnology," said Sadiq.

"Bingo." The biochemist tapped his nose. "Specifically nanorobotics."

The crowd groaned. "Clap your hands if you believe in fairies," said Radkin.

"I *do* believe in what I can't see," said the biochemist. "While you're traveling all over the world to carve up old people, there's an engineer somewhere building nanorobots that will be able to reverse every cause of death known to man."

"Unless the cause of death is 'murdered by nanorobots,'" said Sadiq.

Radkin shook his head. "So let's say these nanorobots can, indeed, replicate healthy cells. I would ask, in such a case, whether they are bringing *you* back to life or simply a *copy* of you?"

The fire popped.

"Whatever happens in the next century," said another of Radkin's crew, "eventually we'll be uploading our consciousness to computers. We'll use our bodies for reproduction and then discard them."

"Amen to that," said Catherine.

"I concede the possibility of robotic avatars," said Sadiq. "But we won't be uploading our 'consciousness,' whatever that is. We'll be implanting our actual brains into the machine."

In the distance, someone climbing the steps of the pyramid-temple was singing the theme from *Rocky*. Sammy could see the man's silhouette framed against the moon, his arms raised, fists clenched.

"You've been awfully quiet," Radkin said to Sammy.

Sammy held up his hands. "I'm just here to learn."

Radkin kept his eyes fixed on Sammy, but Sadiq gestured to Catherine. "How about you? What does the future hold?"

Catherine took a drink. "You're all talking big, but here you are, a bunch of men, sitting among the ruins and poking at a fire with sticks. *This* is the future."

Most of the men laughed, but Radkin didn't. He was still looking at Sammy. "You're not off the hook so easily."

Sammy cocked his head. "What are you fishing for?"

"I'm wondering why you're here."

"I told you, I'm writing a book." Sammy hoped this sounded
truer to others, to Catherine, than it did to him. "Don't you think
your work should be part of it?" Sammy drank from his bottle.

Radkin licked his lips, which had been dried out by the fire.
"Maybe. But I'm still wondering why you're *here*. We could have
met in the States."

Sammy considered what to say. Obviously, Radkin knew.
Sammy wasn't interested at all in Radkin's research, which was the
same sort of Big Pharma approach that bred the countless, endless antidepressants that had done so little to help Sammy. He'd
brought him to Belize to play a different role: drug mule. Radkin's
credentials gave him medical clearance to carry biological samples—
Anna's samples—across international borders. Sammy had arranged for several ingredients he needed for his elixir to meet
him there in Belize and to be placed in the same container that
held Anna's specimens. These materials included Heartorex, a
dietary supplement banned in the United States; a recently discovered species of Belize feather worm; and, most embarrassingly, the dried scrotum of the endangered Mesoamerican river
turtle. The issue was not just about protecting his secret, but also
his dignity.

"Maybe we should talk in private," Sammy said.

Catherine looked on, alert and confused.

He was rescued by the sound of shouting near Structure D2.
The group of them quit the fire and ran toward the noise. They
found two men at each other's throat. One was a microbiologist
from Belize, the other a microbiologist from Guatemala. A few
months prior, a Belizean patrolman had shot and killed a Guatemalan national just a few miles from Sammy's hotel.

The men grappled with each other at the base of the tower.
The smaller one wrapped his arms around the other's neck and
pulled him into a headlock. They wrestled in breathy silence,
stumbling across the grass like a four-legged animal, their feet

tangled with each other's. Their movement carried them too fast
to stay standing. They went hard to the ground, and this gave the
larger one the advantage. He pinned the smaller man under his
knees and landed one, two, three, hard blows to the face and ribs.
His victim moaned and spit blood.

The rest of the scientists watched with the apathy of the
bystander, but Sammy stepped forward. The Mayans who built
Altun Ha believed the human body was created from maize—
white corn for bones, yellow corn for flesh, black corn for eyes,
red corn for blood. These two men were beating the corn out of
each other, and one of Sammy's thoughts came to him, with its
usual suddenness: he wanted a piece of it. He threw himself on
the men.

"Sammy!" said Catherine.

He wedged himself between the two combatants. The small
man was happy for the assistance; the tall one, less so. The three
of them kicked and clawed at one another. Sammy felt an icy pain
in his gut, but he stayed on, pried at the tall man's hands. He
pushed him off the beaten man and to the dirt of the causeway.
With the two men separated, Sammy rolled away and clutched
at his stomach. He'd been stabbed with a penknife, right above
the belly button. Not too deep. Just enough to bleed through his
fingers.

Catherine ran to him and helped him sit up. She removed her
sweater and held it against his stomach. "The hell was that?" she
said.

A month later, the tall man would send Sammy a surprisingly
heartfelt e-mail of apology, but that night he ran into the woods
as though anyone cared enough to chase him. Sadiq offered his
hand and pulled Sammy standing. Sadiq guided him back to his
truck and treated his injury while Catherine returned to the fire
to fetch their belongings.

"Interesting night for you," Sadiq said. He cleaned the cut
with antiseptic. Sammy's shirt was on the hood of the car.

Sammy breathed through his nose. "I'm not always myself."

Sadiq pulled the gauze tight. "Catherine thinks your research
is theoretical."

"Yes."

"But you're actually making . . . what do I call it, an elixir?"

Sammy was too tired, and too stabbed, to lie. Maybe a part of him felt, *I can trust this man.* "Yes, I'm actually making it."

"Is there even a book?"

Sammy remembered himself and the stakes of this discussion. He pushed Sadiq's hand away. "How do you know all this?"

"Dr. Radkin doesn't take money from just anyone. We looked into you. Can I continue with the bandage, please?"

Sammy reluctantly lowered his guard. "What does that mean, looked into me?"

Sadiq finished dressing the wound and inspected his work. "My people have a saying. Don't try to solve your problems when it's the middle of the night and you've been knifed by a Guatemalan."

Sammy chuckled, and it hurt. "So what happens to my materials? Will Radkin smuggle them for me?"

"He won't. But I'll take care of it."

"Why would you do that?"

"I'm not sure yet. I guess you interest me."

"Well, thanks." Then, to Sammy's own surprise, he placed his hand over Sadiq's. They touched that way for five seconds, then Catherine returned with a fresh change of clothes.

Sadiq kept his word: Sammy's drugs and feather worms and turtle scrotums made it safely to New York. Ultimately, after all that trouble, they proved totally worthless.

Back in America, Catherine and Sammy waited in line for a taxi, exhausted, leaning on their luggage. It was evening. Catherine hadn't spoken to him the entire flight. She just jammed those little earbuds in her ears and scowled at the clouds through the window. When they landed, she strode immediately off the plane, leaving Sammy to pull their heavy suitcase out of the overhead. He thought she might leave him and go back to their apartment alone—he thought it might be over—but a part of him knew that she would allow him to explain this incident, too, just as he'd explained the time he forgot her days after meeting her, the time he attacked her in her own home, the time he dropped out of NYU and began writing a book she'd never seen. She would forgive him because love is like that: it *convinces*.

It was their turn to get a taxi. As the cab pulled up to the curb, Sammy pulled Catherine's headphones out of her ears. "Hey," he said when she turned to him, "maybe we should get married?"

13

My Husband's Diagnosis

The day after my husband's medical chip sounded its alarm, we went together to the doctor. My husband's case history was downloaded from the chip, blood tests were taken, MRIs administered. We sat in the doctor's office, where he had all the scans displayed on the screen behind him—rotating, glowing, color coded. He was older, early eighties, the only doctor in Winterville.

My husband's brain looked like a fetus in ultrasound: rounded and small with the potential for bigness. A depthless gray—the color of the ocean in winter. Our doctor swept his hands across it like a weatherman tracking a storm system. "You have a pontine glioma. Which means you have a cancerous tumor on your brain stem."

"I want a second opinion," my husband joked.

To my surprise, our doctor took it as one and smiled. "Listen, if we were having this conversation ten, twenty years ago, I would be telling you to call your loved ones and make arrangements. That's how bad this was."

I squeezed my husband's hand. "But now we can go home, make dinner, and it will go away on its own?"

"Ha." The doctor tapped his computer and sent some literature to our phones: *Difficult Cancers of the Brain.* "The difference is we could never operate on these, but now we can. It's all chip guided."

My husband was touching dumbly, adorably, at the back of his head, as though he might feel the tumor pushing through his skull. "So what's next?"

"Before we consider surgery, we try radiation. It probably won't work, but that's where we start."

I looked up from my phone. "This says we should go straight to surgery. As soon as possible."

Our doctor looked surprised. "You read fast."

I could feel my husband watching me, glowing with pride. He loved this side of me—this smart, bumptious kid who would do intellectual combat with anyone. Through his eyes, I loved it in myself.

"It's true that it says that. But the people who wrote that are out of touch. They've only seen the brain through a computer." The doctor was talking to himself as much as to us. "The brain seems like such a powerful thing, but I'm telling you, when you pop open the skull and see one, it's just a little raisin in there."

"So you're saying surgery is riskier than the pamphlet says?" asked my husband, trying to mediate.

The doctor sat forward in his seat. "I'm saying a lot can go wrong. You could come out a different person. Or with slurred speech. Or not able to open your eyes."

I wasn't sure if that was a euphemism for being dead or if he meant my husband's eyelids might actually stop working.

So we scheduled the radiation and went home. I told my husband to sit, relax, let me make dinner. French onion soup—his favorite. But he stayed in the kitchen with me while I cooked, which is exactly what I wanted. When it was ready, we wrapped ourselves in blankets and ate our soup outside. We watched some fat squirrels chase each other up and down the trees. We threw bread at them, and they squawked at us, strangely angry, and carried it up to their nests.

I felt powerless—and angry, too, to have found myself once again at risk of losing someone I loved. *Case history* was not a phrase I wanted associated with my husband. Sitting there in the dark woods, I thought of Sammy, of the year I turned sixteen, of everything that had happened. When I first began to tell Sammy's story, it had become clear to me right away that I would need to go deeper, further—to Ge Hong, to Trithemius, to all of the people who had stoked the fires of Sammy's mind long before I met him, who had walked, even briefly, the same path. But that was a world of sickness and pain and self-destructive pursuits. I didn't want my husband anywhere near that world.

"I called my mother," he said, interrupting my thoughts. He held up a hand before I could say anything. "I couldn't not tell her. She's coming to visit."

I stared into my soup. "Did you know that an anagram for *mother-in-law* is *Hitler woman?*"

"It wasn't worth arguing with her."

I could see him direct all of his energy into being patient with me. It made me wonder, as I sometimes did, if I was much too selfish to deserve my husband. I remembered the bartender I met in college who let me drink for free all night. When I rolled off him sometime around two in the morning, sweaty and satisfied, he'd fixed me with his narrow green eyes and said, "Let me guess. You're an only child."

14

Necropsy

The day after my visit with my father, I asked RJ to meet me in the lab. Even with Sammy gone, I had my run of the place. The substitute hired last-minute to replace him would literally sprint out the door when the final bell rang, and though no one said this, I believe some of the other teachers felt uncomfortable in there— it was like wearing a dead man's clothes. While I waited for RJ, I petted and fed Number 5, Number 7, Number 37, and Number 42. They squeaked and chewed and cuddled my finger.

Time was moving strangely. Between LHS's acts of remembrance (our glee club sang Boyz II Men's "End of the Road" over the intercom) and the suicide prevention assembly, I'd become accustomed to hearing Sammy spoken of in the past tense. Yet if I stood by his desk in the little office that abutted the laboratory, I could still smell him, and I could still see the little chocolate thumbprint he'd left on the computer monitor the day we ate grocery-store brownies. He was *present*.

RJ arrived. He was the only kid in school who wore, instead of a backpack, a messenger bag, and he removed it not by lifting the strap over his head but by simply unclasping the strap and catching the bag by its handle. He was known for this, and he did it now, throwing the bag onto the table.

"So here's the deal," I said. "We may not have the Appetizer, but we're going to run some tests on Sammy's Entrée. If we're going to figure out what was missing and give this stuff to Steph-

anie and my dad, we need to learn as much as we can." I was also
thinking of Sadiq's arrival. When he landed in Littlefield, I didn't
want to look like a child playing with his teacher's toys.

For RJ, Stephanie's safety was more than enough justification
for this after-school workload. He nodded once—agreed—and we
set about unpacking the box from the storage unit and organiz-
ing our materials. As RJ removed the CATHERINE medicine, he
tapped the vial and frowned. "There's hardly any left."

I took it from him. "It's not enough for a person. But it's
enough for a rat."

RJ picked up Number 37 the same way Sammy used to pick up
his grade book: as if it might bite him. It was Friday evening. Almost everyone else had gone home. The sun was still out, but we
had the lights off in the lab, and it was dry and cool. Three days
had passed since I'd pressed RJ into service as my lab assistant.
He was a leader by nature, but he played his new role gamely,
fetching me ingredients when I called for them, transcribing our
data in his juvenile jock penmanship. I'd taught him how to hold
the rats, how to feed them, how to clean their cages. It was nice
sharing this side of my life with him, but it was also strange, watching RJ interact with the rats. It was like having two different
groups of friends meet.

The first day, we'd done baseline measurements. These were
compromised by the rats' participation in my now-aborted study
with Sammy, but compromised would have to do. Watching
Number 37 swim his directionless laps, RJ had the same reaction
as I first did, beginning with amusement before giving way to
pity. The metaphors were too obvious to acknowledge: Number
37, swimming in circles, finding the platform, and immediately
forgetting it; RJ and I, searching through the ruins of Sammy's
life, always a step behind, completely unsure what we were chasing or who was chasing us.

The second day, we made and administered the Entrée. I adjusted the doses for the rats' weight, and we set about following
Sammy's instructions. I used a mortar and pestle to grind the

B. rossica into powder until the air was fragrant with the smell of chocolate and pine. In a Griffin-form beaker, I used a glass stir rod to mix the powder with the *P. cupana* extract and the tribal medicine, whose heavy green coloring, even in such small quantities, quickly overtook the other ingredients. Finally, I added the quicksilver, which provided a mineral sheen to what previously looked like vegetable soup.

I had been prepared to force-feed this concoction to Number 37, but rats are opportunists, and when I placed the mixture in his cage on a plastic spoon, he devoured it instantly, then went back to sleep. I felt a twinge of guilt, but I reminded myself of the image of Number 50, brought back to health.

My guilt was further soothed the next morning, when we found Number 37 still napping and pooping and going about his lazy day as usual. He appeared entirely unchanged. Only as RJ carried Number 37 to the water maze did I begin to notice a difference in him. Although I'd previously teased RJ for his tentativeness with the rats, Number 37 *did* look more on edge—his eyes showed an alertness that contrasted with his usual oblivious good nature. Healthy rats will scan the environment as you carry them, searching for markers they can use to orient themselves in the water maze. This had never been Number 37's strength. If he was doing it after just one dose of Sammy's elixir, then it might be working. Number 37's escape latency would still be slow this time, but the next day . . . that could be interesting.

I'd added fresh paint to the maze that morning, so the water had a slightly synthetic, balloonlike smell. I took a seat beside the pool and made sure the timer was reset to zero. When I was ready, I nodded to RJ, and he lowered Number 37 into the water.

With no hesitation, Number 37 churned his muscular legs and rocketed to the platform. Escape latency: three seconds.

"Holy shit." I was so startled that I forgot to turn off the stopwatch. The numbers ticked upward.

"Hell yeah!" RJ pumped his fist. "That's good, right?"

Number 37 sat still on the platform, his ribs expanding just slightly with shallow, easy breaths. For him to do so well in the water maze, this quickly, meant he wasn't just making new memories. He was reclaiming old ones—memories he'd lost. I smiled at RJ. Yes, this was good.

The next morning, Number 37 was dead. He'd collapsed onto his side near the water bottle, his eyes open and empty. His little pale feet were limp. His tail curved out and away from his body, the tip of it protruding just a millimeter out of the cage. His mouth was slightly open, revealing his uneven teeth and the wide, flat pink of his tongue. In the opposite corner of the cage, Number 5, Number 7, and Number 42 stood close together watching his body, not moving at all, not even when they saw me. On Number 37's stomach, I could see the slightly slick patches where they'd groomed him after he died. I had interrupted a funeral.

"What happened to him?" RJ asked.

"What does it look like?" For the moment I allowed myself to blame RJ, to pretend that I was only doing this for him.

RJ cast furtive glances around the laboratory and lowered his voice. "Do you think someone did this to him?" he whispered. "The same people who destroyed his apartment?"

I stared at RJ in disbelief. "Someone? *We* killed him."

We returned to the lab during last period, when the room was free. RJ was done for the day, but I was skipping class—trig, maybe—despite Captain Carson's warning. I had in front of me the body of Number 37, a pair of stainless steel medical scissors, tweezers, and a scalpel. I'd asked RJ to swipe some pliers from the Tech Ed workshop, and he deposited those onto the table with the rest of the instruments.

"What are we doing? Like, an autopsy?"

"*Necropsy*," I corrected. "An autopsy is for people."

RJ puffed his cheeks. He could be surprisingly squeamish about this kind of stuff. The day we dissected frogs our sophomore year, he'd stayed home sick.

"You don't have to be here."

"No, I'm in." But as I put on the latex gloves, he added, "I might not look."

The body of Number 37 was lying stomach down on the table. In death, his pink ears looked slightly darker, and they were low and flat against his head. His eyes were red, empty slits. I told myself that there was no real tragedy. We would have put down all of the rats at the end of our study—lab rats are not like racing horses or show dogs; they don't "retire"—so Number 37's death by elixir was only a slightly earlier death than scheduled. Still, I felt bad.

I picked up the scissors and gave them a couple of quick test clips to make sure the mechanism was smooth. I'd read about how to do this in the books Sammy gave me at the beginning of summer, but I could have done it without them. Taking apart a body is not difficult. The tricky stuff is purely psychological—the realization that everything that holds us together, that keeps our insides on the inside, can be so easily dismantled.

I pinched Number 37's head and brought the tip of the inner blade to the pale pink fur between his eyes. I pressed just enough to pierce the thin skin and cut a straight line to between the ears. I placed my index fingers on either side of this wound and tugged gently until the skin spread apart and I could see the rounded top of the skull. There was a little bit of sound as the skin gave way, and I could see RJ wince.

"The next part is probably the worst."

"Cool." He stared straight ahead. "Do your thing."

I picked up the pliers. They were light, needle-nosed, and scuffed from the friction of the wires in the workshop. I placed them against Number 37's head and squeezed until the bones of the eye sockets crunched and cracked. Reaching Number 37's brain was now just a matter of using the tweezers to poke, tug, and remove the broken bones of the skull and braincase. I did this quickly, even carelessly—I wasn't going to be graded. Soon, I exposed the brain. It was red and blue and gray, slightly snail-like. I slid the tweezers to the bottom of the brain cavity and popped the brain out, laid it gently on a paper towel beside the body.

RJ sensed this moment of accomplishment and peeked through his fingers. "That's it?"

I tapped the front and back of the brain with the scalpel. "This is what we're interested in the most. The cerebrum and cerebellum."

If I were in RJ's shoes, I would have asked more questions, but his curiosity did not extend that way. He wanted to help, and when he couldn't, he stayed out of it. I used the scalpel to cut small disks from these areas of interest, no thicker than a fingernail. I had expected I would need to plate them and examine them under the microscope, but it was immediately clear that the naked eye would do.

I must have made a frustrated sound, because RJ said, "Everything okay?"

"Look." I directed his attention to the biopsies, but he couldn't see, at first, what I was seeing. "The dark spots. That's the quicksilver." It had accumulated in the brain right where it always does. It had suffocated the tissues. The necropsy wasn't finished, but I was ready to make my ruling: Number 37 died of mercury poisoning.

Despite his disgust, RJ leaned in to where I was pointing. "This is bad?"

"Yeah."

"Because you didn't expect it?"

"Because it's exactly what I expected."

I sank onto one of the uncomfortable lab stools and asked RJ to get me a box of rat food from the supply closet. When he returned, I emptied the packets from the box and began to line it with tissues. RJ sat next to me, and for the fifteen minutes we had left until the final bell rang, we made a casket for Number 37.

Andres J. Fisher Attends
His First Meeting of the
New York Society of Numismatics

New York, AD 1911

Andres J. Fisher sits on the floor of the bathroom, watching his father bleed from the nose. It is night. His father has his head tipped back, and the blood is a blooming rose in his nostrils. He is tall and lean—leaner now than ever—and he has a face like a shut window in December, square and dark, with blue eyes so cold they are gray. For all of Andres's young life, his father's aloofness has seemed impenetrable, like a very long book. But as the sickness takes him, it is like an opening of the window, a turning of the page. Andres is eight years old and not at all frightened.

When the bleeding stops, his father readies himself for the meeting of the New York Society of Numismatics, of which he is chairman. He packs his robes, which are long, silk, and the color of a copper penny. He shaves and puts on his shoes. In every room there is a window, and the last light of the day turns purple as it suffocates under the grip of the borough. Andres likes to read the paper after his father discards it, and this morning's edition of the *New York World* said there are, every minute, twelve new Americans.

"Well, come on then," says his father.

"Yes, sir," Andres says, and his mother fetches his coat.

Outside, the air is thin and dry, the sky a cloudy darkness. Andres holds his father's hand. Until the year prior, Andres had a horse, and his name was Lancelot. When Lancelot fell sick with influenza, he lathered and cried and chewed the air. When they shot him, there was the haze of black powder, the shine of his wet coat under the sun, and a deafening noise that stained the dirt red. Through these things, Andres saw Lancelot's soul depart his body, and it was the shape of a horse—but smaller, like a glass miniature. It was only an illusion. It was only the powder and the lather and the dizzying report of the pistol. But every night, he imagines he will someday ride Lancelot into heaven.

First it was the porcelain mantel clock Andres's mother had inherited from an uncle. Then it was the eighteen-karat-gold French candlesticks that had sat, for all of Andres's life, in the center of the dining room table. Finally his father sold his wedding band, along with Andres's mother's, to a jeweler only two blocks from their home. At night, Andres hears them argue.

"I have to walk past my own wedding ring!" his mother complained. "He has it right in the window!"

Whatever money his family once had, Andres's father has spent it. Andres has pieced together the story through his parents' late-night quarrels, the tale of his father's selfishness leaching through the walls like mold.

Several months after his father's diagnosis, a dealer approached the society with a rare set of ancient Egyptian coins—rare precisely because ancient Egyptians were not known to use coins. The dealer allowed the society to authenticate the first in the series. A younger member, an Egyptologist, spent a week with the coin and returned with a translation of the glyphs on the reverse: "Here is the way to cure any disease of the body."

Last week, his father bought the coins for an enormous sum. "The society said I would be a fool if I didn't!" Andres heard him say.

"You've been a fool all your life," his mother replied.

Since the purchase, the Egyptologist has been hard at work finishing the translation. Tonight, he announces the result, and Andres's father will learn whether he lives or dies.

•

When Andres and his father arrive, several men are arranged in
a circle, all in their robes. Most of the chairs remain empty. It is
not what Andres imagined. The meeting hall is not even a hall,
but simply the back room of a library—a library Andres has seen
hundreds of times from the street. The chairs are mismatched and
cheap. The men are just men; he recognizes the watchmaker who
always eats pears. The only interesting thing is Andres's father's
face—the expression of it. His father is disappointed, too. This
is not what *he* expected.

"Where is everyone?" his father asks.

The watchmaker comes near. "Most of them didn't have the
stomach," he whispers.

His father is confused, but all at once, Andres understands:
despite his father's claims, no one wanted him to buy these coins.
Andres would guess they begged him not to. What the watchmaker means is that not everyone has the stomach to see his father
humiliated.

The few of them in attendance take their seats, and the young
Egyptologist makes his way to the head of the room. He is small
and plain and, to compensate, wears a large pince-nez of unusual
brightness. In his left hand, he holds one of the coins. It is dark,
nearly black—the blackest coin Andres has ever seen. It is so
darkly colored he finds it hard to believe it contains any readable
material at all. It would be like trying to discern a man's thoughts
solely from the contents of his pupils.

"As you know," the man says, "the coins originate from the
Fifteenth Dynasty of Egypt, circa 1550 BC. The obverse contains
the cartouche of Khamudi, the last Hyksos ruler."

"What of the *recipe?*" Andres's father demands.

The young Egyptologist nods in a capitulating way. "The coins
do contain a recipe. It is a lotion of fenugreek oil that eradicates
liver spots on the skin."

"And?"

"I'm sorry. It's moisturizer. My wife uses something just
like it."

Andres's father stands and leaves the room. Everyone looks at Andres, waiting, as though his father were already dead and the society were a kingdom he inherited. Andres knows he should weep for his father—just as, when Lancelot's heavy head went limp on the autumn earth, the man who shot him said, "There's no shame in crying." But all Andres can think of is that black sphere, an empty sun, held between the fingers of the man still at the head of the room. A darkness that is the shape of a common thing—a coin—but its darkness makes it strange. He imagines all kinds of objects blotted this way: a black watch, a black pear, a black wedding band held behind black glass. He thinks, *That's my heart.* A thing that is not the thing it looks like.

He thinks, *What's wrong with me?*

The Journal of Sammy Tampari: March 8–April 1, 2003

March 8

Arrived today in Bucharest with S and C. We flew first to London and spent two days there as tourists. I should have held firm and said no, let's push on to Romania. But I'm grateful to S for helping me, and when he said he wanted to show us around his home city, how to say no? I asked C that actual question, and she stared into her hands and said, "Do you want to know if *I* want to see London?"

While we were there, C turned twenty-six. "My last birthday as your fiancée," she said, and I knew what this meant: set a date.

What's wrong with me? Recently I described it to C like light. What's wrong with me is the absence of feeling the way black is the absence of light.

What's wrong with me is this: ██████████████
Good night.

March 9

S arranged for us to have a private tour of the Romanian Center for Health and Life-Extension. He knows the former research director of the center, someone named Bogdi, and organized this trip after I mentioned the center in an e-mail. I'll meet Bogdi in a few days. For reasons I look forward to hearing, he quit the center to form a sort of rogue scientific consortium known as the Immortalist Underground. They have a website that requires a password log-in, and if you get the password wrong, the website crashes your computer.

The people who work at the center call it the Constantin, after the woman who founded it. In the 1950s, Cristina Constantin developed Rejuvitol-X5, an antiaging treatment that is now illegal in the States. C thinks I'm writing a chapter on the Constantin for my book, but I'm really here to heed the Belgian's advice, to search for an injectable to go along with my ingestible. An appetizer to my entrée. I tried to convince C to skip this trip, to stay home and rest, but she is stubborn and suspicious, and I'll have to be careful. S promised he would prep Bogdi on my lie.

Alarm set for 7:00 a.m., EET. An hour later, S arrived from down the hall. I was already showered and dressed. S was wearing a sweater vest over a blue button-down with the sleeves rolled up. He has forearms like a race-car driver.

The Constantin is located a few miles north of the city. The place is described as a research facility, but it reminded me more of the health spas that line the Black Sea, places where celebrities sunbathe on the golden sand while paparazzi disguised as beach vendors take close-up photos of their famous breasts.

In the scientific community, no one takes this place seriously. The center produces a lot of wild claims and almost no verifiable research. But for the people who spend the last of their retirement savings on the Rejuvitol-X5 Life-Prolonging Program, the Constantin is anything but a joke. As we approached the entrance, I watched a queue of old people snake its way from the outer steps to the welcome desk.

"Waiting list hundreds of names deep," said Alex, short for Alexandru, our tour guide while on the grounds.

In the late 1940s, Cristina Constantin, a biologist, discovered that procaine hydrochloride, i.e., Novocain, seemed to promote antiaging effects: increased wound healing, reduced cholesterol, even hair growth. The problem was that the body hydrolyzes procaine too quickly for these benefits to take hold. The numbing effect of procaine results from its disruption of neuron communication, like cutting the cord of a landline phone, and the body responds to this disruption with cholinesterase, an enzyme that breaks down procaine in about an hour. Constantin theorized that if she could stabilize the procaine by eliminating its anesthetic function, the body would tolerate its presence for longer periods and allow the antiaging properties to do their regenerative work.

In 1951, Constantin premiered Rejuvitol-X5, a compound of procaine, benzoic acid, disodium phosphate, and a variety of antioxidants. In one of her earliest papers, Constantin documented a case study in which a sixty-year-old man with diabetes and severe eczema began treatment with injectable Rejuvitol-X5. In the "before" photographs, the patient looks oily and corpselike, as though someone made a wax sculpture of a mummy. In the "after" photographs, he looks like Tom Selleck from *Magnum, P.I.*

For a little under a decade, Hollywood celebrities and European political leaders flocked to Romania. The peer-review process allows for the emergence of fads such as this—it takes time to debunk them. But when it happens, it happens fast. In quick succession, the *British Medical Journal* released one, two, three articles proving that Rejuvitol-X5 offers no life-extending benefits. The FDA banned the drug in the United States. It was strange, in Bucharest, to walk into a convenience store and see little vials of the stuff hanging right there on the shelves, next to the spearmint gum. But if you want the really strong version, you have to attend the Constantin and get it shot into your veins.

I never doubted the studies discrediting Rejuvitol, but the center has continued to develop and test new formulations of the drug, or so I'd heard, and they've done so without the kind of regulations that plague medical technology in America. In the 1970s, at the height of the regime of Nicolae Ceaușescu, the dictator ordered Cristina Constantin to make him immortal. Even after his execution, the center continued to operate with a kind of vaguely threatening authority. What did I think I'd find here? Maybe large vats of Rejuvitol bubbling in cauldrons, monkeys in cages undergoing highly unethical tests, the kind of experiments I would never condone, but if someone else happened to be doing them, ideally in a faraway country . . .

As Alex showed us around the facilities, it didn't take long for my outlaw spirit to fade. The first floor was mostly examination rooms, and these looked like anything you'd find in a small-town private practice: blood pressure gauges, privacy screens, clear plastic jars full of tongue depressors. The room Alex showed me had a bookshelf stocked with bootleg DVDs, almost all of which starred Sandra Bullock.

"Where do you do your research?" I asked Alex.

He didn't even understand the question. "We keep track of our clients here."

"But who's working on the Rejuvitol?"

"Our distributor is in Hungary. We just redesigned our logo!"

S moved to my side and touched my elbow. "Just wait until you meet Bogdi." S's fingers on my skin were electric. C took a picture of my unhappy face and smiled at it in the viewfinder.

As we approached the eastern wing, I heard the sounds of Ping-Pong echoing between the columns. Two old men, shirtless and in matching white shorts, volleyed the little ball back and forth between them. Their old-man breasts jiggled with each hit. They looked tan and happy—the men, I mean, not their breasts.

Alex sensed my growing disappointment and turned on the charm. "Listen, you know of President John F. Kennedy?"

"I *think* I've heard of him," said C.

Alex paused for dramatic effect. "He spent three days here in 1960."

"Not the best example," said S.

Alex waved this away. "Come on. Rejuvitol does not stop gun-shots." He led us to a back office where a comically anachronistic row of secretaries—all young, pretty girls in tight-fitting sweaters—typed away on desktop computers. Behind them hung a large photograph of Cristina Constantin laughing and drinking tea with a beautiful and slightly androgynous German woman whom I recognized as Marlene Dietrich. Alex pointed to her.

"Also dead," I said.

Alex realized that we were committed to giving him a hard time and smiled his first natural smile of the day. "Okay, but she is alcoholic and still lived to ninety? So, not bad?"

As if to court further dissent, he showed us a photograph of

Constantin and a haunted-looking Spaniard with a mustache as thin and black as an underline.

"Salvador Dalí," said Alex.

"Also dead," said C and S in unison.

"But seriously," Alex said. "Dalí was poisoned by wife, tried to set himself on fire, et cetera. Rejuvitol does not make perfect world, only healthy body."

When he'd first introduced himself, Alex proudly announced his age: "Fifty-nine years young." He looks closer to thirty, and I have to assume this explains his prominent position at the Constantin. He's a walking advertisement for the benefits of Rejuvitol. As a PR man, he seemed easily rattled.

"How often did Ceaușescu come here?" I asked.

Alex's smile went away. "I don't know."

"You didn't work here, then?" asked S, in a tone that suggested, yes, Alex did work here, and, yes, S knows he worked here.

"I was very low level, an assistant to an assistant. Basically a boy secretary."

"What kind of experiments did Constantin have you doing for Ceaușescu?" I asked.

Alex shrugged again. "I don't know. I was very low level."

On our way back to the lobby we again passed the row of young women at computers. Their typing ricocheted off the sleek metal desks and made it seem as if there were many more of them than they were.

Alex saw us fixate. "It used to be official policy: only young, beautiful women for clerical work. It really said that in the office handbook! Now that is not the case, but it is like a . . . trend now. We'll hire anyone, but only young, beautiful women apply."

"Was that a Ceaușescu policy?" I asked, even though I'd decided to stop asking about him.

One of the typists, a blue-eyed girl with an ergonomic wrist pillow, turned her head slightly and said, over her shoulder, "I don't know," completely out of instinct. Immediately the girl spun back to her computer, but I could see the back of her neck turn bloodred in embarrassment. We stood in awkward silence, during which I realized that *this* was the company policy now, to answer every question about Ceaușescu with a prompt "I don't know."

Alex's old, smooth face flushed the same color as the girl's neck.

"It's okay," I said. "I was just curious."

Alex didn't say anything. He stared for a second at his loafers and then took a deep breath as if he'd decided on something. Without a word he led us to his office, which was large and overlooked the volleyball net outside. He leaned against his desk and asked C to close the door behind her. When she did, he said, "Listen, for the girls the policy is just policy. No talking about Ceaușescu. But for me it is not just policy. It is also"—he weighed his words, searching for the right English phrasing—"a bad memory, like something you don't want to talk about?"

I started to say something apologetic, but Alex continued without letting me.

"Some years, Ceaușescu visited every week. You could hear the bulletproof car coming miles away. It went very fast and sounded like a helicopter. He would bring many soldiers with guns, and it was like being invaded, only the invaders were your own countrymen. I remember 1978, Ceaușescu turned sixty years old, but you could not mention this. No 'Happy birthday, General Secretary,' unless you wanted to be taken out back. He pretended he was in his thirties, always. If you looked at him, you would be fired. If you took a picture of him, you would be taken out back. If you talked to him, taken out back. Only Dr. Constantin could speak to him, and imagine the difficulty! She could not say to him, 'As a man in your sixties, you must do such and such to be healthy.' She had to say, 'You are so young and healthy, so here's what you do to stay that way.' Remember that Dr. Constantin was herself very old at this time. She was terrified of forgetting the rules, of saying something that would offend him. The second he left in his helicopter-car, she would cry and cry.

"Okay, and experiments? We had to develop new drugs and give them to our other patients without even telling them, to see what would happen? And it was sometimes very bad? Once we give an old woman a kind of Rejuvitol, but with bemegride. Her name was Camelia. Very old face, but young eyes, like our typists. She thought she was taking the regular medicine, but we gave her the new one, we had no choice, and she took it for three weeks. 'I don't feel good,' she'd say, and we had to lie and say, 'It's fine, drink some water, be happy.' And then one day, when I'm walking her to her room, she has such a bad seizure her eye removes from its socket and bounces against her cheek like a tetherball. This is what I think of when I think of Ceaușescu. Camelia's eye dangling from the socket, because of something we did."

S stepped forward as though he were going to comfort Alex, but when Alex looked up from the floor, it was clear that he wasn't sad but angry.

"So you are disappointed," Alex said. "So be it. We are not what you expected. You think you are the first to come here expecting weird science? We are actually much better than what you expected. We don't hurt anybody, okay, or do things we shouldn't based on the greed of one man. People come, we give them medicine—controversial, yes, but certainly safe, no one says otherwise, and they leave feeling good.

"You seem like nice people. But if you're doing this research, then you already have more in common with Ceaușescu than most. You should look closely at yourself to make sure you are not too much like him, and also allow others to see you, not keep yourself hidden like Ceaușescu. So I thank you for coming to the Constantin and for giving me the chance to show you around. Be honest with yourselves and each other, always."

On the way home, we stopped at a Kaufland supermarket and bought enough Rejuvitol for all of us. "Now in vials!" exclaimed the English packaging. We toasted one another's health, tipped back our heads, and squirted Constantin's elixir into the backs of our throats. This was the weak stuff, just vitamins. It tasted like apple juice. As we drank, I replayed Alex's words. I *am* keeping myself hidden—from C most of all.

We polished off the Rejuvitol and threw the empty vials onto the floor of the rental car. S drove, C in the passenger seat, me in the back. More than once I caught S watching me in the rearview, and I thought, *Do you see me?*

Good night.

March 10

Rain and discord. Trapped inside. The plan was to spend two days sightseeing until the meeting with Bogdi. But in the morning the thunderstorms came and rattled the windows, and by afternoon, when the weather cleared, the streets were chaos. When we asked the concierge for a taxi, he just laughed. The Transport Workers Union has staged what's called a warning strike, where they stop working for two hours in the middle of the day.

Dinner at the hotel, out of necessity. S came downstairs in jeans and a black T-shirt, the most casual I've ever seen him. I had dressed down myself, and C was practically wearing pajamas. It's as though with the transport union on strike, we all went on strike. We laughed when we saw one another.

The dining room was dark, candlelit, with light piano music bubbling from wall-mounted speakers. The only other table was a group of Swedish real estate agents who are here, they announced to us loudly, on their yearly retreat. It was two guys alone with fourteen women. The guys sat at opposite ends of the table, sucking in their stomachs and grinning at their own luck. I tried ineffectively to order some wine, and S got involved, and C got involved, and somehow we ended up with two bottles.

After several glasses, S grabbed C's hand and pretended to read her palm. "This is your heart line. You see how it's all wavy? That means you'll have many lovers but not many serious relationships."

"Oh, yeah?" I said. "Honey, is there something I should know?"

C traced the line with her finger. "My palm thinks I'm a slut?"

"I'm afraid so, yes." S kissed her fingers.

C cooed in a funny, exaggerated way. She made a loving face at me, letting me know that their flirting was just for laughs, but she didn't need to. Here were these two people I am maybe in love with, being their wonderful selves with each other. What could be better?

"Okay," S continued, "and here is your fate line. This tells me you're going to be trapped forever in this hotel."

"I wonder which one of you I'll kill first," C said.

We finished our entrées and sat back in our chairs, exhausted and full. For dessert, the waiter brought a massive cheese plate that I don't remember any of us ordering. I know cheese, and this was the good stuff. S slipped a cracker into his mouth and closed his eyes in happiness.

"It's delicious," C said, "though I always struggle with the idea of cheese as dessert."

S looked up from his plate. "Whatever you eat last is dessert."

For a moment I wondered, *Is this really going to happen? All three of us, together?* I sat rigid at the table. I didn't know if I wanted to ruin the mood or encourage it. C dabbed her lips with her napkin, and S motioned to the waiter for the check.

My worrying was for nothing. By the time we hit the elevators, the feeling was gone. Maybe I was the only one who ever had it. As the doors dinged open, S went right, and we went left. I allowed myself a final image of S's body wrapped in the soft cotton sheets, of me waking up next to him, C already brushing her teeth, completely approving of what we'd done.

March 11

The strike continues. When we approach the concierge, he laughs and shakes his head. There is fighting in the streets, he tells us. Later, a bus driver hits a cop with a brick and is punished for it, badly, by a police dog. "Maybe stay in and enjoy the pool?" says the concierge. So we stay in and enjoy the pool. C swims laps. S reads submissions to the *Journal of Gerontology & Geriatric Research.* I am bored, bored, bored.

procaine

March 12

Totally. Crazy. Day.

Woke up early to meet Bogdi. "It's going to be tough," S said, since Bogdi is on the other side of the city in something called Sector 4. "Sector 4, malfunction," said C in a robot voice, and they laughed together. As we left the hotel, the doorman swung the wide, heavy doors open for us but raised his eyebrows while he did it, as if to say, *Are you sure you want to leave?*

Outside, a couple of cabdrivers had lined up their cars to block access to a side road. Someone in a moving van was shouting at them and laying on the horn. S led us away and made a call on his cell phone. Above us, on the small balcony of an apartment complex, an older couple was slow dancing to the cacophony of the street noise.

"Bogdi knows someone who lives right here," S said. "He'll give us a ride."

We waited. It was a nice day, sunny but with wind. C was wearing a tank top. She burns and then tans, which isn't good for you, but it's what she does.

We heard a short, trumpety honk, but a honk directed at us this time, not at traffic. (How could we tell the difference? I don't know, but all three of us did at once, turning our heads to the sound as if our names had been called.) Bogdi's friend arrived in a pickup truck with flames on the side and a large, wooden utility trailer. The door opened, and a heavily bearded, heavily gloved man popped out.

"Yo, yo. Friends of Bogdi?" He was wearing a black T-shirt with white lettering that said BIKES, BITCHES.

"That's us," said S. "Thanks for your help."

The man waved this off and moved to the back of the truck. He opened the gate of the utility trailer, slid the ramp down, and hopped inside. I was worried that he expected us to ride in the trailer like that, but the reality was worse. One by one, Bogdi's friend removed three single-speed bicycles from the back of the truck. He lined them up in front of us and clapped his hands together, the way people do when their job is done.

"They are small but very good," said Bogdi's friend, misinterpreting our expressions. "New tires on all three."

"I don't mean to sound ungrateful," said S, "but we thought you'd be driving us."

The man gave him the crook eye. "I mean, by car, with traffic and roads closed, we're talking maybe three hours? By bike, thirty minutes no problem. Straight shot."

I'm proud to say that it was not C, not S, but me, of all people, who first grabbed one of the bikes and took it for a test spin. I rode a quick lap around the street sign. I hadn't been on a bike since I was ten, eleven years old? I wobbled and almost fell as I navigated the curb. The old couple on the balcony were watching me now, and as I came to a stop near my friends, they applauded me in a way that was both friendly and insulting.

"There you go!" said Bogdi's friend. He gave us the directions quickly and without further discussion. It was not a straight shot, as he'd promised; rather, he unfolded a map and drew on it what appeared to be a whirlpool. When he accidentally guided his pen the wrong way down a street, he chuckled to himself, crossed that line out, and drew a skull and crossbones next to it.

"We're actually doing this?" asked S, as the three of us retied and double-knotted our sneakers.

We lined up like ducklings, me in front, and pedaled our way toward Sector 4. As we made our first right, I experienced a brief moment of confidence: a freshly painted bike lane emerged from the curb like a red carpet. We rode it for half a mile before it disappeared, unceremoniously and without warning. I slammed on my brakes. C crashed into me, S into her. I tipped over and skinned my elbow bloody on the deckled surface of a concrete planter.

We persevered despite the rocky start and despite the bloodstains that were already coating the sleeve of my shirt. As we neared Sector 4, the road congestion began to clear, just enough for the streets to feel more dangerous. We came to a multilane roundabout, a spiral of chaos and screeching brakes. We tried repeatedly to time our entry into the road, failed, and in this failure left ourselves vulnerable: neither on the sidewalk nor moving in the right direction.

I was about to cry when I heard a whistle from behind us. A police officer was beckoning us over. The whistle hung from his mouth. We walked our bikes over to him like schoolchildren about to be scolded.

He stashed the whistle in his front pocket and put his hands on his hips. "This is not good. You are going to die."

"What should we do?" I asked.

"You should stop doing this," he pleaded. "Be reasonable."

"It's not illegal to ride a bike," said C sharply.

The officer only shook his head. "It makes me very sad to watch what you're doing."

"We need to get here." I showed him our crazy map.

The officer gestured to his car. "I can take you, but you'd have to lose the bikes."

We debated this. We were only halfway to Bogdi and had nearly killed ourselves. On the other hand, abandoning the bikes on the street would be a supremely shitty thing to do.

"The bicycles belong to you?" asked the officer.

"A friend," said S.

The cop made a face, recognizing the moral quandary in which we found ourselves. "A good friend?"

So we ditched the bikes. We left them unlocked at a bike rack outside a pharmacy and jumped happily into the police car as if we were arresting ourselves. The officer punched on his siren to ease his reentry into traffic, then turned it off and guided the car expertly down side streets, alleys, and once or twice through parking lots as a shortcut. The three of us sat in the back with our knees and elbows touching.

We arrived at Bogdi's address, which was a packing warehouse within spitting distance of Tineretului Park. The officer pointed to the metro station we would have used had the metro been operational—a fifteen-minute ride from our hotel. Out on the water, parents and children were paddleboating from one end of the lake to the other. I could hear the sounds of klezmer music, kids laughing, and underinflated soccer balls being thwacked by cleated shoes. The wind carried the oily smell of fried dough.

We thanked the officer and stared up at the warehouse. The building was unmarked and without windows, the kind of place

Batman might go to fight the Joker. It was an industrial district, and several much larger warehouses surrounded Bogdi's, with hardly any space between them. A metal chain hung outside the roll-up door. I remembered Bogdi's booby-trapped website and wondered if, when we pulled that chain, a piano would fall on our heads. But S tugged the chain, and I heard a bell resonate deep inside the warehouse. Thirty seconds later, the door mechanism began to whir and the door lifted slowly open. I exchanged a look with C, positioned myself defensively behind S, and entered the headquarters of the Immortalist Underground.

Imagine a college dorm room occupied by freshman boys. Posters cover the walls: athletes in motion, terrible rock bands, a scantily clad woman holding a stack of textbooks under her breasts, and beneath those, a jokey line: I LIKE BIG BOOKS AND I CANNOT LIE.

Now take that dorm room and double it in size. Then double it again, and again, until it's roughly the size of a Romanian packing warehouse. At first glance, the Immortalist Underground comprised approximately eighteen people, seventeen of whom were asleep. Their bodies littered the sofas and the floor. One of them was literally sleeping under newspaper. Bogdi sat front and center with his legs stretched out on a plastic jug he was using as a footstool. A small, mousy brunette lay with her head on his lap, dressed in a jean jacket and old-school, pump-up Reeboks. Like the rest of them, she was asleep.

"Sadiq and pals!" Bogdi shouted at us from across the cavern, with no regard for the naps taking place around and on top of him. "It's soooo crazy to see you!" He looked long and hyper-skinny, with an elasticity to his arms that suggested double joints. (Later, to show off, he would twist his legs up over his head and walk around on his hands, like a sentient pretzel.) His face was clean shaven and not unattractive, if a little gaunt. He wore a backward baseball cap with sunglasses resting on the rim. I guessed he was around thirty-five years old.

"Boggers, my friend!" S called as we navigated the mess. "When does your decorator graduate from primary school?"

Bogdi tipped his head back and laughed silently. "Whatever,

whatever." His voice was high-pitched and slightly feminine, accentuated by his way of speaking, like an American Valley girl. He struck me immediately as someone who was so intelligent, and so assured in his intelligence, that he adopted zero of the typical affectations of intelligent people.

Bogdi asked if we had any trouble finding the place. As we explained about our ill-fated bike ride, I expected two reactions from Bogdi: (1) "Oh, boo hoo, you spoiled American babies, bicycling here is not that dangerous"; followed by (2) "You left my friend's bikes in the streets? You dicks!"

Instead, Bogdi seemed even more shocked by our misadventures than we had been. "Omigod!" He punched his girlfriend on the shoulder, waking her up. She moaned and hissed something at him in Romanian. "Dumitru tried to kill these guys!" he told her.

She looked at us. "Again?"

I wasn't sure what that meant.

"He was just trying to help," said S.

Bogdi scrunched up his face. "Um, no. It's all about his stupid organization. What's it called?" He snapped at his girlfriend, but she wasn't listening.

I remembered the T-shirt. "Bikes, Bitches?"

"Right! They are activists for bicycles. They want the city to make, like, bike lanes and other such conveniences. The mayor will not do it! He says Romanian drivers are too uncivilized to coexist with bikes."

"What does this have to do with us?" asked C.

Bogdi sat forward, serious now. "Because you have a resource more powerful than gold, than oil, than weapons-grade plutonium. You have American blood. Can you imagine if it spilled on the spokes of a bike in Romania? Bikes, Bitches would go straight to ProTV News and say, 'See? This is why we must have bike lanes!'"

"Jesus," I said. We had taken seats on foldout chairs and pulled them close to Bogdi.

He surprised me by reaching across and taking my hand. "You gotta believe me. I told him to drive you. I would never give a bicycle to someone I care about."

I told him it was fine. Reassured, Bogdi began to toss loose change at one of the sleeping bodies on the floor.

The little coins pinged off the man's back and head until he stirred and shot an angry look at Bogdi. *"Tâmpit!"* Motherfucker.

Bogdi ignored the insult. "Where did you put the refrigerator?"

"Under the Toyota. I've shown you a hundred times."

"Do we have any American beer left?"

The man stood and shuffled off in the direction of what was likely, once, a foreman's office, but now seemed to be a graveyard for rusted automobile equipment. "We have only American beer," he said as he went.

"We have a friend who's, like, big shit at Michelob," Bogdi explained. "He pays us in beer."

"Pays you for what?" I asked.

Bogdi indicated the space of the warehouse, as though that were an answer. "Poor guy has Huntington's disease."

"What happened at the Constantin, Boggers?" S asked. "It's a bit strange in here."

Upon hearing the name of the center, Bogdi curled his lip. "You went there already?"

"A few days ago," I said.

"Okay, so, like, why are you asking? The center is where old people go to play lawn darts until they die."

"So you . . . upgraded . . . to this?" S asked.

"Don't be such a downer! Wait till I show you."

The other man returned with the beer. He introduced himself as Gavril and popped the tops off the bottles with a cigarette lighter. Gavril's face would have been unremarkable—brown hair, brown eyes, fortysomething—except for a tattoo of Mickey Mouse that crossed from his neck to his face, with just the tops of Mickey's ears peaking above the jawline. Bogdi's girlfriend had fallen back asleep, but he poked at her until she woke and said her name, eyes half-open: Livia.

Bogdi held her beer and offered her sips like a baby goat. "She's as important as she is lazy. She's the key to the whole thing."

One thing was for sure: *something* was happening here. "We're eager to hear about it," I said.

Bogdi's face grew serious. "Sadiq calls me out of the blue and says he has a friend interested in my work. Remind me what I said, Sadie?"

"I believe you told me to go fuck myself."

Gavril laughed. "That sounds like you."

Bogdi shrugged: guilty as charged. "Gav had Parkinson's when I met him. Now he has, like, a clean bill of health. That's the kind of results we're talking about." Bogdi paused for dramatic effect. "You'd be protective, too?"

"Sure," I said, "but from Sadiq?"

"Sadie is an angel, but he works for a devil."

"Radkin?" I waited for S to say something, but he didn't, so I continued, "I don't care for him either, but what does he matter to you?"

"Anyone who isn't us is an enemy," Gavril said.

"Because they can't be trusted," Bogdi finished. "Radkin is a snake in scientist clothes. There is nothing he wouldn't do for money. Steal our research, sabotage our operations. He could, like, send someone who works for him, but whom I consider a friend, to see what we're up to." Bogdi looked pointedly at Sadiq.

"Securing research funds is part of the work we *all* do," S said, "and Radkin does not apologize for being good at it." It sounded like an argument S often made to himself. "Honestly, though, and no offense, he couldn't be less interested in what you are doing."

Bogdi shook his head, more sad than disbelieving. "You are both naïve. Never trust anyone driven by greed."

As we talked, I'd been taking in more of the warehouse. Along with the sleeping bodies, the warehouse contained several dozen pallets and one wall of tall metal shelving. Many of the boxes resting on these things were either unlabeled or labeled in Romanian, and the boxes I *could* read did little to explain the work being done here: several boxes of baby aspirin, gallons and gallons of lye, enough sparklers to host a large Fourth of July party. I tried to combine the ingredients in my head, to make recipes from them that had something, anything, to do with the elixir of life. But all of my recipes, every single one, produced a weapon: acid bombs, poison gas, maybe even a crude sort of napalm. I began to seriously worry for our safety.

C wasn't impressed by any of this and certainly wasn't in the mood to see S or me interrogated. "So what's *your* motive?" she said. "American beer?"

Bogdi's eyes lit up. "You're just like Livia!" He nudged his girlfriend, but she only burrowed deeper into the couch. "Not American beer, though that's funny."

"What then?" S asked. "Pure scientific curiosity?"

Bogdi opened another beer. "Let me ask you a question: Why did Cristina Constantin pursue immortality?"

"From what I've seen," I said, "Rejuvitol is first and foremost a business."

Bogdi made an incorrect buzzer sound, like from a game show. "I'm talking about when the real experiments happened."

"She didn't have much of a choice," S said. "Ceaușescu."

Bogdi sat up in his seat. "Bingo! Some people search because they want riches and power. And some people search because a rich, powerful person told them to."

"I don't understand," I said. "You're working for someone?"

Bogdi touched his nose. "We're all working for someone."

"Uh-oh," said C, catching on before I did.

"What's going on?" I asked.

Bogdi pointed up at the ceiling.

"Oh, Jesus," said S.

"Oh, Jesus, exactly!" Bogdi said. "I have spoken to God."

I began to fear, in light of the bomb-making equipment, that the Immortalist Underground was not a rogue scientific community but a divinely inspired terrorist organization.

S grunted, the muscles in his jaw beating like a pulse. "Boggers, you're making me nervous. Was it a mistake for us to come here?"

Bogdi closed his eyes. What S said seemed to actually hurt his feelings. "It's only in your countries that science and religion are enemies. Everywhere else they are BFFs."

"I don't think that's true," I said.

"Okay, follow me." Bogdi stood and led us toward a side door. "I used to search for the elixir because of money, like Radkin, and maybe also fame. I wanted everyone to know my name the way they know Constantin's."

"What changed?" S asked.

"I had a religious experience," Bogdi answered, as though it were the simplest and most natural thing in the world. Then he opened the door.

We gaped. The door led not to the outside, as I'd guessed, but to a whole other warehouse.

"Holy shit," I said. The building contained everything I'd hoped to see at the Constantin. From the outside, it looked like a warehouse, but inside, Bogdi had built a fully functioning medical center. To my right, a svelte, pink-haired woman was running a treadmill stress test, electrodes suctioned above her sports bra. An IV dangled from her lean, muscular arms. She nodded at us, completely unfazed, as the EKG tracked her vitals. A gamma camera sat in the corner, which meant the woman had radioactive dye coursing through her veins, ready for nuclear imaging.

Every room contained something fun and expensive: an eighteen-liter console lyophilizer, an electrosurgery unit, an X-ray generator. This glorious and seemingly random collection of equipment was so random it could only be used for one purpose: the elixir. In one room I recognized a 1960s, frighteningly analog ECT machine. I hadn't seen one of these devices since the day I nearly killed C. I could feel my face go white, and C put a comforting hand on my arm.

"What on earth do you need this for?" I asked Bogdi.

"Nothing yet. But you never know."

We were interrupted by the appearance of Livia, who emerged from behind us and threw her arms around Bogdi's thin waist.

"Hey, baby," she said, eyelids heavy.

"My love! Now I can show them your hard work."

For this we returned to the first warehouse. I felt like a kid being taken from the toy store. Bogdi marched us back to the shelving units and removed a narrow blue box of sparklers. He set it on the ground, and we stood in a circle around it as if we were about to start praying.

"I should probably, you know, prepare you for this," he said. "So you don't think I'm crazy."

It's a truly terrifying thing when someone such as Bogdi is nervous that you'll judge him for what he's about to show you.

"You've seen Rejuvitol," Bogdi said, "so you get, like, the basic idea. Our product is called Dor, which is a Romanian word. Impossible to translate."

"It's *impossible*," Gavril added, as though we'd challenged Bogdi.

"So for today let's think of it, like, Super Rejuvitol. We've pushed Constantin's ideas to the next level."

"I take it there's more than sparklers in that box," said S.

Bogdi looked at me. "At the center, it became clear right away that procaine is too weak. It is medicine for babies. So I asked myself, 'Bogdi, what is like procaine but stronger than procaine?'"

Bogdi removed a sparkler, ripped it in half, and out fell a stream of white powder.

S took a step back. "Is that cocaine? Say that's not cocaine."

"No, it's Dor!" Bogdi twirled his hands theatrically. "Which, yes, includes quite a bit of cocaine."

"Okay," said C. "Time to go."

"Aww," Bogdi said. "Don't overreact."

C ignored him. "Time to *go*," she said to me.

But I couldn't. Not yet. "How do you get it?" I asked. From the corner of my eye, I could see C staring daggers at me.

"I'm an army brat," Livia said.

Bogdi squeezed Livia's hand. "So she gets all the stuff. Some we use for the Dor, some we sell to fund the Dor."

"You're drug dealers," said S. "Boggers, what's happened to you?"

Bogdi stared at the floor. "It is not awesome, from an ethical perspective. But this feels like an ends-justify-the-means situation?"

"Well, thanks for having us," said C.

S bit his lip. "She might be right," he said to me. "Maybe we should go."

Instead of protesting, Bogdi adopted a stance of indifference. "Okay, go home and discuss. If you want, come back tomorrow. You can try some."

C actually gasped. "*Try some?*"

Bogdi shrugged: *Why not?*

"What's in this for you?" C asked him. "If you're drug deal-ers, and so secretive and all that, why would you even want to be in his book?"

"His . . . book." Bogdi had forgotten about this stupid lie. To cover his uncertainty, he altered his performance. "Look, you guys, like, came to me."

Feeling suddenly exposed, I coordinated a swift exit. Back in the hotel room, C and I played our roles perfectly.

Me: It's been a long day. Can we talk about this tomorrow?

C: Tomorrow? Before or after you've done cocaine with a drug dealer?

Me: [trying to joke] After?

C: [not amused] You would agree that I've been extremely sup-portive of you, even through some pretty dicey stuff.

Me: Of course.

C: You would agree that I've never held our relationship hos-tage to make you do something or not do something.

Me: I agree.

C: You would agree that I don't get upset easily, and that I don't sound the alarms for no reason.

Me: Yes.

C: Then I hope I've earned some credit in your eyes when it comes to giving me my way, in this particular situation.

Me: [silent, a coward]

C: I'm telling you: this might be a deal breaker.

Me: It's not like that. Bogdi has two Ph.D.s. I'm talking about trying his medicine just once. I might learn something.

C: Medicine. Really.

Me: Yes, really.

C: Do you understand what I'm telling you?

Me: Nothing bad will happen. I promise.

C: You're really going to do this? It's worth more to you than me?

Me: You'll see. I'll go, I'll come back, no problem. We'll enjoy the rest of the weekend.

C: [her heart breaking, you fucking idiot, you've finally done it] I'm going to bed.

Now it's time to lie down. Tomorrow is March 13: the day
Sam Tampari, the King of Idiots, does cocaine.

Good night.

March 15

April 1

Back in NY. It's late, or early. Four in the morning. C came home
yesterday and moved out. I haven't written since I left Romania.
No energy for it, and it's taken a while for the memories to crys-
tallize. Every day they grow sharper and more painful. It's as if
my life has been cut in half—one side of the fridge is stocked; the
other side, her side, is empty.

Here's what happened:

Slept in late on the thirteenth. Woke up on the floor. I showered and dressed, but C stayed in bed with her back to the room,
clearly awake but not moving. I didn't say anything when it was
time to go. Just left. Met S in the lobby. He looked like British
fucking royalty, Prince William on vacation. White slacks ironed
to a perfect sheen, tight blue polo shirt that hugged his strong
arms.

Outside: lovely. Like the day after a storm. The strike ended
overnight, a compromise reached, and suddenly there were too
many taxis to choose from. When S stood on the curb and signaled, two cabbies came at once, and I expected them to argue
for us. Instead it was all:

"You take them, Mihail!"

"They are all yours, Radu!"

To the point where I wondered if both of them might leave
without us. On the way, I asked S how he first met Bogdi. They
didn't seem to have much in common.

"Oh, that's a long story," S said, pretending he didn't want to tell it.

In the early 1990s, S was a student at the Imperial College London. The AIDS crisis dominated the news. In a press release, Freddie Mercury announced he had the disease and died twenty-four hours later. S studied HIV/AIDS during the day, held candlelight vigils all evening, and practiced safe sex at night with two students from his intramural racquetball club. When he was only nineteen, he published his first study: "Protective Role of Progesterone in HIV Vulnerability and Progression." He could diagram the structure of HIV by memory, the nucleocapsids arranged like question marks in a floral wreath of docking glycoproteins.

He graduated at the top of his class and moved to America for graduate school. That's where he met Bogdi—a doctoral student who seemed to be an expert on everything. Soon after S's arrival, they coauthored a short editorial in *Medical Hypotheses* in which they posited the need for drug therapies that could interfere with the interaction between HIV and C-C chemokine receptor type 5. Without much fanfare, they had predicted the CCR5 antagonists of the future, an achievement that went mostly unrecognized, except by an older, acclaimed molecular biologist who had spent the last several years exploring the relationship between levels of gene expression and aging. Joseph Radkin invited them to join his research team at the University of Oregon. Working for Radkin would mean S distancing himself from AIDS research, and his attachment to that project was serious. He'd seen his friends fall ill, grow paper-thin and paper-colored, including one of those racquetball boys, who had recently made headlines in England by filling an art gallery with time-stamped Polaroids of his own shrinking face.

"But Radkin had the money and the prestige," S told me with a heavy sigh. "It was a postdoc many of my classmates would have killed for. I told myself it was a stepping-stone, that in the long term my own research would benefit. That it was better to work within the system than outside it. Bogdi, well . . . he went another way."

Another way indeed. When we arrived at the warehouse,

Bogdi was there, and Livia and Gavril. The sofas were arranged more coherently, the floors swept of trash and bodies. The warehouse had skylight windows—had I not noticed them before, or were they covered?—and Bogdi sat in a spotlight of warm sun. Livia was awake. Her jean jacket had been replaced with a brown leather one, but the Reeboks were the same. Her pants had holes at the knees.

Bogdi asked after C, and when I said she wasn't coming, he clapped. "So can we stop pretending you're writing a fucking book?"

With a silent apology to C, I told him we could. We followed them to the other warehouse, the better warehouse. It was emptier of people than the day before—the running girl was gone—but the equipment was still there. Bogdi was all business: striding purposefully down the corridors, pausing to snag folders and printouts. This was a side of him we hadn't seen yesterday.

We reached a sort of conference room—as much of a conference room as I could have expected in the Immortalist Underground. There was a square table, a projector pointed at a blank wall, a large conference phone. But the strangeness of the place was not entirely absent. I'm not sure the phone was plugged into anything, and while half of the chairs were standard black rollers, the other half, amazingly, were beanbags.

Bogdi indicated for us to sit, gesturing at a chair and a beanbag as if he were a waiter offering us a table or booth. When we were seated, he nodded to Gavril, who pressed a series of buttons on a small silvery remote. The lights in the room dimmed, and the projector whirred into function.

An image appeared on the wall, a mammogram of a woman's breast. The calcifications and fibrous tissues speckled the image with white. Near the nipple was a bright, branching lesion, maybe 1 cm in width. Its irregular shape and architectural distortion suggested it was malignant—as did Bogdi's showing it to us. This woman had breast cancer.

"This is from a year ago," he explained. "But you saw her yesterday, on the treadmill."

"With the pink hair," I said.

Gavril pressed a button, and a second mammogram appeared alongside the first. The tumor was gone.

"We all know what we're seeing." Bogdi slid a folder across the table to me, and it was interesting that he did not have a second folder for S. It was only me he was trying to convince.

I opened the folder and spread the stack of papers in front of me. Like the mammograms, they were before-and-after, but these were tables and charts and tall lists of numbers. The data showed the results of an extensive series of blood tests, measuring the quantities of various cells in the running girl's blood. The first page compared the number of lymphocytes before and after one year of treatment. The second page, her monocytes; the third, her B cells; and it went on this way, page after page: T cells, NK cells, gamma globulins. These cells were further subdivided into categories—for B cells: CD45, CD19, $CD21^{low}$.

"Measurements of her immune system," I said to S, keeping him in the loop. "After treatment, she has one of the strongest I've ever seen."

"That's, like, the beauty of Dor." Bogdi's wide, gummy smile announced his pride. "Dor didn't kill the cancer. Her own immune system killed the cancer. We just gave it a little boost."

"A *big* boost," Gavril said, failing to grasp ironic understatement.

"And for what it's worth?" Bogdi continued. "She's also lost forty pounds and can run a five-minute mile."

"Okay," I said, "so how are you doing this?"

Gavril clicked again, and a digital line-drawing of a needle appeared on the screen. The needle was filled with colors in different amounts, with labels identifying each substance. It was a kind of pie chart—a needle chart—showing the composition of Dor. Except at the top of the image, it said, *PARTIAL List of Ingredients*, and then, in parentheses: *For Non-Members*.

Even in this incomplete format, the list of ingredients was long, complicated, and highly syllabic. Compared to my elixir, it was like looking at the ingredients of processed food versus organic. There was deoxycholic acid, ipilimumab, brentuximab vedotin, sipuleucel-T. There were items even I didn't recognize, some natural, some synthetic. Still, I got the gist: Dor was a cocktail of immunostimulants, designed to trigger the body's natural defense systems. To synthesize all of these things into a single intervention would require an incredible amount of expertise and an incredible amount of money.

"How many treatments of Dor did the running girl receive?" I asked.

Bogdi grunted like someone who has just eaten a large meal. "Many, many, many. Close to a million dollars' worth. This is one of the problems: to make it so a single dose will do."

"I don't understand," S said, speaking for the first time since the presentation began. "How does the cocaine factor in?"

Gavril clicked to an animated GIF of the human body, which cycled through that body's response to an injection of Dor. The cartoon figure lit up with bright reds and blues as it coursed through his veins.

"I don't need to tell you about cocaine's effect on the blood-brain barrier," Bogdi said, as the animation showed the BBB growing porous and thin as the cocaine entered the central nervous system. "We want the Dor hitting the brain like a high-speed train, and the cocaine clears the tracks."

As the drug circulated through the figure, the animation began to glow redder and redder: the body temperature was rising. "Another side effect of cocaine that we use to our advantage," Bogdi said. "What happens when the temperature in the body rises?"

"The immune system activates," I answered.

The blue blood of the figure began to pulse, faster and faster. "Cocaine also raises the heart rate," Bogdi said, "along with the blood pressure."

I could see it: the Dor was speeding through the circulatory system, unimpeded, screaming and shouting and waking up every immunoresponse in the body.

"To cure all sicknesses," Bogdi concluded, "we need all of the alarms sounding at once."

My mind signaled caution, but I felt the same sensation as when I attended my first meeting of the numismatists: *Finally, I have found my people.* I had more questions for Bogdi—thousands of them—but he held up a hand. "If you want to know more, you join us."

"So that means you *want* me to join you?"

Bogdi sat down. "Sadie has told me about your work. What you're doing with mercury is, like, cousins with our research, albeit much more barbaric."

"Different approaches to a similar problem," I said as diplomatically as I could.

"There's no shame in how far behind us you are." Bogdi indicated the expanse of the warehouse. "You don't have Livia."

From her beanbag, Livia made a jerk-off motion with her hand.

"I definitely don't have Livia."

"Of course, if you join us," Bogdi said, "you quit with the mercury and focus on Dor."

I could feel S's eyes on me. "Actually," I said, "I'm thinking of the two in combination. Dor could be a valuable appetizer, increasing the permeability—"

Bogdi cut me off with a laugh, loud and long. "No, no, no, no. No, no. Dor is not an *appetizer*. Dor is the whole meal, it is dessert, it is breakfast the next morning. It is your mama picking out your undies and your papa driving you to school."

"With respect," I said, "that's shortsighted. Your approach relies on the immune system being able to recognize threats, to identify targets. Not every disease makes itself visible." *What's wrong with me?*

"And mercury is the answer? That's, like, some medieval, flat-earth shit. Your elixir will create the healthiest, most vitamin-rich corpses in all the world."

"Do I look like a corpse to you?"

"You two are like long-lost brothers!" Gavril said, which he meant as a compliment but is easily one of the scariest things anyone has ever said to me.

The appeal to family seemed to have a mollifying effect on Bogdi. He lowered his voice. "Okay, maybe for now, we agree to disagree?"

"Let's say I do want to join. What's next?"

This time, Livia answered. She hopped up from her beanbag. "Next, we get *high*." She waved us on, already halfway out of the room.

"Wait. If it's so expensive, why spend a dose on us?"

"Ugh, bro." Bogdi drew out the words. He did not like being distrusted; he took it personally. This was a weakness, but one that made him more dangerous, not less. "Yes, we want something from you. You cracked the case. Can we show you our work now, please?"

Livia snapped her fingers. "It's Dor time, bitches!"

Back in the first warehouse, Gavril appeared with the Dor—no joke—on a silver platter. There was a needle for each of us. Bogdi tried to explain the sensations in store. It would "knock you right out," he said, "and when you wake up, you'll have so much energy you'll go around looking for heavy things to pick up." But then he gave me a hard look. "You have to be careful. Even in Dor, cocaine is still cocaine. Too much will kill you."

Somehow, I thought, he knows about my childhood overdose, maybe even my fall. He knows I live on the sill of the window, looking down.

"Ready?" Gavril asked.

I closed my eyes as Livia slapped my forearm. I felt S's hand on my shoulder, warm and damp. He was nervous, too. Livia flicked the needle and brought it to my skin. Pinch. Ouch. Hum.

"Prepare to get your bell rung," said Livia.

My bell rang. Next thing I knew I was lying on the couch with my feet in S's lap. He was staring up at the skylight. Bogdi and Livia were on the couch across from me. They were sitting like Catholic-school students: spines straight, hands folded in laps. Gavril was facedown on the floor, mumbling into the cement. Dark spots crowded the edge of my vision and occasionally launched themselves in front of me, as though my right eye and left eye were playing a spirited game of Pong.

S's head came forward. A lot of my images from that day are blurry, but this I remember: His mouth. His lips parted and dry.

I'll wet them for you, I wanted to tell him. *Bring them here and be mine.*

"Am I dreaming?" I asked.

"Dor is like a dream," Gavril mumbled into the floor. "It's something you can't explain."

"What is that word?" I asked. *"Dor?"*

"We told you," Gavril answered. "Impossible to translate."

"Try." My father was running laps through the warehouse, weaving in and out of the stacks. When I was a child, he would jog every morning, always the same route: the FDR from 120th to East 81st. He ran so slowly that people walking their dogs would pass him. I would say, "Don, what's the point of running if you're running slower than you walk?" And he would say, "Samuel, let me explain to you Dr. Robert Trivers's theory of self-deception."

Gavril push-upped to his knees and sat cross-legged with his back against Bogdi's couch. *"Dor,"* Gavril said. *"Dor, Dor, Dor.* It's a word you see in poetry and songs. It is to miss somebody, or to want something you can't have. It is desire and sadness. It is your heaviest pain." Gavril put his hands over his heart.

"Mm," said S, either moved or asleep.

Livia ran her toes through Gavril's hair. "Only romantics think Dor is some great mystery. It's very simple: Dor is when you regret not fucking someone when you had the chance. Which, thank you very much, is what most poems are about."

Gavril swatted her foot away. "You are an animal, really. There are monkeys with deeper thoughts. I sang a song about Dor at my mother's funeral."

"Okay, okay." Bogdi's impatience suggested he'd listened to this debate before.

Gavril stood and serenaded us with the song. By the time he reached the final verse, he was in tears. "'Mi-e dor de tine . . . [sniffle] . . . mamă.'"

For the next thirty to sixty seconds, all I could hear was *sssssssssss.* Like bacon sizzling. When the sound stopped, I was standing far from the couches, eyes closed, lifting a box of baby aspirin. I held it over my head like the Larry O'Brien Championship Trophy.

"I told you," I heard Bogdi say. "It makes you want to pick stuff up."

I opened my eyes. Livia was attached to Bogdi's neck like a lamprey. Her hands caressed his chest. He was having a conversation with S as if nothing were happening, but I could see his eyes go glassy. Bogdi said he was pursuing an elixir of life because God told him to, but really he was just in love, and that love came with a price: the dread of losing it.

"You need to tell me everything that's in here," I said.

I expected an immediate no, but Livia surprised me, saying, "That can be arranged."

"I'm pumped you like it," Bogdi repeated. "Because we have a request."

I saw S blink himself to alertness.

"We need to get more Dor to the States," Livia said. "The Underground is growing."

"I'll do it," said S immediately. "No need to involve him."

Livia shook her head. "American citizenship required."

"Plus you look like a terrorist, Sadie," Bogdi added. "No offense."

I was looking at my hands. I felt as if there were multiple versions of us—many Sadiqs, many Bogdis, a hundred Livias—having this conversation at once. I felt as if I were being pulled apart. "What would I have to do?"

"Very simple." Bogdi sat forward in his seat. "You give Livia a photocopy of your passport. She gives you a bag. You check the bag. That's it. You don't even need to pick it up at baggage claim."

"And then what?"

"And then you're one of us," Livia said.

S touched my hand. "If you're caught . . ."

"Never happen!" Bogdi protested. "No way."

Livia leaned her head on his shoulder. "If you want to work with us, that's what it takes."

So I agreed, and amazingly, that turned out to be the least interesting part of my trip. It went exactly as Bogdi described. I checked the bag, had anxious diarrhea the whole flight home, and then returned to my apartment as a member of the Immortalist Underground.

But let's go back:

S and I left the warehouse around midnight. It had rained while we were inside, and the streets were shiny. We leaned against each other and breathed deeply. Silver lindens shed pollen onto the road. Their leaves broadcast the sweet smell of honey and lime juice. S threw his arm around my shoulders. From up close I could see his bristly nose hairs, the imperfections in his skin. We had to walk to the subway.

"So what do you think?" S asked me. The streets had been busy when we arrived, filled with sidewalk vendors selling cotton candy and snow cones and multicolored shoelaces. It was quiet now.

"I don't know. I definitely feel something."

"Me, too."

We followed the stairs belowground, paid our fare, and waited for the train to arrive. This was the hard part—to sit with our feelings, to keep the flame of our happiness kindled. It's how all of my experiments go: I feel good, the way I've always wanted to feel, but then that goodness slips away like a tide going out. I can't hold on to it. And what's worse is that the loss I feel isn't something being taken from me; it's my brain *healing* itself. It's my body trying to *help*. I can't tell it, *No, don't you understand? By healing yourself, you're killing me.*

The train came, and S took my hand and led me inside. We sat in the rear of the car, and he leaned his head against the scratched plastic window. The intercom spoke to us in Romanian. Lights from the tunnel whizzed by.

"I feel like I could outrun this thing," he said. "Or pick it up like the Hulk."

"I'm not tired at all."

An image of C came into my mind. Her cute nose. Her round, pale eyes, blue and soft like shallow water. By the time the train arrived, S and I had been touching for as long as we'd ever touched. Our hands were entwined, sweaty and grimy from the stale underground air. When we emerged topside, it was as if a test had been passed. Heracles escaping from Acherusia.

We walked to the hotel but lingered in front of the doors. I could see the receptionist staring at us, unsure if we were guests.

I wished we had cigarettes or something to explain why we were just standing there, delaying the decision we were about to make. S stared at our feet, uncharacteristically nervous. "Do you want to come to my room?" he said at last.

My mouth went dry, and I said nothing. In my mind I was already in his room, but S took my silence as reluctance.

"It doesn't have to mean anything," he said. "I would never tell anyone."

"I know."

"We can tell her we slept at Bogdi's."

I didn't want to think about what I would tell C. I wavered.

"I'm sorry," he said. "It's just, I don't want you to be my Dor."

Two minutes later we were in his room. We rode the elevator, willing it to be faster, and when we reached our floor, crept as quietly as we could away from the room I shared with C and toward his. I held my breath as he swiped his card. Red light. Red light. He blew on the magnetic strip and tried once more. Green light. Inside, he offered me a drink from the minibar, which I declined, then he sat on the bed while I pretended to admire the view from his window. I closed the blinds and switched off the bedside light.

I sat next to him, and he found my face with his hands. He gathered my shirt and used it to guide me on top of him. I kissed and kissed and kissed him. He breathed heavily the way English people do, with a hint of something, a groan, as if the whole world were too hot for them. He took off my pants and somehow knew to take his own off for me. My fingers barely worked.

I started to turn him around, but he said, no, like this, and I felt his leg land on my shoulder. The hair on his calves tickled my cheek. When we started, in earnest, I didn't last long.

Afterward, lying next to me, he said, "I was telling the truth when I said this doesn't have to mean anything. But for the record, I'd like for it to mean something."

I rolled onto my side to see him better. "Doesn't my life bother you? What I'm planning with Bogdi?"

"It should, probably. No, it does."

I didn't know what to say, so I let him keep talking. I liked knowing this about him: he would always keep talking.

"I worry for you," he said. "But I think I can be okay with it. It's worth being okay with it if I can be with you."

The next morning, I woke up early so that I could sneak back into my room. S didn't stir. I opened the door to leave his room, and there was C, sitting on the floor in the hallway with her back against the wall. Crying.

"Oh."

"Asshole," she said through her tears. "Asshole, asshole, asshole."

I had no words. My vision pixilated. I sat next to her on the floor.

"Don't sit next to me," she said, but didn't move away. "And don't deny it. I've been sitting here all night, like one of those girls who does that."

"I'm so sorry."

"All I want to know is, how long? I've seen you two flirt, but, Jesus, everyone flirts with you."

I tried to take her hand, but she pulled it away. "It was just this once. I didn't mean for you to know." In spite of myself, I asked, "How *did* you know?"

"Are you joking? When you got off the elevator, you were *singing*."

I didn't remember this at all.

"Some Romanian song. I heard your voices and came to check on you. He was unlocking his door, and you were draped around him, kissing the back of his neck. So that's an image I have, now. Forever."

I blushed, ashamed, not just that she'd seen me but that I'd been so forward with S. In my clearly unreliable mind, I had been more reserved. But apparently I threw myself at him as if it were prom night.

She was waiting for me to say something, but I didn't know what to tell her, or what I even wanted. So I said, "I'm not writing a book." When she didn't respond, I said, "I haven't taken my antidepressants since the day I hurt you."

"The day you hurt me," she repeated quietly. "Which one do you mean?"

An hour later, the cab came and took her to the airport. I'll never see her again, probably, and I don't know what to think or feel. I am alone and on drugs. I have Dor. It must have been Gavril's song we were singing when C heard us. The funeral song. I've since looked up the lyrics. I miss my village, the song says. I miss my country. It's about someone who wants to go home.

Good night.

The Tourist

I sat across from Sadiq at Big Wharf Fish 'n' Chips, a seaside diner for tourists. Before he arrived, I tracked his flight from London, watched the little airplane avatar blip across blue ocean. It was Saturday. I'd spent the morning pacing my bedroom until I couldn't wait any longer and left for RJ's. In his car, I kept peering over the seat in case anyone was following us, kept checking the side mirror as if I were on the run from the law. Maybe I was. We still didn't know who had broken into Sammy's apartment and storage unit, and I carried my fear of this person like a collar around my neck. We arrived at the restaurant a full hour early, and as I walked to the entrance, alone, I half expected to find the door destroyed.

By the time Sadiq showed up, scanning the claw-foot tables with tired eyes, I'd already apologized to the waiter on ten separate occasions. My mood was penitential. When I saw Sadiq's body in the doorway, damming the light of the sun with his baggy T-shirt and duffel bag, straight from the airport, I almost slid under the table. This wasn't a name on a postcard, an S in a journal. This was Sadiq, Sadie, flesh and blood, the man Sammy loved long before he met me and who had no earthly reason to help me—but *must*.

"I saw your postcard," I told him as he sat and arranged his bag under the chair, saying whatever I could to fill the silence, which had settled over our table the moment he saw me wave to him and went slack-jawed—me, the one entrusted with Sammy's journals and research; me, the one entrusted with Sadiq's phone number; me, a fucking teenager. "From the Republic of Guyana."

"Well, it was nice of him to keep it. He sure as hell didn't respond."

Over the phone, I had told him that Sammy had died and that I, his best friend in Littlefield, was in possession of his research, his storage locker, and a cryptic note. My use of the phrase *best friend* should have given away my age. Just as I certainly looked young to him, he looked old to me—Sammy's journals never mentioned that Sadiq was ten years his senior. He was handsome, but the clean-shaven face described by Sammy was gone. His beard was heavy enough to make him look older, more foreign, more out of place in a small Maine town.

"When did you last see him?" I asked.

"Oh, not for years. I only had his address here because I sleuthed for it in a moment of weakness. After his betrayal, he went incognito."

He would use that word repeatedly throughout our conversation, and soon it became capitalized in my mind: Sammy's Betrayal. After Sammy dropped out of NYU, his journals became denser, slower reading, full of scientific theories and terms. I'd only read far enough to know that Sadiq and Sammy became a couple after the events of Romania. If a betrayal was coming, that was news to me. But Sadiq seemed to assume Sammy had *talked* about this betrayal, his mind so wracked with guilt he would confess his past sins. I didn't have the heart to tell Sadiq that Sammy had never talked about him, even when I pressed for details. "He's just a guy," Sammy would say, his voice going hollow. "An old colleague."

"I can't imagine him teaching high school," Sadiq said. "You were his star pupil, I take it?"

"I guess so." I had decided before Sadiq came that I would be honest—the kind of honesty, like a deathbed confession, that arrives only when one is truly desperate. "At least, that's how it started."

Sadiq stared. "It."

I didn't say anything. Outside, through the window, I watched a motorboat eddy in tight circles around the pier. Beyond the bay was marshland, and beyond that, the Atlantic.

Sadiq put his head in his hands. "Oh, Sam."

He was the first adult to know about our affair. Watching him, I was glad no one else knew. I was thankful, too, for RJ, who had never judged me, and who was, at that moment, waiting outside in the car.

"I'm sorry. It's just . . . you're how old?"

"Sixteen."

"Oh, Sam." Sadiq glanced nervously at the other tables, as though he'd just realized what an odd pairing we made. The restaurant had a thin lunchtime crowd—most of the tourists had left before September. "Well, I'm here." Sadiq steeled himself. "You better catch me up."

I filled him in on everything that had happened. Sadiq sipped his ice water through a straw, watching me with eyes that looked intermittently alert and jet-lagged, their brightness coming and going like a flashlight turned on and off. He hadn't been to the States in years. "I assumed I'd be tenured in an American Ivy by now. But after his Betrayal I ended up back home, with nothing. I teach at the only place that would have me: Online England University. Can you believe that name? It's like something from a spam e-mail."

The waiter delivered our food. The french fries were served in little replica lobster boats, their acrylic hulls emblazoned with the Big Wharf logo. Sadiq turned his gaze from me to the window. The noonday sun reflected off the water, which was more gray than blue, like sharkskin. Above our table, a decorative buoy was suspended in a fishing net. "We talked once about moving to a place like this. Somewhere on the water."

"So you were a couple, after Bucharest?" I knew the answer, but something told me to let Sadiq speak, not to overwhelm him with how many details of his life I'd learned from Sammy's journals.

"Not immediately." Sadiq leaned back in his chair and wiped

a bit of lobster roll from his beard. The cold mayonnaise stained the edges of his mustache. "He wouldn't return my e-mails when he first flew back to New York. He blamed me, along with himself. He could hold a grudge, as you know."

"Yeah," I said, even though I didn't.

"I called Sam when I arrived back in the States, but he wouldn't answer the phone. He'd changed his voice mail to nothing but fifteen seconds of John Bonham's drum solo from 'Moby Dick.' Zeppelin was my favorite band, so this had to be a message to me. He was saying, 'Enjoy this recording, because I'm never answering the phone.'"

"Did you want to be his boyfriend?"

My childish phrasing narrowed Sadiq's eyes. "Yes, I wanted to be his boyfriend. In October, the AGE held a conference in New York. I camped out in front of his apartment building. He had a racist doorman who wouldn't even let me wait on the steps. I sat on the curb. When Sam came back from wherever he'd been, he took one look at me and burst into tears. It confirmed the doorman's worst fears about me.

"The dishes in Sam's apartment were piled so high in the sink that later, when he was asleep, I just threw them out. He'd removed the furniture from his living room to make space for laboratory equipment. It's really just the smell I remember. Did you know you can predict the offensiveness of an odor using its molecular weight and electron density?"

I could practically smell my dad's breath. "Yeah."

"Well, let's just say Sam's apartment was very electron dense. Can I eat the last of your chips?"

I sailed my lobster boat across the table. My phone vibrated in the pocket of my corduroys—RJ texting to make sure I was okay—so I typed a quick *i'm fine.*

The waiter came with our check, which Sadiq paid absentmindedly with crisp American bills. I didn't say anything. We sat quietly, absorbing the clatter of knives and forks and stainless steel lobster pliers. Neither of us belonged there. We'd been brought together by Sammy, but even our conceptions of him were different; the holes in our hearts were different sizes, different shapes. An amputee and a widow have both lost something, but how much do they have to say to each other? It was a weird, sad scene—the two of us tourists in each other's life, in a restaurant for tourists.

Sadiq nodded, as though he'd decided on something. "I want to make it clear that I'm not promising anything. But tell me what you need."

"Why would you help me?" I didn't want to dissuade him, but I was too curious not to ask.

Sadiq looked at me as though the answer were obvious. "Because he asked me to."

A jolt ran through me—another secret of Sammy's, passing through my body. "When?"

"He called me, well, a week before he died. He said that if a friend of his contacted me, I should help that person. That I *had* to help."

I tried to hide how much this news hurt me. Everything that had happened—the package left late at night, the infuriatingly vague note—suggested *suddenness*. But if he'd called Sadiq, how long had he been planning this? My anger with Sammy made me resentful of Sadiq. "He asks you to help, so you fly from London? Just like that?"

Sadiq laughed. "Was anything with Sam 'just like that'? Of course I resisted. We hadn't spoken in years. He said it was important, that it was the last favor he'd ask of me. What could I do? I said okay, and he hung up."

I didn't know what to say. Sammy had enlisted help on my behalf, but I felt as if I'd been bartered for—a debt to be settled.

Sadiq leaned back in his seat. "Only now I see the trap he was setting. He's dead, and you're a child. So either I ignore his dying wish and read in the papers that you've killed someone, or I stay."

My phone buzzed with another text from RJ, and Sadiq glared, suspicious. "Who keeps pinging you?"

"Just my friend. He's waiting for me outside."

Sadiq froze. "He knows?"

"He's been helping me." I was scared Sadiq might leave, fly home, and never talk to me again.

Instead, he rubbed his full stomach and pushed back his chair from the table. "He's just waiting out there? Let's go get him, for God's sake. I might as well meet the whole crew."

Sadiq rapped his knuckles against the faux-mahogany nightstand of his hotel room. He did this, I would learn, when he was thinking. RJ stood with his hands in his pockets. The recipe book was open on the table.

"Can you get us the ingredients?" RJ asked.

"There's only one way to get the Dor, but I haven't spoken to Bogdi in years. I'll put out some feelers."

"What about the Entrée?" I asked.

Sadiq sat at the edge of the bed. He had two teenage boys in his motel room, and I could see, in his careful movements, his awareness of how it would look to an observer. "We still have enough of the mercury and *cupana*?"

I nodded.

"The *rossica* we can just buy online, but the rapamycin will be tricky."

"Which thing is the rapa—?" RJ asked.

"In the pill bottle," I reminded him.

"Write it down," RJ said. "I'll get it."

"How's that?" Sadiq asked, skeptical but already scribbling the information onto a Post-it.

RJ pocketed Sadiq's note. "My dad."

"Can he be trusted?"

I don't know what I would have said to that, but RJ didn't let me respond. "If I tell him I need something, he'll get it for me."

It was hard for me to imagine, this kind of trust. When I'd left for RJ's that morning, I'd given some excuse to Emmett I no longer remember, but I do remember he'd said, "If you don't want to hang out with me, I don't care," and I'd said, like a baby, "Fine!" When I approached RJ's house I could see, through the window, his family eating breakfast together. All of them were eating food that came out of one box or another: Pop-Tarts for RJ, cereal for Stephanie, instant oatmeal for his mother, a breakfast bar for his dad. They were all on their phones or their laptops, not really talking. Still, they were *together*.

As if he could sense me judging him from afar, my dad called, the number from St. Matthias appearing on my screen. I excused myself and stepped outside to the parking lot.

"Hi, Dad."

"Kiddo. What's the latest?" His voice sounded distant and hoarse. I imagined him in his room at St. Matthias, his fuscous skin turning the color of cigarette smoke in the dim light of the cabin.

"Just working on school stuff."

He laughed and coughed. "Every time you lie, an angel loses its wings."

"Okay. Thanks for calling."

"Wait," he said quickly, with enough distress in his voice that I removed my thumb from the END button. "When are you going to come visit again?"

"Did Dana tell you to ask that?"

He paused. Even if he wanted to, the Copper Code was making it hard for him to lie. "Well, actually she did."

I almost hung up again, but something kept me from it. If I could finish the elixir, could I convince my father to take it? Did he trust me enough, and love me enough, to accept my help?

"Dad? If at some point in the future I asked you to do something, but I couldn't explain why, but it was really important, would you do it?"

"Is this a riddle? Should I be asking for clues?"

"I just need to know."

"Is it bigger than a bread box?"

"Dad."

There was a moment of quiet as he considered what to say. "I think it's usually the person dying who gets to Make a Wish," he said finally. "But okay. Anything you ask me to do, I'll do it. But it can't involve murder. Or spiders."

"Thank you," I said, surprised by the relief I felt.

"Do I even want to know what's going on with you?"

"I'm fine."

My father gasped theatrically. "Did you hear that? An angel is screaming in pain!"

I hung up. As I did, I glimpsed, in a distant patch of trees, someone watching me. I squinted. Yes, someone was there. I told myself I was being paranoid—it is not inherently sinister to stand among trees—but as I started to move in that direction, the figure ducked, this motion was *clear*, and then bolted. I stood in the emptiness of the lot, much too far away to chase him. I looked back at the motel. My fear was a sickening weight in my stomach, but Sadiq's help, his presence in Littlefield, still felt tenuous. If I told him what I'd seen, would he stay?

"The next problem," Sadiq said as I returned to the room, "is this tribal medicine."

"What do we do?" I asked, trying to hide my unease.

Sadiq bit his lip. A shadow had passed over his face. "There's no way around it: we'll have to call Catherine."

I stared at him.

"Okay, here's what we'll do," he said. "Let's run some tests on the ingredients we have left—if we can understand the tribal medicine, perhaps we can re-create it ourselves. We have time to kill, anyway, while I track down Bogdi. Deal?"

"Deal," I said, and as if any of this made sense, we shook on it.

Over the next week, Sadiq and I studied the recipe book during every free moment I could muster. He kept the book when I would leave, and I didn't like this—surrendering custody. When I left for Dana's or, more rarely, for school, I was always gripped by the fear that when I returned, Sadiq and the recipe book would be gone. But no, he was always there, dependable and honest Sadiq, with the book spread to Sammy's final elixir.

ELIXIR OF LIFE #101
Yield: 1

INGREDIENTS
THE APPETIZER
1. Dor (1 sp)

THE ENTRÉE

1. Quicksilver (200 ml)
2. Tribal medicine (100 ml)
3. B. *rossica* (3 oz)
4. Rapamycin (15 mg)
5. P. *cupana* (100 mg)

PREPARATION

Inject Appetizer. Combine Entrée and drink.

HOW DID IT TASTE?

still not strong enough. what's missing?

"'What's missing?'" Sadiq read out loud. "He must have thought he was very close if he believed you'd be capable of finding the answer. No offense."

"It's okay. I thought that, too."

I'd been describing my experiments on, and necropsy of, Number 37. I finished the story with Number 37's brain, strangled by quicksilver—just as anyone could have predicted. Reading Sammy's account of his trip to Romania had given me a better understanding of Dor, but I still couldn't grasp its interaction with Sammy's Entrée. "I don't get it. Even if I'd given Dor to Number Thirty-Seven, how would that have stopped the mercury poisoning?"

"That's an important question," Sadiq said. "How does mercury accumulate in the brain?"

This, like so many of the questions Sammy once asked me, wasn't a question but a quiz. Luckily, I'd been studying. Remember: mercury crosses the blood-brain barrier by adopting a sort of disguise; it pretends to be an amino acid. But once inside the central nervous system, the chemical features of the brain fluids cause the mercury to demethylate—in other words, the brain dissolves the disguise. Mercury can sneak in, but it can't sneak out.

"Good," Sadiq said. "And you're correct that a boosted immune system alone couldn't solve this problem. How about cocaine? How does that interact with the blood-brain barrier?"

I was starting to get the picture. "It tears it apart."

"Mercury does damage to the barrier, too, but cocaine, especially when injected, is like a hole punch."

"So Sammy thought the Dor would allow the mercury to escape."

"Look." Sadiq turned the pages of the book. "After his early overdose, Sam used very low quantities of mercury. We can even call him cautious, if we overlook the absurdity of the whole endeavor. After he incorporated Dor into his regimen, you might expect him to use less of the mercury, since the cocaine was doing some of the same work. But no."

I followed his finger. "He almost doubled it."

"And in his final recipe, he doubled it *again*. Somehow, that brought him close enough that he thought a teenager and his old, fat ex could find the missing piece."

Sadiq and I smiled at each other, but these were sad smiles, of the left-behind.

The focus of our research was the CATHERINE vial, the tribal medicine. Sammy's journals said only that the medicine's centerpiece was the *Zamia nesophila*, a cycad grown in the Bocas del Toro region of Panama. But a search for the plant in the scientific literature revealed almost nothing, and the few articles we did find reported not on its medicinal value but its conservation—apparently, *Z. nesophila* was extremely rare.

If we scraped the walls of the vial, we had just enough to run a few tests. For this, we needed some of the equipment from Sammy's storage unit, which I retrieved with RJ's help and set up right in Sadiq's motel room. We hung the DO NOT DISTURB sign on the doorway, and considering all of the broken locks and the figure stalking me in the distance, this seemed a futile gesture, like strapping on a seat belt before driving off a cliff.

To start, we ran a sample of the tribal medicine through Sammy's mass spectrometer, which we had set up on the desk beneath the wall-mounted TV. The device looked like a large printer, with an ugly industrial casing that disguised the beauty and intricacy of the inner components: the filaments, magnets, and vacuum pumps, the repeller plates, focusing plates, and electron traps. A spectrometer is a precision instrument that demands a clear, contaminant-free environment, so having it set up in a cheap roadside motel was painful, almost sacrilegious—any good scientist would have seen it and winced.

A mass spectrometer destroys whatever you feed it: inside, the sample of tribal medicine was vaporized and blasted with electron beams. This allowed the machine to dismantle and sort the sample, the results of which it then reported to a computer—in this case, Sadiq's laptop. It didn't take long; we sat at the edge of the bed, watching the monitor grow fat with data.

Interpreting that data took longer, so we ordered a pizza, which we ate noisily, using tissues from the bathroom as napkins. Sammy had done well to bring me Sadiq, whose research on HIV/AIDS had prepared him to see something I would have missed. *Z. nesophila*, we discovered, had an amazing quirk: it was filled with progesterone, a hormone typically found only in humans.

"Protective Role of Progesterone in HIV Vulnerability and Progression" was the title of that first paper Sadiq had published when he was only nineteen. "Look." Sadiq pulled up the article on his browser. "Progesterone repairs the blood-brain barrier."

"But why would he want that? The whole point of the elixir is to break down the membrane." It would be like trying to light a fire and douse it at the same time.

We sat with this question. RJ texted to check on me, as he so frequently did, and Emmett wrote to see if I was up for a movie. I typed my responses wearily. I was sick of making excuses to Emmett and scared of disappointing RJ, but most of all, I was just tired.

One benefit of exhaustion is that when you're too burned-out to think, you have to trust your instincts. I hopped off the bed and scraped another dab of the tribal medicine from the vial, likely the last it would produce. In the bathroom, we had a microcentrifuge set up next to the hand towels, and I placed the sample in it, flipped on the machine. Sadiq watched this silently, understanding that if I was using the equipment, I must have had an idea. The centrifuge began to whir, spinning the sample like a high-speed merry-go-round, separating fluids of different densities.

This is what I was remembering, as it spun:

On Monday, July 12, I met Sammy in the chem lab for another round of testing, and I had no way of knowing that it was also his birthday. He arrived slightly late, wearing his usual clothes: twill pants, dark shoes, a button-down with the sleeves rolled up, a cardigan or sweater that he would remove, put on, remove, put on, somewhere between four and five hundred times a day.

It was injection time, so I lifted Number 50 from his cage and held him belly up in my palm. He squirmed against my hand, his big teeth showing. I poked him with the needle and scratched his ears until his eyes closed and he didn't want to bite me. He held his tail straight against my arm, and I could see the network of veins.

"All good?" Sammy called from the closet. The rules of the science fair said he had to be watching me anytime I interacted with the rats invasively, but Sammy wasn't big on rules. It was clear to me that he didn't care about the science fair at all. My love for him transformed this indifference into further evidence of his enlightenment. He didn't waste time worrying about science fairs, prizes, or publications; he was seeking a higher form of truth. Even as I saw my chances of winning slip away, I was never, not once, mad at him about it. I only loved him more.

As I carried Number 50 to the water maze, I could see small indications of how the *P. cupana* had strengthened his memory. Before we even reached the pool, his paws started air-swimming, anticipating the feel of the water. I indicated this to Sammy with a flick of my chin. Until then, Number 50 had shown improvements in escape latency, but these differences were small and nonlinear. His last escape latency, two days before, was thirty seconds.

I placed him in the water, and for a moment he paused, doing nothing. My pulse quickened. Was the stress too much for him? No, he was doing everything I hoped he would do: thinking, orienting, *remembering*. When he was ready, he spun his tiny paws and propelled himself directly to the hidden platform, where he sat, his breathing only slightly elevated, looking up at me, like, *What else you got?*

I smiled at Sammy. "Ten seconds."

I rescued Number 50, dried him with a hand towel, and placed him back in the cage, where he curled up immediately and slept with his face pressed into the warm haunches of Number 5.

Later, as we were testing Number 37, watching him swim his happy, high-speed, directionless laps, Sammy startled me by saying, "What sort of effect might *Annona muricata* have on our rats?"

Annona muricata was soursop, the key to my previous science-fair project. I was surprised he even knew the subject of that study—he'd never shown any interest in its specifics or, honestly, in anything about my life before I met him.

Seeing the surprise on my face, he said, "Yes, Conrad, I read your study."

My report on the study *would* have been online, deep in a PDF on the web page of that year's science fair listing all the losers. The idea of Sammy googling my name was thrilling, strange, and sort of erotic.

"Well"—I thought hard, not wanting to sound stupid—"it's a strong anti-inflammatory, so—"

"It's interesting how your study noted the slow-acting nature of the treatment. Are there any potential benefits to this?"

I didn't know if this was a question or a quiz. Either way, I didn't have the answer. Although soursop was the strongest-acting treatment I tested, it was also the slowest acting. When it comes to scarring, you typically want something quick. This was partially, probably, why I had lost.

"Well, give it some thought," Sammy said, when it was clear I was coming up empty. He gestured to our soggy Number 37. "Now rescue this poor bastard, and let's go home." It was the first time he'd done this—refer to *his* home as *our* home—and even if it was just a slip of the tongue, it left me lightheaded as we walked to the car.

•

It didn't take me long, once the centrifuge finished its work, to plate the newly separated samples and examine them under the microscope. My instincts had been right. The primary component of Catherine's tribal medicine was Z. *nesophila*, but in a close second place was soursop.

"Son of a bitch," Sadiq said, when I finished explaining. "We sorted ourselves right into a queue for him, didn't we?"

Sammy's problem was that he needed some way to repair the blood-brain barrier following its encounter with Dor and mercury, but he couldn't repair it too quickly, otherwise the Dor and the mercury wouldn't work. The Z. *nesophila* could play that restorative role, with soursop like an anchor, slowing it down. Some compounds adhere more slowly to the cells; it's the same reason methadone is used to treat heroin addiction, even though methadone is, itself, an addictive opioid: it's just slower.

When Sammy had asked me about my project and the soursop, I had told myself he was simply getting to know me and my work. I even took it as a sign, maybe, that he was falling deeper in love. But no. He had been steering me toward his elixir before I even knew it existed.

"Can I see his final journal entry?" Sadiq asked one evening during a snack break.

I wiped the cheddar cheese from a cracker off my lips. I'd offered Sadiq full access to the journals, but his relationship with them was so different from mine. I carried the hurt of being absent in those pages, of gaining no insight from them into Sammy's true feelings for me. Sadiq carried the *fear* of Sammy's true feelings, of discovering that their relationship, to Sammy, was a small and sunless thing. When Sadiq asked if he could see the final entry, what he meant was *Should* I see it? In some cases, I had to tell him no—you really shouldn't.

"Sure," I told him, in this case. "But it's nothing."

The final entry, and this seemed not an accident, was the only

one, across twenty-two journals, that Sammy did not begin with
the date.

> Frustrating day. Sometimes the world makes so little sense
> that it feels like a conspiracy to confuse me.
>   It is a *fact* that 92% of Daily Doubles are located in the
> bottom three rows. The top two rows almost never con-
> tain Daily Doubles; the very top row, less than 1% of the
> time. It is a *fact* that most Daily Doubles are located in
> the fourth row from the top (38%). In Double Jeopardy!,
> the two Daily Doubles are never located in the same cat-
> egory. And yet, contestants who locate the first Daily
> Double generally do two things next, in sequence: (1) They
> finish the category in which the Daily Double was located,
> and (2) They start at the top of a new category. I can only
> guess that most contestants employ a suboptimal strat-
> egy because they don't want to seem overly "cutthroat" in
> their methods of game-playing. But where does this come
> from, this inane desire to *compete* without appearing
> *competitive?*
>   My mom had an insult for basketball players whom
> she considered to be too friendly toward and too accom-
> modating of their opponents. She would say, "He is not a
> basketball player."
>   Good night.

We both felt it at once, Sadiq and I: the arrival of a crossroad.
We'd run the tests available to us, done as much research as we
could from a motel in southern Maine. I could see the gears of
the elixir in motion, could understand, at least, the *theories* behind
Sammy's approach. But Sammy was dead, and nothing we'd accomplished had helped us understand what was missing or why
we could expect the outcome for my father to be any different.
    Surrounded by Sammy's equipment, we had not much space
to maneuver. It felt as if we were in the command room of a sub-
marine, and I wondered if the feeling between us was not unlike

that shared by the men and women who lived on such vessels: kinship, but also the claustrophobia of that closeness.

"The good news," Sadiq said, "is that we understand the mechanisms of the tribal medicine. The bad news is that the *Z. nesophila* is a truly unique plant."

I knew what he meant by this: to continue, we had to call Catherine.

Part of me did want to give up. When I slept, which was rarely, I dreamed of Sammy's ravaged apartment, of a broken padlock, of a figure in the trees. I would dream of Sammy turning the same color as my father, turning *mean* like him—showing me I am not loved. Maybe I wasn't. Sammy never said those words. But he'd given me these things, trusted me with them. He'd sent me a message, in his own infuriating way. He believed I could save my father.

"Okay," I said. "We keep going."

"The other benefit of reaching out to Catherine," Sadiq said, as if trying to talk himself into it, "is that she may be able to provide more certainty on what exactly was in his system when he died."

I wasn't sure what he meant. Why would she know more than we did?

Sadiq rubbed his beard and looked at me with dull eyes. "Conrad, his parents are dead and he has no siblings. Where do you think his body went?"

"I don't know. An aunt or something?"

"No. Not an aunt or something. It went to his next of kin."

"But Catherine isn't family."

Sadiq's mouth opened and closed. "Oh. There may have been things he didn't tell you."

I waited.

"When I say next of kin, I don't mean Catherine. I mean her son. Sam's son."

The Blood-Brain Barrier
Is Discovered in Dogs

Freiburg, Germany, AD 1913

When Edward was a boy, his father said life is like the ripples of water from a cast stone skipped across the surface of a lake. There's no *end* to a ripple—not really. There's only an absorption, a *subsumption*, as the ripple rejoins the body of the whole. An individual life, his father said, only seems distinct from the sum total of all lives for the brief period in which it is visible.

That day by the lake, Edward had asked a simple question—"What is it like to die?"—but such had been his father's way, choosing to interrogate the premise instead of answering. At the age of fifty-one, Edward owes much to the influence of his father. He has enjoyed a long career in the sciences: degrees from London and Breslau, an honorary professorship at Freiburg, a position as head of surgery at Deaconess. Still, in the case of that one, particular question, Edward wishes his father had answered more clearly. *What is it like to die?* The question has resurfaced, and the memory with it, because Edward has cancer and will soon be dead.

You will soon be dead, he tells himself. *Edward will be dead.*

But for now he is short, thin, and huddled over the body of a dog he killed earlier. It is noon on a Wednesday—lunchtime, if Edward could bring himself to eat. But the cancer is in his stomach, a tumor the size of a lemon, and there's no room for food. At night, he dreams of *Apfelstrudel* and *Rumkugeln*, cooling in rows

near an open window, and of anchors settling to the bottom of
the ocean. During the day, he spends most of his time at the hospital, finishing as many projects as he can. His lab at Deaconess
is long and narrow, like a train car, and he thinks of it that way
now more than ever. He is only a passenger.

"Edward," says a woman's voice. "Are you awake?"

Edward stirs. "Yes. Were my eyes closed?"

"Briefly." She is Marie, his lab assistant. She has the pale hair
and wide blue eyes typical of the women of Germany, including
his own wife. Edward was born in South Africa, but Germany is
his home. He will be buried here.

"Could I trouble you for some coffee?" he asks her. Marie's
work is research, and it is not her job to fetch him drinks, but
she says yes, of course. She is half his age and very smart, and he
thinks of her like a daughter. He has already secured a position
for her after his death.

When Marie is gone, Edward returns his gaze to the dead dog,
a beagle, whose little brain is the size of a newborn's fist. Earlier,
Edward carved a window into the dog's skull, like the porthole
of a ship, so he can see the shoulderlike curve of the cerebral
cortex. Other than its size, the dog's brain is similar in shape to
that of a human's, and there is either comfort or unease in this
similarity, depending on your opinion of dogs. Edward maneu-
vers his scalpel into the porthole and uses the blade to carve a bi-
opsy sample from the brain. He balances the specimen on the flat
edge of the scalpel and rolls his chair to the microscope, where
he plates the sample and examines it. Through the lens of the
eyepiece, the cells of the brain are blue.

Edward returns to the beagle's body, holds it flat against
the lab table, and digs a larger scalpel into the back of its neck.
Under all that fur, a dog's skin is thin and dry, much less stubborn
against the blade than a man's. Edward cuts until he has exposed
the cervical vertebrae, and the cells of these, too, are blue under
the microscope—the color of Marie's eyes, and his wife's eyes,
and the sky in June.

He flips the body over and cuts into the stomach. There is the
squish and stench of a belly exposed, the warm, hot smell of

innards. He plunges his hand into this opening and removes the organs as he finds them, cutting deeper as he needs to, and places their samples under the lens. The liver: not blue. The kidneys: not blue. The heart: not blue. Nothing is blue but the brain and the spine, and this is good. The experiment was a success.

When you're dying, memories are like teenagers: they come and go as they please. So there was no reason, several months prior, for Edward to have remembered a minor experiment conducted by a former mentor at Breslau. In the experiment the mentor injected blue dye into the blood of a dog, killed the dog, and examined which organs had been stained. The liver: blue. The kidneys: blue. The heart: blue. He worked his way up the body, finding blue wherever blood travels, until he reached the central nervous system. The brain and spine were untouched.

Edward's mentor hypothesized that by the time it reached the cranium, the dye was too diluted to turn the brain blue. He further speculated that the chemical properties of the dye made it less adherent to the tissues of the brain and vertebrae; the blue coloring slid off those organs the way raindrops run off a pane of glass.

Only many years later, when he could pinpoint the month he would die, did Edward consider an alternative theory. In his own practice, he had noticed the difficulty faced by himself and his colleagues when trying to deliver drugs to the brain. What if, he wondered, some sort of protective membrane, an invisible barrier, separated the central nervous system from the rest of the body?

Once he had the question, finding the answer was simple. He reversed his mentor's process. Rather than injecting the dye into the bloodstream, he inserted it directly into the cerebrospinal fluid of the brain. If the dye still couldn't stain the brain cells, then the hypothesis about adherence to tissue was correct. If the dye stained the brain cells and every other organ, then the theory of the dye becoming too diluted proved true and his mentor was right. But if the dye stained *only* the brain and spinal column, then Edward could prove that the central nervous system shielded itself with an invisible fence heretofore unknown to science.

Edward's nose detects the bitter, burnt smell of coffee, and then Marie appears, holding two mugs. She joins him at the microscope, and he moves aside for her to see. She bends at the waist and presses one eye to the eyepiece, her mug of coffee still steaming in her hand. Edward sips his own, just enough to get the taste of it, to wet his tongue. His fingers around the handle are the fingers of a stranger, skeletal and sallow. He used to be a man of substance, but now, as Marie pulls back from the microscope and blows cool breath onto her coffee, he thinks she could breathe him right out of the room.

"Oh, Edward. You did it."

Who is he, and what has he done? What can possibly be accomplished in a life so short?

"It seems so."

She laughs at his modesty and places a hand on his shoulder. "You are one of a kind."

It is Edward's turn to laugh, and here is the joke: Edward's specialty is the removal of cancerous tumors. If Edward were some other person, some layperson—a bricklayer, perhaps, or a butcher—he would have gone to see his family doctor. He would have said, "Doctor, I have no appetite, and there is blood in my stool." And the doctor would have said, "I will make you an appointment with Dr. Edward Goldmann at Deaconess."

The joke isn't funny—not because it's morbid, but because it's much, much too familiar. A joke told every day loses its punch line, and the history of medicine is filled with jokes like these. For instance: the dye Edward used in his experiment is called trypan blue. It was developed by an American biologist who was searching for a drug to treat a particularly nasty brain parasite called African *Trypanosoma*. At the turn of the century, an epidemic of these little critters killed more than a quarter of a million people. They enter the brain through the bite of the tsetse fly, and once there, it's impossible to remove them. The American hoped the trypan could infiltrate the brain and wipe out the infection, allowing him to save countless lives. But the trypan didn't work. The drugs couldn't reach the parasites—they were somehow protected.

That *somehow* was the invisible barrier Edward just proved. In trying and failing to solve one problem, the American created the substance that would be used, in another decade, on another continent, to explain his failure.

It is only the beginning. Edward has proved the existence of the barrier, but what does the barrier *look* like and how does it work? He will never know. He will never get to see it. He is aware of a man, a fellow German, who has begun to experiment with focused electron beams, and these may allow for microscopic views of incredible detail, turning the invisible visible. Then, he supposes, the dye itself will become obsolete, replaced perhaps by radioactive atoms that operate with such precision that Edward's work will appear clumsy and crude. People will read the brain the way they read a city map, and these maps will prove his own knowledge laughably incomplete.

He can only glimpse the contours of these things; he can't even imagine them so much as he can imagine someone else imagining them. There's too much he doesn't know! What is the exact relationship between the brain tissue and the invisible barrier? When will cancer of the stomach be nonfatal? When will anyone be able to say, definitively, that Edward's work mattered?

For now, imagine the surface of a lake. Edward's father said life is like the ripples on the water—diffusing, suffusing. There is no end. Soon, Edward will see his father, and he'll tell him, *Father, you were wrong.* Life is not the ripples. Life is simply the throwing of the stone. By the time it touches water, you're gone.

17

My Husband's Radiation

A few weeks after my husband's diagnosis, I sat next to my mother-in-law in the waiting room at Northern Maine Medical Center, Department of Radiation Oncology. Her name was Kimberly, and she hated me. She felt that I had been selfish to bring my husband up here to "the arctic," as she called it, away from his family and his friends and the life he'd built in New York. She was right to think so. My husband lived a good life in the city. *We* lived a good life. At some point, and I don't know when, that goodness stopped working for me. My roommate in college had been an army brat, and I remember asking him, of the ten different places he'd lived, which one he considered home. He told me what his father had told him, that he wouldn't know until he was older, until wherever he was, whatever he was doing, one of those ten places called to him. One day I was lying in bed, awake, my future husband asleep beside me, and I knew I had to listen to the voice I'd been ignoring. I knew it was time to go home to Winterville.

I'd said to my husband, "I'm hoping that you'll come with me. Also that you'll marry me."

"You're proposing," he said, not a question.

"Yes."

"Winterville." He took out his phone. "Let me find it on a map."

Kimberly pulled her jacket tight around her little body. She was in her late seventies but had the body of a much older woman, the frailty. "It's too cold in here," she said. "It can't be good for him."

A nurse and her patient emerged from behind the heavy doors. I tried to picture my husband at the end of this long road, after radiation round one, radiation round two, and the inevitable surgery.

Kimberly's mind was in a similar place. "Will his hair fall out?"

"Yes and no." That was only the start of my answer, but she turned back to her reading, either satisfied or determined to remain unsatisfied.

After our first visit with the doctor, we entered my husband's treatment plan into his medical chip, and it responded with his odds of survival: 93 percent. Such a high number! We toasted to 93 percent. We joked about it ("There's a better chance *I'll* kill you"). We made love in the glow of it. The number was so high it seemed almost vulgar. Some people in the world were truly suffering, and here we were, worrying ourselves over 93 percent. Then we woke up one morning, scanned the chip as usual, and the odds of survival were 92.5 percent.

We called our doctor in a panic and asked him what had changed.

"Nothing's changed," he said. "Time is passing."

The thought of that morning upset me. I turned to Kimberly. "He's going to be fine." I hoped that if I gave her some comfort, she might respond with some for me. What better opportunity for us to bond, at last, than this? But I was wrong to think Kimberly's heart could be thawed. She was a sheet of ice, and behind that was another sheet of ice, and behind that, another. "He's going to be fine," I said again, into the emptiness of the waiting room.

Kimberly looked at me sideways. "God willing. My doctor said he's never heard of your doctor."

I studied the etched lettering on the door by the reception desk: ONCOLOGY. From the Greek *onkos*, for "mass," the Latin *onco-*, for "tumor." The study of. I allowed myself a moment of anger at Kimberly's doctor, who would feed her neuroses and give her ammunition against me. But most likely she had tricked him into it, asked him a seemingly harmless, offhand question, "Do you know Dr. So-and-So?" And he'd answered honestly, no, never heard of him.

The doors opened, and they rolled my husband into the room. They had told him to dress comfortably, so he'd worn sweatpants, a flannel shirt. He looked like a lumberjack after a bad fall. I went to him and touched his face, which was cool, clammy. He gazed up dreamily, happy to see me but not quite himself. Kimberly nudged me aside and kissed him on the cheek.

My husband touched the thick spokes of the wheelchair. "I feel like Bruce Banner."

"Who's that?" Kimberly asked, annoyed, as though Bruce Banner were a friend of mine who, like my husband, I had lured to northern Maine and deliberately given brain cancer.

"A physicist," I said.

I let Kimberly push him through the doors while I ran ahead to get the car. When I pulled up, my husband stood and waved us off, but we helped him into the passenger seat anyway. As I drove, I put my hand in his lap, and he put his hand over mine. Then Kimberly leaned forward from the backseat and put her hand over his, as if we were in the huddle, moments before the big game.

"Let's get you home fast," Kimberly said, and her message to me was clear: *Step on it, sister.*

So I stepped on it. We sped like teenagers through Wallagrass and along Eagle Lake.

"Which direction are we traveling?" Kimberly asked.

"South," I answered.

"Hm." Her tone was skeptical, as if to say, *You're telling me you can go farther north than Winterville?*

My husband was sleepy when we came home, so I put him to bed and lay next to him, staring at the back of his head.

Four hours later he rolled over. "Ugh. I can't wake up."

At first I smiled, relieved. It was a familiar line: "I can't wake up." He said it practically every morning. I always laughed to myself because even as he said it, he was checking his e-mail, sending text messages, planning his day. I started to ask him how he was feeling, but when I looked back down at him, he was fast asleep, his mouth open. He really couldn't wake up. I put my face close to his face, felt the reassuring puff of breath on my lips. I watched him sleep and wondered if our doctor's prophecy was true—if somehow, this quickly, my husband's eyelids had already stopped working.

18

The Rapamycin Trials; or, Sammy's Betrayal

Sammy and Sadiq, kissing in a tree.

It was late fall 2008, in Puna'auia, Tahiti. Sammy and Sadiq lay in bed in their tree-house cabana, watching the sun rise. Big-bellied moths fluttered against the mosquito net, their wings shiny and damp from the sea air. Sammy and Sadiq had been a couple for five years, give or take. They had forged a severe, committed, battle-tested love. They had survived Bucharest and breakups and Bogdi, with whom Sammy was now well and truly mixed up. They had the kind of love that could arrive at a tree house and see the toilet, which sat in the middle of the bedroom, with no walls around it, and say, "Well, who needs secrets?"

They weren't perfect. If Sadiq was being honest, their relationship could, at times, seem so dreadfully *serious*. He considered himself a funny person, so why, when he made the joke about the chemist who had to quit school (he was out of his element), did Sammy rub his eyes and stare into the middle distance? It was *supposed* to be stupid, Sadiq wanted to say. That's the joke! And if Sammy was being honest, he could have used an extra five to six hours of alone time per week, just to decompress. Sadiq was not quiet, and sometimes Sammy dreamed of earplugs. Plus, and he wasn't sure when or how this had happened, but Sadiq had become kind of *religious*.

Still, if you saw them there, shirtless in the humidity, you could mistake them for perfection. Even Sadiq's mother, who had accepted Sadiq's sexuality the way one accepts a cancer diagnosis, displayed a picture of the couple in a prominent position on her mantel and once, for reasons unclear, e-mailed Sadiq a photograph of herself posing *with* the picture. There was Sammy, obsessive and depressive, always ready to retreat inside himself, and there was Sadiq, warmhearted and expansive, like a planet, using his gravity to pull Sammy back out.

"I should get up," Sadiq said, stretching. "I have to meet Radkin in half an hour."

"Same. Bogdi."

Normally this was a place for beach bodies, but that year, Tahiti was filled with scientists. You could walk the beach and see nothing but middle-aged researchers, their faces painted white with sunscreen, dressed in a uniform of khaki shorts and sandals with socks. Earlier that year, a group of biologists at the University of Wisconsin had published a groundbreaking study in *Nature*. Their research showed that rapamycin, a macrolide typically used to prevent transplant patients from rejecting their new organs, slowed aging in a large sample of mice. When treated with the drug, the mice lived as much as 38 percent longer. For the first time in history a pharmacological treatment had extended the maximum life span of a mammal. The study would have made waves in any scenario, but rapamycin had a uniquely alluring mythology: it was first discovered, forty years prior, in the soil of Rapa Nui, aka Easter Island.

Sammy had begun to experiment with the drug in his elixir. An enzyme in the body known as a kinase acts as a sort of negotiator: it mediates the transfer of a hostage—a phosphate group—from a high-energy molecule to a substrate. One of these kinases, mTOR, mediates growth and helps the body navigate changes in nutrients and stress. For this reason, mTOR is essential to a young, growing body—it helps turn children into adults. But even after the body reaches adulthood, mTOR just keeps working, and people keep aging. If Sammy could capitalize on rapamycin's ability to inhibit mTOR, it would help make his elixir stronger and longer lasting.

Soon after the article appeared, the science community

descended on Rapa Nui. There were medical researchers and biologists, such as Sadiq and Radkin, who hoped to study the descendants of the Rapa Nui people, some of whom still lived there, while others had moved to Chile or Tahiti. Some of these communities had been claiming for decades to have members as old as 140. There were fringe groups, such as the Immortalist Underground, and there were all manner of businessmen and entrepreneurs, including the owner of an all-natural-energy-drink company, who recognized a moneymaking opportunity when they saw one. There were amateur scientists and detectives—this, perhaps, being the largest group—who had always wanted to go to Easter Island, it seemed like a cool place, and what better time than now?

Sadiq stood to pee. He could see the waves crashing outside and then, a second later, hear the sound of them.

"Why do you stand to the side of the toilet?" Sammy asked. "That's so weird."

Sadiq flushed. "Our flat growing up had a very narrow bathroom. Eventually we moved to a bigger place, but the habit stuck."

"This is illuminating. You do this at home?"

"I suppose."

Sammy rolled out of bed and beat Sadiq to the small kitchen sink, the only place to brush their teeth. They didn't have a shower, but it was too hot to matter. The minute Sammy dressed he would start to sweat through his clothes. From the sink, he could see the line of tree houses stretched along the coast. In one of those, Bogdi and Livia were likely still asleep.

Sammy spit and rinsed. Sadiq took his place, already dressed in his khaki shorts and wrinkled, collared shirt. In the sunlight, Sadiq's big shoulders seemed impossibly broad; at his neck, his skin was so smooth Sammy wanted to tackle him then and there. Instead, Sammy put on his jeans and the T-shirt Sadiq had bought him when they first moved to Houston. It had a picture of a waffle in the shape of Texas, and on the back it said TEXAS BREAKFAST.

Sadiq turned and frowned at him. "You should really wear shorts."

"You didn't pack me any shorts."

"That's because you don't own any."

Sammy tied his sneakers, and Sadiq watched him with the same ache in his stomach he always felt when Sam went somewhere without him. Even though Sadiq would never say this to Sam—it would be cruel and hypocritical—Sadiq always worried that what had happened to Catherine might someday happen to him. She let Sam out of her sight, and Sadiq had taken him.

"Be safe today," Sadiq said. *Please, God, take care of him.*

"No worries," Sam said, and was gone.

Sammy walked the beach toward Bogdi and Livia's. He didn't look forward to seeing them. He preferred them in Romania, himself in Houston, with the Atlantic between them. Even worse, they'd arrived in Tahiti with a Celebrity Client, who referred to Sammy, always and without exception, as "Samster," or "the Samster."

The sun was fully up and cooking him. He walked near the water, where the ocean cooled the sand. Some dorky children of scientists were trying to skimboard, unsuccessfully, in the shallow foam. They were sunburned and bruised. This reminded him of Catherine, who never understood that the skin needs thirty minutes to properly absorb the lotion. And if they were somewhere with mosquitoes, he would say, "Are you using bug spray? If you are, you should apply a sunscreen that's at least fifteen SPF stronger than normal." And she would look at him as if he were very, very far away and say, "I love you, but maybe it's time you returned to your home planet."

Thinking of this made him wonder, as he often did, how Catherine was doing, and where she was. When he first returned from Bucharest, she had already flown home to North Carolina. They talked every day on the phone, sometimes for so long his voice would grow hoarse, and she would hear this change and think he was angry, when he was just tired. She made three demands if he wanted to be with her: no more Sadiq, no more Bogdi, no more Dor.

A secret: it wasn't Sadiq, but Bogdi, that Sammy wouldn't give up.

He knew he'd lost Catherine forever when she returned to New York but still wouldn't see him. She wanted only to stay on the phone and narrate her disappointment. But after nearly a month of this, he'd begun to wonder if her sole objective was to punish him for as long as he would take it. It's possible her insults were meant to soften him, like the bludgeoning action of a meat tenderizer, until he agreed to her demands. But all they did was harden him against her, until his love for her was like a bullet, small and painful, in his heart. When you're shot and bleeding, there's only one thing to do: take the bullet out.

So when she said she was coming to move the last of her stuff out of his apartment, he left her a goodbye note—as nice as he could possibly muster—and hid on the roof until he saw the moving van drive away. When he climbed back down the fire escape, he was unprepared for how different the apartment looked. It was like a shadowy version of its old self; everything appeared suddenly flat. One morning, he woke up and could see his own body plummeting by the window. He blinked away this image, but it kept coming, again and again: just a flash of himself, falling to his death from the roof. He could see it so clearly (and hear the impact it made, like a sopping-wet towel dropped into an empty tub) that he climbed back onto the roof to re-create it. As he stood on the lip of his building and looked down at the street below—plenty Sammies high enough to kill him—a woman saw him from the sidewalk and screamed. She pointed at him until several other people joined her. Humiliated, Sammy ran out of view, down the stairs, and back into bed. He found his phone and considered calling for help, but when he turned it on, the home screen reported fifteen missed calls from Catherine, and fifteen voice mails. He deleted them.

One afternoon, he dragged himself out of bed to buy coffee filters, and when he returned, there was Sadiq on the sidewalk. It was as if the sun had come out. Sammy cried, and some amount of time passed, and they made love again. Radkin received a job offer at Rice University, and Sadiq asked Sammy to move. To Houston. In *Texas*.

"Fuck it," Sammy said. "Maybe that's just what I need."

Over the sound of the ocean, he heard someone calling his name, or a version of his name. "Samster! Ahoy!"

Celebrity Client was reclining on the ramp to Bogdi and Livia's tree house. He claimed to be twenty-eight years old—same as Sammy—but Sammy wasn't sure he believed him. His sunglasses and vacation beard covered his tan, tight skin, which was swollen around the eyes from Botox injections. He waved at Sammy and smiled, and his skin pulled tight against his skull.

"Are they in there?" Sammy asked.

Celebrity Client shrugged. "I knocked twenty minutes ago. I'm gonna peace the fuck out of here if they don't show up soon."

Sammy climbed the ramp and hammered the door with his fist. "Open up! Police!"

"That's not funny!" came the immediate reply.

Behind Sammy, Celebrity Client groaned. "They were in there the whole time?"

The door opened and Bogdi appeared, dressed in only a towel. He grimaced at them. "I love both of you very much, but it's, like, seven in the morning."

"It's noon," Sammy said.

"Past noon," said Celebrity Client.

Bogdi rolled his eyes. "Okay, so you're both on time."

Sadiq took a cab to the hotel, where he would meet Radkin as well as the AGE's special guest: Bucky Baker, Jr., an oil magnate and chairman of the board of trustees at Rice University. It would be a long day for Sadiq, trying to impress them both. It's not that he didn't like Bucky, who often found ways to surprise him—your stereotypical oilman in some ways but not in others. He had a gay daughter, for instance, and his acceptance of her had softened his cold, conservative heart. The way he said *LGBT* made Sadiq smile, every letter emphasized so distinctly, so as not to forget one. It reminded him of Keanu Reeves in his favorite American movie: "I am an F-B-I agent!" Sadiq's favorite thing about Americans was how they never shied from putting two completely random ideas together. Surfer? Bank robber? Yes, okay. In the end, Keanu throws his badge into the ocean.

Sadiq, too, sometimes thought about quitting. The move to Rice had come with better pay, but also an intense, unyielding pressure. Bucky had lobbied the university to make Radkin a godfather offer. The funding was insane; the facilities, brand-new. Before the move, Radkin had been supportive of Sadiq's efforts to devote some of his research to HIV/AIDS, but after, Radkin said, "I need you totally with me."

Plus Sadiq had to convince Sam to move to Texas, and, holy hell, could he be stubborn. Once, when Sadiq asked him to use soy milk in his coffee, just to *try* it, he had said, "I'd rather die." Sadiq's heart had just about stopped. Did Sam mean it? With Sam, you never knew. Being with him was like that feeling you get when you see someone standing near the edge of a cliff. It's a kind of vertigo via empathy—a feeling that *you* are falling, because *he* might. Do you rush forward and pull him away from the edge? By moving so suddenly, you risk startling him, and you will see the surprise in his face as he plummets. Or, worse, by approaching him you force him into a decision: now or never. If he jumps, you will blame yourself: if only you could have lived with the vertigo, the constant fear, then he would still be alive.

In the end, Sam agreed so quickly that Sadiq became suspicious. He even began to search the internet for information about Catherine, whom Sadiq hadn't seen since Romania. He wasn't sure what he was looking for, exactly. He hoped to see her married, maybe, or living somewhere far away, such as Siberia. The last time he looked, he found her working for a company that made all-natural energy drinks. Her name appeared not in academic papers, as he'd imagined, but in press releases and corporate profiles. She had become, he realized with a laugh, filthy stinking rich. She was not married, but she did have a son. Sadiq began to do the math, calculating the boy's age against when Catherine last saw Sam, but Sadiq did not like where this equation was taking him, so he put it out of his mind without ever solving for x. If the boy had anything to do with Sam, Catherine would have said so.

Sadiq tipped the cabdriver and walked across the courtyard

to the hotel. The sun was high and hot, the color of orange sherbet. Radkin and Bucky were waiting for him in the lobby. Bucky was wearing a baseball cap with the logo of the Houston Texans and a tight black T-shirt that showed, at the biceps, a hint of his old navy tattoos.

"Sadiq-o-saurus Rex!" said Bucky, rising. "We were just talking about you."

"If you were wondering if I'll accept a pay raise, the answer is yes."

"Ha ha," said Bucky. "It's good to laugh. No one in this place has a sense of humor."

Sadiq wondered what awful things Bucky had been saying to the hotel staff.

"We're meeting Lorenzo in an hour," Radkin said, his voice cool. Sometimes when he spoke, Sadiq imagined his words coming out of an air conditioner.

Lorenzo was a descendant of the Rapa Nui who lived with his grandmother in Māhina, on Tahiti's northern side. The grandmother, Lorenzo claimed, was 132 years old. She was also dying, and the point of today's visit was twofold: (1) secure the rights to her autopsy before someone else did, and (2) document Lorenzo's preparation of the rapamycin tincture his grandmother credited for her long life. Radkin had been studying the drug, tangentially, since the late 1990s, when one of the supercentenarians he'd autopsied had a rapamycin-coated coronary stent, and whose tissues, in the area of the stent, showed surprising vitality. Over the next decade, Radkin had made occasional, brief mention of the drug in his work, suggesting it might have benefits as an antiaging therapy or as a treatment for autoimmune disease.

This last point had attracted the attention of Bucky Baker, Jr., whose gay daughter had adopted a son with a rare autoimmune disease known as Canale-Smith syndrome. In a few scattered case reports, drug therapies using rapamycin had shown some progress in treating the disease. But the research never went anywhere. Pharmaceutical companies weren't going to spend billions of dollars to develop medicine for a disease that only affects a few hundred patients worldwide. There is a name for treatments that go unexplored due to a lack of corporate interest: orphan drugs.

So the AGE came to Houston with a clear understanding: they would continue to pursue antiaging therapies, but they would also devote some of their energies to rapamycin and Canale-Smith. Sadiq had not participated in any of the rapamycin trials—Radkin said he wanted Sadiq focused on their "real work"—but Radkin's team reported promising results with the drug, and Bucky was happy. And then those twats at the University of Wisconsin published their study in *Nature*.

When Bucky sent Radkin and Sadiq an e-mail with the *Nature* article attached (as if they weren't aware of it already), his question was obvious: Why, if I'm donating millions of dollars to Rice University, is a research team at a school that *isn't* Rice University getting the scoop on rapamycin? His e-mail didn't actually say any of that, of course. It said only, *Interesting.* —BB Jr. But when Radkin decided to go to Rapa Nui, and Bucky invited himself along, it didn't take a mind reader to know that he was checking on his investment.

"We should go," Radkin said to Bucky. "Sadiq thinks we're getting the first crack at Lorenzo, but who knows what the Chile people have been up to."

Two airports in the world offered flights to Rapa Nui—one in Tahiti, to the west, one in Chile, to the east. Most of the scientists stayed in one of those two countries. There was no real meaning to it. But still, it was hard, in a juvenile way, not to think of the two groups as opposing teams in a contest. There was the Tahiti side, and there was the Chile side, and only one could win.

Catherine arrived in Chile with her boss, an entrepreneur with the temperament of a five-year-old, and Theo Charles Knoll, her actual five-year-old. The entrepreneur, Keenan DeCosta, owned a minor league baseball team, a health spa chain, and the company Catherine worked for, HeyO DayO, a line of all-natural energy drinks.

"It's not an *energy* drink," Keenan said to the cabdriver, who hadn't asked and barely spoke English. "It's a *nutritional* drink."

"Keenan, give it a rest," Catherine said. "Theo Charles, don't unbuckle your seat belt."

"But!" they whined.

"Enough." Catherine turned in her seat and watched as non-native bottle palms whipped by the window, their long leaves curved and bushy like an arched eyebrow. Keenan had hired her straight out of graduate school, which she had stretched to nine full years. She kept waiting for the academic job market to improve, but it never did, and least of all for anthropology. When Catherine searched the job listings, her queries returned either no results or visiting positions at schools she'd never heard of and which sounded, frankly, made up: Southwestern Alabama College of the Environment, Goblintown Community College. She could adjunct at NYU for $6,000 per semester. That might just be enough, she explained to her cooing, oblivious toddler, to pay for their bankruptcy attorney. She'd never been good with money, she would admit that, but the really hard part, the thing that made her skin feel raw if she forced herself to think about it, was that Sam had always *encouraged* her to be bad with money. "Just buy it," he would say. "I'll take care of you."

When he proposed—something she'd never pressured him to do—it simply stopped occurring to her that the future might be something she'd face alone.

And then he had sex with a man and became a cocaine smuggler.

At least it was an unbeatable breakup story. She'd be the envy of all her girlfriends, if she had time for girlfriends, which she didn't. All she'd needed to forgive him was a promise: No more Sadiq, no more Bogdi, no more Dor. It didn't seem like a lot to ask, and Sam agreed so quickly to cut Sadiq from his life that she felt wounded on Sadiq's behalf. But even though Sam claimed to love her, too, he wouldn't give up Bogdi and the Underground.

When she realized she was pregnant, that the knot in her stomach wasn't grief but a baby, she didn't tell him. Not right away. She made a temporary arrangement with herself. She needed to know what *she* wanted first. When she decided to keep the baby, she still didn't tell him because, well, they spent all their time arguing. Soon she would have to move her stuff out of his apartment, and that would be a better time. She would tell him in person. She nursed the obvious fantasy: she would tell him, and he would beg her to stay.

Instead, when she showed up with the moving van, Sam was not there. She called him three times before letting herself in. She found a note from him on the counter, saying goodbye. It was one sentence long.

So she took her stuff and her embryo and moved into a new apartment she shared with two master's students from her department. Her roommates were both straight out of college. She took energy from their youthful, stress-free happiness, and they seemed to appreciate her presence as a cautionary, worst-case scenario. She called Sam every day, and every day his phone went straight to voice mail.

At seventeen weeks, when the baby was four inches long, she gave up on calling and wrote him an e-mail explaining the whole situation. She attached a picture of the first ultrasound. Five seconds later, her in-box dinged: message returned undelivered. Sam had either deleted his e-mail account or blocked her from reaching him. At thirty weeks, when she was well and truly fat, she decided to go see him. She arrived at his building and was forced to wait in humiliated silence as the doorman tried to recognize her. When he did, he said, "Sorry, sweetie, Mr. Sam moved weeks ago." She asked for a forwarding address, and the doorman went to get the super, who came out in his bathrobe.

"Do you know where he went?" the super asked *her*. "He owes me money."

"That makes two of us," Catherine said, and left.

So that was that. She was a single mother, as her own mom had been. Her mother said she should hire a private investigator to track Sam down, sue him for child support. She was obviously within her rights to do so. But it hurt too much to think about, how completely he'd vanished. Did she even want him in her baby's life?

She took this question with her into the hospital, where she squeezed her mother's hand and delivered a giant, screaming baby, who arrived facedown and with his arms above his head, as if he were diving out of the womb. She named him Theo Charles, after her grandfather. He was a smart, sunny, unpredictable child: crawled late, talked early, could walk backward at fourteen months but wouldn't try stairs, even with help, until twenty. When he turned two, and her job search was at its most hopeless, she took him for his first trip home to North Carolina. He slept the whole flight, so Catherine was in a good mood as they deplaned and rode the escalator down to arrivals. Her mother, waiting for them at the bottom, quickly spoiled it.

"Jesus H. Christ," her mom said into Catherine's ear, after hugging Theo hello. "He looks *just* like Sam."

Yes, he was Sam's son: blond hair, slanted smile, long, womanly eyelashes offset by a jaw growing in strong and square. He sometimes reminded her of photographs she'd seen of old Russian generals—but, like, a *nice* Russian general. The Russian general who says, "Comrades, we will catch more flies with honey."

She spent the rest of their visit anxious. Her mother took them to the Blue Ridge Mountains, to a place where the ground was soft like mud but also somehow dry. Catherine watched Theo face-plant onto the spongy surface and come up laughing, but she couldn't laugh with him. Her mind was with Sam. Yes, she'd tried to reach him. But whenever Theo started to ask about his father, could she look him in the eye and say she'd tried her *very best* to find him?

So she and her mother searched the internet for a private investigator. Catherine imagined a man in a trench coat snapping pictures with a huge telephoto lens, but the PI—who looked like a dentist, or a vice principal—only needed thirty minutes to find Sam through the computer. Sam lived in Houston.

"Houston?" Catherine repeated.

The man nodded. "It's in Texas."

She booked her flight and left Theo in North Carolina. She didn't know what she would find or even what she was planning to say. *You have a son; want to meet him? You have a son; you can write to him, if you're clean? You have a son; go fuck yourself?*

In Houston, she followed the emotionless instructions of her rental car's GPS. The satellite street view of Sam's address showed a large, Spanish-style building offset from the road. She had to admit that it looked nice, so she was prepared for the possibility that Sam was doing better than she'd imagined.

She was not prepared for what she saw when she pulled to the side of the road across from his mailbox: Sam drinking a cocktail on the porch, and next to him, Sadiq. They lived together. This was their home. Sam leaned back and draped a leg over Sadiq's knee, and Sadiq pretended to eat it like a baby back rib. They clinked glasses and drank. Sam looked thin and slightly translucent; Sadiq looked fat and happy, like a squirrel in the suburbs. She dreamed back to the night of their drug-induced hookup, the way she crumpled in the hallway and forced herself to listen to them—first to the sounds of Sam coming, and then to the louder sounds of Sadiq. It was the worst night of her life, but she had never considered, not once, that the two of them would have a real relationship. Sam had promised her: no more Sadiq. These two idiots had betrayed her love and her friendship, fine, but they weren't supposed to build a life together.

Catherine opened the car door and stepped out. Her legs were weak, as though she were returning from space. On the porch, Sam stood and shielded his eyes from the sun. Was he looking at her? Did he recognize her so soon? No, he hadn't—he was watching as a postal van rumbled down the road and turned into his gravel driveway. The driver had a package for them, and Sam stepped off the porch to retrieve it.

Catherine began to cross the street. It was good if Sam had his life together. It was a good thing. She imagined introducing Theo to "Uncle Sadiq," and then she started to laugh, like a crazy woman, in the middle of the road. She stepped onto the sidewalk and was almost to their driveway—almost past the point of no return—when Sam tore open the packaging to reveal a narrow blue box. Catherine froze in place with a suddenness that surprised even her. Why was she having déjà vu? About a *box*?

The answer came from the same wounded place in her memory where the image of Sam kissing the back of Sadiq's neck still resided. The answer came from the Immortalist Underground, from the stale, cavernous air of Bogdi's warehouse. She pictured the six of them—herself, Sam, Sadiq, Bogdi, Livia, and that other one—what was his name? Gavin or something—standing over a box of sparklers, and inside it, the cocaine she and Sam would fight about until she was too tired to keep her eyes open. Well, her eyes were open, and she was staring at that same box of sparklers.

She watched as Sam surrounded the box with his long, skinny arms and carried it up the stairs to the porch. Any doubts she had left about the contents of that box were erased by Sadiq and his reaction to seeing it. As Sam passed him on the porch, Sadiq's face darkened, and he downed the last of his drink.

And then she was walking back to her car, getting into it, and driving straight to the airport. When she returned the car, the guy in the garage said, "You didn't refill the gas?" And she said, "Nope!" and paid the exorbitant service charge with a smile. Anything to get out of there faster. Anything to get home to Theo, her beautiful boy, who did not have a father and never would.

Keenan DeCosta arrived in New York only two or three months later. Catherine was on campus, holding her perpetually unattended office hours, when she received a phone call from the program administrator saying a man was there to see her about a job.

As she walked down the hall to the main office, she imagined a wizened anthropologist waiting for her, someone who looked like Clifford Geertz, with white, windswept hair and an avuncular beard. Instead, there was Keenan: goatee, cargo shorts, sport sandals. Only the sandals truly shocked her, and she tried to avoid looking at them the same way she avoided staring at people with prosthetic limbs.

"Can I help you?"

Keenan stared at her. "Let me answer your question with a question. When was the last time you had a smoothie?"

Catherine was too confused to do anything but answer sincerely. "Last weekend?"

"Exactly. In twenty years, no one will be eating solid food. Liquid diets are the future."

From this improbable premise, Keenan pitched his new company: a line of all-natural nutritional drinks based on tribal and folkloric medicines from around the world. They would take goji berries from Tibet, and Sango coral from Japan, and anything else Catherine wanted, and mix them all up in the world's first health beverage *system*. Before she could blink, he was telling her about the trips they would take, all over the world and at his expense.

"It's called HeyO DayO."

"HeyO DayO."

"It's like you're saying hello to the day," he said. "The day-o," he clarified.

Three years later, as they rode in the cab to their Santiago business hotel, she was pretty much rich. She still couldn't believe it. She hadn't flown coach since that trip to Houston, but she would sometimes walk right past her first-class seat and keep walking, deep into the plane, until Theo tugged her hand and said, "Mommy, you said 3B. This is *not* 3B. We are *lost!*"

Her thoughts of Theo were interrupted by Theo, who was trying to start a slap fight with Keenan. She had been worried, in the early days, that Theo would come to see Keenan as a father figure, but instead they were something like brothers.

"Could this hotel be any farther from the airport?" Keenan asked as he grappled with Theo.

"It's been twenty minutes," Catherine said.

"It's been twenty minutes," Theo said, in perfect imitation of her voice, then laughed so hard he lost the slap fight.

Their goals for the week were simple, as usual. The University of Wisconsin study had created a lot of buzz, and HeyO DayO needed some photographs of Catherine and Keenan, but especially Catherine, in front of the moai, the stone statues. They also had a meeting with someone named Lorenzo, who had positioned himself as a kind of Rapa Nui historian, the keeper of records. She hoped he would have some good stories that they could use in their TV spots or on the website. In truth, none of their drinks would undergo any actual changes. Several of them already included ingredients from Chile and French Polynesia, and these would be highlighted more prominently for as long as the excitement lasted. For obvious reasons, they could never add rapamycin to an energy drink available at gas stations.

Sammy became suspicious when, at 1:00 p.m., Bogdi was still wearing the towel. His ribs appeared every time he laughed at something, his skeleton flexing against his skin like gills. Livia was dressed but in no hurry; she reclined on the bed with her sneakers on the pillows and her head in Celebrity Client's lap. Sammy watched as Celebrity Client ran his fingers through her uneven bangs and wondered if the poor fool was in love with her.

"Shouldn't we get going?" Sammy said for the third or fourth time. According to Bogdi, the Underground had made contact with a Tahitian pharmacist who was using rapamycin-loaded nanoparticles to effectively, but illegally, treat children with muscular dystrophy.

"You gotta relax," Bogdi said. "This is, like, island life. We're on island time."

Sammy closed his eyes. "Please stop saying 'island time.'"

"It would be nice to get some sun," added Celebrity Client, trying to be helpful, but Sammy could tell his heart wasn't in it. Earlier, they'd been allies, but with Livia in his lap his impatience had mysteriously faded.

"It would be nice if everyone stopped bitching," Livia said. "You two are like my sisters."

"I didn't know you had sisters," said Celebrity Client. He'd been a member of the Underground since early in his career, when he came to Romania to shoot a low-budget adaptation of a video game about a World War II soldier with swords for arms.

"Okay, seriously," Sammy said. "What's going on?"

Bogdi and Livia shared a look.

"Listen," Bogdi said. "The pharmacist didn't check out."

Sammy stared at him. "What does that mean?"

"It means he was on the crazy side. His e-mails were actually pretty funny."

"When did this happen?"

Livia twisted her head so that she was looking at Sammy upside down. "Hey, dickhead, we *told* you not to come."

"I—" Sammy stopped. She was right. They said it wasn't

worth the trip, that they knew flying made him anxious. He had
thought they were just trying to be nice. "I don't understand.
What are we doing here?"

"You aren't doing shit," Livia said.

"Bucky Baker, Jr.," said Bogdi.

"Bucky Baker, Jr.," Sammy repeated.

"We know something you don't know," Livia said in a sing-
song voice.

Bogdi explained. The Underground had acquired the results
of Radkin's research into rapamycin as a treatment for Canale-
Smith syndrome. The results were not encouraging: None of Radkin's trials had shown that the drug had anything but a slight
ameliorative effect on the disease. According to Bogdi, Radkin
had hidden these results from Bucky Baker, Jr., in the fear that
Bucky, when he learned of them, would withdraw his consider-
able financial support from the AGE. Bogdi was hoping he would
do just that when he and Livia showed him the results. And
maybe, if all went well, they could help him find a new outlet for
his wealth.

"We want that American oil money!" Bogdi said. "We're
gonna swim in it like your Scrooge McDuck."

"How did you get these results?" Sammy asked. "You stole
them?"

Bogdi shrugged. "We steal from him, he steals from us. It's,
like, the nature of the game."

"I seriously doubt Joseph Radkin has ever stolen anything
from you."

"You're more naïve than my sisters," Livia said.

"She's right," Bogdi said. "You're too horny for Sadie to see
the kind of man he works for."

"Seriously, how did you get this information?"

Livia rolled her eyes so hard she actually flipped over on the
bed, with her chin now hooked over Celebrity Client's thigh. "If
I say 'computer hacking,' will that shut you up?"

Sammy curled his lip. If she'd said "computer hacking" it
absolutely *would* have shut him up. "You know I can't let you
do anything that would hurt Sadie."

"Sure," Bogdi said. "That's why we didn't want you to come."

"Even if I let you do this, which I won't, there's no way some-one like Bucky Baker, Jr., will listen to you."

"He'll listen if we're with *him*," Livia said, pointing her chin toward Celebrity Client.

"We read an interview," Bogdi explained. "Bucky Baker's favorite movie is *Trigger Finger 2*."

Celebrity Client nodded as though this fact were inevitable.

"It doesn't matter," Sammy said, "because we're not doing any of that."

"I hear you," Bogdi said, "but I don't agree."

Bogdi and Sammy stared at each other. The two of them were no strangers to arguing, but that was about formulas, chemical equations; it was like two computers barking at each other in bi-nary code. This time—and Sammy had seen this exact phrase on one of Celebrity Client's movie posters—it was personal.

On the way to Lorenzo's house, Sadiq received a text message from Lorenzo: *No, don't go to my house. Meet me at the University.* So Sadiq gave the new instructions to their driver and explained the change to Radkin and Bucky, Sadiq's anxiety rising in a way he couldn't quite articulate.

He'd been the sole liaison between Lorenzo and the AGE—Radkin had never even spoken to him—and that was the start of the problem. Anything that went wrong would fall squarely on Sadiq's shoulders. He had spent much of the last decade asking people for things—most often, access to their dying bodies—and so considered himself skilled in identifying the needs in people. Some wanted to be made to feel important, as if the future of human life hinged on their cooperation, and Sadiq would tell them, yes, you're important—the *most* important! It really was that unsubtle. Others wanted favors: cash, medical treatment, scholarships for their grandchildren to prestigious American schools. Others, such as Lorenzo, just wanted a friend.

But rather than welcoming the three of them into his home—where he lived with the grandmother—Lorenzo wanted to meet them alone in the cold confines of a university laboratory. Had Sadiq read him wrong?

When the driver first pulled onto the university campus, Sadiq thought he'd taken them by accident to the airport. But then he saw the university signage and realized, no, the campus was only airport*like*, with long, industrial outbuildings and what really, really looked like an air traffic control tower. From the car, he spotted Lorenzo waving to them outside the science building. They walked the ten or so meters to meet him, and he waved the whole time, as if they might lose sight of him on the way. They shook hands and introduced themselves. Lorenzo was light skinned, short, and broad chested. In America, he would likely be mistaken for Hawaiian, though a barista in Houston once asked Sadiq if he spoke Japanese, so you never knew.

"Is everything okay?" Sadiq asked. "We were worried the change of venue might mean your grandmother had taken a turn."

Sadiq saw Radkin give him a look, as if to say, *We were?*

Lorenzo shook his head. "Honestly, my *mémère* took that turn many months ago. But I do have some difficult news. I've decided to work with the University of Wisconsin people."

Next to Sadiq, Radkin's body went stiff, and Bucky's hands formed into fists.

"You've been very kind. UW just has better . . . resources."

Sadiq knew what this meant: they'd offered Lorenzo something. How had Sadiq read him so wrong? For some people, any offer of payment was an insult, the quickest way to lose them. He had thought Lorenzo was one of those.

Bucky was breathing hard. "Now, okay, we can always negotiate—"

"I'm sorry. I signed all the papers."

"A phone call to us would have sufficed," Radkin said, his voice low.

"I wanted to tell you in person," Lorenzo said, offended by the very idea. "It was the honorable thing."

Lorenzo took his leave, and Bucky stormed back to the car, muttering to himself. Sadiq had the urge to run and hide, as if he were a little boy who'd broken something.

Radkin stood close, with his arms crossed. "Well?"

"Lorenzo misled me." Sadiq wasn't sure that was true. "What am I supposed to do?"

"How about your job? Which is to not put me in situations like this one, where my time is wasted."

"We've followed bad leads before." Sadiq didn't know why he was arguing. It *was* his fault.

"Your head isn't here. Not since *him*." Radkin walked to the car, where they had a long drive ahead.

Him. The word hung in the air like smog. Maybe things weren't perfect with Sam, maybe accepting his work with the elixir, the dangers of it, had been easier to do in theory than it was in practice. There was the day, last year, when Sadiq helped Sammy take a brain scan and run blood work on himself immediately before and immediately after a dose of the elixir. In the afterimage, Sadiq watched Sammy's brain glow green and red with happiness: the prolactin, serotonin, and endorphins lighting up the twilight blue of his mind like fireworks. This should have been a good thing: Sammy and Bogdi's elixir was working, was getting stronger by the day. But since then, whenever the elixir wore off and Sammy's eyes went dull, Sadiq would picture those happy colors draining from his lover's mind like bathwater.

Still: they loved each other. Sadiq felt this love in the deepest part of his heart. He reminded himself of something his mother once told him: "There's no point in looking for the badness in goodness. You'll always find it, and what then?"

They landed on the island sometime before noon. Catherine checked her watch. Counting their connecting flights, they'd flown over six thousand miles to reach Easter Island, yet, after all that effort, the time difference between here and New York was only an hour. She felt betrayed by this, and saddened—time had followed her.

As she stepped onto the sidewalk, the cool air of the island hit her face. It smelled of mud and meadows and gasoline. With no planes landing or taking off, she could hear the screechy, whistling

broadcast of hawks circling. Their airplane had rattled like a cold
body the entire flight, breathing its icy, pressurized air onto her
bare arms. On their descent, she'd seen the yellow grass of the
island, the pockets of rock near the coastline. From the sky, the
island had a thirsty look. But at ground level, she could appreciate the greenness of the grass, flat as paper near the parking lot
but rolling upward into hills on the horizon. Near the exit, one
of the moai stared back at her with big googly eyes.

She scanned the parking lot until she recognized the logo of
their rental car company. "There," she said to Keenan, and he led
them toward it. He was wearing a backward baseball cap and
carrying a huge bag of photography equipment around his shoulder. On her trips with Sam, Catherine had been the photographer.
She wasn't an expert, but she liked lining things up, and it became
a challenge for her, to take a picture that could make Sam smile,
or, better yet, a picture *of* Sam smiling.

She gave their name to the man at the outdoor reservation
kiosk.

"Hmm," he said, in a heavily accented baritone. "I have you
here for car *and* mountain bikes. Which you want?"

"Right," she said. "Both."

"Hmm. The island is small, like this." He used his index finger and thumb to indicate a space roughly the size of a black bean.
"No need for both."

They wanted the car and the bikes for a silly reason—with
time constraints, and with Theo, they needed to drive, but in the
photographs for the website, they needed to be on mountain
bikes. It was part of their brand.

But how to explain this to the rental guy? So she said, "I know
it's crazy, but we're Americans."

They followed the road away from the airport, driving along
the ocean. A man she'd seen on the airplane had beaten them to
the water on his rented ATV, and he was unfolding a collapsible
kayak near the cliffs, which was so cool, Catherine thought, like
a big piece of origami. She would love to do something like that,
but it would mean leaving Theo on the shore and watching him
shrink into a pinprick as the ocean carried her out. The thought

of that made her want to scream herself awake, like from a bad dream.

It wasn't long until the road brought them near an *ahu*, a stone platform, with a row of moai facing inward with their backs to the water, as if they were bracing themselves against the wind. She stopped the car. Keenan unpacked his camera, whistling. Theo unlocked his own seat belt. Catherine told him to stay near the car as she unloaded the bikes from the rear-mounted bike rack. By the time she was finished, Keenan was on his knees in front of the moai, snapping pictures, though it looked from behind as if he were praying to them. Catherine wheeled the bikes into place. A few hundred feet down the road, two men were drinking beer in the back of their jeep, and she thought they might be laughing at her. She did feel ridiculous, swinging her leg over the bike for the first time, tousling her hair to create an appropriately wind-swept coif. She had never expected to become such a *visual* part of the company. What kind of person reads the websites of corporations? Weirdos, she guessed, and maybe business majors at poorly ranked schools.

Keenan was already snapping pictures. He looked up from the viewfinder. "Theo, buddy, can you stay out of the frame for just a second? . . . Good. . . . Lean back a little, Cat. Wow. How many years have we known each other? How have you not aged?"

Five miles to the west, back toward the airport, Sammy and Sadiq were standing on the lip of the Rano Kau crater lake. Ear-lier, Sammy had been cold, but the volcano had its own climate, separate from the island's, and so he removed his cardigan and slung it over his shoulder. The sky was still gray, speckled with streaks of sun. The heavy clouds, matched in color by the basalt at ground level, looked augite and agitable. The whole place, and he realized this was foolish to think about a volcano, being much too obvious, had an overcooked appearance. He wondered about that name, Rano Kau, and he dreamed a translation: Bowl of Mud.

"Beautiful," he said.

"I wonder how deep it is." Sadiq didn't actually care. It was just something to say. On a better day, he could have found beauty in the way the waves struck the outer edges of the Rano Kau, and how, like a hand cupping wet clay, you could see exactly how they'd shaped this place over thousands and thousands of years. If she were here, his mother would have said, "God is great, God is *so* good," and Sadiq liked that about her, how in the way she said it, she privileged goodness over greatness. But today was awful, and this whole trip was *so* awful.

"You've been a complete waste since we came to Rice," Radkin had said over the phone yesterday morning, while Sadiq waited with Sam for their flight to Rapa Nui. "You're distracted, and I need to know why. Is it Sam?"

"I don't agree with your premise that I'm distracted," Sadiq replied, though he didn't know what he believed. It was true, for example, that the last monthly report he'd written for the AGE newsletter had contained an unusual amount of typographical errors, including an omitted comma that implied, mistakenly, that a symptom of Guillain-Barré syndrome was being unable to eat diarrhea. *Was* Sam to blame? Sadiq spent so much time worried about Sam that he did sometimes forget to perform basic self-care, such as toothbrushing or toenail maintenance. Some months ago, he'd called his doctor to ask about something to help him sleep, and the receptionist—or was it the nurse?—said, "He'll want to see you first." Sadiq had felt a rush of warmth at those words— *he'll want to see you*—as though the doctor simply wanted the pleasure of his company. Such was the depth of his need to be loved: it made him gullible. When the woman said what she said, he let out a small, involuntary coo. Hearing this, the woman said, "Um," and he was so embarrassed that he never went in for the sleeping pills.

He watched Sam step closer to the edge, too close, and felt his stomach tighten. Sadiq asked, "Should we head back to the bikes?" They'd left them near the road, at the bottom of the trail.

"If that's what you want."

"That's why I asked, because it's what I want."

Sam looked over his shoulder with a boyish, wounded expression. "Why are you snapping at me?" *He'd feel bad*, Sammy thought, *if he knew I've spent this entire trip protecting him.* Bogdi had been steadfast in his plan to sabotage the AGE's relationship with Bucky Baker, Jr., and so Sammy had gone to work on Livia, who, despite her meanness, was more logical and could be reasoned with.

"Okay, fine," she'd said after two days of pestering. "God, you're such a pussy."

Sammy reached the bottom of the volcano, and the bikes came into view, held upright by their kickstands. He stood with his hand on the vinyl saddle while he waited for Sadiq to catch up. The dirt road split in the distance, one way leading to the airport, the other hugging the coast. A group of tourists on horseback crested the nearest hill—six people on five horses, all of the horses plump and long-legged, with tawny, dappled coats, like sunlight breaking through a screen door. He watched a gust of wind push the grass in his direction, then the wind hit him, and he was cold. He put his cardigan back on and immediately began to sweat.

Sadiq arrived, and they mounted their bikes in clumsy, angry silence. The man at the rental place told them the island was small and dense with things to look at. "You can't go wrong," he'd said. "Every road leads somewhere good."

They set off, the wind beating against them. To their right, a man was kayaking in the rough water, pushing his boat through the choppy ocean. The man waved at them, and Sammy knew that Sadiq must have waved first, probably to make sure he was okay. The moai stared at Sammy, stone-faced, and he remembered his trip to Puerto Rico, a vacation he'd taken with Catherine early in their relationship. They had gone to a beautiful white sand beach, but they couldn't decide where to set up their umbrella—she wanted to be close to the public restrooms; he wanted to be far from people—and an older man, a native, had called to them, "What are you arguing for? You're in paradise!" Even then, Sammy had known: *This moment will never leave me. I'll have this man in my head, judging me, forever.*

Sadiq watched Sam pedal, the back of his neck glistening, and thought, *If Sam is a distraction, so be it.*

Sammy heard the sound of an automobile and saw a large luxury SUV approaching. He moved off the road to make room for it. As it neared, he could see a woman in the driver's seat, and in the passenger seat, a man. As it passed, he saw a child in the backseat, face pressed to the window. It was an unremarkable sight, except that less than a second after the car drove by, Sammy heard the sound of its brakes being applied, hard and fast, as if in distress. He stopped his bike and turned. Sadiq had stopped as well, and so had the car. One at a time, three of the car doors opened—the car was still sitting there right in the middle of the road—and three people emerged. One was a boy, blond haired and handsome. One was a man, in sport sandals and baggy shorts. One, the last, was Catherine.

How long did it take Catherine to recognize Sam, there on the side of the road, his skinny arms rattling on the handlebars—three seconds, five? *You could actually calculate this*, she thought as she sat in the car, her door open, Keenan and Theo already outside. You would have to know how fast she was going, and you would have to measure the distance from when she first saw him to when she stopped. She had been driving, probably too fast, when she saw two men on bicycles, one leading the other. She had thought, *That guy looks a lot like Sam.*

Even after stopping, which was involuntary, she might never have left the car were it not for Theo. In her side-view mirror, she saw that he was running loose and headed toward the cliffs. So she hopped out of the car and caught him by his sleeve, swinging him into her arms and releasing him back in the direction of the car. He charged at Keenan like a bull, and Keenan, her sweet idiot boss, knelt to receive him. She almost smiled, but then she remembered herself and what was happening. Just a few yards away, Sadiq—*Sadiq*—was off his bike and closing the distance between them. Behind him, Sam had not moved a muscle. He was frozen in place like a moai, staring at her as if she'd beamed down to Earth from a spaceship. She *did* feel alien, in her own way. The girl they'd known, all those years ago, was gone. She'd been abducted by time.

Sadiq drew close and took both her hands, squeezed them. He was big and beautiful, like a tree. "Catherine," he said, not really looking at her. He was watching Theo with a pained, sickly expression, and she knew right away that he knew. Maybe he'd already known. This thought hurt her and dazed her, like a blow to the head. Did Sam know, too?

"Hi, Sadie," she said to him, surprising herself at this use of his nickname.

He looked back at her, his eyes grateful. He must have been having a bad day.

Theo had found something to occupy him in the grass, so Keenan left his side and shook Sadiq's hand. They introduced themselves, and Catherine said something about having worked with Sadiq in the past. Keenan just smiled and nodded, not really caring. In the distance, she could hear the ocean hitting the rocks, attacking and retreating. Sadiq made an awkward, throat-clearing sound, and the three of them stood there and stared at Sam, waiting for him to do the human thing and come over. He took a long time dismounting his bike, lowering the kickstand, and looping his messenger bag around the handles. She studied his face as he pretended to be busy with these simple tasks. He was still the man she remembered. Blushing lips, pale blue eyes the color of forget-me-nots. People are so *pretty* when they're embarrassed, and Sam was embarrassed by everything. If she was less stunned by him than she used to be—which she was, or so she told herself— it was not because he'd aged but only because she saw him more clearly. Time had explained him to her. All those years ago, when she loved him, she believed she did so in spite of his unhappiness, which had seemed to her soundless, unknowable. Now, and perhaps because she'd watched a child grow, *their* child, from a speck of cells to a boy, she could see the shape and size of his sadness—she could measure it, same as she could the movement from seeing a man you don't know, biking on the side of the road, to realizing, *Yes, I do know him—it's* him. And the shape of his sadness was this: his body, every inch of it, head to toe. This whole time, that's what she'd loved in him. That's what she'd missed. He was like a shadow box, where the darkness and depth makes everything on the surface more beautiful.

He was close enough that she could hear him breathing. He was so handsome she blinked.

"Hi," he said.

"Hi," she answered.

Again, she introduced Keenan. She tried to read Sam's face as he made small talk, as they agreed, yes, the island was wonderful, the people, too. He was terrified, that was plain as day, but she saw nothing of the terrified *knowingness* she'd seen in Sadiq, none of the awareness that everything was about to change. Just a few feet away, Theo was talking nonsense to a bug he'd found in the dirt, and Catherine thought the sound of his voice must be for Sadiq like a train approaching when you're tied to the tracks.

Before anything real could be said among the four of them, Sam registered the sound of Theo's singing. He tilted his head, puppylike, and Catherine watched his eyes track the grass until he found Theo, squatting on his heels, saying, "Hi, bug. Hello, Theo," doing both voices, his and the bug's.

Sam swallowed. "Yours?"

She smiled. "Yes. That's Theo."

Keenan touched the small of her back, which was not a supportive gesture but simply his way of saying he was ready to go.

Sam was looking at her again. "He's gorgeous." It took her a moment—a moment of pure disbelief—to realize he was saying this not just to her, but to her and her impatient boss. He thought Keenan was the father. Keenan! With the sport sandals! The anger she felt then was like a strong analgesic. It felt really, *really* good. *You stupid shit,* she almost said. *He looks exactly like you!*

Instead, she turned to Keenan. "Can you give us a second?"

"Just one?" This wasn't funny, but he did as she asked and excused himself. He joined Theo on the ground, and she was grateful for the noise they made. No one else was on the road.

"I'll let you catch up," Sadiq said, and his eyes were saying, *Don't tell him.*

But she had to tell him, and she smiled in a way that communicated, she hoped, that she was sorry. When it's time, it's time.

Sam turned his whole body to watch Sadiq leave, reminding her of Theo, who would do the same thing when she dropped him off at school. Sadiq stood near the bikes, studying his shoes. Sam faced her, eyebrows raised. He seemed startled to find himself alone with her.

"So listen," she said, and began.

"So listen," Sadiq saw her say, and then Sam shifted, blocking Sadiq's view of her face. He couldn't make out any more of their conversation. He could only stare at Sam's back, wondering, wondering, while that man with the goatee spun Sam's child in a wide, nauseating circle. The moment that boy emerged from the car, smiling and expectant, Sadiq had *known*. If he hadn't wanted to cry, he would have laughed at Sam's failure to recognize his son, who looked so much like him you would think Catherine played no role in his conception. But she *had* played a role, and she'd raised the boy into this laughing, goofy tadpole. The boy was like a joyful version of Sam, which was so odd, because Sadiq had convinced himself that no such thing was possible.

Sam was nodding, slowly. The information was sinking in. Sadiq's only hope—and he was ashamed to be hoping for this, but self-preservation is not moral—was that Sam would screw this up, say the wrong thing, and Catherine and Theo would be out of Sam and Sadiq's life forever. He and Sam could go on as they'd been going. And how had they been going? Happily, Sadiq thought, and terribly. In love, but not really taking care of each other.

Sam and Catherine were embracing, and he was whispering something into her ear. Sadiq's breath caught in his throat. They pulled apart, and he could see Catherine smile. *So that's it*, he thought. For once in his life, Sam hadn't screwed things up. Sadiq wanted to kick over the bikes. But then Sam turned and came closer, and he was sick looking, white-faced like a ghost. Sadiq held out his hand, and Sam took it. Catherine was motioning to Keenan, heading for the car.

"Are you okay?" Sadiq asked.

Sam rubbed his forehead. He was so pale. "Oh, Sadie. I screwed that up. I really botched that."

"He's your son?"

Sam nodded. "I could tell she was waiting for me to say something. To say I wanted to be in his life. Jesus Christ. Did you *see* him?"

"I saw him."

Sam took a long, shaky breath. "Why aren't you freaking out? Am I wrong to be?"

At no point in his life, not even decades later, could Sadiq explain why he said what he said next. Exhaustion, maybe, or lingering resentment over the fallout with Radkin. Or maybe he was simply done standing on the cliff with Sam and decided to give them both a push. "I already knew. I mean, I didn't *know*. I heard she had a kid, and I did the math. I suspected."

"You suspected." Sam's eyes went cloudy. Behind him, Catherine had started the car. The engine coughed to life. They were surrounded by ocean, and Sadiq could hear it on all sides. Sadiq waited, and when Sam's eyes finally refocused, they were filled with tears, and the love in them was gone.

In her rearview mirror, before she drove away, Catherine saw Sam bent at the waist, crying, while Sadiq steadied him and talked. It looked as if Sadiq was apologizing, but Sam was shaking his head, over and over, while he sobbed. Catherine's eyes were dry—she'd told him, and that was all she needed. Whatever happened next would happen.

Still, a part of her wanted to throw the car in reverse and go to him. But no, those days were over. He wasn't hers to take care of, not anymore. She put the car in drive.

No, she wouldn't go to him.

But if he called . . . ?

Sammy and Sadiq sat in the terminal, waiting for their plane back to Tahiti. Sammy remembered flying in to the island, what seemed like ages ago, and savoring that private, hopeful feeling he always had before landing. The wheels of the plane hit the runway, and his heart stirred—somewhere new! *This could be the place you've been waiting for.*

.

Four hours later, after two short delays, they boarded. Catherine, Sammy knew, was still on the island. When she told him they'd be spending the night there, he was relieved.

The plane took off, and Sadiq gripped the armrests, looking ill. Sammy knew a few comforting words would make all the difference, but he couldn't bring himself to speak. He thought of Dr. Huang, his old psychiatrist. He pictured her: those severe, side-parted bangs, the thick, rectangular glasses. She would say, "Sam, here's what's scaring you: If you can't find a way to love your son, and be loved by him, then you'll know you were right all along—that you aren't meant to love or be loved. You'll know, once and for all, that you lack the capacity for happiness."

The plane landed, and they hired a taxi.

"Please talk to me," said Sadiq.

Sammy didn't want to talk, which would mean saying the name of his son out loud. The taxi driver, perhaps sensing the awkwardness, put on the radio. The station played "I Want a New Drug" by Huey Lewis and the News, and then, absurdly, played it again.

They arrived at the tree house. Before Sadiq could beg, or plead, or say whatever he wanted to say, Sammy kissed him and pulled him onto the bed. There, they made love for the last time. Did Sammy know it was the last time? If he was being honest, yes.

He woke before Sadiq did. He put on his jeans, a black T-shirt, and sneakers without socks. He walked down the ramp to the beach. The air was already hot, the ocean flat and green like a dollar bill. Those boys with skimboards were back at it, and one of them, the shortest, had his arm in a sling. *Damn right*, Sammy thought, and what he meant was that no one should leave this place unharmed.

He entered Bogdi and Livia's without knocking. He found them in the bedroom, still sleeping, their bodies intertwined. They were naked, but their embrace looked more consanguine than sexual, as if they were siblings who had fallen asleep holding each other against bad dreams. On the floor, Celebrity Client slept on his back.

"Wake up."

And they did—Livia first, Celebrity Client second, and finally Bogdi, who said, "Sam? The fuck?"

"Give me the stuff on Radkin. The rapamycin trials."

"Ugh." Livia kicked her pale legs out of the covers. "We told you we'd drop it."

"We're giving it to Bucky. *I'm* giving it to Bucky."

"Huh?" Bogdi said.

Sammy nudged Celebrity Client with his foot. "Are you still flying home today?"

"Yeppers." He rubbed his eyes. "Flight is at four."

"Can I ride with you to the airport? I'm going to try to get on your flight."

Celebrity Client grinned and offered his hand in a high five. "Travel buddies!"

"Am I, like, the only one who's confused?" Bogdi started to say more, but Livia shushed him.

She looked hard at Sammy, as if trying to see through him. "You want us to go with you? To Bucky's?"

Sammy shook his head. "I don't need you. I'll say Sadiq sent me."

A smile touched her lips. "Which is not true?"

He met her eyes, and he felt, for the first time, that he truly understood her. Livia was an agent of destruction. She grabbed her phone from the side table and typed until his own phone vibrated.

He looked at what she'd sent him and nodded. "I'll be back in an hour."

She stood and embraced him, fully nude. "I take back every bad thing I ever said about you."

After they landed in New York, Sammy and Celebrity Client parted ways at the taxi line. Sammy gave the cabbie his parents' address and dozed on the way. Sadiq would still be in Tahiti, dealing with Radkin. He would almost certainly be fired.

Sammy rang the doorbell, and both of his parents answered the door together, the way only parents do. They hadn't seen him in five years.

"Leena," Sammy said, his voice breaking. "Don."

Leena embraced him, and Don placed a warm hand on the back of his neck. They brought him inside. As the door closed, Sammy heard the artillery-like sound of a misfired piston, felt the hot blast of air from the sidewalk grate. He was home, and the house was too cold. He shivered, fighting the urge to laugh. *I'm from New York*, he thought, *and there is no peace for me.* The city followed him the way time followed Catherine—he, closing his eyes, searching his mind for quiet; she, watching her son grow up so fast she was sometimes scared to wake him, not knowing what new thing he would do, what change in him would announce itself.

Anna Agrees to an Autopsy

San Ignacio, Belize, AD 2002
Anna opens her eyes. Her great-great-granddaughter is inches from her face. Always with the Eskimo kisses, this one!

"Please," Anna scolds. "Not so close, Francie."

The child is oblivious to rebuke. "Love you, Grauma!"

"Go away now," Anna tells her, even though what she really wants is to say, *Your love is small compared to my love for you, Francie. I love you more than my own daughter.* But it would delight the child too much to hear these things. There would be painful hugs.

Not to mention Anna's own, less loved daughter is in the room. Anna can see the shape of her, hazy and dark, like a shadow behind a curtain. She's not so bad, fat Samantha, just old, too old for a daughter. What she hates in Samantha is only Anna's own stubborn living. When a daughter is past ninety, the mother should be dead!

Also in the room is Francie's mother, who is Edith or maybe Ellen. If she is Edith, there was also an Ellen, perhaps a cousin who died? Next to her, standing in the doorway, is a man Anna doesn't know. He looks like Anna's first husband, her little night bird, who flew away in the storm. The Hurricane of 1908. For three hours the sky turned black. She counted every second: one *help-me-Jesus*, two *help-me-Jesus*, three *help-me-Jesus*, four. The next morning she wept, hard and painful, her lungs and forehead burning. The doctor said she would kill herself, crying this way, so she began to cry inside herself only, her body growing fat with tears. Then she met Second Husband, who kissed away her heaviness and gave her all the babies she could handle, plus two more.

"You have a visitor, Grauma," says Edith-or-Ellen.

Anna tries to see the man better, but Francie is dancing around the room to the music of the American singers on her tiny radio—every day for months the same ones, over and over so that even Anna's memory can hold them. Her favorite is the rapper Eminem, who sings so fast Anna can pretend he is speaking Kriol and fall asleep to him. She prefers to dream in Kriol. Her English dreams are not so nice and are filled with jungle cats.

The man leaves the shelter of the doorway and comes to her side. Up close, he is too fat to be First Husband. Samantha, who rides a wheelchair, also comes closer. "Muma, this is Sadiq. He wants to talk to you about some doctors."

Now they have Anna's attention. "Someone to fix my hands?" Of all her pains, the hands are the worst. For thirty years, they have been locked into fists. There is physical pain, yes—like a scorpion sting between the knuckles, every second of every day—but even more cruel is the pain of the heart. How she misses being able to *hold* things: a hot cup of tea, a paperback book, a child's hand.

Everyone looks guilty. "No, Grauma," Edith-or-Ellen says. "Not for your hands."

Sadiq smiles at her. "You are an important woman. There are doctors in America who would like to learn from you."

Anna feels sleep coming in the distance. It makes a sound in her head like footsteps. "Okay, so bring them? I'm not going anywhere."

Sadiq makes an uncomfortable face. He's holding some papers.

"They won't come now," says Samantha. "They'll come . . . later."

If Anna had the energy to laugh, she would laugh at this. Don't they know how old she is? If they wait too long, she'll be dead before they get here.

The fat man looks pained. "I'm not explaining this well."

Samantha has fallen asleep in her chair. Her mouth hangs open, gargling oxygen. Samantha is the daughter of First Husband. When she was young, she looked so much like her father that it became painful for Anna to see her. Now she looks like Anna—like an old woman.

"After you die," Sadiq says, "the doctors want to study your body. To see how you lived so long."

Oh, Anna thinks, *an autopsy.* Why didn't they say so? Her family assumes you cannot be old without also being dumb. It makes her long for the days of Samantha's childhood, when Anna was prized for her intelligence. "Muma speaks *four* languages," Samantha used to brag. "English, Kriol, Spanish, French." At the time, Anna turned red-faced at these compliments—women were not supposed to be smarter than their men. But she did not marry First Husband for his brains! He had big, stormy eyes and a stomach as smooth and hard as a granite countertop. She remembers the day the German motorcyclist drove his noisy bike into the river. While everyone else stood gaping, First Husband stripped off his shirt and pants and dove into the glassy water. He threw the German to shore and dragged his motorcycle out of the river with one hand. She can still see him high-stepping in the shallow water, his stomach glistening in the afternoon sun. Praise God! She took him home with no time wasted, climbed on top of him, and punched that stomach until they made Samantha.

Also, she could *barely* speak French. More like three and a half languages, she used to tell Samantha. But now that number feels too small. It feels as if she's had to master many more languages. She's learned thousands of new words, adapted to changes in meaning. She's 123 years old, born in 1879, but go ahead and ask her what a cell phone is. She'll tell you and get it right. She knows what it means to *web surf.* In one of Francie's magazines, Anna has seen a photograph of a boy wearing a fauxhawk. Samantha was born in the spring of 1907, which was the same year Anna first heard the word *moron.* It was used to describe a child, but it was not such an insult then. It was just a way to categorize people. This child is a boy. This child is Guatemalan. This child is a moron.

Sadiq clears his throat, and Anna realizes she has been speaking out loud. To distract from her embarrassment, she asks, "They'll cut me open?"

"And stitch you right back up," says Edith-or-Ellen.

Anna first learned to read from an American priest, who taught her the meaning of *grabby* in more ways than one. Good riddance! He died in the hurricane with First Husband, though he was old by then. They found his entrails wrapped like baby snakes around the frame of his wooden bicycle.

So she says, "No thank you."

Edith-or-Ellen chews her lip. "It would be good for us if you agree to this."

"It would be good for young Francie," adds the fat man.

"Where is my Francie?" Right away Anna knows the answer: they've taken her from the room while they discuss the gruesome details of her great-great-grauma's dissection.

"They will admit Francie to the QSI," says Edith-or-Ellen. "Free tuition!"

Ah, Anna thinks, so a deal has been made "under the table," as Second Husband would say. The QSI is the best private school in Belize. Very expensive. It would mean a world of possibilities for her Francie. Anna imagines the girl at her desk in the brightly lit school, learning maths from a woman in a colorful dress. A woman with an American university education. She imagines Francie herself with an American university education. She sees Francie, all grown-up, striding purposefully down the halls of some important building—a bank, a courthouse, the National Assembly! Men line the hallways, and they whisper to one another as she walks by. "Don't mess with Francis," they say. "She's one badass chick."

Imagining this, Anna feels as if her heart were about to explode. Can love kill you?

She remembers her hands. She shows them to Sadiq, who is still clutching what she now knows to be contracts. "Can't sign."

No need to sign, he explains. Her family can sign for her. She agrees to this. They call Francie back into the room, and she comes in dancing, singing, an angel.

•

Anna is dreaming English dreams. The Jungle Cat roars.

She is a child. The American priest shows her what it means to conjugate. *He gropes. He groped. He will be groping.* He shows her what it means to feel disgust. She conjugates her disgust until it becomes something different. She is disgusted. She had been disgusted. She is ashamed. She had been ashamed. She is angry.

The American priest rides his bicycle from the market to the mission house. Papaya and sea grapes bounce in his basket. The Jungle Cat watches him from the trees. Its black fur is caked in mud. Its mouth drips with sea foam. The Jungle Cat sprints from the gray and green of the logwood and deflates the tires of the bicycle. It climbs onto the back of the American priest and scalps him with its teeth. It opens the stomach of the American priest. The American priest screams, but soon his screams are strangled by the space-constricting volume of his own blood. The Jungle Cat gathers the intestines from the American priest as if it were re-spooling a ball of yarn. It strings the intestines on the bike like Christmas lights.

Anna cheers from her hiding place. But then the Jungle Cat turns its emerald eyes onto the road, and onto First Husband.

Anna is a young woman. She dances with First Husband. He boogies side to side like a fiddler crab. She laughs so hard she spits. He twirls her. Anna has more thickness than the other women, but in his arms? She's lighter than a leaf.

The Jungle Cat stays low to the ground. It sneaks through the crowd on the soft pads of its feet. It is 1908. One hundred and ten years ago to the day, an army of woodcutters and black slaves defended Belize from the Spanish. Anna comes from the woodcutters, First Husband comes from the black slaves. First Husband's great-grandfather fought side by side with his owner; he aimed his musket at the waifish bodies of the Spanish soldiers— starved to the ribs by yellow fever—and watched their stomachs explode onto the pale sand of the beach. First Husband dances and says something Anna can't hear.

The Jungle Cat takes flight. It extends a single claw on each of its front paws, curved and sharp like a pair of parentheses. For a moment it looks like this: (First Husband). But then the parentheses close, and the Jungle Cat divides First Husband into halves. Red mist coats Anna's hair and face. First Husband's top half disappears into the night air, his big eyes blinking in the rain of his blood. Anna screams and runs as if she were being hunted, but the Jungle Cat has no interest in her. It lifts its pink nose and smells Second Husband. It trots all the way to San Ignacio. Second Husband's house is big and yellow. His neighbors call it Mustard House. Second Husband is not like First Husband, who was young and strong and required careful approach. Second Husband is eighty-six years old. The Jungle Cat walks in as if it owns the place. It strolls to the couch and breathes hot air onto Second Husband's face. Second Husband wakes and opens his mouth into a silent O of surprise. The Jungle Cat crawls into that O. It swims Second Husband's veins to his left ventricle. It shakes the blood out of its fur and extends a single claw on each paw. For a moment it looks like this: (heart).

The Jungle Cat sleeps for a long time. When it's done, it stands and stretches and turns its emerald eyes onto Anna. It goes to her bedroom. She wakes up the moment it passes through the door. When she sees the Jungle Cat, she's so happy she cries.

Finally, she says. *Finally.*

The Jungle Cat lolls out its tongue and licks her salty cheeks. Anna closes her eyes. *You remembered me.*

The Jungle Cat uncurls her hands—at last—and kills her.

19

The Rule of Three

Sadiq and I sat on the edge of his bed, my laptop on the table in front of us, watching a video called "Cocaine Preparation and Injection: How to Get High LIKE A BOSS!!!"

"Look at that little spoon." Sadiq pointed. "It's actually quite cute."

In the video, the faceless man sucked the cocaine solution into a needle, flicked the side to evacuate the air bubbles, and clenched and unclenched his hand until his veins were dark, angry ducts. I felt a little nauseated, and the needle wasn't even in yet. Watching the video was, sadly, our idea of a break. I'd made an offhand remark—"Even if we get our hands on the Dor, I have no idea how to actually *use* it"—and Sadiq stood, with his finger in the air, and said, "To the Web!"

When the video finished, I closed my laptop, and we returned to the little table where the recipe book sat open.

"What happened with the AGE and Immortalist Underground after you left Tahiti?" Now that I'd read about Sammy's Betrayal, I could pretend I'd known about it all along.

"I don't totally know. Bucky Baker, Jr., dismantled Radkin's career with the viciousness of the very rich."

"And the Underground?"

"How should I know? Bogdi never even called to say sorry."

Sadiq was about to say something more when his phone rang. We stiffened in our seats, hopeful and afraid. Sadiq showed me the phone. It said, *Catherine.*

•

Thirty minutes later, she knocked on the door. Sadiq and I had been waiting in nervous silence, watching the clock, running our sweaty palms over our pants. Emmett had already texted me twice that morning, asking where I was. In spite of Captain Carson's warning, I could count on one hand the full school days I'd attended.

Sadiq opened the door, at once revealing and blocking my view of her. I saw only her small hands encircle his back in a quick, obligatory hug. Then he stepped to the side, and I was staring at the woman I'd read so much about. She was wearing a blue wool coat and black jeans that flared a little around her sneakers. She unwrapped a thin scarf from her neck and wiped her nose with the back of her sleeve. She had short, heavy eyelashes, like those of a child's doll. I studied her so hard that it took me a moment to realize that she had begun to study me, too. Over the phone, Sadiq had told her everything.

"Ah," she said, looking at me. "Now it makes sense."

I wanted to ask her what she meant, but instead I offered her my hand. "Hi."

She ignored me. "I don't have long," she said to Sadiq.

Sadiq nodded, trying too hard. "Of course, of course."

She shook her head, and it seemed as if she might be on the verge of laughter. I had so much to say to her, but my voice was like a fist in my throat. The room, like all hotel rooms, had a staged, theatrical quality—here's a painting of a lighthouse, and across from it, on the opposite wall, a *photograph* of a lighthouse—and we stood in silence, as though one of us had forgotten our next line. Through the window, I tried to peer out across the parking lot, to the trees, where I'd seen the figure watching me.

Sadiq put his hands in his pockets and sucked in his stomach. "Was your flight okay?"

Catherine did laugh then. "I can't make small talk with you." Her mouth was stretched thin like a knife. "I mean, what on *earth* are you doing here?"

I could tell it was a great release for her to say this. The tension in her body deflated like air escaping from a balloon.

"I called him," I said, coming to Sadiq's defense.

Catherine wouldn't even look at me—she'd seen me once, and that seemed to be enough for her. Sadiq was trying to avoid her eyes, but she wouldn't let him. "Look at yourself. You're staying in a hotel room with a sixteen-year-old. You flew from *London?*"

"I'm not staying here," I said. "I just—"

Catherine held up a finger. My father used to do this, in the good years, whenever I talked back. But then he would bend his finger as though it were speaking and say, in a weird, high-pitched voice, "Redrum, redrum!" That I didn't get the reference only made it funnier, more random. But there was no humor when Catherine did it.

Sadiq sat in one of the desk chairs, defeated. I tried to imagine this big, sad man as Sammy had described him: loud, joyful, cheesy. Always the optimist. He looked sunken and embarrassed. We exchanged glances, and I felt so, so young. We were seeing each other through Catherine's eyes.

"I'm only trying to ensure he doesn't hurt himself," Sadiq said. "And, yes, I flew from London, where I don't have much waiting for me, in case that matters to you."

Catherine closed her eyes. "I don't know if it does, Sadie, honestly. Not long ago I told my son he'll never see his father again, and then I had to leave him in New York to come be a part of whatever *this* is."

Perhaps sensing my discomfort, Catherine lowered her finger, finally. "I'm not going to talk to you," she said to me, her voice softer. "It's not to be rude, or because you've done anything wrong. You're just a kid. What *is* wrong is that you've gotten mixed up in this awful thing, stupid fucking Sam, and rather than helping you, Sadiq is encouraging you to pursue it. And I'm not much better. I'm not going to help you, either."

"You're helping if you've brought the tribal medicine," Sadiq said.

Catherine rolled her eyes at him. "I did, but you know that's not what I mean. And seriously, shame on you."

"His father is dying," Sadiq said to the carpet.

"Sam killed himself, Sadie. Nothing he did is going to save anyone's life."

"He didn't kill himself," I said. "Not like that. He was trying to help me."

Before I knew what was happening, Catherine had taken my hands. Her fingers were cold. "Okay. Sit down."

So I sat, and she sat next to me. It was so familiar, being treated this way, being braced for bad news. The hotel bed, with its awful puce bedspread, felt like a time machine we'd entered together. I traveled back—the year was 2004, and my father was saying, "Sit down," exactly as Catherine had said it, and then trying to tell me something, but failing, half-talking and half-sobbing, and all I could make out was the word *cigarette*.

Catherine smoothed the bedspread. "I'm sorry. But no. His death had nothing to do with the elixir. It was suicide."

I looked to Sadiq, but his face showed the same surprise as my own. "What?" I said. "But—"

"He told me he was going to do it. On the phone."

I was about to deny this, to call her a liar to her face, but then the memory surfaced. The night before he died, our last night together, when I told him I loved him. He'd gone outside to make a call. I had watched him from the window, pacing along the tree line. When he climbed those steps and came back to me, his eyes full of need, I believed he'd truly come back.

"What did he say?" I asked.

She hesitated. I wasn't sure if she was protecting her privacy or protecting me from the truth. Sadiq was watching us from the chair, where he sat with one arm resting on the clear glass desk. It was like a joke. *Three widows walk into a hotel room . . .*

"He told me to say goodbye to Theo."

"But why did he do it?" It was time to ask the question—for the first time, out loud—that I would wonder for the rest of my life. "Was it because of me, what we did?"

Catherine gave my hand a squeeze. "Honestly, Conrad, I have no idea. I hope there's nothing worse than what he did to you, but I'll never understand him, and you won't, either. I tried—well, it doesn't matter. He wouldn't listen to me."

I stared past her. Finally, I could complete the scene in my mind. Finally, I could watch him die and torture myself with that image. He was in the car, and it was a hot, early morning—the windows were rolled down. He was sweating, but when the breeze came, he shivered. He undid the seat belt, trying to get comfortable. Was that an oxymoron: to die comfortably? The sun was only just rising. Bogdi's words were in his head, from all those years ago: "Even in Dor, cocaine is still cocaine. Too much will kill you." Other words were in his head, too, the words spoken to him by a sixteen-year-old boy. Three simple words. He had done to that boy what he did to anyone who loved him. Through the windshield, the Methodist church was a wide, white triangle. Its slogan: A CHURCH WITH A HEART. To the sixteen-year-old boy, he made a vow in his mind. If there's an afterlife, and someday I see you there, I promise: I'll stay far, far away.

In a strange way, I'd never seen Sammy more clearly. It was the moment I should have felt furthest from him, when the elixir should have seemed the most like a delusion. Instead, I could see the final recipe in my mind, and it was as if something began to shift, to open, to *unlock*. What's missing? An answer was forming on my tongue.

"It's not your fault," Catherine said, interrupting my thoughts. I looked into her eyes, which had before been hard and closed, the pupils constricted into periods. They were open. "Whatever happened, it was Sam's doing."

This wasn't the first time I'd been told that someone's death wasn't my fault, but it had never felt more hollow.

"I called the police after he hung up," Catherine said, as much to herself as to me, "but I didn't even know where he was."

"He had a studio apartment," I said stupidly, weakly.

This information seemed to interest her. "Really."

I wiped my nose. "He didn't like it."

She took a deep, slow breath. "Okay. Show me."

We stood outside the widow's house, the three of us lined up in a row. The sky was clear and colorless; the sun was warm, but the air carried autumn. The widow's wind spinners blew counterclockwise.

"The garage?" Catherine said.

I pointed. "Above it."

"This is where you . . . ?" said Sadiq.

I didn't answer. The curtains in a window of the widow's house shifted, and I wondered if she saw us and if she recognized me. It seemed like a long time ago that I was scared of her.

As if sensing my lack of concern, Catherine said, "Let's go."

So we walked right down the driveway, in broad daylight. At the top of the steps, the police tape was gone, and the busted door had been removed. The entry was sealed with a blue tarp affixed by duct tape. Without hesitation, Catherine sunk her painted fingernails into the tape and peeled one strip away, allowing us to squeeze past, one after the other. I went last, and before I even followed Sadiq through, I could feel the emptiness of the room. Inside, all of Sammy's furniture was gone, and the place had been cleaned of debris. The room looked smaller than ever. Catherine turned on the overhead light, revealing every ding and scratch. I moved to where the bed used to be and felt as if I were floating in space.

"My son's bedroom is bigger than this whole apartment." Catherine was touching the walls, her fingers circling the hole above the missing headboard.

"Can I see a picture of him?" I asked, expecting her to say no. But she was distracted, and a mother, so she reached absentmindedly into her purse.

The picture showed a boy, maybe seven years old, smiling for a school portrait. He wore a checkered button-down and a thin mauve tie with a pattern of the periodic table. As he'd grown, he'd acquired a little more of Catherine in his looks, though these changes were more about mannerisms than genetics. He smiled her even, thin-lipped smile, and his posture—a little slouched, completely unself-conscious—certainly wasn't his father's.

As I handed the photo back to her, she gestured to the hole in the wall, which she'd been inspecting. "Did Sam do this?"

"Yeah," I said, my face warm.

Catherine put her hand through it. "Please tell me he never hurt you."

I shook my head. "Never. It wasn't like with you."

Catherine flinched. It was a cruel and petty thing for me to have said, but ever since she'd arrived, I felt powerless.

Sadiq was studying a particularly worn section of the floor. I could see Sammy there, hunched over his desk, sighing to himself as he assigned another F to a student.

"That's where he wrote," I said to Sadiq. "Your postcard was there."

"You were in touch with him?" Catherine's voice was neutral.

"I tried to be. But no."

Catherine opened and closed a cabinet. Like the rest of the apartment, it was empty. Did Sammy ever imagine this, all of us in one room?

"I know you don't want to be involved," Sadiq said to her. "If you could give us the stuff, I know Conrad will agree that we'll never contact you again."

"Yeah," I said, even though I had every intention of contacting her again.

"I brought it. But it's a trade. The medicine for the journals."

I felt my legs weaken. What was it about me that I was so easy to take things from?

"He gave them to Conrad," Sadiq argued.

Catherine gave him a savage glare. "Trust me, I don't want them."

"Then why?" I asked.

"Why are any of us here? Sam told me to bring you the medicine and take the journals. He wants Theo to have them, when he's grown. It was his last request."

I could no longer stay on my feet. I slumped to the ground with my back against the wall, just a few feet below the hole. I wanted to crawl inside that hole, disappear forever. It was painful enough that Catherine was one more person Sammy had warned without warning me, but this was so much worse than that: the journals were never really mine. I was just a placeholder, and in so many ways. I was temporary.

Catherine ran her hands through her hair. "I don't like it any more than you do. But I loved him, too, and this is what he wanted." She hadn't yet convinced herself—I could hear this.

"Someday Theo will be older than his father," she added, but in a different, less confident tone, as though she'd only realized this fact right then, and it surprised her.

Sadiq came to me and put his hand on my shoulder. "It's up to you."

Catherine stood in the middle of the room. "What I should really be doing is figuring out who's responsible for you and telling them everything you're up to."

I gave her a panicked look.

She waved it away. "I'm not going to do that. I'm also not going to try to convince you that Sam was crazy, which he was, or that the elixir is make-believe, which it is. I'm really sorry that instead of doing those things, all I'm doing is making this deal with you. But I'm tired, Conrad, and I've been living with Sam, in one way or another, for many years. All I want is to do what he asked me and go home to my son."

I imagined handing her Sammy's journals, and it was as if I'd be giving her my soul. But she was right: Why were any of us here? Because none of us could say no to him. I had pushed myself up from the floor when my phone reported a text message from RJ. The school day had ended, and I assumed he was asking where I was.

Instead, the text said, *911!*

Sadiq and Catherine dropped me off at RJ's just after two in the afternoon. I was in the backseat, and Sadiq turned to face me. "We'll go back to the motel and wait for you to call."

"I leave for my flight at nine," Catherine added, facing forward, and I knew what she meant: the clock was ticking.

I walked from the car to RJ's front porch and rang the doorbell, pressing hard, my fingers trembling. From inside, I heard the echo of the bell, the barking response of the dog, and the sound of the dog being scolded. I listened to the hum of Sadiq's rental car as he pulled away from the curb. I remembered what Radkin said, reported by Sammy, about how aging is a loss of information. That's not how growing up felt to me. If anything, my life had been an accumulation of painful details—one after the other, or one contained *within* another, like nesting dolls. There was so much information I wished I didn't have.

The door swung open, and it was not RJ, but his father, who greeted me. RJ's dad was smallish—shorter than his son—but sturdy and solid-looking, like a wrestler. He was dressed in a light, thin sweater and earth-tone cardigan, with all of the color in his outfit centered, in an un-American way, on the pants. His slacks were green.

"Come in," he said, his voice friendly but purposeful.

I followed him out of the foyer and into the living room. There, I found three other people waiting for me: RJ, looking dejected and apologetic; a fortysomething man standing at attention like a bodyguard behind the sofa; and an older man I didn't recognize—not at first, not until he rose to greet me, and I saw the two sets of glasses around his neck and the outline of shin pads behind the pants of his suit, and then he shook my hand, smiled, and called himself Joseph Radkin.

20

Immortalists at War

I was sitting in an armchair, as scared as I've ever been, trying to process the sound of Radkin's words. He spoke in a voice that was both monotone and insistent, like the horn of a car, and he had a gift for sustained, focused eye contact that I've come to associate with guidance counselors, car salesmen, and sociopaths. It was a trap.

"I've been looking for you," Radkin was saying, "though I was expecting someone considerably older."

I stared at him, my lips and throat dry. He was a small, gray scientist—smaller even than Sammy had described him—but he was too fastidious to be taken lightly. His peppery beard was shaved in sharp, straight lines, and his dress shirt was so pressed and clean he would have looked almost mannequin-like if not for the heavy wrinkles around his eyes and the way his hands, which he kept folded in his lap, had the leathery quality of a belt. His shirt was yellow, almost bronze. He reminded me of an antique sword.

"You're not in trouble," said RJ's dad, though I'm not sure everyone in the room agreed with him. "Dr. Radkin thinks you and RJ have some materials that belonged to Mr. Tampari."

"That belong to *me*," Radkin corrected.

"Right, okay," said RJ's dad, too relentlessly good-natured to realize he was participating in a shakedown.

Behind Radkin, the man I'd been thinking of as his bodyguard shifted on his feet. He was dressed in black trousers and a red turtleneck, but I could see, poking just above the top of his collar, part of a tattoo: mouse ears. I remembered something from Sammy's journals.

"Gavril?" I said.

He recoiled at this, his dark eyes registering surprise. "How do you—?"

Radkin held up a hand, silencing him. "It doesn't matter."

The rapamycin—the drug RJ had asked his father to get—had revealed me to Radkin. He explained this, lying through his teeth. Sammy had stolen his research, he claimed, fled to Littlefield, and killed himself, and Radkin was merely trying to recover his property. RJ's dad had requested a sample of rapamycin from the company that controlled its market in the United States, and this company—Radkin said with a hint of embarrassment—is where he worked. Radkin, for all his menace, had a nine to five.

RJ was sitting on the same couch as Radkin, on the opposite side. "Sorry, Con," RJ said, his voice as defeated as I'd ever heard it.

"Whoa," said his dad, surprised by the despair on his son's face. "No one needs to be apologizing for anything."

"I have to go to the bathroom," RJ said, and without waiting for a response, he was gone. I watched him leave with my eyes wide and wounded. How could he desert me? My only relief was that I knew, finally, who'd been working against me this whole time. My enemy had a face. "You're the one who broke into his apartment?" I asked Radkin.

"What?" said RJ's dad, startled.

Radkin's mouth twitched. "I don't consider it breaking in when I was seeking my own property."

"And the storage unit?"

Radkin turned to Gavril with annoyance on his face. "Apparently there's a *storage unit*."

Gavril hung his head.

I didn't know what it meant, that Radkin had done one and not the other. "Have you been following me?"

Radkin's face showed real surprise. "I told you: I just learned about you this morning."

"I don't understand. Why come now? He lived here for a year."

Radkin threw up his hands. "We came because he *told* us to come. He said he had something to give me. And then I came all this way to find him dead and his apartment full of high school tests and paperbacks."

"I don't believe you," I said, but I really meant that I didn't want to believe. Sammy had killed himself, and before he did, he called Sadiq and Catherine and Radkin. He'd engineered all of this.

"Oh, no," Radkin said, his voice deadpan. "You don't believe me."

I sat back in my chair, and the room seemed to grow quiet. Again, the final recipe came to me, and it was as if, if I just reached, reached, a little further . . .

Radkin was watching me with a cryptic expression, but before he could say any more, RJ's father intervened.

He'd finally realized that there was more to this story, so he ended the conversation by literally placing himself in the middle of the room. "Okay. I made a mistake. I should have called Conrad's aunt before we had this discussion."

For obvious reasons, this outcome was not desirable to me. "It's fine." I leaned around him to speak to Radkin. "I'll give you everything."

"Are you sure?" said RJ's dad.

"Perfect." Radkin clapped his hands, not waiting for me to change my mind.

We stood, and Radkin approached me for a handshake. He gave me his phone number and the address of his hotel, which was less than a mile from Sadiq's.

Before he released me, he leaned in to whisper in my ear. "If I don't hear from you tonight, I'm calling the police."

I knew he wasn't bluffing. Whom would they believe—me or him? I pulled my hand away. I didn't even wait for RJ to reemerge; I bolted out the door, without any plan other than to start walking home and call Sadiq on the way. Instead—I should have known better than to discount him—I found RJ waiting in his car, parked across the street, waving me over.

I hopped in the passenger seat. I was so happy to see him that I felt my eyes go damp, and he mistook this for sadness.

"It's okay. Check this out." He held up a clear plastic bag filled with cylindrical pills.

"Is that the rapamycin?" I asked, hope returning to my body.

He grinned. "Where to?"

I considered this. "Dana's."

When I pushed through the front door and into the living room, I found, in a bizarre reenactment of the scene I'd just fled, Dana, Emmett, and Captain Carson waiting for me in the living room.

"Honey, we need to talk," Dana said.

Captain Carson was on the couch, and he shrugged his eyebrows, like, *I told you not to keep skipping.* Emmett wouldn't look at me, but I knew he was angry from the way he picked at his cuticles. RJ was still outside, the car running, and I had texted Sadiq about the developments with Radkin. We were headed to meet him and Catherine.

"I can't right now," I said.

Emmett scoffed, his face red. "See?" he said to Dana. "I told you."

"Huh?" I said.

Dana gestured for everyone to calm down. "Just sit, please. You're not in trouble."

It was a big day for me not being in trouble. "Fine," I said. "Just let me change."

Dana agreed to this, and I went to my bedroom. There, Number 5, Number 7, and Number 42 were resting in their cage. After Number 37 died, I'd taken them home with Dana's permission, though I'd told her it was only temporary. In reality, I planned to keep them as long as they lived—their lab days were over. I knelt down to their level and promised I would come back as soon as I could. I refilled their food and water, retrieved Sammy's journals from under my bed, and escaped through the window.

.

By the time RJ and I arrived at Sadiq's motel, Catherine had parked her rental car right outside his room, like a threat. I knocked on the door, and Sadiq answered.

"We don't have much time," I said, hurrying past him.

He closed the door and locked it behind him. "Conrad," he said, speaking slowly, "The game is up. Even if we had everything we needed, there's no way for us to work with Radkin breathing down our necks."

"No. We keep going."

A kind of calmness had settled over me. *still not strong enough. what's missing?* It's a common sensation, when a word is on the tip of your tongue, but I've always found two different versions of that feeling. In one, you know no matter how hard you think, how tightly you shut your eyes, the word isn't going to come, not then, not ever. And in the other version, yes, it's *right there.*

I turned to Catherine, who was watching me and RJ with a sad, curious expression. I think she was experiencing, or re-experiencing, the shock of my age. It's an observable phenomenon: the more teenagers you put together in a room, the younger they look.

I held up the journals, which I had placed in a canvas super-market bag. I felt as if I was carrying Sammy's remains. I handed them to her, and she slid her hands through the loops of the handles, her arm staggering a little under the weight. They were hers to carry, and I wondered if she was trying to imagine a day when she could give them to her son. She must have been because she said, "How bad are they, honestly? What am I in for?"

It was an impossible question to answer. "He's harder on him-self than we could ever be."

She hesitated, and I realized what it was she really wanted to know—*needed* to know, if she could even conceive of showing them to Theo.

"There's nothing about me in there," I promised.

Her face betrayed a flash of guilt for having made me say this, but all she said was "Thank you," and she produced from her coat a one-quart plastic container half-filled with what looked like green batter, or a thick pea soup.

Sadiq was at my side, inspecting the liquid with me. "Is it still good?"

"I don't know, Sadie. There's no expiration date." She looked up at us, and she must have seen in our faces how much we had at stake. So she added, "Keep it cold, I guess."

Before she could say goodbye, I hugged her. Behind me, Sadiq and RJ were silent. Catherine put a hand on my shoulder, patted twice, and withdrew.

"I really am sorry for everything you've been through," she said. "Nice to meet you," she said to RJ, who repeated those words back to her. To Sadiq, she gave a quick kiss on the cheek. "Don't be a shithead. Talk him out of this."

"Catherine," I said as she opened the door, and she must have thought I had changed my mind because her grip tightened on the bag. "He really killed himself?"

"Sweetheart, if it wasn't you, it would have been someone else. If it wasn't me, if it wasn't Sadie . . ." She gestured with her free hand to all of us, then she shrugged—*What can you do?*—and was gone.

"Don't despair," Sadiq said, after the door closed. "I was able to reach Bogdi."

Sadiq had barely finished this sentence when his laptop began to chime with a message: *Incoming call: Boggers.*

We gathered around the laptop, trying to fit ourselves into the tiny box that showed our faces. Sadiq occupied the middle of the frame, with me on his left and RJ to the right. In comparison to the two of them, I was struck immediately by how awful I looked— greasy, pale as birch, almost corpselike in the blue-white glow of the screen.

The video hiccupped in a burst of pixels, and there was Bogdi. He blinked at us as though he'd been sleeping for years. He was not at all like Sammy had described him—a science prodigy dressed as a frat boy. Instead, his hair was long and lawless, jutting off his head and disappearing at the top of the screen. He had a thick, Cold War mustache. His eyes were small and dull. He had placed himself close, unusually close, to the camera. He seemed to huddle over the screen, and his haggard appearance made me think that either he was afraid of being overheard or that he needed the laptop for warmth.

I tried to identify his location, but few of his surroundings were visible. I could see a dark gray wall behind him, right up against his back, and my first thought was *prison cell*. The light on his face was bright but low, and strangely angled, as though he'd placed a flashlight just out of the frame. What sort of prison allows its inmates to video chat?

"S . . . Sadiq?" Bogdi's voice was thin. "Is that you, old friend?"

Sadiq was shaking his head in disbelief. "Boggers. My God. Are you all right?"

Bogdi's voice, too, was nothing like I expected. Gone was the Americanized, Valley girl lilt of Sammy's journals, replaced with a heavily accented, raw-throated weariness. "Don't worry about me," he said unconvincingly. "Winters are hard, that's all." He closed his eyes. "Winters are hard."

"Where are you?" Sadiq asked.

Bogdi looked around suspiciously, licking his lips. "I can't tell you that. It wouldn't be safe for either of us."

Sadiq was too stunned to speak, so I said, "I'm Conrad. This is RJ. We were friends of Sammy."

"I'm sorry for your hardships. I know what it's like to feel loss."

"Had you already heard?" I asked.

Bogdi bit his lip as though fighting back tears. "Yes. No matter where I go, bad news finds me."

In the awkward silence that followed, it was hard to know if the connection was still stable. Bogdi's wan face watched us from the other side, barely moving.

Sadiq cleared his throat. "We were going to ask for your help, but maybe you're the one who needs it."

"No one can help me." Bogdi's voice was hard and tinny. "Tell me your troubles."

Hesitantly, Sadiq told him our troubles. "We need Dor. We thought you and Livia might be able to help us."

Bogdi's eyes went wide with hurt, as though he'd been struck with a bullet offscreen. "Livia is dead," he whispered, his voice *this* close to breaking.

"Oh, Boggers," said Sadiq. "How? When?"

"There was an accident. She was in—I don't know your American word for it. A . . . dirge . . . a floating . . ." Bogdi's hand appeared, miming the act of something taking off, flying away.

"A dirigible?" I said.

Bogdi nodded, his mouth twitching. "Yes."

Sadiq leaned into the camera, covering my face with his own. "Livia died in a blimp?"

Hearing this, Bogdi burst into hysterics, and it took me a moment—a good five seconds, maybe more—to realize he was laughing. "Yes," he was trying to say, but the game was up. He leaned back, grinning, and the gray background pulled away in a disorienting act of showmanship. It wasn't a prison wall, I realized, but a gray piece of what looked like poster board that someone had been manning behind him. I could guess who that someone might be.

Bogdi held his computer at arm's length, and a woman appeared over his shoulder, howling with laughter. Livia. They were on a bed—I could see the headboard and pillows—and she was rolling around so fast she became a blur of images: a long, dark ponytail, a jangle of hoop earrings. Bogdi contributed to the pandemonium by shaking the camera, and I saw a flash of Livia's bare feet and the briefest glimpse of her face—delicate nose, rounded chin. She was a wild, adorable thing.

"You fucking *dorks*," she said. "You thought I died in a blimp!"

"You scared me," Sadiq said. "God, you scared me."

Livia stopped writhing and joined Bogdi in the frame. His eyes were shut with laughter. "Poor baby," Livia said to Sadiq. "Poor sweetie."

RJ was looking at me, like, *What?*

"Where are you, really?" I said.

Bogdi angled the computer toward a tall window, but all

I could see was his reflection and Livia's. She was wrapped around him like a vine.

"Welcome to the Hilton Hotel of Boston, America!"

"How are you in the States?" Sadiq asked.

"It's not, like, superconvenient," Bogdi said. "But Samster said he would give everything he had to Radkin if we didn't fly over here."

Of course. Sammy had called them. And what better bait than Radkin?

"So you're okay?" Sadiq asked.

"Um, the pool here has a waterslide," Bogdi said.

RJ made a frustrated sound. In all of my life, I've never met another teenager with less patience for adults. "Can you help us or not? We need Dor."

Livia showed her teeth. "Relax, PJ.'

"Okay," Bogdi said, "we'll be there in, what, three hours? Two and a half?"

"Just like that?" I asked.

"Sure," Livia said. "We help you, and you give us the recipe book."

"Oh," I said. This was my life: whenever there seemed to be nothing left to lose, someone would say, *Just one more thing . . .*

Bogdi clapped his hands, understanding that I had no choice but to agree. "Cool cool cool." He reached for the mouse to close the call. "See you bitches soon!"

Sammy must have told Bogdi and Livia about the storage unit, because they asked to meet us there. I told them there was nothing of value left, but they insisted, so that's where we went—RJ, Sadiq, and me—in the early evening. There was a drizzle, so we lined up with our backs to the building, taking shelter in the slight overhang of the roof. I had only a few hours, I figured, until Radkin acted on his threat.

RJ's phone sounded. "Shit," he said, grimacing. "My dad. He says *he'll* call the police if I'm not home in ten minutes."

"Go," I said. "We'll be fine."

RJ looked at me, hearing the lie, and hesitated.

"I'll take care of Conrad," Sadiq promised.

After RJ departed, Sadiq and I had a final moment of quiet, just the two of us. I was still working through everything I'd learned in the past twenty-four hours. It seemed Sammy had used the AGE and the Immortalist Underground as lures for each other, to bring them to Littlefield, but why? And who had been following me, if not Radkin?

As I stood outside of the storage facility, a more immediate question came to mind. "If Radkin didn't know about the storage unit," I asked Sadiq, "who broke the lock?"

Sadiq thought about this for a moment, then he laughed. "Here's a hypothesis: What if Sammy left you the package, with the key, and then realized he still needed something from the storage unit? Perhaps what he used that night to, well . . ."

"So he could drive back to my house and risk someone catching him, or he could break the lock?" It made a kind of sense: Sammy's final act of forgetfulness.

Sadiq's smile had faded, and it reminded me of Sammy and how brief his happiness always seemed. "We've both done a lot for him," Sadiq said. "Probably more than we should have."

I said nothing. Even if he was right, I couldn't let myself think that way. To get through this, I had to believe I was making the right choices, for the right reasons.

A moment later, Bogdi and Livia pulled into the lot. I had expected the two of them to show up in one of those psychedelic 1970s vans, or, who knows, a golden tank. But it was just a blue sedan, a two-door, with New Hampshire plates. It was completely anonymous except for the rear windshield, where they'd affixed a small decal of the Romanian flag. Three vertical stripes: blue, yellow, red.

Bogdi, in the passenger seat, was the first to step out of the car. He took a moment to examine Livia's parking job—she'd parked horizontally across two separate spaces—and greeted us with a wave. He'd pulled his long hair up into a bun, which bobbed on his head as he jogged toward us. He went straight to Sadiq and wrapped his skinny arms around Sadiq's big body. Sadiq returned the hug with one arm.

Bogdi held Sadiq at arm's length. "Pal," he said gravely, "I'm so sorry I ruined your life in Tahiti."

"Just try not to ruin anyone else's." Sadiq glanced at me.

I was watching Livia tug an empty-looking duffel bag out of the car. She was wearing a neon-green ski jacket and parachute pants with a bright, vaguely floral pattern. She planted a foot on the front bumper of the car and tied the laces of her Reeboks. She looked over at me from this position, and in the brief moment before Bogdi blocked my view of her, I knew: no matter how strangely she might act, she was serious, and dangerous.

Bogdi encircled me in a hug, and I felt the brittle hairs of his mustache on my cheek. "Little Conrad," he said into my ear.

By the time he released me, Livia was upon us. Her hoop earrings rotated slightly as she moved. "You have the book?"

"Yeah." I gestured with my head to the backpack looped around my shoulders. Then, because she was scary, I added, "It's nice to meet you."

Livia made a snorting sound with her nose. "Storage unit. Storage unit. Storage unit." She ushered us toward the double doors of the building.

"There's nothing useful here," I said, but I led them anyway to the unit, where Bogdi crouched into a squat, his bony knees touching his chest, and lifted the door by the handle. It was only halfway up when he emitted a squeal of delight.

"Bingo, bongo!" He motioned theatrically for Livia to enter.

She strode inside and made a beeline for one of the boxes in the far corner. When I saw what it was, it was the stupidest I've ever felt in my life, and there has not been a single moment since that's come close.

The sparklers.

Sadiq looked at me, and I could see him trying to keep the frustration off his face. "You didn't tell me that was here," he said evenly.

We'd had all the Dor we needed—a whole box of it—sitting unguarded in the storage unit. "I didn't know about the Dor when I first came here," I said, but that was no excuse. What's worse was the measurement in Sammy's final recipe: *Dor (1 sp)*. One sparkler.

Livia pulled a switchblade out of her ski jacket and jabbed it unceremoniously into the box. She carved open the packing tape and flipped the lid. Watching her, I remembered that first night I opened the box of Sammy's journals. Back then, I believed my only problem was heartache. Bogdi was watching her, too, and I saw it, like a dark eddy behind his laughing eyes: his widow self. I knew then that despite his resources, Bogdi had needed Sammy much more than Sammy needed him. When it came to the elixir of life, Bogdi had the curse of happiness. He had too much to lose.

Livia dumped the sparklers into the duffel bag. When she was done, she pushed the knife closed on the meat of her thigh and tossed the bag out of the unit to Bogdi, who slung it over his head. Livia returned to the hallway, and she was holding a single sparkler, waving it back and forth as if it were lit, as if this were a celebration.

She held it out to me, but when I reached for it, she pulled it away. "Book."

"I need two." One for my father, one for Stephanie.

Livia's face assumed a puzzled expression, but this was another act. "Oh? Two sparklers? Do you have two books?"

"You know there's only one."

Livia mimed wiping sweat from her brow. "Phew! Because there is only one sparkler, so everything is fair."

"Livia, please," Sadiq said. "He's just a kid."

Livia motioned to the debris of our surroundings, as if to say, *Look where we are.* "This is not a place for children," she hissed, "so if that's what he is, you shouldn't have brought him."

"Please," I said. "They're dying."

"No offense," Bogdi said from behind me, "but, like, everyone is dying."

Livia's argument was less philosophical. "One of these is worth more than your life. Than Papa's life. Than PJ's crippled sister's life."

I looked back and forth between them. They had traveled so far to get here: Romania to Boston, Boston to Maine. They'd put on that ridiculous show on the computer. They said they wanted the recipe book, and maybe that was true, but it was the Dor that had activated Livia's greed.

"I saw Gavril," I said.

They paused. Livia's lip curled, and Bogdi held the strap of the duffel bag with two hands.

"You didn't know he was working for Radkin when you sabotaged the AGE in Tahiti."

"How could we have?" Bogdi asked, and I felt that he was talking to Livia more than to me. They'd had this conversation many, many times. "He was our oldest pal."

I pointed with my chin at the duffel bag. "How much Dor do you have left?"

"You don't know *anything*," Livia said, which was answer enough. They'd taken down Radkin not knowing how much he had against them. In destroying the AGE, they'd destroyed themselves.

Sadiq had followed along. "The warehouse? The equipment?"

Bogdi spit on the ground. "Seized. An 'asset of the government.'"

It was nice for at least one thing to make sense. "You didn't know Sammy had any left until he called you. You're just as desperate as I am."

"If you're so smart," Livia said, "you'll stop talking and take the sparkler."

I shook my head because I knew what it would mean if I took only one. I knew the decision it would leave me. And I knew, although I hated to admit it, what choice I would make. "No, I need two."

Livia was on me so fast I can't even describe the motion of her body. We had not been far apart—an arm's length—but then her face was right in front of me, and she held in one hand both the sparkler and the collar of my shirt. In the other hand, she had the knife.

"Give me the fucking book"—her words were hot on my face—"and take the sparkler, or I'll cut you open and leave the sparkler inside you."

Bogdi dropped the duffel bag and sprang forward, tried to fit

his skinny body into the narrow space between us. I could see it
in his face: if she had to, she would do it. "Let's relax," he said.
"But you should also, like, take the sparkler."

I looked to Sadiq, and he nodded. So I took the backpack off
my shoulder, unzipped it, and offered her the recipe book. She
let go of my collar, even straightened it for me. We made the ex-
change. I held the sparkler between my forefinger and thumb, and
it was so skinny and so light. It was like holding nothing.

As Bogdi and Livia began the walk down the hall, Livia paused
midstep. Bogdi took another pace before he realized she wasn't
with him and turned with a questioning look. Before he did, I realized why she'd stopped: he'd left the duffel bag on the floor.

"Darling?" She curdled the word with sarcasm. "What's
missing?"

Bogdi blushed and ran back for the bag. Once he had it secure around his shoulder, Livia made a clicking noise with her
mouth—*Let's go*—and the two of them started again down the
hallway.

As they went, Sadiq stood next to me and examined the sparkler in my hand. He asked me something, but I don't remember
what. I wasn't really there. Livia's question was hovering in front
of me: *What's missing?* I let the words—and the *sound* of them,
like a frustrated tutor—hang there, solidifying. Then I pulled up
Sammy's final recipe in my mind, placed it alongside Livia's
question.

still not strong enough. what's missing?

Darling? What's missing?

It wasn't a question. It was a quiz.

All this time, I had thought Sammy died on the precipice, so
close to something he couldn't quite reach. I thought he needed
my help. Maybe I wanted to believe that. But I had to be honest
with myself: He knew he was going to die. He put in motion a series of events—phone calls, packages, cryptic notes—that brought
everyone to Littlefield together. All of the data he had left me
were forming a constellation, a shape that held meaning.

What's missing? Sammy had known the answer; he had died
knowing it. I'd been thinking of the missing component as some-

thing he had overlooked, when really it was something he had been trying to show me. We had the Appetizer, we had the Entrée, and it wasn't some rogue ingredient we lacked, some random plant from a faraway country. It was a third course. It was Dessert.

Without saying anything to Sadiq, I ran down the hallway to stop Livia and Bogdi before they left. I found them at the end of the corridor, waiting for the elevator.

"Wait!"

Livia threw her head back in agony. "We will never leave this place!"

Bogdi took her hand in his, squeezed. "What do you need, little Conrad?"

I caught my breath. "Do you know how I can get an ECT machine?"

Livia and Bogdi exchanged looks, and then she asked, "Where are we, again? Kentucky?"

"Maine."

Livia wrinkled her nose and said, "I have cousin near here," as though this was an answer to my question. She pulled out her phone and began to search through it, but then the elevator doors dinged open and revealed, staring out at us, Joseph Radkin and Gavril.

Gavril had a gun.

Instinctively, I stepped back. Gavril shook his head, and I took this to mean I shouldn't move any farther.

"Honey, look!" Livia said to Bogdi, in a sunshiny voice. "It's two dumb assholes."

Radkin moved out of the elevator, flanked by his spy. He began to say something, but spotted, over Bogdi's shoulder, an old friend he hadn't known was here. "Sadiq?"

Sadiq stepped two paces forward, and I did not fail to notice that he'd placed himself between me and the rest of them. "Dr. Radkin. What are you doing?"

"We're all here for the same thing." Radkin gestured at the duffel bag around Bogdi's shoulders.

"But why?" Sadiq asked. "You always said their work was bullshit."

I became aware, as Sadiq spoke, of Livia easing the switch-blade out of the back pocket of her pants.

To Sadiq's question, Radkin made a dismissive gesture with his hands. "If it's worth money, then it's real."

Gavril held the gun steady, though it wasn't clear to me that he was pointing it at anyone in particular. His mouse ears rose over my sight line of the gun, and they made me remember a ques-tion I'd forgotten to ask them—an absurd question, but one that mattered to me.

"Did you find a rat?" I asked Radkin and Gavril. "In Sammy's apartment? A Wistar rat?" It was one thing I still didn't know: What happened to Number 50 after Sammy revived him?

"Why are you *talking*?" Radkin asked, but Gavril caught my eyes, and something passed between us.

"I let your rat outside," Gavril said, and maybe it was only the dramatic nature of the scene, but I felt I could hear in his voice everything he'd been through: the experiments he'd en-dured, the friends he'd betrayed. "He's free."

I remember Livia, in the seconds that followed, pulling the knife and charging Gavril with a battle cry that could stop a beat-ing heart. I remember Bogdi dropping the duffel bag on the floor, freeing himself to fight. I saw the bag, and I went for it, thinking if I could only take one more sparkler, it would spare me from making that terrible choice. But Sadiq was in front of me, with a head start. He was reaching for the bag when the gun went off—and my God, a gunshot is so much louder than movies had told me—and he whirled away, the force of the bullet pushing him toward me, and the blood puffed from his arm like a firework. *He's dead*, my mind was screaming, *Sadiq is dead*, but I was taking his hand as I thought this, guiding him in the direction of the stairwell. We descended the stairs, half-running, half-falling, to the bottom floor. By the time we reached the doors, he was breath-ing so hard I wondered if *that* would be what killed him.

We burst into the parking lot. I ran to Sadiq's rental car, but I had to wait for him to catch up. When he finally made it, he unlocked the car, and we threw ourselves inside.

"Are you okay?" I tried to inspect him.

"I think so. It only grazed me." He took his hand away from his arm. The bullet had ripped his shirt, and the wound was an angry line on his skin—more than a graze, but so much less than it could have been. He put his hand back over it. "But you'll have to drive."

"Right."

We exited the car, switched sides, and reentered. But we didn't leave, not right away.

"Wait," he said. "Should we call the police?"

"We need to get you to a doctor."

"I'm fine." I heard for the first time how annoying it is for someone to say that when it obviously isn't true. "Can we just sit for a minute?"

"Okay." I still had the sparkler. I placed it on my lap.

The right thing to do was to give it to Stephanie. RJ was my friend, and his sister was so young. She was a good person, not like my father, who was old and cruel. Stephanie deserved my help, and RJ deserved my loyalty. But I was only torturing myself with these thoughts because my mind was made up.

"So." I assumed Sadiq was going to tell me to get moving already. Instead, he asked, "Electroshock therapy?"

"He'd been leading me toward it all summer. The *P. cupana* has one purpose: to restore memory after a brain burn."

Sadiq was working it out in his mind. "He thought ECT could finish the job of the cocaine and mercury? To eliminate the blood-brain barrier?"

I nodded. "It takes all three."

"But if he already knew, why put you through this whole charade?"

I would never know, completely, the answer to this question. That day in the lab, Sammy had said, "Never just take my word for it. You have to see for yourself." Maybe that was part of it—Sammy playing teacher, one last time. I pictured, too, the journals in Catherine's hands, the recipe book in Livia and Bogdi's. Maybe he used me to get these things where he wanted them. And then there was Radkin, the AGE squaring off against the Immortalist Underground, whatever violence was happening behind the bright white walls of the storage facility. There must have been a part of Sammy that was saying, to all of them, *You deserve each other.*

I was starting the car when I saw Livia come running out of the building. Her face was completely calm. She wasn't covered in blood, hers or anyone else's. It looked as if she was holding the knife, but as she came closer, I saw that it was only a pen, and in her other hand, a Post-it. It was as though I'd dreamed everything I'd seen inside.

I rolled down my window as she approached. "What happened?"

Sadiq leaned over so she could see his face. "Is anyone hurt?" It was just like him, to be asking this question as he bled through his fingers.

She tucked the pen behind her ear. She was not out of breath in the slightest. She had many fights left in her. "My cousin thinks he can help you. He knows where to get the shock machine."

"Oh my God," I said. "Where?"

She looked down at the note in her hand. She looked up at me. "Do you know a place called . . . Winterville?"

Sammy Feels a Spark

New York, 2009

Celebrity Client does one shot, two shots, three shots. Boom, boom, boom. Fireball, cherry bomb, buttery nipple.

The bartender is, like, *Hey, are you Celebrity Client?*

Celebrity Client is, like, *Fucking right!*

To celebrate, they do a Fireball.

Celebrity Client puts his back to the bar. He's in New York shooting a movie called *The Geometrist*, about an assassin who, like, uses geometry. The bar is a big rectangle at the head of the room, and the dance floor is a triangle with round edges, and the music is the . . . is the *vertex*. At the top of the hypotenuse is a girl who looks sort of like Livia. Yes, just like Livia. He feels this similarity in his pants. Her lips are half-parted, showing just a hint of her tongue, and it's like a dare.

What club is this, anyway? What neighborhood? Bushwick. Brooklyn. Buttery nipple.

Bzzz. His phone vibrates against his thigh. He slides it out, and it says, *The Samster.*

He answers, shouting into the phone, and he's, like, *Samster!*

And Samster is, like, *Celebrity Client.* With a period at the end. That's what makes Samster so funny! He's the kind of guy who uses semicolons in text messages. Celebrity Client has seen him do this. Celebrity Client still has the message, and he shows it to himself when someone is mean to him on Twitter. It makes him laugh every time.

The text said, *Thanks for the invite, but I can't come to the wrap party; I'm not feeling well.*

Hahaha.

Now, Samster is, like, *Do you have any Dor?*

And Celebrity Client is, like, *Fucking right!*

And Samster, all hesitant, is, like, *Can we meet up?* He says it as though Celebrity Client might say no! Some people just don't understand friendship.

Celebrity Client hands the phone to the bartender and is, like, *Tell this guy where I am.*

The crowd has pushed almost-Livia closer. He goes to her, and she stays put, fighting the geometry of the crowd. He's dancing, head rocking, and she's receptive, she knows who he is, and those half-parted lips are, like, *I dare you.*

Sammy boards the Staten Island Ferry at Whitehall. It is late, almost midnight, and one week exactly since his encounter with Celebrity Client at that stupid club—the night Sammy had solved the elixir of life.

There is not much fog, so it will be a good ride, where you can see the city. The other passengers are mostly drunks and young people. Sammy no longer considers himself young, though he is only twenty-nine. He's *never* felt young, not really—never known how it feels to have the stupid, innocent happiness of a child. Once the ferry has taken him farther from the terminal, he will dump his parents' ashes into the water, and then he will follow them down.

He was at his parents' home, where he's lived for a year, when the doorbell rang. He doesn't have a job or any of his own money. He sleeps in his old childhood bedroom, and just like a boy he keeps secret things under his bed. Mercury. Dor. After Tahiti, he's no longer in contact with Bogdi, so the Dor he has left is all he will ever have. It's like a big red timer, counting down. Whenever he can stomach it, he calls Celebrity Client and mooches.

When he answered the door, after checking the peephole, the police officer on his steps asked him if he was a relative of Don and Leena Tampari's. Sammy said that he was. The police officer asked to come in. Sammy said okay. The officer stepped inside and told him his parents had died in a car accident caused by an intoxicated driver. The intoxicated person was also dead, though Don and Leena's taxi driver had lived.

After the police left, he called Catherine, the mother of his boy.

"Oh, Christ," she said. "I'm so sorry."

"Can I speak to him?"

She hesitated. "It's two in the morning."

"Okay. Of course."

Catherine hated when Sammy did this, asking for Theo when Sammy knew he wasn't available. When he's actually around, she says, you're nowhere. Once, they took the boy to the zoo, and they'd done one of those photo booth pictures together, a set of three. In all of them, Catherine is looking at the camera (the right place), Sammy is looking at the monitor (the wrong place), and Theo is looking at *him*. Don and Leena put the printout on the refrigerator.

On the ferry, he thinks of Theo and feels good. The boy will sleep more soundly without someone calling at strange hours to wake him.

Celebrity Client reclines with almost-Livia on a red sofa in Sour Room. The club is Sweet&Sour, and it's two big rooms: one for dancing and one for everything else. He feels the pillowy softness of the cushions against his back, the heat and wet of the girl's leg hooked around his own.

The Samster arrives. He's almost as handsome as Celebrity Client, which is fine, it's good. He unhooks the ropes that separate Celebrity Client's sofa from the other, lesser sofas.

Celebrity Client is, like, *Nice!*

Samster, to almost-Livia, is, like, *I'm Sam.*

She introduces herself, and when she turns her face to the Samster, Celebrity Client knows: Samster sees it, too, the similarity. But then rather than give Celebrity Client a high five, Samster gives him a look, a sad look, that makes Celebrity Client want to see the semicolon.

Celebrity Client is, like, *Yo! How's things?*

Samster sits, mumbling an answer, and Celebrity Client is no dummy. He knows Samster didn't come here to chat.

A tray of shots. Three Wise Men.

The Samster is wearing a black T-shirt and pants that are not good. But the shot girl smiles at him anyway, and Celebrity Client thinks, *Yeah, baby! Get it!*

So to the waitress, he's, like, *Do you wanna do drugs with us on this couch?*

And she looks at Samster, but he doesn't say anything, and she's, like, *Something something something my shift!* She's got red hair, it's not natural, and she's wearing one of those black midriff shirts. Her stomach is smooth and muscled, and this is unbelievable, but she's got an *outie belly button.* You never see this! A shot girl with an outie!

The Samster moves over. He's just being polite, but she takes it as encouragement and slides in next to him. Their shoulders are touching. But now almost-Livia is jealous, so Celebrity Client tucks her hair behind her ear and gives her a little kiss on the nose.

With their faces still close, he's, like, *I want you.*

And she's, like, *Oh, yeah?*

Samster nudges him. *Do you have the Dor?*

The shot girl is, like, *What door?*

Celebrity Client is, like, *Samster, want to try something new?* Celebrity Client takes a little metal tube out of his pocket. It's called a Zapper, and it is small and sleek and stainless steel.

Samster is, like, *What is that?*

Celebrity Client is, like, *You've never heard of zapping?*

It's the newest thing. Just before the high kicks in, you give yourself a little jolt. It makes doing drugs more, like, interactive.

Samster's face goes so white it looks as if he might puke. He's, like, *No, thank you. No.*

Celebrity Client is, like, *You'll love it!*

Samster is talking fast, something about electricity, fragility, and the "brain structures."

He looks as if he might cry, but Celebrity Client is, like, *Trust me.*

Almost-Livia runs her fingers along the Zapper. She's, like, *Should we?*

Celebrity Client is, like, *We should.*

Sammy peers over the side of the ferry. Who would have guessed that Celebrity Client, of all people, would show him the answer? That golden retriever of a man. Sammy had felt the Zapper tickle his neck and discharge, and when he woke up, he just *knew*. The missing piece of the elixir was brain burn—the very thing from which he'd been running.

I'll huff and I'll puff and I'll blow your house down. To destroy the blood-brain barrier, he needed three big breaths: Dor, mercury, electricity. The Zapper wouldn't do it—that was nothing more than a toy. It would have to be brain burn. Once the barrier was down, he could safely double the volume of quicksilver—it would sneak in and then waltz right out, having completed its mission. It was Sadiq who said it, all those years ago in Romania: "Whatever you eat last is dessert."

Sammy peers over the side of the ferry. He doesn't know how to swim, so the chances of accidental survival are small. But he doesn't want to get sucked under the boat and churned up by the machinery. A few years ago, a New York stage actor killed himself this same way, and his body washed up mostly intact. If Sammy jumps from the rear of the boat, he should be fine.

He hasn't told anyone what he's going to do. He considered calling his old psychiatrist, Dr. Gillian Huang, but she is too smart, too resourceful. She might talk him out of it. The ferry is nearing the halfway mark. He removes the ashes from the pockets of his coat. He has them in a plastic bag, which he unzips. He checks his surroundings—no one is watching—and throws his parents into the water.

Celebrity Client is, like, *Imagine an ocean. The ocean is made of orgasms. You're floating in the ocean of orgasms, but you're also, like, high as fuck. That's Dor.*

Almost-Livia is, like, *You convinced me!*

The shot girl sticks her tongue into Samster's ear—he doesn't react, dude isn't ticklish, Celebrity Client has tried—and she's, like, *You go first.*

Celebrity Client hands him the Dor. *Just do your thing, bro.*

The Samster shoots the Dor and takes a drink of something from a bottle—something green. Celebrity Client plants the Zapper at the base of Samster's neck, right where it begins the curve into shoulder. He presses the button—there's only one button, no voltage settings, who wants the hassle?—and the Zapper is, like, *BWANG.*

Celebrity Client turns to almost-Livia, and she kisses him. Her tongue touches the roof of his mouth. When she pulls away, he's, like, *You're the best, most beautiful girl.*

And she's, like, *Aw,* and they kiss again.

The Samster's eyes roll back, and he's, like, *Something something something.*

The shot girl is, like, *Whaddidhe say???*

Celebrity Client is, like, *Your turn!*

She takes the Dor, and he zaps her. Next he zaps almost-Livia, who is not his true love, and then he just sort of sits with the Zapper, smelling the smells of Sour Room, wishing he were in Sweet Room. He didn't tell them the Zapper only gets three charges before it's empty, didn't tell Sammy that the Dor is running out, that he doesn't have enough for himself. Yesterday someone on Twitter was, like, *Your movies are the worst. You should kill yourself.* And he wanted to write back, *I can't think of one time I've been truly cruel to someone. How many people can say that? How many people, when it comes to kindness, to the giving of kindness, can honestly say they have no regrets?* But the gossip blogs would mock him endlessly if he said this. Plus it was too many characters.

Maybe forty minutes later, Samster is, like, *What's wrong with me?*

Celebrity Client thinks, *You still don't get it, Samster. There's nothing wrong with you, or with anyone, because imperfection is the only reasonable state of being. Who cares about living forever? Let's live! If a line is parallel to any line on a plane, it is parallel to the plane. That's the first rule of geometry, or at least it's one of the rules, and to me it means we are all brothers and sisters. We should celebrate this, not try to fix it.*

But Celebrity Client doesn't say this. Instead, he's, like, *Be cool, Samster. Everything is great. Soon we'll be dancing in Sweet Room.*

Naturally, Sammy would have to test his theory. Another rat study: something to confirm that ECT attacks the blood-brain barrier, that the elixir would work more strongly on a brain-burned subject. He would need to be sure the elixir could counteract the memory loss from a high-voltage, bilateral burn—a new ingredient, perhaps. But these thoughts are purely academic. They don't change what he has come here to do.

Sammy has his hands on the railing, ready to disembark, when he hears a fart behind him.

"Oh," says the source. "Thought I was alone."

Sammy just nods, humiliated on the man's behalf.

The man is short and pale, wearing jeans with an elastic waist. But rather than flee, as Sammy would have done, the man joins him at the railing. "It's my dialysis. It makes me gassy."

"I'm sorry." Below, the waters swirl in the wake of the ferry.

"I couldn't sleep. I figured I might as well go for a ride." When Sammy doesn't respond, the man explains, "I'm only in the city to see a specialist."

"Ah," Sammy says, and maybe because he's feeling bad for the man, or maybe because a small part of Sammy is scared of what will happen once the man leaves, he asks, "Where's home?"

"Maine." The man points in the direction of Maine. "I teach high school physics."

"I was never any good at physics. My master's is in chemistry."

A smile breaks across the man's face. "You know, we need someone to teach chemistry. I've been too sick to even place the ad."

At first Sammy doesn't say anything, but then he realizes the man is serious. Sammy laughs. "I don't know."

The man, who still hasn't introduced himself, places a light hand on Sammy's shoulder. "High school kids aren't that bad, and you're fifteen minutes from the ocean."

Before Sammy can stop him, the man is telling him about his hometown, which Sammy will remember as Littletown, but then he'll get a phone call, and the man will say, no, it's Little*field*. Sammy will decide that disappearing is just as good as dying, so he'll pack up his stuff, without telling Catherine, and leave.

21

Home

By the time I reached my father, I had missed fifteen calls from Dana, five of which had produced voice mails.

"I'm sorry if you felt ambushed," said the first, "but you're not in trouble."

"Get your ass home," said the last.

I was driving Sadiq's rental car, alone, with nothing but a learner's permit. I'd left Sadiq at the hospital, barely stopping to say goodbye. Despite my urgency, I'd spent the entire drive to Cumberland in the far right lane, getting passed by tractor trailers and, once, most embarrassingly, by someone in a driver's ed car. In a cooler in the trunk, I had everything I needed to create the elixir of life.

It was almost midnight when I hit the long dirt driveway that led to St. Matthias. The moon was big above the trees. I took my foot off the gas, and the car rumbled past the little nighttime animals whose eyes flashed in the headlights. It was so dark I nearly missed the parking area and drove straight onto the lawn. I turned off the car, killed the headlights, and sat in the growing cold to see if anyone would emerge from the main house to investigate my arrival. While I waited, my mind drifted to RJ. When we started this adventure, I assumed he would be here with me, if we even made it this far. Instead I was alone, and he would never, ever forgive me.

I slipped out of the car and followed my memory to my dad's room. As I walked, rocks and wood chips crunched under my sneakers, the sound bouncing off the lake. It felt as if I were the only person in a five-mile radius making noise, but either everyone was asleep or nighttime strolls are common among addicts, because no lights turned on, no doors opened. The narrow path led to my father's steps, which I climbed quietly, testing each one with my weight.

At the top, I tapped the wooden door with my finger. "Dad," I whispered. "Dad."

Nothing.

I risked a louder knock, two quick raps. Inside my dad's room, I heard the creak of a spring-supported mattress, and through his window I saw the glow of a cell phone or bedside clock. I knocked again.

He opened the door a few seconds later, a blanket wrapped around his bare, impossibly thin shoulders. I've never, ever seen a person look the way he looked that night. His body, in the porch light, was yellow and gray—not yellow*ish*, not gray*ish*. I stepped back, catching my foot on the step and nearly tumbling to the ground. Just in time, I caught myself on the railing.

My dad squinted at me. "Con?" he said too loudly, standing aside in the doorway so that I could come inside. "What are you doing here?" He closed the door behind me.

I whispered, hoping he would follow my lead and lower his voice. "Do you remember when you said you'd give me one Make a Wish?"

He picked a sweater off the floor and began to turn it right-side out. "Vaguely. Yes."

"I need you to come to Winterville with me, and I need you to do whatever I say when we get there."

"That sounds like more than one wish. I'm not going to Winterville."

"Please."

He sat on the edge of the bed and made me wait as he stuck his pallid head through the sweater. "Your mother always said it was hard to say no to you, but I never felt that way."

"You promised." I took his arm, pulling him back up.

He steadied himself against me, coughed. "If I do this"—he

looked right at me—"it comes with full immunity. All past crimes forgotten."

"Sure," I said, not really understanding, heading for the door.

"Hey." He stopped me. "I'm saying you have to forgive me for being a shit dad."

I stared at the floor. I didn't know if I could do what he was asking. I'd carried my hurt and anger at him for so long; it wasn't like luggage I could simply leave on the side of the road.

"Okay. But you also have to call Dana and tell her I'm with you and that I'm spending the night here."

He laughed himself into coughing again. "Oh, she'll love that. I'll do that for free." He grabbed his phone from the table and pointed me toward the closet. "Get my jacket, and we'll go."

It was a five-hour drive from Cumberland to Winterville, almost three hundred miles. My father lay in the passenger seat, his seat reclined to the maximum, dozing on and off. I drove, gripping the steering wheel so hard I would later find bruises on my palms. At that hour, it was just us and the trucks driving I-95 north through Brunswick, Augusta, Waterville. It was too hard to find a radio station, so we drove in silence, interrupted only by occasional bursts of my father's snoring. He didn't ask why I was taking him to Winterville until hour two, when we hit Pittsfield and he was woken by the distant sound of a fire truck.

"What's the plan?" he said then, popping his seat upright, stretching his arms above his head. I could see how hard it was for him to be crammed into this tiny car. He grimaced and adjusted his seat belt.

"It's better if I don't tell you."

"You're running this show, but a hint would be nice."

A truck passed me on the left, and I moved a little into the breakdown lane to make room for it. "You're going to die before they let you out of St. Matthias," I said once the truck had merged back into the right lane in front of me.

He turned in his seat, half-startled, half-amused. "You've gotten really honest."

"Do you think I'm wrong?"

He sighed, though it was more of a wheeze, dry like the desert. "No, I don't think you're wrong."

"Okay, so would you agree that if you're going to die anyway, it would be worth trying anything to save yourself, even if that thing is kind of insane?"

His eyebrows shot up. "Wait, that's what this is about? You're trying to help me?"

"Of course. What else would it be?"

He looked out the window. "I don't know. I just didn't realize."

I didn't say anything. His uncertainty reminded me of how little we understood each other, how rarely we'd even talked—really talked—over the past few years.

"Sorry, kiddo," he said after a minute, "but I need to sleep."

"It's okay."

He reclined again and was snoring in seconds.

We hit Bangor and Old Town, and the interstate led us away from the ocean and deeper into lake territory. The air grew thinner and sweeter then, less salty. I cracked my window, just a fraction of an inch. The speed limit changed to 75 mph, and seeing this, I said screw it, what's left to lose, and stepped hard, and then harder, on the gas.

The moon was still up but low in the sky when we passed Portage Lake and saw the sign welcoming us to Winterville. Bad weather came early up there, and the ground was hard with cold. If my dad had been awake, he would have protested as I turned right onto Dubey Lane, but he wasn't awake, so I switched on the brights and followed my heart home.

The road to our old house was paved, technically, but so long ago that the icy winters had cracked the pavement in huge, strangely uniform chunks, revealing the dirt and stone beneath it. Maybe the light was right, or maybe I was just sleep deprived, but I could *see* our old life. There, on the side of the road just before our mailbox, was where my mother, in heavy sweaters and pale, high-waisted mom jeans, had hung bat houses that never attracted bats, being much too low and facing the wrong direction, and instead housed only spiders and long green caterpillars. And there, halfway down our driveway, was where my dad had tried so hard to grow peas in square wooden planters, but deer would come with their whole families and eat them, roots and all, straight out of the dirt, burping as they did it and flicking their ears. You can buy deer repellents—and we tried those—but the owner of the convenience store said, "Honestly, if you aren't prepared to shoot them, they're going to eat your peas. Are you prepared to shoot them?" My dad said no, definitely not, and the man said, "Me neither, and that's why I buy my vegetables from the grocery."

I stopped the car when I saw another car, a minivan, parked in the driveway. My father sold this house after I moved out, and he sold it cheaply, so it went fast. A new family lived there now—a husband and wife, a boy about my age, just a little younger. Dana had given me this information when they made their first offer, and she said it happily, as though it would please me to know that a boy my age was living in my house. For years I'd pictured that boy in my bedroom, sleeping soundly, lulled by his confidence in the world's moral truths.

I kept my lights on and studied the house for changes. They hadn't repainted, but they'd done something to the roof, and the shingles looked bright and bloodred. They'd installed a second exterior light on the side of the house, and this shone onto an empty doghouse, a big one, such as for a German shepherd.

Next to me, my dad woke up, sensing the car's lack of movement. He was disoriented, and he clutched at the dashboard. "What's happening?" His voice was breathy and panicked.

"It's okay. We're in Winterville."

He nodded and began to relax, but when he saw the house, his face darkened. "What are we doing here?"

"I don't know. I just wanted to see."

He elevated his seat. "Well, let's go. People live here. You're going to scare them."

Foolishly, this hadn't occurred to me. How could anyone be scared of us? This was our home.

"Christ"—my dad reached over me—"at least turn off the lights."

"I just wanted to see."

Whatever softness in him I'd found earlier, he seemed to have slept it off. "This is the last place I'd want to be. Living here alone with you was the worst part of my life."

I was too hurt to say anything, and too angry at myself for letting him hurt me. I put the car in reverse and did a slow, careful turn until the car was facing the road and I could switch back on the lights.

My dad settled in his seat. "I didn't agree to side trips. Let's just get where we're going."

"Fine." I reminded myself that I *wasn't* saving him, not really—I was *killing* this version of him. I steered the car back onto Main Street, into and out of town, and toward the ruins of the now-defunct Aroostook County Health Organization, the conversion camp for homosexual boys.

My dad made me stop for coffee on the way, and we refueled, so it looked something like morning by the time we reached the camp. The sight of the sun peeking over the tree line tricked my body into thinking it was time to wake up, and I felt, if not energized, at least less nauseatingly tired. My dad's only advantage over me was that he'd become accustomed to bad, interrupted sleeps. He hummed quietly to himself as he sipped his drink and worked the phlegm out of his lungs.

"This place?" he said as I turned into the camp and drove right past the open gates.

"I told you it was crazy."

I parked the car and circled around the hood to help my dad out of his seat. He clasped my forearm and groaned as I pulled him standing. Prior to its use as a camp, the building had served as a packing and shipping facility for a Canadian company that made snowshoes and cross-country skis. When the Health

Organization took over, they'd painted the building a soft, pretty shade of blue. As a kid passing by on the bus, I could see the small outbuildings, like barracks, where the children slept at night. Those were missing now—having been torn down, I assumed, when the place closed.

When we first pulled in, I hadn't noticed the tiny white two-door parked with its nose kissing the building, but a man was coming out of it, tall, heavy, and dressed in a square black suit. He flashed an even-toothed smile as he approached, his hand extended long before he reached us. He pumped my dad's arm once, mine twice.

"You the folks come to see the place?" It was just past six in the morning, but he showed no signs of tiredness or of having been put out.

"Are you Livia's cousin?" I asked.

"I don't know who that is," he said cheerfully. "My pal Sergiu called and said to wait for you here. That guy has bought a *lot* of property from me, so when he says jump . . ."

I started to thank him, but he was already leading us to the front doors. "I'm Frank." He unlocked the building. "You'll see there's oodles of space in here." He held the door for us and punched some switches on the wall. The entry room lit up in a wave of bright, sterile light. "Kind of a creepy vibe, but never let decorations keep you from buying a place."

Those decorations comprised two separate mobiles of construction-paper snowflakes, a column lined with postcards, and a feature wall with a pastel mural of Jesus touching ten to fifteen boys on the tops of their heads. Jesus had been drawn so that he appeared to have a separate arm for each boy, and while I think the idea was that his two arms could move at a speed beyond sight, he nonetheless looked like an octopus monster, his happy eyes glowing as he made sparks of light shoot out of yet another boy's head. At the foot of the mural, a box of blue-handled safety scissors lay next to a box of crayons, all in primary colors.

"I'm sorry," said Frank to my dad, studying him, "but are you Ned Aybinder?"

My dad blew his nose and groaned from the exertion. "You recognize me from my acting roles or my modeling work?"

"Ha ha. I believe I sold your house."

My dad looked at him. "Oh, that's right. Frank." I couldn't tell if my dad actually remembered this.

Frank swatted one of the mobiles, setting it in motion. "That was an easier sell than this place. Though it really is a lot of space for the money."

I said nothing, and my dad had stopped listening. He found an old swivel desk chair and claimed it for himself.

There was an awkward pause.

"Listen, should I leave you two with my card? Or is this a forget-you-ever-saw-us type of situation? Like I said, Sergiu has bought a *lot* of property from me." Frank was looking at my dad for an answer.

"Ask the kid."

I felt like the least intimidating criminal in history. "You should probably forget us."

Frank held up his hands: *Say no more.* "Just leave the key on the desk. And enjoy your stay, et cetera."

I waited until I heard his car pull away from the building. Signs for the restroom pointed one way, for the barracks, another. A third sign said CLASSROOMS →.

My phone buzzed with a text from RJ: *Dana knows u & dad not in Cumberland. She MAD.*

"Upsy-daisy," I said to my dad.

His fingernails, as he reached for my arm, were the color of mustard. "I feel like you're bringing me to a surprise party."

"It's just us," I promised.

We navigated the long, dusty corridors. At each doorway, I stopped to investigate the contents of that room while my dad leaned against the wall, breathing hard. One classroom contained an art-therapy studio, the walls still covered with crayon drawings of boys and girls holding hands. Another was a small library, which held not many books but a lot of pamphlets. By the door, a copy of *Hamlet's Father* lay atop an illustrated children's Bible. In the halls themselves I found a jump rope, a toothbrush, and a stack of origami paper. There was a flashlight with no batteries, and farther down, a box of unmarked cassette tapes. This place, like many similar places, had been shut down following allegations of abuse, and it was impossible not to see every object in every room in terms of its potential to harm a child.

In the back of the building, in the classroom farthest from the entrance, I found a 1960 Siemens Konvulsator.

I'm not sure if my dad recognized the machine. "Can I sit?" he asked. Next to the Konvulsator was what looked like a brown leather dentist chair, but with wrist, chest, and foot restraints. I helped him settle into it and then knelt in front of the machine.

The device was white and about the size of a large microwave. A series of switches and knobs adorned the front panel, and these were labeled in German, though someone had scribbled English translations in red Sharpie along the side. I didn't need them. An ECT device is surprisingly, frighteningly simple, and its design matches its function—you're shocking someone, not launching a spaceship. One knob controlled the intensity of the current, and two knobs acted as timers: one to control the duration of each shock, and one to control the amount of time between shocks. There was a power switch, and in the center of the panel, a square yellow button marked ANFANG—in Sharpie, BEGIN.

RECIPE #102

SAMMY AND CONRAD'S ELIXIR OF LIFE
[ANNOTATED]
Yield: 1

INGREDIENTS
THE APPETIZER
1. Dor (1 sp) [cocaine weakens the blood-brain barrier (first attack) and triggers the immune system; immunostimulants strengthen the body's defenses]

THE ENTRÉE
1. Quicksilver (200 ml) [sneaks past and dissolves the

blood-brain barrier (second attack) and clears the lobes of the
brain like a forest fire (destruction breeds creation)]
2. Tribal medicine (100 ml) [*slow-acting soursop restores the*
blood-brain barrier once the elixir has finished its work]
3. B. *rossica* (3 oz) [*free radical scavenging activity combats*
the effects of aging]
4. Rapamycin (15 mg) [*inhibits the kinase mTOR to slow*
future aging]
5. P. *cupana* (100 mg) [*targets hippocampal NMDA recep-*
tors to aid memory formation and retention]

THE DESSERT
1. Brain burn (bilateral) [*third and final attack on the*
blood-brain barrier, allowing the mercury to escape]

PREPARATION
Inject Appetizer. Combine Entrée and drink. Dessert until
seizure.

HOW DID IT TASTE?
My father would have to tell me, if he survived.

When I came back to the classroom with the cooler, my father
was asleep in the dentist chair, his mouth open. He looked like a
boy. Quietly, I tore open the sparkler and dumped its contents
into the spoon. I used the syringe to draw up water from my bottle
and sprayed it onto the powder. With the top of the plunger, I
stirred the liquid clear. I pulled the Dor into the syringe and
flicked the needle, depressing the plunger until all of the air was
out of the rig.

I took my father's arm, gently, trying not to wake him. I rolled
up his sleeve and wiped his arm with an alcohol pad. With shaking hands I tied the elastic tourniquet around his arm, secured it
with a slipknot. My father's eyelids fluttered, but he didn't wake.
I pinned his arm against the chair and reminded myself of Sadiq's
instructions: *Go slow, but be confident.*

I found a vein, held my breath, and stuck in the needle. I removed the tourniquet and injected my father with the Dor. His nose pinched, reacting even in sleep to the pain.

As I withdrew the needle, he opened his eyes. "Con? What's happening?"

"You're okay."

"We're in Winterville. You took us to the house."

"Yeah."

He licked his lips. "I feel weird."

"I need you to drink something."

He didn't respond. I squeezed his hand and took the Entrée out of the cooler. This, we'd mixed back in Littlefield. I'd transferred it to a stainless steel travel mug so that he wouldn't be able to see the color.

"Can you sit up?" I didn't really ask, just pulled him up by the shoulders.

He groaned.

"I need you to drink this, and I need you to keep it down. That's really, really important."

"Roger that," he said thickly, and I know he was trying to give a salute, but he wasn't in full control of his body. His right arm just sort of hung there, twitching. He looked down at it in surprise.

"Open up." I held the mug and tipped it back slowly, not wanting to spill. The taste of it made his eyebrows squeeze together, but I kept on him, held the bottle against his lips. He drank the whole thing. When it was done, he closed his eyes, panting.

"Are you going to throw up?"

He took several deep breaths. "Only if we keep talking about it."

"Okay, sorry."

He fidgeted with the armrest as if he were still in the car. He was trying to recline. "The house looked good," he said dreamily. He closed his eyes.

I checked the knob beneath his chair, but he was already as far back as he could go. Even though he was falling asleep, and that was good, I said, "They made the roof so red."

"Mm," he said, surprising me. "It's cedar."

"What?"

He didn't open his eyes. His voice was as thick as peanut butter. "With cedar you buy it brighter. The weather will dull it
down."

"Oh." For some reason, even though I would never live in that
house again, I was flooded with relief.

"Good night," my dad said.

"Good night."

When, after five minutes, he still had a pulse, I opened his mouth
and inserted a mouthguard I'd bought at a pharmacy. The Dor
had kicked in by now, and I could have poked my dad right in
the eyeball without waking him. I attached the electrodes to his
temples and fastened the restraints on his body, which was easy,
like putting on a belt.

What's missing? Brain burn. Dessert. Sammy's theory, now
mine, was that ECT disrupted the integrity of the blood-brain
barrier. But that's all it was, as I hooked my father up to the
machine—a theory.

Many years later, as part of my undergraduate thesis, I proved
it. I designed an experiment based on Dr. Edward Goldmann's
initial demonstration of what was then called the hematoence-
phalic barrier. I injected trypan blue dye into the bloodstreams
of Wistar rats, some of whom were then treated with ECT, some
not. In the untreated rats, the dye failed, as expected, to reach the
central nervous system. In the rats treated with ECT, the brain
turned blue. You can find my article on the subject in the *Journal of Neurochemistry*. In the acknowledgments section, I thank
Sammy.

When everything was ready, I set the dials on the machine. I
watched my dad sleep, allowing myself a few seconds of quiet to
consider the magnitude of the occasion. I'd spent a lot of time
thinking about what would happen if the elixir didn't work, but

not until I had my finger hovering over that big yellow button—
ANFANG—did I understand how much of a killer I would be if
things went wrong.

I punched the button. My dad's jaw clenched and puckered
as if he'd bitten into a lemon. His arms pulled against the restraints, his shoulders rocking. For an awful second, his eyes
opened, and I could see only the whites of them, like the bark of
a birch tree. He dug his fingernails into his palms, and I tried to
reach in, to pry his fingers apart.

After what felt like forever but had only been four or five seconds, his body went slack. I thought for sure I had killed him. I
threw my face against his chest, listening for breath, for a heartbeat. It was there, but faint. I reached for the machine, turning it
up to 600. My dad was so quiet I wanted to punch him right in
his slack, yellow face. The safety features required a delay of ten
seconds before I could press ANFANG again, and these seconds
I counted out loud: "One Mississippi, two Mississippi, three
Mississippi . . ." Normally, a heart-rate monitor would beep or
flatline, making noise, speaking for my father. But none of that
equipment was here. It was just me and my dad and the Konvulsator, surrounded by dust.

". . . ten Mississippi." ANFANG.

My dad's body surged again, and he was alive, twitching
and rocking. This time, a seizure took hold. His fingers waggled
and danced as if he were playing the piano. His jaw worked around
the mouthguard, trying to spit it out, but the mouthguard held.
He tried to roll over in his seat, and I was worried he'd break his
shoulder, so I threw myself on top of him, weighing him down
against the leather padding. He didn't make any noise, other than
the sound of his body rubbing against the fabric. He just fought
and fought, and I fought back, gripping his arms, leaning into him,
giving it everything I had—because fuck him, that's why. Because
live. I needed someone to live.

When the seizure passed, he relaxed again, still sleeping. I
could hear his heartbeat with my ear on his ribs. I turned off the
Konvulsator and slumped, exhausted, to the floor. The adrena-
line left my body, and I felt as if it had taken my lungs with it. I

looked at my father, and I shook, and I asked myself if this was a
journey you don't come back from, even if you do.

An hour later, my father woke up. I'd removed the restraints, and
he used his left hand to wipe the drool off his chin.

"Ugh," he mumbled, his eyes barely open.

I pulled myself off the floor and stood over him. "Hey, Dad."

"Conrad? We should get you to school."

"No school today." That was a lie. "How do you feel?"

He scooted himself up in the seat, but barely. "Like I've been
drugged."

He slept until noon.

At eleven, the color of his skin began to change, subtly at first,
just a small, hesitant brightening. I tried different things to test
it. I covered one eye, I put my own skin next to his. Everything I
did stoked the fires of hope: my father was losing his yellowness.

When he first began to wake, I studied his eyes as he blinked,
moisture forming in the corners. His pupils were small and pure
glossy black, and the whites of his eyes were white only. The dark
rings around his irises had faded. They were wide and brown.

"Whoa," he said, after a moment. "Not so close, Con."

I pulled away and touched his hand, which was upturned on
the armrest. The redness and swelling in his palms had faded,
though I could still see it there. "How do you feel?"

"Good," he said casually, as though *of course* he was good,
what else would he be?

"Okay," I said hesitantly, not wanting to jinx it. "Can you
stand?"

He looked around. "We're in Winterville."

"We drove here last night."

He touched his head where the electrodes had been, but he
didn't ask any of the questions I was expecting. I helped him stand.
His legs were firm under his body, and he led me down the hall,
not asking why we were in the Health Organization.

Before we stepped into the cold sunlight, he turned to me. "Hey, mind if we stop by the old house before we go?"

"Okay?" I said, confused.

"Awesome. *Vámonos*."

When we reached the car, he hopped into the driver's seat.

"You hungry or anything?" he asked me an hour or so later, as we headed south toward Littlefield. We were in the part of Maine where all the lakes have either Native American names—Molonkus, Mattawamkeag—or literal ones: Pleasant Lake, Long Pond.

"I'm fine." I was watching him, as I had been all afternoon. He was driving easily but attentively, checking his blind spots and using his turn signal. The color in his face was still good, but when he coughed—why was he still coughing?—I could hear the weakness in his lungs. He drove the speed limit. He hadn't asked me a single question about what we'd been doing, or why he felt better. He didn't even acknowledge that he did feel better.

We passed a police officer at the bottom of a hill who was camping for speeders, and my dad made the joke he always used to make, holding a shushing finger to his lips and ducking down in his seat. For me, it was like sharing the car with a ghost—my old father, back from the dead. When we'd gone to the house, just before leaving Winterville, he told me again about the red cedar roof, and when I didn't say anything, he squeezed my shoulder and said, "Is it too hard for you to be here?" It had been so long since he'd shown real, nonsarcastic concern for me that I'd almost recoiled from the weight of his hand. If he noticed, he didn't say anything. He just watched the house for a few more seconds, then put the car in reverse.

"Have you talked to Dana? She'll be worried."

I didn't tell him that last time I'd checked, I had over thirty calls from Dana, plus an additional ten to fifteen texts from Sadiq and RJ. I turned on my phone and quickly typed a message to all three of them, individually, letting them know we'd be back at St. Matthias by seven. I pictured my dad a few months from now, working again, living on his own. I pictured him back at school, in front of a classroom.

"What are you smiling about?" he asked, stretching one arm, yawning. The car strayed into the breakdown lane, the tires catching the rumble strip.

When we reached St. Matthias, we were greeted by the flashing lights of an ambulance in the parking lot. The sky was pink and purple, the sun low against the water. We parked as far from the ambulance as we could, not wanting to be in its way. St. Matthias was full of sick people, and I assumed the ambulance was for one of them.

"Is that Dana?" my dad said as we exited the car.

It *was* Dana. She was running across the parking lot, Emmett behind her, signaling to someone. She was wearing her scarf like a bonnet, which made her look old, like a person who shouldn't be running.

"They're over here!" she was yelling.

The rear doors of the ambulance opened, and two EMTs emerged in reflective black-and-yellow jackets. They pulled a gurney out of the back and fell in line behind my aunt, and seeing her lead this team of men toward us was such a weird sight. As they came near, I braced myself for Dana's anger, but she was too hurried for that.

She wasn't even looking at me. "Ned, where the *hell*—it doesn't matter. You're going to the hospital. Now."

"Whoa," he said.

The EMTs were circling the car.

"What's happening?" I said to my aunt.

She was trying to pull me away. "I'll explain in the car."

"Wait," I said, freeing myself from her. The EMTs were laying my father down, securing him to the bed. I ran to him. He was watching the EMTs strap him in with a surprised but affable smile.

He raised his eyebrows to me. "This got interesting!"

The EMTs started to wheel him away, but I held on to the

bed. "He's fine!" I said, though I wasn't sure if that was true. "He's better!"

My dad uncurled my fingers from the frame. "Go with Dana. I'll see you there."

As he took my father away, one of the EMTs touched my arm. "Don't be scared. This is a good thing."

I could only stare as they loaded him into the back of the ambulance and shut the doors. What was I going to say? How could I possibly explain? Dana was standing next to me, with Emmett waiting to the side, strangely aloof, strangely angry.

Dana wrapped her arms around me. "We're going to talk about where you've been. But I'm very happy to see you."

Nothing made any sense to me. I hadn't slept for almost thirty-six hours.

"Let's go." Dana released me from the warmth of her hug. She took my wrist and dragged me to her car, and we rode together to the hospital, where, by the time we arrived, my father's liver transplant had already begun.

22

Goodbyes

Here's that clue again, the Copper Code:

$$Cu^+ + H_2O_2 \rightarrow Cu^{2+} + \bullet OH + {}^-OH$$

This is what Dana told me in the car, though she expressed it in words: *Wilson's disease.* It was a genetic disorder, and my father had it. He'd had it all along.

I'm not sure I said one word the entire drive. For a minute or two we hung close to the ambulance, its siren lights reflecting off our windshield. But then it ran a stop sign and we watched its red lights reduce, winking and disappearing. Dana talked and talked, and I listened to her voice, trying to follow it the way we followed the ambulance, failing hopelessly.

The Cu is copper. The human body takes in more copper than it needs, and to fix this problem, the stomach sends excess copper to the liver. There, transport protein ATP7B2 helps the body get rid of it. For this reason, ATP7B2 is known as the copper pump. My father had a broken copper pump, and this meant his liver and brain were being poisoned by copper deposits. The excess copper reacts with hydrogen peroxide (that's the H_2O_2) to produce a hydroxyl radical ($\bullet OH$) that destroys human tissue. The liver fails. The eyes turn yellow. And sometimes, though not often, Wilson's disease produces remarkable changes in personality. Later, I would read the case of a twenty-five-year-old who had been

prom king in high school and pursued a graduate degree in physics at MIT. Upon the onset of Wilson's disease, he dropped out
of school, renounced all ties to his family, and tried to kill himself by jumping into a sewer.

The disease is treatable, but first you have to diagnose it. In my
father's case, that proved difficult for a few reasons. First, Wilson's
disease typically arrives in much younger patients. Second, it's easy
to confuse the disease's psychological symptoms with depression,
which, since the disease manifested alongside my mother's death,
seemed the more obvious diagnosis. Third, my father's DUI and
recently developed drinking habit meant that every doctor viewed
his symptoms through that lens. In short, everything about my
father's condition said depressed alcoholic widower, and no one
was looking for the signs that pointed elsewhere. It was caught
only because a nurse, who had just started working at the hospital, checked his last round of blood work and thought, *You know,
this looks more like* . . .

The hospital, recognizing the screwup and potential for an expensive lawsuit, pushed my father to the top of the transplant
list. This had all happened in less than a day. He would get a new
liver, and he would be himself again—or something like himself—
and I would never know for sure which aspects of his cruelty had
been him and which he could blame on the disease. The car crash,
the way he abandoned me, all the horrible things he'd ever said—
those were *real*. They *happened*. I would have no choice but to
swallow them, to begin revising every memory of him since the
day my mother died. And yes, I would never know if the elixir
had worked.

Hours later, I sat with Dana and Emmett in the hospital, our chairs
pulled tight together. That talk Dana had staged for me earlier was
about to happen. She'd intended to hold off until we were back
home, but Emmett had been acting so coldly to me in the hospital that finally she said, "Okay, let's huddle up."

It was late, and the hospital mostly empty. My father was still
in surgery. It would be another hour or more until I could see

him. I kept waiting for a doctor to rush out, his eyes dark, and
stare me down, saying, "What did you do to him?" But so far,
nothing like that had happened. To everyone but me, my dad was
just a really sick guy finally getting the help he needed.

I slouched in my chair. I was in desperate need of sleep. The
world was blurry and gray, and only Emmett's meanness kept my
eyes open.

"What's your problem?" I said to him before anyone else had
the chance to speak.

"What's *your* problem?"

"Boys," Dana said.

"You're acting like a jerk," I said.

"Oh," he stammered. He was almost too upset to speak. "How
about this." He began to tick off my offenses on his fingers. "One,
you totally ditched me all summer and since school started. You
and RJ never invite me anywhere. Two, I know what was going
on with you and Mr. Tampari."

"What—" I said, but he was still going.

"Three, you've been working on some kind of . . . potion with
RJ." Here he looked at Dana for effect. "Doing *drugs*. And four,
you've been meeting with weird Middle Eastern guys about it."

"Okay," Dana was saying. "Okay—"

"That's not true!" I said. The room was spinning.

"Yes, it is," Emmett fired back. "I *saw* you."

"You're the one who's been following me?" At the storage
unit, at the hotel—it had been Emmett.

Emmett stared at the floor, and his voice went small. "Going
where you guys go didn't used to be *following you*. It used to be us
hanging out."

I opened my mouth to reply, but my anger had been silenced
by guilt. On his list of offenses, I'd been most stunned by his
knowledge of Sammy and me, but I realized he'd listed them in
order of importance. Number one: I'd ditched him.

"All right," Dana said. "Emmett, I'm going to speak to Conrad alone for a second. I think he has some things to tell me."

Emmett began to protest, but she held up a finger, so he threw
his headphones on and moved to the other side of the room. I
looked at Dana, and I was much too tired to run.

"Listen," she said. "I know a lot of what he said isn't true. But clearly some of it is. Starting with the fact that you probably haven't been including him lately."

I lowered my face.

"Captain Carson told me you've been skipping class." She took a breath. "You're not on drugs, are you?"

I shook my head, happy for the chance to be truthful.

"I didn't think so. And I know a lot of this stuff is just Emmett's imagination. He felt left out, and he constructed this fantasy. That's just him. That's how he is."

I shifted in my seat.

Over the intercom, a crackling voice summoned a doctor, but it wasn't to surgery. Someone else's crisis. Dana gave me a serious look. "I think we *all* could have done a better job paying attention to each other. What Emmett said about you and Mr. Tampari—it made me realize that relationship, and how much time you were spending together, is something I should have paid more attention to." She paused, bracing herself. "That part of the story is true, isn't it?"

I began to cry.

"Okay," she said quickly. "Listen to me carefully: Whatever happened isn't your fault."

I shut my eyes. Even though the waiting room was empty, I felt as if everyone were looking at me.

"Hey." She touched my arm. "I'm not mad at you. I'm really not. But I'll be honest: some of the stuff I'm going to do next is going to *feel* like punishment, starting first and foremost with taking you to see a therapist."

Immediately my mind flashed to Dr. Gillian Huang. I imagined a person like that seeing all the way through me, seeing all of the things I'd done. My therapist, however, would turn out to be a friendly, heavyset woman who made jams as a hobby, and whose little office smelled like blueberries.

Dana had said she wasn't angry, but she was, just not with me. "That *bastard*," she was saying under her breath.

I wiped my eyes and rubbed my nose on my sleeve. Confession had a hold of me. "I'm gay," I told her, because this was the closest I could come to admitting how much I'd loved him.

Dana nodded. "I thought you might be." She was looking at me but past me, as if she was weighing carefully what to say next. "Maybe I'm just tired now, and a little shocked by everything that's happened, but I'm going to tell you the only problem I see with you being gay, and then I'll shut up and support you for the rest of your life. Here it is: Being gay, it means you've cast your lot with the world of men. You're going to surround yourself with them—you already have—and you've seen more than any teenager should how far that gets you, *what* it gets you. Your uncle was the exception, though I'm not sure you knew him well enough to see that. You always held him at arm's length, and you've held me at arm's length, too. You needed to grieve, and I let you. But that's over now. I'm the woman in your life, God help us. Understand?"

I did understand.

Dana sighed. "I'm going to be very important to you."

I had only a minute or two in the bathroom to recover from my talk with Dana when I received the text from RJ: *S and I outside.*

As I exited the hospital, I zipped up my jacket. The air was chilled, the stars muted by clouds. All of the light came from streetlamps. Sadiq and RJ were waiting for me by the entrance, hands stuffed in their pockets. As I approached, they looked up from their feet, their eyes questioning.

"Is your father okay?" Sadiq had been to the hospital himself, for his wound. He was still wearing the bracelet.

"Did it work?" RJ added.

"Maybe," I said to both questions. I told them about the surgery, about the Wilson's disease. I told them it looked as if my father would recover.

Sadiq looked up at the sky. "Thank God for that. I'm very sorry for what I've done, Conrad. I wanted to protect you, but that should have meant stopping you. You could have been killed, and I led you right into the line of fire."

"Don't apologize. You helped me."

"No. Catherine was right. It was the wrong thing to do." Sadiq laughed at the self-evidence of that. "Sammy left me a long time ago, but I'm still trying to please him."

I told him to go back to the motel, get some sleep. He gave me a one-armed hug and departed. RJ was watching me with an uncharacteristically guarded expression. Part of him must have known something was wrong.

"I don't understand," he said. "Was it working or not?"

I wanted to tell him that it was all, definitely, a hoax. That it did nothing, and that without the surgery, my father would be dead. But I owed him the truth: "I'm not sure. He seemed better."

"Awesome." A heartbreaking smile spread across RJ's face. "When can we do it for Steph?"

I forced myself to meet his eyes. "Hey. Thank you for helping me."

"Psh, I'll steal drugs for you anytime."

Among teenage boys, it doesn't get much sweeter. "I love you," I said. I can only hope, even now, that he understood all the ways that I meant it.

He grimaced, because of course. "You're so girlie."

I was glad I told him how I felt about him, but don't mistake that moment for a selfless act, or a kind one. It was selfishness. Because I knew that would be our last conversation. "We can't do anything for Stephanie. I don't have any more."

RJ scrunched up his face. "What?"

I confessed everything: Bogdi and Livia, the single sparkler.

"You didn't even tell me? You just took it?"

There was nothing to say but "I'm sorry."

He was squinting as if he couldn't see me, as if I were disappearing to him. I could see his sister in his face. "How could you do this?"

There was so much I could say, but only one thing that mattered: "He's my dad."

What happened next was exactly what I deserved. RJ swore at me, insulted me. He threatened to tell all of my secrets, though he must have known this threat was empty—no one would believe him. I watched all of this happen from above my body. When someone you love begins to hate you, it's like one of the cords tying you to earth has been severed.

When he finally wore himself out, he turned away and left me standing there alone. Eight months later we would graduate, and once, during the ceremony, I would look over and see him staring at me, his eyes as full of hurt and anger as they'd been that night, wishing me dead as the principal said, "Conrad Aybinder," and I rose to the sounds of my family cheering my name.

I returned to the waiting room and slept until someone woke me—Dana, placing a cool hand on the back of my neck. "You can see him. He's awake."

I stretched and stood and followed her down one hallway, then another, to my father's room. She opened the door for me.

Inside, it was dark. The sky outside his window was pure black, and only a soft, yellow light came from a desk lamp near his feet, leaving most of him in shadow. It took my eyes a second to adjust, to find him. When I did, he was squinting at me, his own eyes adapting to the brighter light of the hallway.

"Dad?" I stepped forward.

His hand extended for me. "Kiddo. Come in."

23

My Husband's Surgery

The morning of my husband's surgery, I call my father to wish him a happy birthday. I've barely slept, and to avoid disrupting my husband's rest, I spent much of the night on the couch. Now I'm sitting on a stool in the kitchen, watching the sun rise through the patio doors. I can hear Kimberly stirring in the guest bedroom, applying her makeup, coughing into the crook of her elbow.

"Kiddo," my dad says, answering the phone.

I lay my spoon into my empty bowl of granola. "Happy birthday."

He snorts into the receiver. "Forget that. Tell me what's up."

I give him the timeline: surgery this morning, recovery this evening, no real news until the next day, when more tests will be done. The prognosis is still good, but the likelihood of success, according to the medical chip, no longer starts with a nine but an eight.

"I'm sorry I'm not there."

"It's okay," I promise. My dad has never returned to Winter-ville, and I understand why he can't. When we visit him in Little-field, where he lives with his wife—a retired real estate agent—he is a good, attentive host. It's enough.

"Anyway, he'll be fine. It's not like it's brain surgery."

He's made that joke before, but I smile regardless. "Actually . . ."

In the background, I hear his wife ask if it's me on the phone. My dad tells her it is.

I shut my eyes. "I'm scared."

"Me, too. I'm the one who told you he was a keeper."

This is true. Around month four, I called my dad with some petty, minor complaint: "He doesn't share food. I like when a date says, 'Try this,' and gives me a forkful of his dessert. With him, it's like we're at two separate tables."

My dad took a long pause, though I don't remember if it was before or after he laughed at me. "Con," he said finally, "this guy sounds like a keeper."

Upstairs, the shower turns on, and the pipes under the kitchen sink begin to hum. Everything is connected. My husband is awake.

"I was thinking about the day of your surgery," I say.

"Mm." We've never discussed this day; we've never remembered it together. I'm not sure he understands what happened or what he allowed me to do. It's hard to know where forgetting ends and pretending to forget begins. I don't push it, even though a part of me, sometimes, feels entitled to more gratitude.

He changes the subject. "Is Kimberly still there?"

"Yeah." We both laugh. "I should probably go."

"Call me when it's over, or when you want to."

I tell him I will and that I love him, and he tells me good luck and that he loves me. I climb the stairs to watch my husband getting dressed. When I get there, he's still in the bathroom, and Kimberly has somehow sneaked past me and is laying out clothes for him on the bed. As she unfolds his shirt and spreads it on the mattress, she touches the fabric of the collar, her hands lingering in a way that is, to me, inappropriately mournful, as though he were already dead.

"Good morning," I say. "Can I get you anything? Breakfast?"

"I just thought I'd pick out some warmer clothes for him."

She is so small; it seems inconceivable that she produced my husband, who despite the weight loss still has twenty pounds on me. As Kimberly moves about the bedroom, her body hunched over the bed, she reminds me of a praying mantis.

The bathroom door opens, and my husband emerges with a towel wrapped around his waist. "Oh. Everyone's here."

"I was just offering your mom some breakfast," I say, letting him know that I tried, unsuccessfully, to get her out of the room.

"Ma, you should eat." He looks good with a shaved head, though a little monochromatic and weirdly shaped, like a pencil with a perfectly round eraser.

She's laid out so many clothes on the bed you can't see the bedspread. "I had some trail mix in the bedroom."

"What?" my husband asks. "Where did you get trail mix?"

"I brought it. I know you don't usually have any."

My husband throws up his hands, and I think, *Well, at least she's distracted him.*

In the waiting room at the hospital, a nurse appears from behind a doorway and says my husband's name. She's big, dressed in white and blue, and my husband waves to her in a way that suggests they've met before. I've never seen her, and I don't like to be reminded that a whole world is behind those doors—a world he is traveling to without me.

We stand. Kimberly positions herself to be hugged first, and so she is, my husband's long arms encircling her twiggy frame. She tells him good luck, and he says, "You, too," which he can never stop himself from doing.

When my turn comes, I kiss him twice on the lips, not caring that his breath has a stale, hungry smell, the result of his pre-surgical fasting. He orders me not to worry, and I agree there is no need. Eighty-seven percent is, still, a very high number. He gives my hand a final squeeze, blows a kiss to his mother, and disappears behind the door with the nurse.

I sit down. Kimberly flips noisily through a women's magazine, practically tearing the pages as she turns them. It is loud enough that people look up. Ten other people are in the waiting room—two couples, both Kimberly's age, and what looks like a family of six, including a young boy, maybe five years old, who has been driven mad by waiting and is bouncing in his seat, making crazy faces at no one.

I check my e-mails. Not surprisingly, I have one from Dana, who is so reliably supportive you can set your watch to her notes of encouragement. After my dad's surgery, she did exactly as she had promised, bullying her way into my life in the best possible way. She drove me to therapy every week, monitored my social life as if I were on parole, made sure my college applications were finished and sent. Never in all these years since has there been a week that I haven't heard from her. Today's e-mail says she is thinking of me. She says that once Kimberly leaves and there is room in the house, she will visit and take care of us. Reading this, I close my eyes in relief. Even after all she did for me, it took me a long time, much too long, to realize that in every possible way except one Dana was my mother. When I finally did and asked her if I could call her that, her face lit up like a lantern, and we cried.

I hear less often from Emmett, who is now a storyboard artist for a pretty bad, successful cartoon show in Los Angeles. Over time, I think he began to doubt the veracity of his own story about me—it *did* sound absurd, after all, his talk of drugs and potions and strangers from the Middle East—and he began to see it as Dana did, as the product of a jealous, imaginative teen. He never brings it up, never presses for a resolution. But whenever we're together, a thin sheet of ice is between us, and I recognize it as a lack of trust.

I never told him the truth—that Sadiq is not only real but a friend. He has a house outside London, a husband who is locally known for his skills as a gardener. I've visited him there twice, and he came to meet us once in Cape Cod for a shared vacation. My husband loves him, and Sadiq loves everyone. He doesn't like to talk about Sammy.

Catherine I've never seen again. When she left Littlefield, she said she didn't want to hear from me. But whenever I do write to her, she responds, often in long, hurried e-mails that read like prose poems. In her letters to me she sounds lonely, but I suspect *my* letters sound lonely, and that doesn't mean my life isn't good.

Theo, she told me, is not much like his father, and I know what this means: he's happy.

Then there's RJ. The day we graduated from Littlefield High is the last time I saw him. I never went to him, never begged his forgiveness. Maybe it wouldn't have mattered. *A fantasy*—that's what Dana called it, when Emmett told her my sins. It feels that way now more than ever. How, as an adult, do you say, "I'm sorry I withheld the elixir of life from your sister"? How do you find forgiveness in a dream?

Still, I should have apologized again, and again, and kept apologizing. I should have fought for that friendship and spent my whole life repaying the debt I owed him. I've tried to keep track of him. I know he lives in Philadelphia and makes enough money to have bought a car whose top comes down. After grad school, I learned online that RJ had married Jennifer Smith, and I had a moment of panic. RJ and I had gone to high school with Jenny Smith, and she was known to eat at lunch what she called "licorice sandwiches." But then I saw a picture of RJ's wife, and it was a different woman, just with the same name—a coincidence. Ten years ago, his sister died.

An hour after the nurse took my husband, she reemerges to tell us his surgery has begun. I thank her and start the timer on my watch—in four hours, I can see him again. The little boy on the other side of the room is throwing his action figures on the floor and then, when their little limbs pop off, acting as if he hadn't intended for that outcome.

His mother smiles apologetically at the couple sitting across from her. "We've been here a long time."

"How old is he?" the older man asks her, which is the only thing you can say to someone who is apologizing for a child's behavior.

"Five," the woman says, her eyes wide, as though she never expected such a number.

Five. I was that same age when we moved to Winterville— the decision that has come, in my mind, to be the catalyst for everything that followed. If we had never moved to Winterville, my mother would never have taken a job at a camp for troubled teens. If she hadn't died there, my father would never have started drinking, and when the Wilson's disease came, any doctor with a brain would have seen it. I would never have moved to Little-field, I would never have met Sammy, and maybe—though I don't know—he'd still be alive.

It's a question I'll never answer: Why did Sammy kill himself when he believed he'd finally solved the elixir? Was it our rela-tionship that drove him over the edge, or was our affair a bit of last-night-on-earth recklessness, the act of a man who had already decided? Perhaps that had been the plan all along—to discover the elixir of life and then vanish, leaving others to benefit. Was he driven mad by the mercury? Was it fear of the brain burn? Or was it simply the everyday load of mental illness, which so many people live with, until they don't?

So much could have gone differently. But if I follow that thread to its logical conclusion, I'm a completely different person on the other side, and I never meet my husband.

My husband! He is tall, and he scrunches his nose when he smiles, like a Midwesterner. When his beard grows in, a touch of gray is near the chin, and it makes him self-conscious. He tries to cover it with his hand. When I want to see him blush, which is all the time, I point out this habit to him. To friends, I describe the color of his eyes as autumn, by which I mean they remind me of the woods outside our home, the leaves cooked by the sun and then frozen stiff after sunset, so that when I find them on the porch in the morning, they are smooth and bright. He can chan-nel his love for me into those eyes, so that I can *see* it, and if you meet someone who can do this, keep him.

Two hours have passed. Somewhere, in a room I can't see, they have cut into my husband's skull, exposed the most vulnerable part of him to air. When I think of losing him, I can feel the place in my body where I will carry that loss. My fear of pain is carv-ing out the space for it. I remember the day, not long after I proposed, when the justice of the peace we'd hired to perform the ceremony asked me why I wanted to spend my life with this man. "Because I love him," I said, which had seemed like a tautology, or at least a stupid answer. But now I don't know. Isn't that what love *is*? A stupid answer to a difficult question?

Here's another question, one I've asked myself a thousand times: Could I re-create the elixir for my husband? Could I do for him what I did for my father? I would need to reach Bogdi and Livia, if they're still out there, if there's even a single sparkler left. I would need Catherine's help, without anything to offer in return. Finally, I would need to convince my husband to take it. He knows my interest in the history of immortality comes from Sammy, but it's the one secret I've kept: how *real* that interest became. I honestly don't know how he'd react.

Would it work? Part of me wants to say that the elixir, in the end, was just a figment of my imagination, and before that, of Sammy's, and before that, of the countless men and women who have died in pursuit of a solution to death and illness—because saying that excuses my inaction. It allows me to say that my time is better spent *with* my husband, caring for him, savoring whatever minutes, months, years, we have left.

Since that day in Winterville, my father has aged the same as everyone else—slowly, and then quickly, so that you notice the changes all at once, and they surprise you. And yet, I saw the look in his eyes when he woke up from the brain burn, and that's the memory, all these years later, I can't shake. I'd lost my father, he was *gone*, and then he woke up, and he was back. It was him.

Sammy wrote that people see the elixir of life as against the laws of nature—to wish for it is amoral, to search for it is hubris. But I *have* wished for it, and I *have* searched for it, and here's the closest I've come to a revelation: In hindsight, searching for Sammy's elixir felt no different from searching for a job, for a boyfriend, for a house that's big enough (but small enough) to call home. It's just another thing I've wanted, among many other things, at some point in my life.

I did selfish things after Sammy died. As a result, I lost RJ, and I hurt Emmett, and I could have lost Dana, too, if she didn't love me with a strength drawn from both her own heart and my mother's. I could just as easily have killed my father as saved him. I try to remind myself of this. A selfish act can seem small and local, like a tick bite, but the balance of your life is at stake—your world is at stake.

I didn't fall in love with Sammy in *spite* of his age; that's no insight. I was a sixteen-year-old senior, running from childhood as fast as I could, from a childhood that had treated me badly. Now that I'm older, I want the opposite: to slow everything down. Maybe it's foolish, but sometimes small lessons are the best ones, and that's the lesson I've chosen to take from everything that happened after I first saw Sammy—smiling, gorgeous, much too old for me—striding down the hall and into my life: wait your turn.

My watch beeps, signaling the end of the fourth hour, and as if on cue, the door behind the reception desk opens. I see the nurse in the doorway, but her back is turned—she's talking to someone I can't see. Kimberly sits up in her seat, spine straight, bracing herself for news. I think she's going to take my hand, but she only grips the armrest, squeezing hard. Across from me, the little boy stands up in excitement, but when he sees that it's just the nurse, alone, and not whomever he's expecting, he groans and throws the hood of his sweatshirt over his ears. He looks around the room, and I imagine he's thinking, *How can I show my frustration? What can I destroy?*

The nurse finishes her conversation. To my right, Kimberly is so still I can see the dust particles shifting in the lamplight around her hair. It is time. I take a deep breath and look once more at the boy as the nurse comes to find me, to describe the brightness, or darkness, of my future. The boy is on his feet, eyes narrow, and for a moment I think he is going to scream. But instead he sits, sighs, and leans against his mother, his hands hidden in the pockets of his hoodie. She smiles as she feels the pressure of him on her shoulder, and he closes his eyes, and my God, it's a beautiful thing—a five-year-old boy, learning his limits, surprising himself and his mother with his first act of patience. Watching him, I remember all of those feelings: the fear, the frustration, the hope for the future. I remember being young, when there was nothing worse than waiting.

Acknowledgments

I wrote *The History of Living Forever* over ten long years and with the support of more wonderful family, friends, and colleagues than I could possibly name. Still, I extend my sincerest thanks to the following people, in roughly chronological order:

My parents, Fred and Kathy, and my siblings, Nate and Genny. You are my favorite people.

My in-laws, Andy and Hil and Lauren. I couldn't ask for better.

All of the creative writing faculty at the University of Wisconsin–Madison, especially my MFA advisor, Judith Claire Mitchell, whose support has been a life raft for over a decade.

The graduate program at Florida State University, and especially my PhD advisor, Mark Winegardner, whose voice is nearly as central to this novel as my own. I also thank the rest of my dissertation committee at FSU: Elizabeth Stuckey-French, Jennine Capó Crucet, Dennis Moore, and Aline Kalbian.

All of my brilliant classmates, who have inspired and challenged me throughout the years. Special thanks to the following few, who have commented on early drafts or chapters of the novel: Emily Alford, Marian Crotty, Micah Dean Hicks, Alyssa Knickerbocker, Noreen McAuliffe, and Michael Yoon.

My agent, Adam Schear, who believed in this book, and in me, long before I did. I would never have finished without you.

My editor at FSG, Jenna Johnson, who helped me find the

beating heart of this story and never let me settle for anything but my best. I also thank editorial assistants Sara Birmingham and Lydia Zoells, who kept me on schedule and provided valuable insights during the many months of revision.

Finally, thank you to Lesley. I love you.